QUANTUM BREAK
ZERO STATE

ALSO BY CAM ROGERS

The Music of Razors (as Cameron Rogers)

QUANTUM BREAK
ZERO STATE

CAM ROGERS

TOR

A TOM DOHERTY ASSOCIATES BOOK
NEW YORK

QUANTUM BREAK: ZERO STATE

Copyright © 2016 by Microsoft Corporation

A Tor Book
Published by Tom Doherty Associates, LLC
175 Fifth Avenue
New York, NY 10010

www.tor-forge.com

Tor® is a registered trademark of Tom Doherty Associates, LLC.

The Library of Congress Cataloging-in-Publication Data is available upon request.

ISBN 978-0-7653-9159-9 (hardcover)
ISBN 978-0-7653-9160-5 (trade paperback)
ISBN 978-0-7653-9161-2 (e-book)

Our books may be purchased in bulk for promotional, educational, or business use. Please contact your local bookseller or the Macmillan Corporate and Premium Sales Department at 1-800-221-7945, extension 5442, or by e-mail at MacmillanSpecialMarkets@macmillan.com.

First Edition: April 2016

Printed in the United States of America

0 9 8 7 6 5 4 3 2 1

For Dmetri Kakmi,
the best friend I've ever had,
the best editor I've ever worked with

FOREWORD

I need to confess something. I've always struggled to see the point of a straightforward game novelization. If the experience is already there as intended, why transcribe it? There's more than fifty thousand words of text-based discoverable optional story content in *Quantum Break*, half a novel in itself, and that's without counting the actual performed screenplay. If the player wants a novelization of the story in the game, it's waiting there to be read as they play. Instead, I was interested in creating a work of art that was bold, a bit different, and that would stand on its own two feet.

Cam Rogers was part of the team who crafted *Quantum Break*. The other members of the team were Mikko Rautalahti, Tyler Smith, and myself. As a writer, Cam is a force of nature. The sheer rapid-fire enthusiasm he brings to the table was obvious to us from the very first Skype call we had with him in the spring of 2012. Cam is fast; the way his mind works is staggering. He knows how stories work, and on top of that the man is a walking encyclopedia. When the idea of a novelization for *Quantum Break* came up in the early summer of 2015, I immediately thought of Cam, who at that point had already left Remedy to work on other projects. Cam had intimate knowledge of the *Quantum Break* universe, in a way no outside writer could. I called him, and he was interested.

As with any complex project, *Quantum Break*'s story went through quite a few different versions. Ideas were explored and then, for one reason or another, some were abandoned. Not always because they were not good ideas for the story, but because they didn't work with what we had in the game. Cam suggested that he could bring in some ideas and concepts that were present in the earlier drafts of the story. I liked the idea.

I gave Cam free hands. Use any of the old story ideas that we abandoned along the way. But don't stop there. If you come up with new ideas that you feel would serve this story better, go for it. Make it interesting, make it cool, that's all.

Quantum Break is a story about time travel and branching timelines. Paul Serene sees visions of different potential futures, and he can choose which future comes to be. This opens a door to the idea of a multiverse, or the many-worlds interpretation of quantum physics; the idea that there are branching timelines and with that an infinite number of parallel realities where things went down a different path. As you play the game, you are creating your version of the *Quantum Break* universe via the junction choices that you make. That is your own timeline, different from your friend's timeline, and yet they both exist side by side.

Now imagine many more junction moments, going further back to the time before the game even begins. That's what this novel is. It's an alternate timeline novel. Some things are exactly as they are in the game, some are close, and some are completely different.

I love the idea of echoes and twisted mirrors. We always have multiple layers in Remedy stories. Take the in-game TV series well known to fans of *Max Payne* and *Alan Wake: Lords and Ladies, Dick Justice, Address Unknown, Captain Baseball Bat Boy, Night Springs*. They can be wacky and tongue in cheek, but they always thematically comment and echo the main story. That's what this book is, an echo, a twisted mirror.

This is not the *Quantum Break* you have played. Is this canon? Strictly speaking, no. But, in an experience where the player gets to make choices and shape the story, in a multiverse, what isn't canon? This story contains mysteries and histories of its own. Do the revelations within these pages provide answers to questions raised in the game? We leave that to you.

Sam Lake, creative director, Remedy
Helsinki, January 9, 2016

We are all blind navigators.

In one lifetime a person makes countless decisions. Each choice spawns a new universe. The chosen Present then births its logical Future—but one timeline among a myriad.

My life's mission is to safeguard the universe I have created from the choices I have made.

—From the journals of Dr. William Joyce

QUANTUM BREAK
ZERO STATE

1

When you're young, time is something that happens to other people.

Standing on the lip of Bannerman's Overlook, taking in the view of the city, there should have been all the time in the world. Cold dawn lit eastern-facing windows like bright pixels. Birds lifted skyward from the university campus in a stippled black cloud, thinning as they banked westward toward the river.

Jack Joyce and Paul Serene had known each other all of their lives, a total that would forever remain at twenty-two years if the delicately voiced man behind them lost his temper.

Paul glanced over his shoulder. Orrie "Trigger" Aberfoyle was the calm, kind-eyed murderer responsible for Riverport's small but thriving crime industry, and had the kind of face you'd expect to surface after throwing bread onto a dead pond. At that moment he seemed to be charmed by the relaxed young lady bantering with him. His three enforcers hung back on the verge, with Aberfoyle's black town car.

"He's going to kill us, isn't he?" Paul said.

Zed—that was the only name she gave—had blown into town a few months back, took up residence in an abandoned home, and lived invisibly: no phone, no e-mail, no social media, no Social Security number. Her hair was a shock of dyed black and swept back like a bend-not-break stack of midnight reeds. A jagged tribal design curved behind her left ear and for fun she spent her afternoons bouncing off public property with the parkour crowd by the river.

Jack had placed their lives in her hands.

"Stop checking behind us. It makes us look nervous." Jack tried for a reassuring smile. "I trust her. I know her."

"You should. She's everyone you've ever dated."

"What's that supposed to mean?"

"She's a good-looking disaster who romanticizes your pathologies." Paul kicked a rock over the edge. The four-second delay to impact knotted his guts.

Last night Jack and Paul had taken a six-pack and the dinghy that belonged to Jack's departed dad and went fishing, way out on the Mystic River. Good times, had a few brewskis, Paul crashed on Jack's couch. Then Paul had woken abruptly as he was tossed off Jack's couch by a side of beef with a handgun. And now they were here.

Jack collected a few flat stones from the platform's ornamental Zen garden fringe, just before the dew-slick safety rail. "Look," he said, "those three guys turned up. We got piled into a car. Aberfoyle's phone rings. It's Zed. How'd she get his number? How'd she know we were in the car? How did she know what to say to make him turn the car around and drive us here, rather than some piece of waste ground in the dockyard? I trust her with this," he emphasized. "Five minutes ago she looked me in the eye and told me that all three of us are walking out of here alive. I believe her."

Jack was utterly smitten by Zed, which was why, Paul knew without a doubt, Jack was letting her do the talking for them— which was why Paul was certain they were about to be kicked three hundred feet off Bannerman's Overlook into the Great Mystery.

All Paul ever wanted was to go to business school, for fuck's sake.

"Jack, when you met her she was surfing the roof of a Honda hatchback at one A.M., with the lights off, down the worst road on Mount Greylock. She hangs out with scumbags and her name is a consonant. In two of her four photos the woman is airborne and she looks different in all of them. She has a tattoo on her *head*. That man *literally* gets away with murder several times a year and she's talking to him like he's her dippy uncle. I'm not sure she knows *anything* about *anything*." Now Aberfoyle was wobbling a finger at Zed's bemused face, laying down some kind of law. "If you don't say something to make him happy we are going to *die*."

Jack was Frisbeeing rocks from his left palm into the void, watching them arc and disappear into the foggy woodland that reached toward Riverport's southern border. "Americana." The leather of his jacket snapped as a flat stone spun and descended. "Family businesses. One school. Everyone knows everyone. Riverport, oh Riverport, such a pretty little town."

Paul recognized the refrain from their school anthem.

Jack tossed the remaining rocks over the side. "I hate pretty little towns. I hate this pretty little town." He hooked a thumb over his shoulder, toward one of the most dangerous men in the state. "Once this is dealt with I'm leaving. I mean it this time. This is the last mess of Will's I'm cleaning up."

"You don't mean that. You mean it now, but you won't mean it tomorrow. You'd have grown up in foster care if it wasn't for your brother."

"'Care.' Wouldn't that have been something?"

"Come on . . ."

"Do you remember how many jobs I worked through high school? Because I sure don't. What did I trade to spend ten years working so he didn't have to?"

"Yeah, but Will made your lunches—even if we did have to wash out those Ziplocs every Friday night. He drove us around when we were kids, right? Summers on the lake? I mean, he did his best. You guys are a team."

"He told me our folks were broke. Turns out that wasn't the case."

"But—"

"Hundreds of thousands of dollars."

The fight went out of Paul. "Ah shit."

"He blew it—all of it—in the first couple of years. Then came the loans and now, Paul, my friend, we are here."

The conversation behind them shifted tone. Gone was the music of pleased-to-meet-you. Smiles faded from Zed and Aberfoyle's eyes.

Paul's voice cracked. "Jack. Plan B." He hated himself for the sound of it. "If there is one, now's the time."

Jack took a half-interested look at the scene behind him: Zed and Aberfoyle, standing face-to-face. Aberfoyle's three widebodies propping up his town car, not concerned enough to even draw weapons. One of them looked at his watch. The other one signaled to a third, who sat in the car, listening to the radio. He got out, handed a heavy paper bag to the second, who took out a pre-loved Beretta with a tape-wrapped grip and checked the magazine.

Jack faced the front. To Paul that was an admission: This was now real. This was happening.

Paul swallowed. "They say . . . they say he shoots people with silver bullets," he whispered. "When the coroner finds one the case goes away. The cop who returns it to Aberfoyle gets five grand. They say he keeps the used ones in a jelly jar on his desk."

Jack kept his voice low. "You told me the same story when we were nine. I've still never heard anything that—"

Aberfoyle took a snub-nosed .38 out of his pocket, snapped the cylinder open, checked the contents. The ass-ends of six slugs flashed like mirrors.

"I stand corrected."

The cylinder clicked shut. The wide-bodies sauntered over to Aberfoyle and Zed. Gravity seemed to be charging them double, but they didn't care.

Zed nodded a hello. "Mario. Luigi. Princess Peach."

No reaction from the first two. Princess smiled like a prehistoric fish and held eye contact with Zed way too long.

Paul went white. "Fuck me."

Jack backhanded Paul in the chest. "Take it easy. Wolves dig panic."

Paul nodded, a little too quickly.

"All right. Worst comes to worst, over the side, aim for the slope. Legs first."

"What?"

Aberfoyle's voice suddenly went up an octave. "The universe responds to clear intentions, girl. Mine is to get what's mine. What's yours?"

"Hey, Trouble, c'mere." Zed beckoned Jack over, introduced him in that New Jersey accent. "This is my friend. His name is Jack Joyce. He is the brother of William Joyce, the scientist. The man who owes you all that money."

Aberfoyle turned to Jack. "For a smart man your brother is very stupid."

"Zed?"

Aberfoyle tapped Jack sharply on the side of the head with the silver-loaded .38. "Hey. Over here. You and your brother. You close?"

"He's an idiot and I want this over with. What does he owe you?"

Aberfoyle had a laugh like bad plumbing. "More than he's

got. More than *you* got. You got a spread. Nice piece a land. Nice house. I'm takin' that. But so we're clear: that don't even cover the vig."

"The interest," Zed clarified.

"I watch *The Sopranos,*" Jack said. "So what do we do? No, wait, fuck that. You're not getting the house."

"The fuck you say?"

"Give me a figure, I'll work something out."

"The *fuck* you *say*?" The .38 was up.

Jack wondered if those kind eyes would be the last thing he ever saw. "I said you're not getting the house."

"Mr. Aberfoyle," Zed interjected, smiling. "You're a business-man. Let's business."

Aberfoyle allowed Zed to lead him a few steps away from Jack. "Boys. Eyes on that one." Aberfoyle adjusted his jacket, gave Zed what was left of his patience. "Make it good and make it quick."

"There's a reason I requested you meet me here," she said. "It's the view."

Paul glanced over the side. His depth perception telescoped hard enough to nudge his balance off-center. "Aim for the slope. Right." He felt sick, closed his eyes.

"That gun you carry," Zed was saying. "The one with the shiny bullets. You direct it toward a problem, pull the trigger, and that problem goes away. Click. Bang. Deleted."

"I like that. I'm takin' that one."

"There's a quote—apocryphal—attributed to Michelangelo. The Pope admired Michelangelo's sculpture of David. He asked Michelangelo, 'How did you do that?' The story goes that Michelangelo replied, 'I simply cut away everything that doesn't look like David.'"

"I don't get it."

"Look at Riverport. You control so much of it. You didn't

build that control; you used your magic gun to cut away any-thing that didn't look like control. Businesses. Careers. People." Zed held up one finger. "I have a magic gun, too." Cocked her thumb. "Click click." She stretched her arm toward the hori-zon, pointed her magic finger at a lone warehouse close to the waterside. "A year ago your son was DJ'ing at a house party. A girl needed to charge her phone. He let her plug it into his lap-top. He synched that phone, downloaded her photos, shared a few choice ones with his friends. One of the photos showed the girl and her boyfriend inside an industrial-grade hydroponic setup. Your boys followed her boyfriend, found the warehouse—the same warehouse my magic gun is pointing at right now." She looked Aberfoyle in the eye. "Those two kids are dead. No one knows who did it, never will, and you have two more silver slugs in a jelly jar on your desk."

Aberfoyle's bottom lip devoured his top, blood vessels red-dening around his nose. "Do you believe in God?"

"Click."

Aberfoyle took a threatening step toward her.

"Bang."

The warehouse went up in flames. Aberfoyle went from red to white.

"Calm down, Orrie, it meant nothing to you. You're a child of the fifties. You like cars." Zed's magic gun shifted target. "Click."

"I will fucking end you."

"Bang."

The windows of a downtown chop shop blew out, the cor-rugated roof spewing blackest smoke. Aberfoyle's phone started ringing. He fumbled it out, stabbed it open, shouted, "I know! Handle it!" He disconnected, raised the .38. Zed kept her eye on Aberfoyle while her gun-finger moved to its third target.

"Don't you dare."

Princess snatched the tape-wrapped Beretta from the backup goon and checked in. "Boss?"

"You like boats?" Zed asked.

"Don't you fucking dare."

"Click."

Aberfoyle's gun was shaking. "Don't . . . !"

"Bang."

On the river a yacht exploded.

"Click."

"No—"

"Bang."

And another one.

"Click—"

"STOP!"

Zed looked him in the eye. "To answer your question, Orrie: No. I don't believe in God. I believe in cause and effect." And then, "Bang."

Aberfoyle shrieked as a million dollars turned into a waterborne mushroom cloud. Zed slapped the .38 out of his grip before he could pull the trigger. It hit the deck and went skidding.

"Good-bye, Orrie." She quickly stepped aside.

Princess got ahead of himself, racked the slide, and fired. Sideways, like he had seen in a movie. Princess was no Michelangelo.

The life of Orrie "Trigger" Aberfoyle was taken in hand by a 9mm slug and together they leaped out a ragged window just above his right ear.

Aberfoyle's second-in-command, whose job security had just turned to shit, now profoundly miserable, dumped half a mag into Princess.

In a flash of animal panic the third guy, who now thought

he was caught in the middle of an elaborate house-cleaning operation, blew away Aberfoyle's second-in-command.

This last-goon-standing backed away, hyperventilating and wide-eyed, realizing the depth of shit he was in. He waved the gun across Zed, Jack, and Paul, feeling behind him for the car. Zed picked up Aberfoyle's .38 and blatted off three shots in the goon's general direction, making sure at least two silver slugs landed in the town car's bodywork. The goon turned the key, hit the gas, and their immediate problems vanished in a slamming driver-side door and a long shriek of rubber as the town car fishtailed once and tore out of there. The three of them watched it disappear down the road.

Paul's legs lost their muscle, betrayed him, and he pitched back toward the waist-high rail.

Jack was there, seizing him hard by the arms, keeping him from toppling. Paul wanted to say something funny in that moment, something Jack would have said, but all that came out was "Go Team Outland."

Zed appeared, calm hand on Paul's shoulder as she waited for him to get his breathing under control. "Here." She pressed a single silver bullet into Paul's trembling hand. She gave one to Jack and kept one for herself. "That's the future we stole back."

That .38 slug flashed brightly. "Business school," Paul said, and closed his hand. "I'm going to business school."

Jack pocketed his. "I'm starting over. Somewhere else." To Zed, "Come with me."

Zed looked at her own, softly smiled, and sent that .38 slug sailing into the sky and out over Bannerman's Overlook.

Into the Great Mystery.

2

Saturday, 8 October 2016. 3:33 A.M. Riverport,
Massachusetts. Six years later.

The For Sale sign lay on its back in the dewy grass, the house ragged since Zed occupied its rooms. The illuminated skyline behind the sagging roof was a changed thing: smart office blocks, gleaming high-rises, exclusive apartments.

The monolith that was Monarch Tower dominated it all: a Titan's spear tip of irregularly cut black crystal, lit bright with the burning sign of a geometric butterfly.

Monarch Solutions: many-armed, known by all.

A train rattled along an elevated line that curved around and then through the central business district.

Jack Joyce had been away six years. Yet in that time Riverport had changed almost beyond recognition. The old city was breathing its last beneath all that shiny new weight.

He had picked a cold, miserable night to come back. Thirty-six hours earlier he had been on the island of Ko Samet, about four hours from Bangkok. His boots had been wedged into a white-sand beach, with a chilled bottle of Tsingtao slotted into each one. There had been the silence of the ocean and nothing but the sting in his eyes and the salt in his mouth, as he tried not to think about . . . Riverport.

Jack stepped away from the cab that had brought him here and shivered. Forty degrees was colder than he'd known for

years, and eighteen months in Thailand had left him as tanned
as the upholstery of the car he had been leaning against a short
time ago. Every Monday for the last year he had told himself
he'd leave the next week. But he stayed on. He'd still be in Chiang Mai if Paul hadn't e-mailed.

I honestly thought Will was out of the woods.

Then came the erratic behavior, the outbursts, and then he threatened
me. He's in worse shape than when we were kids, Jack . . .

At one point William Joyce had been a genius, Jack was sure
of that. His peer-reviewed quantum physics articles had net-
ted him fame, attention, and grants. UMass opened its doors
to him. The future seemed incandescent.

I drove by the house. I don't think anyone's been there for weeks. I'm
concerned he's living under a bridge.

Has he contacted you?

Will was a legal adult when their parents had died. On
paper, custody of Jack had gone to Will. In practice, it had been
the other way around: Jack spent his teenage years providing
for Will, making sure his brother ate, bathed, and didn't go off
on a mental tangent and walk into traffic. Being Will's brother
was the hardest thing Jack had ever done.

On a brighter (?) note . . . honestly I can't tell if this is shitty timing or kis-
met, but I've been hoping to persuade you to come home. I have something to show you—but it's time sensitive. You need to be in Riverport
this week. I've taken the liberty of booking you a first-class flight—
open-ended—back here. Day after tomorrow.

Over time Will's quirky personality metastasized. He was a sleepwalking genius, convinced he was unearthing questions people hadn't thought to ask—and none of it made sense to anyone. While Will had spent his days in the barn, tinkering on things that ate years and never worked, Jack had traded his teens for multiple jobs and failing grades.

He still hated himself for having been stupid enough to buy into any of it.

Two birds, one stone?

What I have to show you will change your life. I shit you not.

—Paul

"Hey man." It was the cab driver. "You okay?"

His name was Nick. He stood about six feet in his high-tops and was friendly in a way that suggested no one had ever not been friendly back. Easygoing, broad-shouldered, with a haircut this side of *Jailhouse Rock*.

Jack hugged himself tighter against the cold and nodded at the driver. "I'm good."

Sunday, July 4, 2010, had been a big day for Jack. After everything that had happened on the Overlook he had packed a bag, driven to his brother's workshop, and punched Will square in the teeth. Then he had pointed his motorcycle west and left Riverport with no intention of ever coming back. Yet here he was.

Six years on the road, staying in small towns until he felt people were getting used to him—and then moving on. On some level, he realized, he was doing what Will did: retreating from responsibility, hiding from what he couldn't handle. He didn't care. First Jack had lost his parents, and then he had lost his brother.

And then he had lost Zed.

"How does a house go six years and not sell?" the cabbie said. "The land alone must be worth something."

Nick had done Jack a solid and turned off the meter. His cab was a private operation, unmarked and almost certainly illegal. Jack had exited the airport, loaded his gear into the trunk and was clipping his seat belt shut when Nick had craftily hunched over the ignition to huff into a tube leading to the ignition: a Breathalyzer interlock. "All right," Nick had said before Jack could second-guess. "Let's hit that road!"

Jack now checked the cab for dings. It looked in pretty good shape.

"1968 Dodge Charger," Nick said, noting Jack's interest.

"Expensive."

"Dad's. Strictly a loaner." Nick handed Jack a tiny enamel cup, hot. It even had a saucer. "Though it's not like he's gonna be driving it anytime soon. Diabetes got him in a wheelchair."

"The Christmas lights and espresso machine come standard?"

"That's all me. You ride with The Prez, you're VP till you exit."

The Prez, right. Jack thought he recognized the face. Nick Marsters, aka The Prez, star player for the Riverport Raptors back in the day, headed for the big leagues. Why was he driving a cab?

"This is where she lived?" The question short-circuited the thought.

Jack downed the tiny cup, bitterness stinging behind his eyes, painting warmth through his innards. It had been a while since he'd had coffee without sweet condensed milk.

"Yeah. Took us a couple hours to walk back here from the Overlook," he said, thinking about that morning six years ago. What had started as Nick's rundown on how the town had

changed led to Jack recounting why he had left. Once started
Jack found he hadn't wanted to stop. Maybe it was the Catholic
confessional urge . . . or maybe he just wanted to delay seeing
his brother for as long as he could.

"You know the cops put the Overlook shootings down to
some dead man making a play inside Aberfoyle's organization,
right? Open-and-shut, cut-and-dried. Do you think your girl
meant for it to play out like that?"

Jack shook his head. "She saw most things as judo. Receive
momentum, do what you want with it. I think she was just
doing what came naturally."

"Maybe you should have married her."

Jack pointed to the corner of the block. "That morning we
stood right there. She held on to my jacket . . . leaned in . . .
and whispered . . . 'I could kick you in the face from here.'"

Nick snorted.

"She went inside and I never saw her again."

Nick turned his dumbstruck expression to the dark house,
to Jack, back to the house. "I find that to be a profoundly un-
satisfying conclusion."

"I came round that afternoon and everything she owned
was on fire in the back garden. She was gone. Five years I spent
looking. Nothing. I thought I picked up a lead in Arizona, but
it led nowhere."

"In the nineties that'd be romantic. These days it's practically a felony." Then: "Missing persons report?"

"No file, no paper trail, no name."

"Maybe Aberfoyle's guys got to her?"

"They'd have gone for me and Will first. Zed was an unknown, and the only guy who walked away from the Overlook
that morning was found in the river a week later. Basically
we were never there." Being there, in that moment, with this
stranger, looking at a house that hadn't known Zed and him

for more than half a decade . . . "Maybe she just wanted out. Maybe I was just being a creep, trying to find her. Jesus."

"No place like home."

"If I'm lucky." He felt self-conscious, confessing like a chump and hungover from it. "Family business. Once that's done I'm on the first flight . . . out of . . ."

Jack never finished the thought. A shape crept to the opposite crossroads, one-inch steel plate doing nothing to mute the low-and-slow chug of 300 horsepower.

"Whoa."

Seventeen thousand pounds of intimidation rounded the corner on fat, bullet-resistant tires, passenger-side spotlight snapping on like an accusation. The bright eye surveyed them as the armored vehicle took its sweet time rolling past. A Monarch Security logo leaped out through the glare—a segmented, geometric butterfly—hi-vis on matte black ballistic surfacing. Nick straightened, smiled, and nodded.

After a moment of consideration the light clicked off and the BearCat picked up volume, rounding the corner and melting back into the 'burbs.

"What the fuck," Jack said, "was that? Are we at war?"

"Monarch," Nick replied, taking Jack's cup and saucer, depositing it through the passenger window onto the espresso machine's top-mounted rack. "They moved in about the time you moved out. Shipping: dead. Farming: dead. Construction: dead. Monarch comes in, builds a bunch of stuff, employs a bunch of people. Riverport's got a pulse again. I like 'em, and their uniforms are frickin' *bangin'*."

"In Chiang Mai cops roll on tires with Monarch branding."

"Monarch Industrial, probably. That BearCat was Monarch Security. My sister's kid's daycare is Monarch Child. My dad's meds are Monarch Pharmaceuticals. Monarch's got this loyalty program, lets you rack up points all over the place, whoever you use. Dad's meds paid for that coffee you're drinking. It's a good deal." Nick backhanded Jack's arm, friendly. "Hey, you know Monarch's hosting a huge gala tomorrow night? A shitload of famous people are gonna be there. I could take you up to the parking garage across the way, give you a great view of the red carpet."

Jack's phone vibrated in his jacket. Caller ID came up as Paul Serene. "Uh . . . I think I fly out before then. Just one second." He thumbed the call button.

"Hey buddy." The voice was as familiar as his own. "Six years away and the first thing you do is go and pine outside her house?"

Jack glanced toward the disappeared armored vehicle. "The BearCat."

Paul laughed. "I requested an alert on your arrival. The BearCat scanned the plate of the museum piece you're leaning against. Monarch Security network cross-referenced with the RPD database, checked the photobank of the driver-cam that takes a shot each time Nick needs to blow-start the engine. Facial recog grabbed you in the backseat, the entry was logged into Monarch's system, Monarch's system texted me, I called you."

"Cause and effect." All of a sudden Jack wanted to be on a plane, headed to someplace even he didn't know. Someplace that didn't have loyalty programs. He thought of Zed and her zero footprint.

"Perks of working for Monarch."

"Which Monarch would that be?"

"Monarch Innovations. Subsidiary of Developments."

"It's like you're here with me, buddy."

"The info stays on Monarch servers, but we make it available to law enforcement upon request. Part of our community policing initiative. Some reservations from rights activists, but mostly the town's on board."

Yeah. Leaving. First chance he got. Maybe never coming back.

"You're still meeting me on campus, correct?"

"I'll be there in about twenty minutes."

"Jack? Thank you for making it. This is important to me. You'll be glad you came, I promise." The call disconnected.

"You said something about a Monarch gala?"

"The buzz is they're revealing a new product line. They say it'll 'reinvent life as we live it.' Probably just another game console. You want another espresso?" Nick asked.

"No. Actually, yeah. Can I get it rolling?"

"You're the VP." Nick opened the door for him. "I'll have to take a less-short way around. Big protest at the university today. Thought it'd be over by now or I'd have mentioned it. Students pissed off about the city tearing down some old library. You know how it is."

Jack checked his phone, giving Nick a little privacy to huff-start the car. "Says here Monarch's the one tearing it down, not the city."

The engine kicked over, purring like it had been put together yesterday. "Same thing," Nick said.

Jack stared out the window of the Charger as it pulled up outside the main walk of Riverport University. "It's all gone."

Gone were the few square blocks of lawn dotted with Colonial Revival–style wood buildings, interstitial spaces crowded with maple and birch. This was a modern, high-tech campus. Founders' Walk remained in place, a token gesture to tradition, next to which a slab of locally quarried marble bore, in

gold Sabon font: *Riverport University—Innovations Campus.*
Someone had slapped a HISTORY NOT PROFITS! sticker on it. A
sticker slapped over that one read: NINJAS ARE COOL!

A small black-and-gold plaque announced that the Quantum Research Laboratory was the winner of the 2013 Pritzker
Architecture Prize. The manicured lawn behind that—a perfect green flattop through which Founders' Walk cut—was
strewn with traveler cups, sodden flyers, beer cans, and the
occasional abandoned sign requesting those participating in
the sit-in to not litter the area. A tent city was in place, forming
a frail protective barrier between the old library—a bright-red
Gothic Revival anachronism amid a herd of glass and steel—
and the outside world. Jack flashed back to an incident on the
New York subway a few years back: a group of thirteen-year-
old girls shielding an old lady from some crazy dude with a
screwdriver.

He opened the car door, got out. "What the hell happened?"

Nick stepped out of the driver's door and sprawled his arms
across the car's roof, pleased at Jack's reaction. "Impressive,
huh?"

"It's like a moon base designed by French aliens. All this in
six years?"

"We live in an age of great change." Nick had the tone of
cartoon millionaire. "Something I heard on a podcast."

Jack peeled a wet flyer off the sidewalk. The date of the
library's execution was set for tomorrow. Right now the tent city
was mostly quiet, some of the residents laid out where they'd
passed out. He thought about the BearCat, all those *frickin'
bangin'* uniforms Nick liked so much, the tower overlooking the
entire city, the 2013 Pritzker Prize—and he didn't like the old
lady's chances.

"Where are you meeting your friend?"

Jack pointed to the plaque. "Quantum Research Lab."

"Your brother . . . that all gonna be cool? I have some experience with wards. If you need me to place a call—"

Jack waved the offer away. "Nah, whatever it is it won't be anything I haven't dealt with a dozen times before. "

Nick thought about that. "Listen, I'm gonna take a break and hang around for a while. Here's my card; you need an escape, call me."

Nick had an actual business card, the central feature being the presidential seal, with the eagle holding two hockey sticks.

"Will do. What are your hours?"

Jack's phone rumbled in his jacket pocket: Will. He wasn't ready for a brotherly reunion just yet. Best to get a coherent answer from Paul first. He let it ring out. A text message flashed up:

I'm at our house. Where are you?

"Between meds and errands and where's-the-remote, Dad keeps me going all hours," Nick said. "That espresso machine isn't just for the customers."

Jack watched Nick pull away, then turned his attention to the university. He hoped Paul had answers.

3

On the twenty-ninth floor of Monarch Tower Beth Wilder watched a two-year-old girl take a short staggering run and head butt the palm of her father's hand. Full of beans and still on Kyoto time. Her mother looked like she needed a drink, but happy to be in America and reunited with her husband.

Lorelei Gibson was the unofficial mascot of Chronon-1, Monarch Special Project's pride and joy. The 1 percent. The nine operatives out of 112 candidates who had the experience, adaptability, and mental fortitude to get through basic and advanced chronon training without losing their shit and washing out.

Chronon-1 wasn't the only squad of chronon-enabled operatives. Technicians were trained for lightweight short-term operations. Strikers were heftier, flashier. Juggernauts . . . well, Juggernauts were still in the test phase. They were scary as shit, but overdesigned in Beth's opinion.

Randall Gibson's crew was different. Trained to adapt, survive, and operate at peak efficiency within prolonged zero-state exposure were using minimal gear, with negligible psychological impact. They were rock stars and they were concrete.

Gibson, his second-in-command Donny, then Irene, Reeves, Dominguez, Voss, Mully, Bristol, and Chaffey. Chronon-1—the jewel in Special Project's shiny crown. Proof of what was possible.

Question was, why were they gathered here?

Beth watched as Gibson hunkered down in front of his daughter and held up his palm again.

"What does the billy goat do?" he drawled, thick as molasses. "C'mon now, show me whatcha got."

Beth knew he was playing up to the crowd that had gathered on the mezzanine, groupies from admin, Industrial, Pharma, and all the rest.

Lorelei giggled, toddled at her dad, and flumphed her head into his hand. Onlookers cheered. Lorelei plopped her hands over her face, embarrassed.

Her mother swept her up, blew a raspberry on Lorelei's fat little cheek. Lorelei reached for her dad, grasping inexpertly, all big brown eyes and "Hug Dada!"

Gibson took her, Lorelei pressing to his fatigues, arms clamped around his neck.

"I gotcha punkin' butter, I gotcha."

Yeah, the Gibsons have it all. Beth envied Lorelei's ability to love like that. Beth barely remembered her own father's face.

Horatio nudged her. "Don't feel bad."

Horatio was a white dude in his thirties, handlebar moustache, wearing a theater sports T-shirt. DON'T SHOOT, I'M A PLOT DEVICE!

Hilarious.

"Do I look like I feel bad?" Beth wasn't super tight with most of the other Monarch Security personnel, but the guys over in Innovations liked her just fine.

"Cheer up, dude. Better people than you washed out of the C-1 program."

Beth blinked. "'Better people'?"

Horatio backpedaled. "I mean . . . you know what I mean. Shit."

"Yeah I know what you meant. Do you know what's going on?"

Beth had made it a good way through the tryouts. Further than most. Flaked at the last hurdle. Now she was mid-level Monarch Security. Stable. Vanilla. Unremarkable.

Just how she liked it.

Horatio shook his head. "Nah. I've spent half of today trying to get our product demos into a showable state for the gala tomorrow night, so I haven't been poking around as much. I was banking on Will Joyce helping me to get the platform stable but he totally flaked out on me. Hey, are you free? I need a newbie to run through our flow, see what you get snagged on."

"Sorry. Plans."

"Yeah, right."

The mood on the mezzanine changed, the crowd dispersed. Gibson's smile vanished. He handed his kid back to his wife without even looking at them. Which meant Martin Hatch had just made an appearance.

His wife understood, turning and leaving without a word, child in one arm, dragging her luggage with the other.

Yep, there was Hatch: A tall, good-looking motherfucker with a killer smile he rarely deployed. Luminous midnight skin and a voice that was pure alpha-wave richness.

He scared the shit out of Beth.

"Ugh." Horatio rolled his eyes. "Gibson may be big dog, but Lord he's got daddy issues. The way he looks at Hatch I'm surprised they're not picking out curtains."

The elevator doors opened. Gibson's wife dragged their luggage inside. Lorelei called for her dada. If Gibson heard, he didn't react. The doors closed, and they were gone.

Beth walked out of the project management bullpen and

hung by the door. Next to the elevators, Hatch had one broad hand on Gibson's shoulder, addressing the team. After a while, the chosen nine, Chronon-1, followed Hatch to a glassed-in meeting room.

Beth stayed back, watching.

Gibson never took his eyes off Hatch, hardly blinked, nodding sharply at anything the CEO had to say.

It was a short meeting. Hatch departed. Chronon-1 filed out, marched briskly past project management.

Gibson saw Beth as they passed.

"Yo, Wilder," he called out, all Louisianan.

"Looks like the squad's got something on the boil tonight," she said.

The squad came to a halt while Gibson broke off to get closer to Beth. "Your shift ends around six, yeah?"

"My squad's on call. Monarch Actual didn't say why."

"I'm gonna need to blow off some steam later. I'd like to give you a ride home." He smirked. "You gonna say yes this time, or what?"

Gibson had the corn-fed steroidal physique of a career operator and a face like a thumb. Whatever juice he was on expressed through his sweat, sour and chemical, half-masked by liberal splashes of Green Irish Tweed.

I know about the gym bag in the trunk of your car. I know what you keep under the bottom lining. I know where the blond hair caught in the zip came from.

"No thanks."

"Treat me nice and maybe you'll find out what you're missing. I'm talkin' about C-1 now, punkin' butter."

Irene hitched a smile behind him. She was loving this.

"Y'know, sometimes we still watch your washout footage. For a laugh. All that screaming." He waved his arms around. "Calling for Daddy. Goddamn, Wilder."

"Hey, boss." Donny was lightweight, tightly muscled, shorter than Gibson. "Come on. Almost show time, yeah? Let's do it."

Gibson kissed his fingers, waved her off. "Later, punkin'."

Horatio crept over. "Do you think tonight has something to do with Project Lifeboat?"

Beth turned on him. "Don't ever talk about that. Especially in this building."

Saturday, 8 October 2016. 3:45 A.M. Riverport University.

Jack zipped his jacket against the cold and headed down Founders' Walk, hands stuffed in pockets. Gone were the electrically retrofitted gas lamps he remembered, the '70s-era garbage cans, chattering sprinklers, the occasional stray dog, and the grandfatherly feel of the scattered buildings.

They had been replaced by track-lit paths, trimmed hedges, solar-powered lamplight, and buildings that evoked a Future Europe designed by robots—all steel, glass, angles, and facets. A guy in a letterman jacket rested with his sleeping girlfriend on an ergonomic bench. Behind them an older woman in a Ramones T-shirt twirled a set of LED poi, inscribing Möbius figure eights in the air, strobing red and green. In the distance a three-sided infoscreen wished passersby a pleasant evening and directed them to the nearest campus exit. The only thing out of place in this better, brighter Riverport U was the library: a tottering old dame of a building from a time few cared to remember.

Jack hadn't set foot in there since a senior-year orientation tour. It was a shock to see the changes time had wrought.

The protest camp was in the largest triangular section of lawn he had seen from the street: a collection of tents and canvas shelters, ringed by a makeshift wall of wilted placards, bicycles, sodden bunting, and plastic sheeting adorned with spray-bombed anti-Monarch logos. A few sleepy-eyed protesters shambled from one tent to another, to the mixed soundtrack of acoustic guitar and Rihanna's last hit. Jack wasn't sure if the people inside were winding down or waking up.

In the east the sky was lighting up steel. The last time he had seen dawn over this town was from Bannerman's Overlook.

Again he thought of Zed, wondered where she was, and why life had pathed the way it had. He had spent the first four and a bit years following what passed for leads: things Zed had said, references she had made that sounded like slipups, rather than another fiction.

He was never going to know who she was, where she had come from, or where she had gone. That was just the way it was. After six years, he was beginning to make peace with that.

Or he thought he was, until he found himself here again. Seeing Zed's house. The 7-Eleven where they'd pour vodka into a Slurpee on a Friday night. The bridge where she free ran. The skate park where she spent some afternoons. He could feel that clear ache pouring into his cracks and he needed to get out of Riverport before it set and became a part of him again.

"Hey, if you're waiting for the demolition it isn't happening till eleven tomorrow. Take a flyer." The girl was in her early twenties, scraps of day-old Day-Glo zinc still visible on her cheeks. She was cherub-faced and surly, zipped into a thermal hoodie and proffering a flyer identical to the one Jack had peeled off the sidewalk out front.

"How's it going?" He gestured toward the old library. "Are they still going to—"

"Tear it down? Yeah. If this were happening in Europe cars would be burning."

"Well, I don't know about that. I mean—"

"Oh yeah," she snapped. "No time no time? Got some important importance going down? Your dog walker forgot to pick up Mr. Snuggle's homeopathic Prozac foam? You're looking at history, an abstract concept made real and it's standing right there. It was built in a different world, by people with different values. That library is *more* than the knowledge it houses. It's shelter from another age, a time capsule, and all that makes it irreplaceable. Once it's gone we can't fake it back into existence, like so much other bullshit. For the good of others at least *pretend* to give a fuck."

A trip wire snagged in Jack's head. "Listen," he said, low and even. "Across the ancient world ten-thousand-year-old relics are being jackhammered into talcum by morons from the Stone Age. In Australia three-thousand-year-old rock art is being dynamited to make way for coal that nobody wants. In Tasmania some of the oldest forests on Earth are being wood-chipped for toothpicks. In China millions of tourists are using legions of terra-cotta warriors as gum receptacles. In Africa billionaires are bidding to be the one to kill the last of a species. In Greenland the ice has pretty much vanished. Prime farmland is being fracked into uselessness. Food prices are set to triple. In ten years we'll be eating bugs. By comparison this building was erected last week and has as much meaning as the beer cans your hashtag warriors are sleeping on."

"You're saying this doesn't matter?"

"I'm saying this is a flyover town. You need to get out more and I'm not your therapy."

"This is my *backyard,* fucko. I can't chain myself to a Syrian obelisk, but I can do this. So take your smarmy been-there-done-that high-minded *fucking*—"

"*Hey!* Sir?" A rent-a-cop was marching over, flashlight in hand. He couldn't have been more than twenty-five. "Is this person bothering you? Amy, we talked about this. You and your people can hand out your material, but you were warned: one more incident and you're out." The cloth badge on his sleeve flagged him as Monarch Protective Services.

Ah crap, now the hangover. Guilt. He hated this part. "Wait, wait, wait." Enough to be miserable; no need to be a miserable asshole. "She didn't do anything wrong." He extended his hand to her. "Give me a few flyers. I'm heading into the city later. I'll hand them out."

Amy glanced at him, skeptically.

"Really," Jack said.

Amy handed over five. The guard sighed, clicked off the flashlight. "Can I take you somewhere, sir? If you're not part of the protest you shouldn't . . ." The guard's eyes narrowed. Jack took a half step back. "Jack Joyce, right?"

"Yeah. That's me."

The guard extended a hand. "You and me were in the same year, Riverport High. How've you been?"

Amy sighed.

"Oh, hey . . ."

The guard laughed uncomfortably and waved a downward paw. "Ah, you don't remember me. Doesn't matter. I was carrying more weight then."

Amy surveyed them for a heartbeat, then turned on her heel and walked back to camp. "Don't lose any sleep over it, Jack Joyce. We're just a flyover town." Hand painted in white on the back of her hoodie: RESPECT EXISTENCE OR EXPECT RESIS-TANCE. She tossed the remaining flyers away, a fluttering pink cloud.

The guard sighed. "I hate to see the library go, but folks'll be glad to get these tents off the lawn. Who knows why the board let them camp there in the first place. You know your brother doesn't work here anymore, right?"

An alarm went off in Jack's head: when people he didn't know mentioned Will it almost always meant trouble. "Sure," Jack lied. "Hey, can you point me to the Quantum Research Lab? I wanted to take a look and then I'll get to my hotel."

Since when had Will worked anywhere, let alone in a respectable lab at a respectable university?

"It's almost four A.M.," the guard said.

"Flight just got in." Jack smiled. "Still on Thailand time."

The guard laughed, pointed east. "It's always lit up. Oh and hey, stop by the Tavern on a Friday. Some of us still hang there. Dave's managing, so we get a discount."

Jack gave a relaxed salute. "Will do. See you." He had no idea who Dave was.

A game plan Tetrised into his head: see Paul, clean up after Will, rebook an exit flight. If he did this right he could be back in Asia before Thursday. Maybe he'd move on from Thailand, up stakes and get to Cappadocia; subsidize the whole trip with a few articles on food, politics, and the underground cities. Or he could do a follow-up on the scopolamine trade in South America, or a character piece on the attendees of Lebowski Fest in Louisville, or pretty much anything that let him grab a few more years of not thinking about whether his life was a panicked exercise in fleeing from himself.

"Jack!"

And there he was, right on time, saving Jack from further thoughts: Paul Serene. Less polished than his Facebook photo, way tidier than the frightened kid who thought he was going to die on Bannerman's Overlook six years ago. Clean, healthy, and in a starched shirt that probably cost more than everything Jack was wearing.

"What are you doing lurking on the lawn?"

Paul hopped over a park bench at a leap, bounced onto Founders' Way. "You know that guy?"

"The guard? Didn't even get his name."

"He didn't ask why you were here?"

Strange question. "Just told him I wanted to check out the fancy lab, then head home. Everything cool?"

Paul smiled, extended his right hand and pretended he hadn't heard the question. "How are you, man? You know all that sun'll have your face falling off by the time you're forty right? We're working on treatments for that. The reports are saying we could have Keith Richards looking like Gosling by 2025. Look at you!"

Jack opened his arms. "Bring it in, buddy."

Paul looked at him sideways, gave Jack his best are-you-serious face.

"Ah, right. Massachusetts. Where people don't hug. How'd you survive eighteen months in Paris?"

"Denial, wine, and nightmares. C'mon I'll show you the lab. Gimme the latest. When are you coming home?"

Jack zipped his jacket higher, stuffed his hands in his jeans pockets. "Is it far? It's colder than I remember."

"Just around the corner. Don't change the subject."

"I'm fine. Thinking of maybe moving to New Zealand. I hear it's really . . . livable."

"The last time you messaged me you were talking Kabul."

"The expat culture there's been covered. *Time* was all over it years back. "

"You're still doing that?"

"Being awesome?"

"Reportage."

Ugh. What is that feeling? Oh yes, guilt. He was meant to be a working reporter, not someone making his savings last on a beach in Asia.

"You realize that you've become a manifestation of Zed's fictional idea of herself, right?"

"Beats working at Walmart."

"One day she ran away from home as a kid. The next day her dad was a millionaire astronaut who left her a bundle in the will. After that she was in witness protection. After that she was—"

"On the run from the mob, had amnesia, had a terminal illness, was a retired dental hygienist trying to visit all fifty states . . . I know. I was there. The stories were a game. She was real." He looked Paul in the eye. "She saved your life." A helicopter thudded overhead, spotlight briefly playing across the quad, light turning to spears as it fell through the sparse canopy of elms. "You said you work for Monarch?"

"Yep."

"They're funding you?"

"Monarch Innovations, their fringe R-and-D division. It's been a total game changer for outliers like the Riverport lab."

"Ten years ago everybody lost their minds because someone opened a Wings Over Riverport. Now this."

"People do like chicken."

Jack had to admit: the new campus did a good job of killing nostalgia. It was beautiful, pristine, calm, and confident. It said: *We've got it under control. Things are going to be okay.*

He thought about cops in Chiang Mai, rolling on Monarch tires, and Riverport cops working hand-in-glove with Monarch Security. Monarch Agricultural drones were using seed bombs to replant swathes of clear-cut Amazon, while Monarch Pharmaceuticals subsidized the espresso machines of hardworking unlicensed cab drivers.

"Hey, funny thing: that guard said Will used to work here."

Paul smiled uncomfortably. "Yeah, about that. When did you last hear from your brother?"

Here it comes. "A week ago. He said I needed to come back and talk sense into you, actually."

Paul stopped in his tracks. "That's why you're here? Not because I asked you to?"

"I'm here because he sent me that e-mail and *then* you asked me to. What's going on? The message you left was pretty . . ." What was the word? *"Grandiose."*

"Where's Will now?"

"He wanted me to go straight to the house, but I figured I'd get more sense out of you."

Paul chewed his lip for one thoughtful second, and then said: "It's better that I show you. *Fuck.*" Paul's eyes were locked on something over Jack's shoulder: the security guard had come back, was talking into his radio, looking in their direction and nodding. "C'mon, walk fast."

Walking away from a badge at 4:00 A.M. wasn't something Jack questioned. He and Paul had started with egging houses on Halloween, graduated to breaking into junkyards to shoot zombie footage for high school film class, moved on to a short-lived flirtation with growing weed in his bedroom, and ended in that final scene with one of the state's more serious killers. If Paul said turn away and fly casual, Jack didn't over-think it.

"You mind telling me what's going on?" They reached the end of Founders' Way, turned right, and then: "You have got to be fucking kidding me."

Paul Serene's twenty-foot-high face smiled down. The videoboard was attached to the façade of the old university lab, preserved within the vision-challenging lattice of the new Quantum Physics Building dome. The view pulled back from Paul's mug, revealing him holding a roiling ball of light in one palm, before a benevolent sweeping gesture invited the viewer into what was presumably a brighter future. This was signified by the light ball enveloping the screen and MONARCH INNOVATIONS sparkling into view.

"Before you say anything—"

"Ain't you pretty!"

"Never mind."

"So benevolent. So constipated."

Paul fished out a transparent laminate and moved to a clear security door by the main entrance. "It wasn't my idea. I just turned up for the shoot."

"What is it you do here again?"

Paul swiped his card. Nothing happened. He swore softly, repositioned it, tried again. This time the card swipe was rewarded with one of the most satisfying *clicks* Jack had heard. The brushed-steel frame nudged open. Paul sighed with relief.

"Project coordinator," Paul replied. "They recruited me out of college. I make sure things get done, effectively, on time, and in a way that gets people excited." He held the door open. "After you." The interior of the glassed atrium was warm, containing three stories of extravagantly empty space. "The dome is a double layer of 3-D-printed textured polycarbonate and reinforced glass. The air layer provides insulation. Depending on the position of the sun, the shadows cast by the canopy's asymmetrical architecture take on different aspects: striations, crazed glass, shapes significant to people who know more about math than I do."

"Neat trick."

"On top of that they've got the glass doubling as solar panels, providing a marginally positive carbon footprint. For the administrative sections of the building at least. Some parts of the labs chew power like a motherfucker."

Paul marched left toward the façade of one of the campus's original brick buildings, now contained within the expensive geometric umbrella of the Quantum Physics Building's dome.

"The architect spends every alternate month under a Shinto vow of non-communication in a compound outside Hokkaido.

It made negotiations and milestones a total bitch. Dunno why they gave him that prize; it'll only encourage him." Paul glanced back the way they came. "Follow me, I'll take you upstairs."

Jack glanced back. "Are we allowed in here?" No sign of the guard, but that didn't mean he wasn't waiting for backup. "You're not acting like we're allowed to be here. Buildings this expensive usually have doors that work the first time."

"Whose face is on that screen?"

"I don't know, but he's smiling like there's a gun to his head."

A hazard-striped security door opened onto a freight elevator, which was set into the façade of the old building. Paul waved his card through a scanner. "You've seen a lot of weirdness, yeah?" Paul wasn't shooting the shit: he was double-checking.

A fifteen-inch screen on the elevator's opposite wall flashed to life and provided a rundown of Paul's appointments: none. It advised that he was five hours early for work and that Monarch Innovations does not approve of more than 10 percent employee overtime in a given month. An MIT-sourced graph appeared to support this philosophy, and the screen wished him a good morning.

"I have now," Jack said.

Paul swiped the card again, tapped the top floor. Jack noticed the tension in his face.

"Hit me with the weirdest," Paul said.

"So I was in Belize. That's in South America."

"I know where Belize is, Jack."

"So I was in Belize and made friends with two lady pimps when I helped them save a horse from being beaten to death by some scumbag who owned a racetrack."

"That's—"

"The next morning I officiated when they fought an early-morning duel over the beautiful prostitute they had both fallen in love with."

Paul eyeballed him.

"2011. Straight-up code duello."

Paul considered. "How did it end?"

"Marriage. All three of them, quite happily."

"Huh."

"Life's short. So, does that qualify?"

"Not even close. This is our floor."

The doors shushed open onto a long, dark corridor. A single door was rim-lit at the end.

"This doesn't feel like it fits inside that old building."

"We added a couple of reinforced top floors to suit our needs. We're above the canopy at this level." Recess lighting kicked in at ankle height, following them toward the door. "Once we get inside I'll need your help to set a few things up. How familiar are you with the theory of relativity?"

"I'm relatively familiar."

"You still like sci-fi?"

"We prefer 'speculative fiction.'"

"Well, I'd say you're about to step into it." Clinically white armored doors rumbled open at the final swipe. "Except this is anything but speculative." Paul walked into darkness. Jack followed.

Lights clicked and thudded, revealing the chamber section by section.

Vertigo kicked in, Jack's hands closing on the cold steel of the safety rail before him. He was looking down into an octagonal tech pit, NASA-white and hairy with red and blue cables snaking out of discrete access panels. Suspended at the center of the hollowed-out geometric sphere of a room was . . . another geometric sphere. Held atop a high-tech dais, the sphere was made of a dense-looking dull metal, each face of it jacked and wired with tons of heavy-gauge cabling. The cabling poured from the sphere and down into subfloor cavities, or was draped over and connected to a metal walkway that ringed the sphere. Jack might have thought the walkway might be for maintenance, if it wasn't for the sealed-off airlock chamber sitting out of place on their side of it.

Paul didn't waste time. After swipe-locking the door behind them, he leapt down the steps to the left and headed around the octagonal pit toward a glassed-in observation room.

"How much money did they give you? What am I even looking at?"

The in-room intercom piped Paul's voice from four corners, weird acoustics making him sound like two people at once. He spoke absentmindedly, working a two-screen control panel.

"The beginning of a new age." He stopped abruptly, clattering keys falling silent. When he spoke again his voice was flat with realization. "You're looking at the death of regret." He smiled. "Huh."

Jack studied the construction, trying to make sense of it, and failing.

"Where have I seen this before?"

"Nowhere," Paul said, busy with the monitors. "It's proprietary."

Something was off about this. "Paul, are you bullshitting me? This isn't 'proprietary.'" Jack pointed out the viewplate. "Tell me that thing isn't based on Will's work."

Paul stopped what he was doing, formed a response, opened his mouth, changed his mind, shut it again. "Okay," he said, and went back to his keyboard. "I won't."

"That security guard told me Will used to work here." Paul was the only person on Earth Jack trusted. If there was deception here, he would not be able to withstand it.

"I know you hate being lied to," Paul said, reading his mind. "But I would point out that I didn't lie to you; I just didn't answer your question in a timely manner. So . . . we cool?"

"Why am I here?"

"I delayed explanations until you saw the Promenade for yourself. You have to understand everything in its proper context."

"Don't give me long answers to simple questions, Paul. What did Will do and how bad is it?" Paul was still tapping keys, dragging a finger across viewscreens. It didn't look like he was getting anywhere. It kept reprimanding with error messages. "What are you doing? Do you even know what you're doing?"

"Yes," Paul said, exasperated, and produced a collection of Post-it notes from his pocket. Waved them as evidence. "I know what I'm doing." The viewscreen barped again. "I'm just," Paul said, calmly, "trying to work. Quickly. Because in less than five minutes your security guard buddy is going to come through that door with at least three friends and change the course of human progress forever." Paul returned to what he was doing. "For the worse, just so we're clear."

4

Jack had left behind the relative safety and calm of Thailand for this. Not only was he involved in the commission of at least one felony, his best friend was acting weird and Jack was already being dragged back into Will's mess of a life. What's more, he hadn't even seen Will yet.

Something hard-kicked beneath the floor. As Jack backed away from the machine, the hair on his arms tickled. Thick cords of cabling spasmed, like living things.

"Paul—"

"Here's the deal," Paul's tinny double voice piped over the intercom. "We hired Will as a consultant on this project. It's supposed to do that, relax. So we hired Will. And things were going pretty great. He seemed stable, not too much of that muttering-to-himself stuff, kept a reasonable focus and he ironed out kinks like nobody else on the team."

"But . . ."

"But he became erratic."

"Define 'erratic.' Erratic like that time at Walmart, or erratic like that thing with the council planners?"

"More like that time he found us playing with his stuff in the barn."

Jack closed his eyes and swore. That had been the bad one. It had been pre-medication and Will had really gone off the

deep end: a daylong fit of rage, followed by an inability to process it. Will had disappeared into the barn for forty-eight hours,
muttering and shouting. When Jack tried to make peace, Will
had thrown a plate at him, mashed potatoes flying everywhere.
It was the only time Jack hadn't felt safe around his older brother.

"You could have told me that in an e-mail, Paul."

If there was one thing he learned from the episode with the
two women in Belize it was that nothing is more important in
this life than happiness—whatever it looks like, wherever you
find it. This was no way to live.

Paul leaned against the console. "What did we always say?"

"C'mon . . ."

"What did we say?"

"We stick together or the bastards win."

"Right. Tonight is the most important moment of my life. I
wouldn't be here without you, so I couldn't have done this
without you." He turned and popped the clear Perspex idiot
shield from an oversized black punch-button. "I want you to
be able to say you were in the room when the world changed."

Paul's palm came down, gently, and the room outside blasted
to electric life. Mechanisms activated beneath the curved walkway that circled the core, and from beneath the walkway flat
double-hinged sections swung up, opened, and clicked into
place. In a single wave corridor sections unfurled around the
circumference. In seconds the walkway had become a sealed
corridor circling the crackling geometric sphere at the chamber's
heart.

Jack stepped back.

Paul said, "Put these on," tossing him a pair of photoreac-
tive goggles.

"Shouldn't you have given me those *before* you hit that
button?"

A monitor suspended from the roof flashed a green alert.

"The ground security door's been opened. We've got about three minutes." Paul ran up the steel-mesh stairs to the entry door, slashed his card through the reader, and locked it down tight. "Call it five. Follow me."

The machine was vibrating. The core threw off sparks. The air smelled like burned hair. A shimmering corona, like a heat mirage, rose from the corridor-ring.

"Will bulk e-mailed the entire project mailing list—investors included," Paul shouted above the din, coming to a stop before the gangway. "He expressed his lack of confidence in the project in a very detailed manner. In short he freaked the investors right out. Funding was pulled, Jack. They shut the entire project down."

Jack nodded, understanding, checked the door, glared at Paul. "They fired you. They *fired* you, and you're in here with a hacked code key about to fire up a *reactor* that your only real expert thinks is *massively dangerous*. With *me*."

"C'mon. We've done worse."

"I don't think we have, Paul."

Something under the floor belted against itself, and the sphere at the center of the room started thrumming.

"This is six years of work, Jack! People trusted me to guide this to the finish line. People with families. Once administration sees that it works safely—"

"You'll go to jail!"

"It'll be worth it!"

Jack took that in. "This is just like that time with that girl from summer camp."

"I don't deny that Heather had a few problems—"

"You're white knighting, man! Again! Let's get the fuck out of here!"

"This is about families, Jack! And futures! *The* future! Lives will change if I can make this happen."

Jack pointed straight at the machine. "This *is* based on Will's work, isn't it?" Jack insisted. "He knows what he's talking about. I mean, before he went off the rails, before our parents were gone, he was doing good work, right? He might be nuts but he's not an idiot."

"The team's been over it and over it and there is *nothing,* and I mean *nothing* to Will's accusations."

"Maybe so, but I didn't come back to get arrested. Shut it down, okay? It sounds . . . really pissed off."

Paul shook his head. "Too late. Once the core's activated there's no way to turn it off, short of finding some way to collapse the black hole."

The machine stabilized, soothed; the vibration dropped to a low, comforting hum.

" 'Black hole'?"

Paul held up his damp fistful of Post-it notes. "I told the team: We've done good dev. We know it works. Show me how to start it and I'll take the fall. I'm *sure* that once the committee—"

" '*Black hole*'?"

A sharp quad-tone *snap* fired off as four safety clasps detached from the airlock, the sound finding a dozen flat surfaces to reverberate from. The airlock seal on the circular corridor cracked and heavy hydraulics hauled the blast door aside, venting atmosphere. The distortion around the core at the center of the machine dimmed.

"I should never have turned you on to The Smiths."

Through the airlock door came a shape. A person.

Someone has been in the corridor the entire time.

The figure braced itself against the wide lip of the airlock's seal before taking one trembling step onto the ramp and into the lab. It gasped, chest heaving, and exited the machine entirely.

"Hey me," the figure said, to Jack. "It's you." Then shook his head. "Damn."

Jack took off his goggles. There was no mistake: Jack was looking at himself.

"Holy shitballs," Paul said.

Jack's clone—all smiles—held his palms up good-naturedly. "Hey, it's cool. This all works out. And Paul . . ." His expression darkened. "You still owe me a fucking explanation."

Paul shook his head to clear it, checked his watch, now a man back on mission. To Jack: "Get in the machine." He was at the L-console next to the gangway, making adjustments.

Jack didn't hear him.

"Hey," Jack's clone said to Jack. "Want to see a trick? Watch this." He directed Jack's attention to Paul.

"Paul . . . ," Jack said, deeply unsettled yet unable to take his eyes off the doppelganger on the ramp.

"And go," said Jack's clone.

"What is it," Paul and Jack's clone said, together.

"Wait," Paul and Jack's clone said, simultaneously.

"We don't have *time* for this," Paul and Jack's clone shouted.

"Knock it off," they chorused.

Paul stepped forward, stabbing a finger at his watch.

"Security is on their . . . ," they yelled at each other. "Ah screw you."

Jack's clone spread his arms in a theatrical *ta-da,* utterly pleased with himself. "Huh? Yeah? How about that?"

"We've got two minutes," Paul snapped.

Jack rounded on his clone, snapped his fingers. "Hey! Whoever you are. Inside pocket." He snapped his fingers again, opened his palm.

"Way ahead of you," his clone said, and handed over a key ring.

Jack stared at the key ring, familiar as his jacket, his bathroom mirror, his own bed. They were all there: the rusted old key to his cabin in Chiang Mai, the sixty-four-gig flash drive he used to back up his articles, his iPhone tool, the bottle-opener he picked up from an aeronautics plant outside of Oxford, Mississippi—all attached to a branded key ring that came with the last pair of shoes he bought new. By contrast the silver .38 slug was overdressed, thin leather strap threaded through the forty-eight-gauge hole at the base.

Jack looked at Paul, wanting confirmation. "This guy is me."

Paul produced his own set of keys: Mercedes key ring, two keys, one silver bullet.

"This is a time machine," Jack said.

Jack's clone took back his keys. "I'll be needing those."

"Into the airlock, Jack. That's how this happens."

Jack's clone's head was on a swivel, taking them both in. "Intense. Hey Paul, what would have happened if I didn't do what I did? Y'know . . . screw with you. The parroting thing."

"To answer your question," Paul said to the clone, "it's not possible. You would always have said and done what you have just said and done. You're here as a direct result of what has gone before. Now get off the ramp. You're staying. Jack, you're going."

"Going? Going where?" The real Jack this time.

"I'm sending you two minutes into the past, so that we can have this conversation."

The machine waited, thrumming heavily. "And what if this plays out like the end of *Evil Dead 2*?"

"You're not going to the fucking Middle Ages. You need this machine to step out of, and that wasn't functioning until we

turned it on four minutes ago. That's as far back as this
machine will take you—to the moment it was first activated.
Now move. I've been waiting three years to try this thing."

Jack walked cautiously up the gangway, eyeing the distortion waves emanating from the machine's housing. "If I get
lymphoma I swear to God . . ."

"It's not radioactive; it's chronon-active. Completely revo-
lutionary and entirely clean. As far as we can tell."

"Swell." Jack stepped over the lip, into the airlock, looked
around inside. No controls, no handles. "Hey, if something
goes wrong, how do I reopen this thing?"

"You don't," Paul said. "Once the charge builds up within
the Promenade it needs to be expended before the internal
atmosphere is vented. Failure to do so could cause . . . big
problems." Hydraulics engaged, hefting the door away from
the housing and sliding it toward the seal. "Just walk counter-
clockwise around the core. One full rotation will complete the
journey."

"Fine. But when I get out of here I want a full—" The door
pressed into place, then locked off with a rubbery smooching
sound. A blast of cool air filled the room. Jack's ears popped.
Wiggling a finger in one ear, opening and closing his jaw, he
peered through the viewplate.

Outside, Paul was waving him to the left. The other Jack
smiled and waved beside Paul.

The airlock had two internal doors. On cue the left door
disengaged. Jack stepped into the Promenade, the airlock
sealing behind him. The interior of the circular corridor was
made of some kind of nonconductive white ceramic, feature-
less, blood-warm beneath his fingers and floored with waffle-
tread black rubber.

The thrum of the core sounded louder inside the corridor,

the womb of some furious monster. The thrum transmuted to a sudden whine, the floor kicked, Jack said, "Fuck," and . . .

Silence.

The regular, adrenal pound of the core was gone, though it couldn't have been more than twenty feet from where he stood. The airlock was so perfectly soundless Jack could have believed it was floating in space. Blood pulsed in his eardrums, his breath rasping like it was piped through earphones.

"Jack?"

He took a step forward, peering around the eternal corner. "Hello?" No response. He started walking.

No other sound was forthcoming. The trip around the core felt a lot like walking on a treadmill, like the corridor was moving around him rather than he moving through it. Then the exit door appeared.

Jack hit the red release button, the seal cracked, the hatch slid aside, and he stepped into the airlock from which he had departed a minute ago. Peering through the viewplate he saw the gangway, the time lab, Paul, and his double. His past self.

The airlock hissed open. Jack steadied himself against the lip of the seal, suddenly light-headed. Internal atmosphere vented and he stepped outside, giddy. He knew this scene. He knew what the Jack before him was feeling. He hadn't noticed how utterly dumbstruck Paul had looked the first time around.

"Hey me," Jack said to his clone. "It's you." Then shook his head. Too weird, like vertigo in his own skull, like waking up from a dream inside a dream to realize he was still dreaming. "Damn."

The clone at the bottom of the ramp took off his goggles, peering at Jack with an expression that resembled hostility.

Jack put his hands up. "Hey, it's cool. This all works out. And Paul, you still owe me a fucking explanation."

Saturday, 8 October 2016. 4:17 A.M. Riverport, Massachusetts. Quantum Physics Building.

Jack's past self reentered the machine and peered anxiously from the airlock as the hatch closed. He and Paul waved him off. There was a powerful snap, the distortion effect around the corridor pulsed outward, vanished, and the machine returned to its usual low hum.

"Jack." Paul smiled alarmingly. "With this device, this machine that you're looking at right now, we can put an end to . . . suffering. Disease. Catastrophe. We can . . . we can go back in time before . . . *imagine* if this machine had existed on September 10, 2001. Imagine how different our world would be today if we could go back with enough time to stop those flights. Imagine being able to develop a cure for a terrible disease in the future, and then bring it into the past. Just think."

Jack looked at the machine. "If in the future you know that this works, like you said, wouldn't you come back to this moment, right now, and tell yourself that?"

Paul's mouth opened uncertainly. He glanced at the machine. "I . . . I don't know. I . . ." He laughed it off and made a final adjustment. "Okay, my turn. The destination date's been set for two minutes from now. All you have to do, once I'm inside, is hit the Go button. Got it?"

"Paul, security is about to walk in here and find me alone with eleven billion dollars' worth of bleeding-edge whateverthefuck. They will not buy that I was looking for the cafeteria."

"Two minutes, Jack. The door's locked. You'll be fine." Paul moved up the gangway, pivoted, thrust both arms into the air, and hooted.

"Woo," Jack responded and opened the airlock, realizing

four cameras were filming him in commission of a federal offense.

Paul stepped inside. "Okay, lock me in."

Jack tapped a key; the airlock sucked itself shut.

A green alert flashed: the elevator had just opened on the other side of the lab's security door.

"Paul, make this quick. We don't have—"

The security door beeped, and hissed open.

"Long."

Paul's face fell. "Oh no."

A forlorn figure stood at the top of the stairs, thin and haunted inside a beaten old coat, looking at Jack and Paul like a child betrayed. "What . . . ?" said William Joyce. "What have you done?"

Will clattered down the stairs. *"What have you done?"* He hadn't run a comb through his hair in days; shirt and pants were a calendar of use.

"What's happening, Will?"

His brother rounded on Jack, his thin-fingered grip pinching into Jack's shoulders, gaze flicking over factors and dependencies only he could see. "You have to help me. We have to shut this down. *We have to shut this down, Jack!*" He abandoned Jack, faced the machine. "The core is live, but if we disconnect the Promenade it's useless for transport. . . ."

Paul's voice crackled over the quad-system. "Jack! Stop him! If he damages the network anything could happen!"

"Shears!" Will screamed. "Cut the power to the Promenade at the trunk!"

Jack grabbed his brother before he could run off. Will wrenched himself free. As he did something heavy fell from his pocket and thudded on the deck. A 9mm automatic. Will tutted exasperatedly and picked it up. "Their calculations are wrong, Jack."

"What is that?"

Will disregarded the gun, annoyed, but didn't pocket it. "Jack, you're not listening. The Meyer-Joyce field is being rendered unstable. It will fracture entirely if—"

Will was never any good with his hands. This could end badly a number of different ways. "Will. I need you to look at me. Can I please have the gun?"

A wild sweep of his arm distanced Will from his brother. "Don't patronize me, Jack."

"You're not thinking straight."

"This device has been *sabotaged*. It will—"

"Listen—"

"*Time! Is going! To end!* If you won't work with me, then you must get out of my way."

Jack refused to engage with the madness, an old tactic. "Or what, Will?" Jack moved carefully toward his brother. "You'll shoot me?"

Will raised the gun and fired into the ceiling, a needle in the ear that killed all sound, and then the shot was reverberating from a dozen surfaces. Will shoved his brother aside, knocking Jack to the rubberized floor.

Through his hands and chest, pressed against the rubber, Jack felt the floor suddenly *thump* from somewhere deep in its guts.

"No. No no no no *no!*" Will hammered the controls, the machine's innards shifting from that low signature hum to something different, more alarming. It wasn't the charge building up. This was something else. Something more uneven, distressed, broken. Escalating. Jack scrambled to his feet.

Paul's face was framed by the airlock's small viewplate as smoke filled the internal cavity. "Jack! You have to stop him! *Jack!*" The Promenade vibrations doubled their rpm, the distortion-shimmer shifting out of synch with itself—becoming something more serrated and angry. Paul looked terrified through the clouding glass. Jack was at the hatch, failing to find any kind of manual override. "We can't," Paul said, coughing, the smoke so thick he was little more than a shadow. "Even if you could open this thing the environment in here is chronon-charged. It needs to be discharged in a controlled fashion— which means I take a stroll down the Promenade. It's cool. But you have to hit that Go button." Paul's hand stabbed the glass, pointing at the control bank where Will stood.

The machine shrieked; a ceramic panel popped free, splang-ing to the mesh maintenance floor.

"Will! Hit the button!"

Will was too preoccupied to listen. "Bringing the core on-line: wrong thing. Charging the Promenade: wrong thing. Us-ing . . ." Will's eyes ran over one of the screens, panicked. "You *used* it? You've used the Promenade? Oh God oh God."

"Will!"

No response.

"Paul. Hang tight. I'll—"

Air pressure shifted. Jack felt himself being pressed bodily into the muscle of a giant heart for one monstrous, elongated *beat* and . . .

Boom.

Jack was lifted off his feet, hit the deck.

Twenty-seven tons of metal tortured by torsion screamed like a living thing.

Jack scrambled off the gangway and sprinted for the con-trols. Maintenance grills tumbled fifty feet from the ceiling, bouncing off walkways, cracking glass. Without slowing, Jack shouldered Will to the floor, grabbed the corner of the panel, and slammed the Go button.

The distortion field amplified, leaped outward, broke the air. Every socket in every panel and recess vomited sparks and flamed up. White enamel tiles were painted in upward tongues of char. The machine's whine dropped. Jack gasped with relief.

Then it began cycling up again, harder and harder, faster and faster.

He couldn't see Paul anymore: the interior of the airlock had filled completely with black haze. Abandoning the controls, Jack cleared the distance to the hatch in seconds, slammed into it, pounded against the glass, and screamed, "Paul! Go! *Go!*" He had no idea if his friend was even conscious inside that armored sarcophagus.

Will shouted Jack's name, was back on his feet, bracing himself against the control panel. "We're too late! Get away from the machine! Get . . . !"

The core threw off three-foot sparks in colors Jack had never seen before.

The Promenade buckled inward. Jack's atoms yanked toward the core, for a second. And then the opposite, times ten.

The blast wave punched through Jack, flowing through his cells like water around stones, and into the room. Lights erupted, glass exploded, panels fried, monitors crazed, and everything . . .

. . . *stopped*.

Silence. Like he had known inside the Promenade. Perfect, utter silence.

Lowering his hand from his face, Jack opened his eyes and looked around. Everything was silent because nothing moved. Nothing. Not the shattering glass, not the flying sparks, not the billowing and rising black smoke. Nothing. Not even his brother.

Every last thing had paused, mid-action. Frozen. Perfectly paused, immobile; people, objects, smoke, and sparks locked in time and space—a snapshot of a moment. He reached out, touched a floating shard of glass, felt it resist, watched it budge but remain suspended in space.

Jack was moving, but not a single other thing was.

Will was still behind the control console, hands thrown up to shield him from the console that had erupted in sparks and flame, his face contorted like a badly-timed snapshot. Jack reached out, fingers stretching toward his brother's frozen expression. "Will?"

An alert—bright green—caught his attention from one intact monitor. It read, in no uncertain terms: DESTINATION DATE: ERROR.

If the destination date was an error, then where—when—had Paul gone?

God pressed Play.

Metal crashed into metal as the control panel blew up. Will shrieked and toppled backward as glass shotgunned from the observation deck's frame. Smoke rolled out from the machine in a terrible wave as emergency lights kicked in blood-red and, instantly, the room filled with nine soldiers in hard-chested tactical gear.

They didn't have helmets, they had masks for faces, and those faces leered yellow, circular, smiling.

Green lasers sliced the smog, attached to black rifles that swept the room like terrible eyestalks. Behind each one a black-eyed idiot grin.

The white lettering on their black chests read PEACE.

Oh good, Jack thought. *None of this is real.*

Will was on his feet. "Jack. Someone is still in the machine."

"Targets!"

"'Targets?'"

Every green beam flew home to one of two focus points: Jack or Will. A lethal wall of cartoon smiles.

Jack and Will should have died. They didn't.

One of the men lowered his weapon: barrel-chested, 'roided, confident. Ex-marine bikers, African heterodox Christian militiamen, Israeli mujahideen . . . Jack had seen enough veteran mercs over the last few years to recognize one on sight. Had to be the leader.

"Gentlemen!" He pointed at Will, voice muffled behind the yellow mask. "You I know." Then at Jack. "You I don't."

He grabbed at his mask and snapped it off over his head—the yellow disk attached to the front of something like a tactical hockey mask. "This is fuckin' stupid, I can't breathe." He was in his forties, close-cropped dark hair, laughing eyes.

"Boss." One of them shifted uncomfortably. "Orders are: masks on."

"Voss, dictate to me again and I'll put on clown makeup and fuck your kids. Donny, cuff the egghead. The rest of you, delete the rando."

Blank-eyed smiles swung beams from Will to Jack's chest.

The floor kicked. The core flared. Blast wave.

Everything paused. Everything, and everyone, freeze-framed in an instant.

This crew had flooded through the door, down both sets of mesh stairs, every assault gun pointed at Jack and Will, beams frozen, expressions frozen, shouts trapped in throats. Eight men and one woman.

The Promenade had shed almost all of its plating, half-skeletonized by everything it had endured, its torment tearing it apart from within.

Will was resigned, eyes on the console, heedless of the two targeting lasers still floating over his shoulder blades. Jack reached out, took Will by the arm. The folds of Will's shirt were hard as rock—locked in a submoment. His brother did not move.

"Will," Jack said. "We have to go."

Nothing.

His grip tightened. *"Will!"*

Something palpable transferred from Jack, through his hand, to his brother. Will's profile flared—suddenly shrouded in that familiar distortion field—and Will kicked off talking: "If he uses the machine it . . . !" Will stopped, realizing things had changed. "Jack. I was too late."

"Will . . . we need . . . "

"We're existing within a topological defect in the Meyer-Joyce field. Time, causality . . . all have ceased to function." Shockingly, Jack realized, his brother was about to cry. "The M-J field has been fractured, Jack. *Wounded.* Zero state. Complete, all-encompassing . . . stasis."

"Will—"

"I was warned." Will was gone again. "I knew it. We knew it. I warned Paul, but he wouldn't listen. *He wouldn't listen.* This could have been avoided, but now . . ."

"This happened once before. I don't think it's permanent. When this ends those men in the funny masks are going to come to, kill me and kidnap you." Then: "Why do they want to kidnap you?"

Will didn't hear. "Not the end," he said, nodding. "Just a stutter." Nodding more vociferously. "All right. Let's go. We have to go."

Everything fluttered uncertainly: juddering in and out, sucked back in, paused.

Jack grabbed his brother. "Run."

A torrent of gunfire annihilated the console, tore through the spaces where the brothers had stood, punched through all of that expensive white ceramic. The smoke-wall finished its rollout, flooding across shooters and targets alike, spot fires erupting and hissing amid the haze.

"Lost visual!" someone shouted.

"Under here!" Will shouted. "Beneath the machine. Maintenance recess."

"Pair off," their leader drawled. "Secure the scientist, then get the bodies to the library."

Visibility was down to five feet. Jack kept his hand on Will's shoulder, making their way through the pall. Will was leading them down the side of the gangway, while Jack kept his eyes on the probing green lasers.

"Something's real wrong here, Will."

"Is there no beginning to your insight?"

"These wide-bodies are career players. Why they're dressed for street theater I have no fuckin' idea but you can bet there's a reason. It's the opposite of camouflage. They want to be seen."

Will stepped on shattered glass and four beams slashed toward them. Jack threw himself on top of Will as a three-round burst sang past his neck, hot.

"Under the ramp! They're under the ramp!"

Jack dropped down into the maintenance ring. Will scrambled, Jack followed, his booted feet disappearing over the side as a pair of questing lasers slashed through the space they had just occupied.

Jack hit the grill floor on his left shoulder. The smoke was thinner beneath the machine, the curving recess tight with the machine's core suspended directly above them. Voices above called out their location: Jack and Will had given no one the slip.

The squad leader, the one with the southern drawl, was giving orders. "Irene, radio Actual, have 'em get their bird in the air in five. Voss, Rodriguez, get the roof off this room. The rest of you secure this floor."

A voice overhead barked: "Sir, two targets are—"

"Beneath that contraption, I know. Well? Go on. Go get 'em. *Hey fellas?*"

"Is he talking to us?" Will whispered.

Jack motioned him to be quiet. Listened.

He heard something. Listened again. A second time: *ping*.

"Come on out."

Two canisters rolled over the lip of the recess, clattered to the grill, trailing orange. *Gas.*

Jack scooped up the first, but it was in his eyes and throat before he made contact. Tossed the first one up, blind. A hand popped over the side, holding a Glock. The shooter waved it around, blasting off shots. When it was over Jack was curled fetal, choking, hands pressed to his eyes as the cloud from the second canister swept around the curve.

"Boys?"

Hands on his arm, pulling hard. Jack let himself uncurl and rise.

"He's reloading," Jack rasped, and he slammed Will into the wall as thirteen blind rounds spanged and whined into tens of millions of dollars' worth of technology.

The shooter started coughing. "Ah, fuck, that stuff's got a kick, don't it?"

"Boss? We're meant to capture Dr. Joyce alive."

"I know, I know, was just havin' fun. They're fine. Go get 'em."

Will's face filled Jack's vision: he was wearing the protective goggles Jack had discarded. "This way!" His voice was pretty hoarse, though.

Boots hit metal as two grunts dropped into the recess, impact reverberating, lasers on, slashing upward. One trooper headed left around the ring, the other right. Pincer.

Will had popped open a decent-sized hatch—no crab-crawling through vents for them—dragging Jack behind.

"Is it dark in here?" Jack's nose and throat were on fire. He couldn't even open his eyes, overflowing with caustic tears faster than he could wipe them away. "It seems really dark in here."

"The Techs mostly use headlamps down here. We're inside the machine. The actual machine. The entire building is given over to maintaining and running the core and Promenade, making time travel as safe and accurate as possible."

Jack hacked and spat. The walls were bolted metal, occasional tangles of cables, hot technology, still running. It was fifty degrees warmer in here than in the lab. "I thought small was the new big."

"The Large Hadron Collider has a circumference of seventeen miles," Will replied. "A lifetime of study and sacrifice has allowed me to harness the laws of time and causality within a space no larger than the apartment building from *Seinfeld*. So I, and the greatest minds to have ever lived, would appreciate you keeping your observations to yourself."

Despite the dire circumstances, it was good to hear Will back in form. Jack coughed repeatedly; all he could taste was salt and snot and acid.

"Time travel's one thing; what's harder to believe is that you know what *Seinfeld* is."

"You haven't changed at all. Can you fathom how serious these events are?"

"Will," Jack said, gasping. "Levity is a strategy adopted by many to deal with crisis."

"You're always like this."

"You're always a crisis."

"That's simply untrue."

As if in rebuttal green lasers snapped on over Jack's shoulders. Will shoved him to the ground as two silhouettes snapped off a series of probing three-round bursts. Gun-cracks reverberated down the narrow throat of the corridor.

"I never shot at you," Will said, face-to-face. "I needed your attention."

"We have to get out of this tunnel."

Tactical lights snapped on atop the troopers' assault weapons. They were coming in. Jack reached up, yanked the pistol from the back of Will's pants, rolled, and squeezed. Nothing happened.

"What was that?" The troopers crouched.

Jack flicked off the safety and squeezed again.

His wrist took the kicks, shots going everywhere. Silhouetted and vulnerable against the light from the entrance, the troopers scrambled back into the maintenance loop. Will grabbed Jack by the collar and hauled him upright. By the time the troopers hosed down the tunnel, Will and Jack had crashed around a left-hand turn.

Jack pressed Will against the warm wall and dragged him down into a kneeling position. Pistol braced, he aimed at the corner as best he could, and waited.

The guards didn't pursue. "I need an eyewash station," Jack croaked. "Or a cafeteria."

"Cafe—?"

"Milk, Will. Something alkaline. For the eyes." He stood up, tried to bring the tunnel into focus. It was like staring into hot light.

"Follow me." Will moved off, then stopped. " 'It happened once before,' " he muttered.

Jack blew a nose full of something offensive onto the floor. "Will, we gotta go."

"Back there, you said, 'It happened once before.' The stutter. How could you know that? If time had stopped and restarted, it would have appeared to you as it did to me: seamless. Unless—"

"The world froze, but I didn't. Then I grabbed you and—"

Will's eyes were scanning again, not seeing Jack. "Your proximity to the pulse altered your relationship to the chronon field. My reanimation must . . . there must have been chronon-transference from you to me. Meaning a non-affected person can act as a kind of causality battery, of sorts. Chargeable, yes, by someone who is a causality source, even in a state in which causality has ceased to self-generate."

"Will! What's . . . ?"

"Time go bad! Get it? Causality, the flow of time, of cause and effect, is a lake. The lake contains an ecosystem. We live in that ecosystem. The lake itself is held in place by a dam. That dam is now leaking, thanks to you and Paul activating that machine. Now the cracks are going to widen, and then—"

"The dam breaks."

"No more causality—*stasis*. A forever now. An eternally frozen present moment. Monarch knew this was going to happen. *Banked* on it, I think. The machine was calibrated incorrectly. Monarch blocked my case against activation at each step, refused my evidence. They *wanted* this to happen, Jack."

"Why? If the world goes down, it takes all of us, Monarch included."

"I have a contact inside the company. Horatio. A nice enough person. Boutique muffins, outrageous moustache, you know the type. . . . "

"*Will.*"

"He tells me Monarch's been incubating something, an initiative directly related to the work at the university time lab. Project Lifeboat. Very few know about it. Nobody except the CEO Martin Hatch, a handful of experts inside the company, an unnamed contractor, a single lobbyist in D.C., and a lone recruiter in Europe."

Then it clicked. "Those guys in the masks are Monarch."

"Monarch doesn't need to steal the machine, Jack: they *own* it."

"I told you something was off about this." Jack took Will's arm. Tried to look him in the eye, but it was so dark in there he may have been staring at Will's navel for all he knew. "Where's your car?"

"In the parking lot, of course."

"And the parking lot is *where?*" Just like old times.

"Three hundred feet from the rear of this building."

"All right, let's—"

A pattern of high-frequency noise penetrated the tunnel, from outside the building. It started as a series of three triple-claps, and then became applause.

Panic cut back into Will's voice. "Is that gunfire? From outside?"

Jack moved past Will, feeling his way along the wall.

"Are they shooting on campus?" Will's voice was rising. "Who are they shooting at?"

"It's an announcement. They want people to know this is going down."

Will was breathing harder than Jack, about to hyperventilate. Jack ran his free hand over the 9mm, made sure the safety was off. "Three hundred feet to the parking lot, right?"

"Yes."

In Jack's current condition a flailing or unconscious Will would have been more than he could handle. A lifetime with his brother had provided a number of ways to get Will's shit under control.

"Hey Will, what's the capital of Nebraska?" Feeling along walls of warm steel. A light ahead.

"Lincoln."

"Hey Will, what's the temperature on Mercury?" Okay, that was definitely a door in front of him.

"That's not my field. I know what you're doing. Around five hundred degrees Fahrenheit as an average." Will's breathing was calming down.

"Hey Will, what's a big word for someone who uses too many big words?"

"Sesquipedalianist." He didn't even have to take a breath in the middle of that one.

The corridor ended. "Hey Will, where's this door lead?"

"That'd be the server room on the fifth floor," Will said, taking a deep breath. "We're below the time lab. The corridor beyond that has an elevator approximately a hundred and fifty feet to the right. That will take us to the ground floor."

The elevator was dangerous. If anyone was watching the bays they'd notice the elevator moving. The doors could open and they could walk out into a half-dozen guns. But with Jack half-blind and unable to make out anything farther than thirty feet away would the stairs be any safer?

"Will, I'm gonna need you to keep your eyes open. Tell me everything you see. Quietly."

They stepped out of the tunnel into a cold, dark room humming with quiet purpose.

"No one's here," Will whispered. It was just them and sequential racks of fat vertical servers: midnight-blue twilight speckled with thousands of yellow and green LEDs. There was only one door, manual, domestic looking, and opened from their side.

"Hey, Will?"

"Yes, Jack."

"When Paul went through, I caught a look at the readout. It said 'destination error.' What does that mean?"

Will thought about it. "Oh, dear."

"Can you elaborate?"

"Because Paul did not appear prior to his own departure he

must have traveled forward. I would assume the error indicates
he traveled to a point where a date becomes redundant. It's
likely Paul sent himself far enough ahead to witness the inevitable collapse of the Meyer-Joyce field."

"The end of time?"

"When Paul emerges from the machine he will be stepping
into a moment that is infinitely self-dividing. He will freeze,
and there will be no coming back from that. I'm afraid he's
gone, Jack. I'm sorry."

"Maybe . . . maybe I can use the machine and get him."

"Let's get out of here alive first. If Paul is at the end of time,
he won't be going anywhere."

Jack listened at the door, couldn't hear anything, and Will
risked opening it, gently. The sounds of war outside, still muffled, grew louder.

"I don't see anything," Will said.

The corridor was dark, lit by illuminated exit signs and a
light coming through a wall window at the far end of the corridor.

"What is that?" Jack said.

"A glass wall that overlooks the campus. Ordinarily it's quite
lovely." The applause from outside had become sporadic. "But
I'm not sure I want to take a look, just now."

"Can . . . could I go forward and pull him back in? Like I
did with you? Would that work?"

"You're talking hypotheticals."

Low frequencies from the outside didn't make it through the
glass outer shell and brick walls. Higher frequencies fared better: Pops. Screams.

If Paul really was dead, it didn't feel real. He had to get Will
to safety before it did begin to feel real, and he fell apart. "Anyone . . ." Breathe. "Anyone likely to be working late on this
floor?"

"No."

"Okay. Let's go. Quietly."

One step at a time, gun in one hand and the other on Will's shoulder, they moved toward the light at the end of the hall. Jack coughed up something watery and acrid for the thirtieth time, unable to contain it.

"Hey," he rasped. "What's that?" He pointed toward a dark, man-sized prism against the wall with one illuminated face.

"Vending machine," Will said.

Jack spluttered again. "Does it . . ." Coughed. "Does it sell . . . ?"

"No!"

There was no explanation for what happened next: Will threw himself backward into Jack, Jack stumbled, and then shots rang out from the end of the hall. The shooter ducked behind the corner as Jack and Will sheltered behind the machine.

Jack's heart sank. The vending machine wasn't going to stop bullets. "Will. Slide down. Get small. When I—"

The shooter popped back, squeezed off four shots. Three went wide, punching through a corkboard, blowing out clouds of particulates. One hit the machine, knocked a hole in the Perspex, exploded three cans of soda, and exited two feet above Will's head. Jack responded by whipping out and firing blind, three shots. The shooter responded and Jack slammed back against the wall, air pressure pulsing with each passing slug. Jack's best guess was that his pistol had maybe four rounds left. Maybe.

"Hey!" he shouted. "Is there some other way we can do this?"

The shooter opened up; Jack got low and fired twice. The shooting stopped—nothing but the ringing in his ears.

"Did . . . ," Will said. "Did you?"

"Hey," Jack called out. He got to his feet, iron sights trained on what he was pretty sure was the right place: just to the left of the open doorway to the elevator bay. "Hey, man. Are you okay?"

The shooter popped out, fired. Reflexively Jack shielded his face and fired twice before his pistol clicked out.

They were both done.

The shooter stood there, a silhouette a little darker than the shadow in which he stood. The shooter's gun hit the floor. Eyeshine blinked off, then on, and he toppled back against the wall. Gravity did the rest.

"Hey," Jack said, moving toward the man. The shooter slid down to a sitting position, despondent, like someone getting bad news. "Hey, brother. Are you . . . ?" It was dark, and he was half-blind, but the truth of the situation was clear.

Will said, "Oh dear."

"Will," Jack asked, "why isn't he wearing black like the others? Where's his mask?"

Will's voice was reluctant, deeply sad. "Oh Jack . . . I'm afraid you've crossed a most unfortunate Rubicon."

The shooter was wearing a buttoned beige shirt. Jack could make that out. There was an insignia on the short sleeve.

"Wait here," his brother said. Jack heard something tumble heavily to the bottom of the vending machine. A seal crackled as it was broken, and he felt Will's hand rest on his forehead. "Water. Open your eyes." Will gently tilted his brother's head back. Coolness was palmed onto his burning face. "Does it hurt?"

Jack didn't say anything.

His vision improved. Details were clearer, edges sharper. The dead man came into focus. Jack let out a breath.

Quietly: "He was shooting at us, Jack."

"He was just confused," Jack stated. "Hiding, probably."

The badge on the man's sleeve belonged to Monarch Protective Services. Not Monarch Security. Not a soldier. Just a rent-a-cop. Just a guy with an Xbox and a crappy car and a half-eaten pizza in the fridge. "I saw him outside. He knew me. From school." If Jack hadn't divorced himself from Will and River-port six years ago he would have needed a job as badly as this guy, and he would have been wearing the same uniform.

5

Jack removed the man's gun and two spare magazines from his belt. He stood, walked through the open doorway, past the elevators, and looked out the wall window. Will followed.

The geodesic undulations of the Quantum Physics Building's laminated glass shell, lit from within, illuminated the surrounding grounds. Jack could see masked "Peace" troops down the length of Founders' Walk. At the end of the path: the ramshackle outline of the protest camp. There, too, idiot-faced men, working, searching, carrying away limp forms in teams of two. Occasionally, single gunshots.

"What the fuck is going on?" He turned to his brother, his face an accusation. "Paul told me Monarch Innovations was funding the research. Why attack the building? The protestors? Where are the cops? The media?"

Will struggled to find words. The elevator beat him to it.

Ding.

Smiley-faced troopers flowed into the hallway with practiced precision—implacable, unfeeling—the first three dropping to one knee so the three behind them could also take aim.

PEACE.

This is what it felt like for Jack, meeting his death. Colors were richer, smells stronger, time slowed, each moment a meal. Some clown had posted a Far Side cartoon to the corkboard; the spalling around one hole in the vending machine shone like chrome. A moment returned from ten years ago, now clear as day: he had bought a beer for the man he killed.

Ten years. The Tavern. Jack had finished a late shift delivering pizza. He had met Paul at the end of the bar, a spot that smelled equally of hoppy microbrew and acrid wafts from the nearby men's room. He and Paul had a few, and this guy had appeared and let them in on a secret: the Tavern was named for the owner's love of Dungeons & Dragons. Jack had bought a round. They'd burned maybe a half hour and another round, and went their separate ways.

He remembered the moment, but he couldn't remember the guy's name.

Jack turned his attention to the present.

Behind their masks each of these six men with French-made weapons was still human. None of them questioned what they were about to do. Their armor looked so heavy and clean and important. Kevlar-gloved fingers squeezed.

Jack said, "Stop."

They did.

Jack opened his eyes, his fingers splayed at the end of his outstretched arm. Beyond his fingers, the men, frozen in mid-action. Around the men a dome shimmered, like water. Like the distortion field that had sheathed the time machine.

"Is it weird that I'm getting comfortable with miracles?"

Will took a careful step forward, risked a closer look. "Do you know what you've done? You have *deformed* a very localized pocket of the Meyer-Joyce field." Will extended a hand toward the shimmering bubble.

"Don't touch it! What if it bursts?"

Will stopped. "We have to replicate this. Can you do it again?"

"Not if these guys *wake up*, no. We have to . . ." The bubble began to flicker, shimmer. "It's breaking."

Jack turned, snapped three shots into the window. Will yelped, and Jack kicked the panel out of its frame. It clattered and skidded off the dome outside. "Out the window."

Will hesitated. Jack grabbed Will, reached into the bubble— it didn't break—and yanked something from the nearest belt.

"Go!" He shoved Will toward the window. Jack's brother, Will, braced against the frame. Behind them the ministutter failed.

Jack shouldered Will out the window, then tumbled after, gracelessly, followed by a stream of reanimated bullets. Falling five feet he hit the laminated glass, hard, and then the grenade on the trooper's belt detonated.

Screams erupted from inside the building.

Will was in his face, terrified. "Are you okay?"

"Just glad the glass didn't break."

"It's reinforced. How do we get down from here? They're going to kill us!"

The canopy was an undulating design that tapered toward the ground on the far side. Three hundred feet beneath their shoes waited the hard, polished floor of the atrium. Two panels of glass—reinforced or not—between them and about two seconds of terror.

Will was transfixed, staring at the ground below with an expression of total horror.

"Will? Hey, Will." Tucking the handgun into the back of his jeans Jack shook Will by the shoulder. Will reacted violently, stance wide, struggling for balance. "Will! We're fine. We walk across this, to the far side, into your car, and we're gone. Easy." Will clearly wasn't convinced. "C'mon, this'll be fun."

"Fun?" And then, "Oh, this is your coping strategy manifesting again. I understand."

"I'll go first, you follow." Jack walked twenty feet to the next segmented glass panel, held in place by the ornate geometrical webwork of steel beams. He jumped up and down. "Totally safe."

"Please don't do that." Will took a breath, followed.

The old physics building—that redbrick relic of a bygone era—was mostly enclosed by the crystalline shell of the Monarch Innovations Quantum Physics complex. Only its new top levels jutted above the glass dome, the levels that held the lab and Monarch's time machine. It was from the ground floor of this building that Senior Operative Randall Gibson emerged, into the vast domed lobby of the Quantum Physics complex. On his earpiece was his second-in-command, Donny, now in charge of the squad Gibson had left in the time lab.

Gibson's ear mic pinged—a call from the Tower. "Actual to C-1, activate rescue rigs."

Beneath their armor Gibson's crew wore delicate wire-and-brace filament exoskeletons, wired to the portable chronon battery on their back. Simultaneously slapping a small chrome plate on each hip brought Gibson's battery online. His skin stung sharply along the lines of the wiring.

"Donny, you copy that?"

Donny was a good guy. Gibson had worked with him for years: easy to get along with, happiest when taking orders, reliable in a fight.

"Yeah, boss. We're live."

This is what they'd trained for. Chronon-1 could now move freely. Interruptions to causality flow would have no hold over them.

"Actual, C-1 is chronon-active."

"Boss, heads up. Getting word: gunfire on fifth, and Reaper squad is down. Fifty percent casualties. Looks like a grenade mishap."

"Are you fuckin' serious, Don?"

Chronon-1 was the only squad on-site authorized to deploy rigs. Reaper squad was filled with regulars. Nothing special, but casualties meant leaving DNA, fiber . . . evidence. Ah, Monarch had the best cleaners in the biz.

" 'Fraid so, sir."

"You're in charge, Don. I'm overseeing Guardian's sanitization run. Buzz me if you need me."

Guardian squad was hanging out in the atrium. No rigs, no skills. This wasn't how Gibson had imagined his first live chronon op: coddling a gang of masked chumps. Fuck this, man. Right in the car.

Guardian squad's CO—a young senior operative, carbine strapped across his chest—saluted as he strolled over, like he was still in the Corps. Didn't even take the mask off to do it. *Asshole.*

The light from the double-dome superstructure was throwing down crazed shadows that made Gibson's eyes hurt.

"Boss," Donny piped up over the earpiece. "Be aware: the two strays from the time lab aren't among the bodies."

Stupid idea for a building, Gibson thought, taking it all in: a football field's worth of space between here and the other side of the dome. Racks of Segways spaced around it just so the civvies could get to the stairs. So fuckin' inefficient.

"Do what we do, Don. Lock it down. They'll be in there. . . ." His eyes traversed the geometrical curvature above him, the inner and outer webwork clashing into still more patterns.

Gibson stopped where he was, eyes up. *Well,* Randall Gibson thought. *Ain't that something.* "Don?" he said. "Look out a window."

"Hey, Randall," Guardian's CO said, eye on the time. "You ready?"

Gibson kept his eye on the ceiling. "Sure, sure. Listen, let me borrow that six-pack your boy's carrying."

Donny piped up. "Well shit, boss. Am I seeing what I think I'm seeing?"

"Wait twenty seconds, Don, *then* tell me what you see."

Jack and Will had covered about ten panels—maybe a hundred feet—and were making good time.

"See? No big deal. Close to halfway there and no casualties." No response from Will, so Jack checked behind him. "Will?"

Will was where they'd started.

Eyes screwed shut, frozen on the spot, Will stammered, "I-I can't move, Jack. I . . ." He looked down. "Oh God."

"Will, look at me, okay? Straight ahead. Slow and steady steps."

"I . . ." Will never finished the sentence. He was staring down, fixated by the glass at his feet, the drop beyond it.

"Will?"

His head whipped up, breath snagged in his throat, and, suddenly, Will was running right at him.

"Whoop," Gibson muttered, tracking the grenade launcher's barrel across the underside of the dome. "We got a rabbit."

Forty-millimeter grenades have a casualty radius of about 130 feet, so Guardian squad had hunkered themselves behind the info stand. Gibson had positioned himself as far away from his target as possible, firing at an angle. Mama Gibson didn't raise no dummy.

Gibson sighed and pulled the trigger. The M32 kicked with a satisfying *thoonk*.

Will sprinted straight for Jack.

"Will! It's cool! Rel—"

Three glass panels thirty feet behind his brother shocked white as the entire superstructure smashed into the underside of their feet. Jack was knocked on his ass, the handgun striking sharp against his tailbone, ankles and shins wracked with splintering pain; Will left the surface completely, arms pinwheeling, and came down hard, smashing into the glass. Jack couldn't hear himself shout, *"What the fuck was that?"*

He couldn't hear anything.

Will was hyperventilating, scrambling to his feet, but something was wrong. His feet wouldn't take his weight. Jack's own feet and legs were a riot of tingling excruciation. His bones burned. Facedown as he was, pressed to the glass dome, he saw what was happening below: a smiley-faced squad taking cover behind a curved information desk and a bare-headed trooper with a six-shot rotary grenade launcher, eyeballing Will with the happiest expression Jack had ever seen on a human face.

Cordite stench and hot glass particles settled into the atrium. Gibson rolled his shoulders, cricked his neck, and sighted up a second shot.

Gibson called out his next shot to Donny. "See if I can pinball him off the roof."

"Damn, boss. You know I could just shoot 'em from here."

"Don't you dare. I got me five shots left."

Foonk.

Jack struggled to his aching feet.

"Will, get up."

If Will's body was pressed to the surface when the next one hit it could scramble his organs.

"Get up!"

Will did, sort of. With a desperate heave he got his body off the glass as a section of panels to his left took the hit, knocking him sideways. Jack watched his brother flail, collapse, and slide, his fingers dragging across the glass. He was close to the curve—it was gentle, but another blast like that would send him flying over the edge, three hundred feet down to the university lawn.

Gibson hitched his lip, dissatisfied. "I got a better idea." He switched targets.

Foonk.

Jack got halfway to Will when the shock wave hit—blowing him backward.

Gibson retargeted.

Foonk.

Both brothers shouted as the panel section behind Will that had taken the first grenade hit took a second. Thick, reinforced glass volcanoed upward. The ejecta from the explosion tinkled delicately as it rained in heavy, jagged fistfuls across the dome.

Punch-drunk and battered, Jack struggled to interpret the world around him through senses that had traded places with one other: he smelled pain, felt brightness, heard fear. The world was two images skating atop one another. His head was an endlessly sounding dial tone. He stood on a hot crystal moon that sweated dollops of melted polycarbonate. The atmosphere was sharp and poisonous. His eyes didn't work.

His brother was on his feet, back on top, away from the curve, away from Jack. Will was also standing on unreliable feet—low and unsteady.

Jack said his brother's name. Will seemed to realize that he was not alone in this place, and recognized his brother. He extended a hand, like a child wanting to be lifted from dock to boat.

The fifth round struck exactly between them. Jack flew one way, Will toward the freshly blasted hole in the dome.

Gibson hooted, long and loud, as the body flipped a low arc through the night air, and through the ragged wound in the double-dome. "Hole in one, son!"

Jack's perception of time slowed. He reached for Will, futile as it was, wanting him back and safe more than he had ever wanted anything in his life. His boots gripped the hardened polycarbonate, braking his backward flight, and he kicked off, launching himself toward Will, crossing the space between them—impossibly—in a heartbeat.

The world stopped, Jack ran, and the world restarted a moment too soon.

Inches from Jack's grasp Will's body fell through the jagged maw of the dome's wound. Watching him fall Jack's every thought became singular: *No*.

The air around his brother's limp body buckled. Inverted? And snapped.

Jack skidded, stumbled, kept his footing.

Will floated twenty-five feet below the wounded dome, suspended inside a ministutter of Jack's creation.

"Ah . . . Monarch Actual. This is Senior Operative Gibson at the Quantum Physics Building."

"What the fuck am I seeing, boss?"

"Shut up, Don. You there, Actual?"

"Actual here. What is it, Senior Operative?"

Gibson eyeballed the space-time distortion filling most of the hole he had blasted through eight layers of sandwiched polycarbonate.

"Actual . . . at least one of the two escapees from the time lab are chronon-active. Natively."

"Say again?"

"They're live. Actual. Teleporting. No rescue rig, no Striker tech. Target spontaneously manifested an M-J field deformation, with intent. Check the feeds." Gibson slung the M32 over his shoulder, turned to Guardian's CO. "Good luck."

And walked out the door.

Will's body was an arc, eyes to the stars, mouth open in a silent exclamation. Fragments of heated polycarbonate and acrid smoke were suspended inside the bubble with him, a three-dimensional portrait frozen in a sphere of paused time. He had fallen wide of the walkway that connected the fourth floor of the old science building to the admin facility on the other side.

When the stutter broke, Will would fall 270 feet to the lobby floor.

The six smiley-faced goons on the floor below were done being impressed.

Jack dropped through the shattered dome without a thought, straight into the ministutter. Jack's feet connected with Will's chest, with zero give.

Jack balanced there, above the drop, surfing his brother in mid-air.

"Don't wake up, don't wake up, don't wake up. . . ." It had been a calculated bet. Will held.

The squad opened up, Jack flinched, and a hundred military rounds *vip vip vip*-ed as they impacted the stutter . . . and caught—leaving the outside of the sphere stippled with lead acne.

The squad reloaded.

Gibson's playdate with five rounds of forty mike had the attention of pretty much everybody. Monarch's regular squads had done a good job of preemptively securing the neighborhood—nothing was getting in or out—but now encrypted comms chatter was rattling off sightings of media closing in by road and air. Civvies were congregating on main thoroughfares. It was a cowboy move, lighting up the dome like that, but orders were orders. Monarch wanted the Peace Movement to make an impression; consider it made.

His earpiece pinged.

"Mr. Gibson?"

Shit.

"Receiving, Mr. Hatch."

"Guardian tells me you're responsible for the chaos I'm witnessing. Is that correct?"

"More than likely, sir."

Gibson was marching toward the last remaining BearCat—one of a couple Monarch had assigned to university security six months ago in preparation for this strike. A plausible story about keys stolen from dead guards was ready for the media.

The vehicle was still idling on the lawn. Almost all other Monarch forces had been reassigned to crowd control on a four-point perimeter. He muted his mic, put two fingers in his mouth, and ripped a sharp whistle. The pair manning the BearCat—one on the MG, the other stretching his legs—acknowledged with a salute.

"Explain yourself."

Mic on. "I was given orders to make a scene. The scene has been made." Mic off. "I need your ride."

"You are aware that one of the men you attempted to kill is considered a high-value asset? We need him alive."

The gunner dismounted as Gibson climbed into the cab. "The skinny guy?"

"Dr. William Joyce: a pioneer in chronon theory and the originator of much of the technology you have been trained to use." Hatch confirmed something on another line. "Guardian tells me both targets remain, miraculously, alive."

"Sir, I consider it a miracle that Guardian is reporting at all." The engine woke with a satisfying thud beneath his feet, soundless inside the cab. "And I'm returning forthwith to render them the benefit of my wisdom and experience." One round left. The BearCat spat dirt and leaped forward, toward the dome.

Jack leaped to the walkway and reached inside the stutter. His hand penetrated the sparkling cloud and closed around his brother's ankle. "I," he admitted, "have no idea what I'm doing." Jack drew back his arm. Will didn't budge. How had he done this the first time? What had he been feeling? Thinking? Jack closed his eyes, pulled gently, and still Will remained fixed. "Come on, Will."

He tried again, imagined Will as a black-and-white image, Technicolor soaking into him from Jack's hand.

Something warm impacted against Jack's arm. A short sound snapped from Will's throat: "Aa—!" Some of the shattered glass was beginning to drop, pause . . . drop. Will's exclamation was an erratic sometimes-rewinding stutter. Jack could smell cordite. The bubble was breaking.

Fuck Technicolor. Jack yanked and Will slid heavily out of the deformation. The stutter cracked and failed, half a glittering pound of hot glass clattering back into the atrium as a hundred loosed rounds rapid-smacked into the already wounded dome.

With Jack's grip tight on his feet, Will cleared the gap, shoulder blades and head thwacking on the guardrail. He hit the floor, hard. It hurt, but he was alive. He had no idea what had happened; as far as he was concerned the ground heaved suddenly, Jack had materialized next to him, and now he was . . .

"I can't . . . I can't keep . . ."

Jack's heart hurt for him. Will was not good at reality—and this was way too real.

From downstairs someone bellowed: "Dr. Joyce!"

Will hesitated. "Do they mean me?"

Jack let Will figure it out.

"Dr. Joyce. Are you in good health, sir?"

Jack peered through a gap in the burnished metal sheet that was the main feature of the guardrail. Five goons and their commander had weapons trained on the walkway. Not good.

"No," Will called back. "You shit."

"Sir, there's been a misunderstanding. We have paramedics on standby—"

"Why are you here?" Jack interrupted. "Monarch owns this place. Owns the lab. The research. The people. Why do this?"

"Sir," the commander said. "Jack—"

"Fuck you."

"We have paramedics on standby and can get you clear of this incident in minutes."

From the top floor of the building Don had a clear vantage down to the lobby. With one finger pressed to the mic in his ear he said: "Dr. Joyce is to the left. His brother is to the right. Aim right, two feet above the deck."

Jack, still peering through the gap in the guardrail, saw every trooper shift aim to his side of the barricade. "Sons of bitches."

Pulling himself into the cocoon of a single second Jack sprang from cover, leaped down the stairs, and slammed into the fourth-floor guardrail. To the eyes of everyone else under that dome, Jack had teleported. From his new position one floor down he watched as time reengaged, Jack's side of the steel plate was perforated by a sparking fusillade, sending Will recoiling. Jack tried to expand another moment, to make it to the third floor, but it wouldn't come.

"Will, those powers I had may have been a phase I was going through."

"Uh . . . ," Will said. "Possibly you overdid it?"

Jack pulled the handgun from the back of his jeans. The last time he had used it burned like a brand in his memory, shame so real it felt like it might end him. Through the gap in the guardrail, through the glass dome, past the trees of Founders'

Walk, the Monarch logo burned bright atop the new tower that looked over the sleepy, unimportant town he had grown up in—the town they had all grown up in.

In his mind's eye he saw the dome explode upward. He saw the smile on that bastard's face as he watched Will fall to his death.

Fuck it.

Jack racked the slide and came up shooting. Three snaps, one hit sending a lone trooper spinning behind cover as the rest of the squad ducked. A volley of semiautomatic gunfire tore Jack's cover to shreds as he leaped down the stairs, sparks tracking the underside of the stairwell.

Time slowed. Back in business.

Jack zipped for the third-floor guardrail, knocked his hip into it, and rebounded down the next stairwell. He was upright behind second-floor cover and blasting as the moment caught up to him. This time his aim was better. The moment danced with him, movement and responses becoming as predictable as minutes and seconds. He sighted and fired cleanly. Three troopers went down, slugs smacking into chest plates, punching through one leering yellow mask.

The remaining squaddie took cover but the commander didn't. Jack had lingered a moment too long and Guardian's CO let his weapon shout itself empty—as predictable as minutes and seconds.

Not quite enough though. A channel of air by Jack's chest and face pulsed like a hot artery and, as reflex and panic threw him backward down the stairwell, one slug took a piece out of Jack's left arm. Rotating with the force of it Jack crashed down the first-floor stairwell like a sack of spare parts.

His pistol skidded over the side, clattering to the lobby floor. Guardian's CO moved forward, unhurried, the yellow mask smiling as he reloaded. His grin twin, the last standing squaddie, flanked around the right side of the information desk, weapon leveled.

The CO motioned the squaddie to advance up the stairs. The squaddie moved up, the CO close behind, when the space around him tremble-snapped, trapping both him and the barrel of the CO's assault weapon. The CO wasn't a small man but there was no withdrawing his rifle: it was frozen in space as surely as if the barrel had been set in concrete.

Jack walked down the stairs, holding his wounded arm, blood trailing from his fingers.

The CO abandoned the weapon, drew his sidearm, and backed away. He had learned enough in the last few minutes to know that firing was a waste of time until the bubble popped. Jack stepped into the stutter and took the CO's rifle for himself.

The trapped CO tensed his arm, smiling face doing a poor job of disguising the panic beneath.

From inside the bubble Jack emptied the mag into him.

The ex-marine disappeared backward over the information desk in a spray of blood, ending his life with feet in the air like bad slapstick.

Jack dropped the rifle, took its replacement from the squaddie's static hands. The stutter burst, the squaddie almost overbalancing as he lurched forward . . . then realized his gun had vanished. He took things in quickly: his missing weapon now in the hands of his target, and his CO's legs sticking up from behind a blood-spattered welcome desk.

"Get out of here."

The squaddie backed away, hands up, turned, and ran.

"Will! Will, you okay?"

Will was already at the third floor. "No more, Jack. Your

abilities are completely untested." Will made it to the lobby, panting. "I want to go home. Once the adrenaline wears off I intend to throw up." Still gasping: "Your arm . . . you're wounded?"

"I'm okay. It's not as bad as it looks." Right now, it was little more than a shallow tear.

"Too much blood for a cut so trivial. You've healed, and rapidly. Your relationship to time has changed, there's no doubt." Will moved for the western exit and the parking lot beyond. "None of which will save you from massive organ trauma if someone wounds you correctly. Dead is dead. Bear that in mind."

Will was right about the adrenaline: Jack's teeth were grinding. Thoughts more complex than "find car, leave" were tripping over each other. They needed to get out of there. He couldn't keep this up much longer. He had nothing else in him.

Without warning the double doors shredded off their aluminum frames, info desk blowing to shrapnel. The salvo didn't come close to hitting the two brothers, but it got their attention. Someone on Founders' Walk cut loose with a roof-mounted .50 caliber.

"Hey! You boys weren't about to leave?"

It was him, the guy who led the attack on the time lab, the one the others called "boss." The guy wearing the happy grin as he had blown the roof out from beneath Will.

He dismounted the BearCat, took a cigarette from a sleeve pocket, and snapped open a Zippo. Cupped the light with his hands. Drew a deep, healthy lungful.

"Jack," Will said. "Come on. The car's this way. We can—"

"Wait here."

Will grabbed Jack's arm.

"Wait *here*." Jack shrugged him off.

Will wasn't accepting it. "Do not go out there! We can fix all of this, but I have to—"

"Fix? You heard them shooting out there. How many people have they killed? You saw what—"

"Jack, it wasn't your fault."

The ferocity in his voice surprised Jack. *"What* wasn't my fault?"

"The guard. Your school friend. Attacking this man won't—"

But Jack was gone. *Blink.*

The cigarette fell from Gibson's lips. "Whup. Donny? Go. Go go go."

The target had separated from the asset, covering ground like Gibson had only seen under controlled conditions. Jack rematerialized outside the dome's double door—the one Gibson had machine-gunned into art. Looked like the kid had one more burst in him.

Gibson swung the M32, aimed wide.

Foonk.

Jack took off, watched the grenade ride a contrail of propellant off to his right, toward the dome wall behind him. He covered eighty feet, maybe more, before the round detonated. The blast wave almost caught up to him in slow motion, and then time woke up.

The force belted him flat in the back, took him for a short ride, and smashed him chest-first into the BearCat's antiballistic geometry.

The Joyce kid was lying faceup in the dirt, sucking wind. Gibson took out his sidearm.

"Kid, feel like guessin' what one of my favorite things to do is?"

Choking, gasping: "That dance from *The Silence of the*

Lambs?" He willed time to invert and pop, protecting himself inside a bubble of time-out-of-time.

Nothing happened.

"Nah," Gibson said. "This."

The gunshot cracked, a sledgehammer came down, and Jack's left knee erupted. Jack watched it happen from some cold place above his left shoulder, like it was happening on television. The reprieve lasted two seconds before every nerve and pain receptor in his body lit up and he screamed.

"For starters," Gibson wondered if his cigarette was still around somewhere. "Actual, this is Gibson. Target is neutralized. Donny, what's the sitch?"

"We got the scientist, boss. He just about shit when that last grenade hit. You coulda warned us."

"Get him to the library. Big man wants a word."

"Copy."

Jack's mind was an animal mess: a howling, confused, red-strobed darkness. He wanted escape. He wanted to kill this man. He wanted to go home. He wanted his brother. He and his brother, in their old living room. He was, he realized, never going to use this leg again.

Gibson's earpiece blipped, the frequency switched remotely.

"Senior Operative, good evening."

Gibson knew that voice: the face behind Monarch's face. The Consultant. "Gibson receiving." If the Consultant was on the line things were almost certainly going to achieve an undesirable level of complication.

"Mr. Hatch tells me you've neutralized the target. Meaning?"

"Meaning I was about to help him with his blood pressure."

Head lolling, Jack tried to take an interest in his surroundings, but the grass felt so good. *Will.* He'd fucked up. Why hadn't he listened to his brother? What was it Will had said? *"Do not go out there! We can fix all of this. . . ."*

No, before that.

"Do not," the Consultant said to Gibson. "Secure him. A chronon-containment team will be on scene shortly."

Gibson did not like that. This kid was chronon-active. Taking him down, unassisted, had been balls and luck on Gibson's part. He'd only succeeded because the target had no idea what he was doing. A seasoned chronon operative was more than capable of fucking a body up given half a chance.

Jack reached deeper: what had Will said? *"You've healed, and rapidly."* That was it.

"ETA?"

"Five minutes."

The blood-soaked fabric of Jack's jeans was cleaning itself, the stain crawling back to the hole in his leg, focusing to a point, retreating back into his devastated flesh just before shattered cartilage self-assembled into a working joint. The lips of the wound quivered, vacillated, and closed shut seamlessly.

"I'd say your relationship to time has changed," Will had told him.

The bullet hole stitched itself shut.

Jack's eyes fluttered. "Your name's Gibson," he rasped.

Jack locked eyes with him, and Gibson saw a short future of nothing but eye shine and blood.

"Affirmative, sir." Gibson was already moving, hands gripping the BearCat's roof before swinging double-booted into the cabin and locking it tight behind him. The engine woke, headlights flared, and the target was *right there:* staring at him over the hood. Back from the dead.

Gibson flipped him the bird and threw the truck into reverse.

6

Two Monarch operatives dragged Will, like luggage, out the west-facing doors of the Quantum Physics dome.

Jack lurched back toward the fractured light of the now-vacant lobby. He tried to push himself back into the gaps between seconds, to close the distance in a blink. It didn't happen. He felt wide and hard and heavy, and could do nothing but lumber. He looked again and Will was gone.

The adrenaline left his system abruptly and the tunnel vision of his focus loosened. The reality of where he was and all that had happened rushed in and knocked him to his knees.

A great, wracking sob burst out of him, a kick in the chest and shoulders so hard his ribs flared with bright pain. They had his brother. Paul was gone. He had killed.

Will had begged him to leave with him. He hadn't listened. Everything had gone to shit because he did what he had always done: act first, think later. Get it done because nobody else would. He was in so far over his head he'd need a jetpack and a map just to see daylight.

They had Will. Paul was gone.

There was a cartoon series he and Paul had loved as kids: *Team Outland.* Zed had, too. Six years ago they were on the couch, streaming an old ep. A character had popped onscreen and made the Team's trademark hand signal—the time-out

sign: "Think Before You Act!" They'd chanted it, snarfed pop-
corn, drank beer, and winced at how badly the series had aged.

Good memory, weird timing.

Stop. Think.

These were the facts, as he understood them.

Paul oversaw a time travel project for Monarch. Will was
hired to consult, but was kept largely out of the loop. Nonetheless, the machine was clearly based on Will's research. Then
Monarch either hired mercenaries or used their own troops,
dressed in weird gear, and had them attack the lab *they own*.
They were supposed to "steal" the core of the machine and kill
a bunch of innocent people in the process.

Why?

Kill a bunch of people, but they wanted Will alive. Why? He
was valuable to them. Which probably meant they weren't done
with the machine.

But none of this would have happened if Paul hadn't turned
on the machine. The attack kicked off almost immediately
after, as if the machine's activation had been a signal.

There had to be an answer but Will was the one with the
brains.

Had Jack's involvement been planned? What about his
abilities? Were they intended? Had Paul been in on it?

Was Paul even alive? If he was trapped at some kind of end-
of-time point, could he be saved?

An hour ago everything had been fine. Now the world—the
universe, maybe—was falling apart.

Will. He had to get Will away from these people. He dragged
his face along one filthy sleeve, shook his head again, blinked,
did what he could to banish the killing sense of grief that threatened to undo him, and stood up.

Will first. Then, once Will was safe, Jack would come back.

He was getting back into that lab, and he was going after Paul. End of time or no, he was bringing Paul back. Nobody he loved was dying this morning. Nobody.

Will was taken to the library, Gibson had said. The library was near the protest camp. The protest camp was by the entrance to the university. The entrance was at the start of Founders' Walk. Okay. Jack oriented. Looked around. The library was east. Whoever had taken Will west must be headed for the parking lot.

A university security BearCat tore out from the parking lot behind the dome, along the nearest treelined avenue, headed east, straight for the library.

Jack willed himself into the space between moments, and while the world wasn't looking, he ran.

The entire city was alert to what was going on. Crowds pressed against Monarch-erected barricades two blocks from campus. Police flashbars turned anxious faces into a neon flipbook. The media were issued canned statements. Civilian drone pilots reported their toys suddenly dropping dead once they got within two miles of the campus. Bloggers screamed blue murder; phones and tablets turned to fritzing junk. Families wanted answers. People were missing. Cops yelled at Monarch troops. Monarch troops followed a policy of total non-engagement. An event had occurred, the company had state sanction to contain the event, local law enforcement and the community would be briefed shortly.

The situation made it easy for Jack to blink toward the western face of the library unseen and get inside. Particleboard fencing had been erected around the site. Signs with DEMOLITION IN PROGRESS—DO NOT ENTER were nail-gunned to each one, by order of Riverport Council and Monarch Construction. Every fourth fence panel had a four-by-five-foot employment infographic, actors in hard hats flashing I-got-mine smiles. Most of these were plastered with unflattering graffiti and anti-Monarch stickers.

The squawk and bark of Monarch bullhorns told Jack the scene two blocks away was intensifying.

Jack climbed the hood on an unattended BearCat, leaped over the fence and made for a rear door. He hit the ground on strong legs, head still spinning but eyes clear.

Fixtures and fittings had been stripped from the library, leaving a shell and the lecture theater without a door. He walked in.

It was dim inside the lecture theater, hollow-bodied and sulking. Racked tiers had been stripped of seating, the oak paneling to be consigned to landfill and history. Slack six-foot-long tubes of plastic wrap hung limply from banisters, littering the floor, along with a thick coat of dust. No fittings and no power meant no illumination. Small, gas-powered generators burbled throatily from deeper in the guts of the old place, someplace better lit than here, judging from the glare spilling from the hallway.

"Please. Let me go. I . . . !"

"Will?" Terror had happened here, in this room. He could feel it, his new sense alive to the agitation and fear. It was imprinted upon the chronon flow in the room as clearly as tracks through snow.

"Please. Let me go. I . . . !"

Jack's attention gravitated toward a space at the foot of the racked tiers, in front of an antique oaken podium. His senses pulled toward that point, like iron filings toward a magnet.

Will had been here. Every cell in him knew it.

Figures leaped into existence, no more substantial than the

thin light that leaked into the hall from the world outside: Will, flanked by two Monarch troopers.

"Please. Let me go. I . . . !"

Jack watched the trooper on the left elbow Will in the stomach, dropping him. Then they dragged him toward the hall, where they evaporated into shadow. Gone.

An after echo . . . or a brush with the future?

Echo. Jack didn't know how he knew, but he trusted it. He had so many questions for Will. He needed to know what the fuck was happening to him.

The hallway would have been beautiful a year ago. Now dust gathered against the molded skirting boards, the two-tone floors strewn with discarded insulation and wiring. The hallway ended, open-mouthed, onto the library's main room, bracketed by frosted glass panels. Light stands were arranged evenly around the cavernous space. Shelf-lined mezzanines overlooked the main room, lined with wrought-iron railings. The long oval of the information desk remained in place, but most everything else had been ripped out. Serried lines of chrome lugs patterned the checkered floor around the info desk: the footprints of vanished Internet cubicles.

Jack tried to pick up Will's trail, feeling for another vision, scanning the main hall.

He was so preoccupied that he didn't notice the two smiley-faced troopers guarding an archway in the north wall, until it was too late. He realized his mistake as soon as they clocked him.

Jack didn't think. He warped forward and grabbed the first trooper's weapon, failing to notice that it was strapped to him. The mask smiled at him and then Jack was struck in the face for his trouble. He recovered in time to be staring down the barrel of the gun he'd tried to snatch.

Jack warped, the trooper fired, and his partner keeled over dead—three ragged holes stitched through PEACE.

The surviving trooper's awareness disconnected for a moment as he took in what he had done. He snapped his rifle toward Jack as Jack cannoned into him at warp speed, blasting both of them into a pile of dilapidated wooden bookshelves stacked seven deep against the wall.

The trooper didn't move, smiling vacantly at his own lap. Jack pulled himself to his feet, stepping away from the slack-bodied trooper he'd just used as an airbag.

The northern room, which the two troopers had been standing watch in, was circular and just off the main room. It used to house the stacks, judging from the signage and the ghostly rectangular footprints that fanned the space. Jack heard generators thumping from a small room off to the side, from which cabling snaked.

"Jack?"

It was dim in the stacks chamber, the light from the main hall lighting that gutted room like dusk: clear surfaces, deep shadows. Will was there, quiet and pressed against the wall, hands zip-tied at his waist and clearly terrified. Jack searched the trooper, took his combat knife, and popped the binders off Will.

"Are you okay? Answer me later. You got a bunch of shit I want explained."

"Jack. Look."

Against the curved wall, near the body of the crumpled trooper, was a foot. Sneakered. Chuck Taylors.

"They brought them in here," Will said. "Some of the students from the camp."

The kid wearing the Chucks was propped slack against the wall, hair spilling from beneath his hoodie across the floor, his chest a bloody ruin.

Jack exited, shielded his eyes against the glare of the lamps and moved past their perimeter. Forward was the wide, doorless exit. To the right was the corridor through which he had entered. To his left was a long hall once used for shelves and periodicals.

Now it was a mortuary. Bodies lay strewn across the chessboard floor, not killed here but dumped. Not one of them would have been out of their twenties. Amy, the girl that accosted him in the quadrangle, would be here, Jack realized. Somewhere. He still had her flyers in his jacket pocket. RESPECT EXISTENCE OR EXPECT RESISTANCE. He couldn't bear to look.

"We gotta go," Jack said, marching back to the light. "C'mon, Will, we gotta go."

Two men with the familiar round-faced PEACE silhouette flanked Will. One had a carbine pointed at Jack, the other had his weapon aimed at Will's head.

Jack cursed his stupidity. They had been in the generator room.

He needed to be sure that if he made a play, here and now, that he could warp fast enough to kill the two men in less time than it took to pull a trigger. He didn't know. His powers had been coming and going. But he had to do something.

Then someone said, "Stop. Just . . . stop."

Jack squinted in the light. An avuncular hand rested on Will's shoulder, briefly, before the third person stepped forward: unmarked urban fatigues, broad-shouldered, hair in a buzz-cut. Military type.

This was wrong. This was terribly wrong. Jack was washed through with the nauseating chill of déjà vu.

The figure stepped into the light.

"Paul?"

Jack's lifelong friend emerged from the shadows, familiar features traced with unfamiliar new details: worry lines now creased Paul's forehead, and his hair had stippled salt-and-pepper at

the temples. His build was no longer that of a project coordinator; his was the economically muscled body of a career soldier.

Paul Serene, the passionate idealist, had been replaced by an
older man. Excitability did not vibrate beneath this lean individual's skin, gone was the easy smile. This man's form was his
function, and his function was the imposition of a will that
glittered sharply and certainly from behind clear eyes.

This couldn't be real.

"I'm sorry," Paul said, and vanished. A hard cannonball of
pain impacted the small of Jack's back, collapsing him to his
knees. Will, thoughtless of his own safety, broke free and dashed
forward to protect his brother.

Space buckled around Will. Within that depression time inverted and snapped. A stutter popped into existence around
him, immobilizing Jack's brother in a posture of panic.

Jack was numb, body and mind. Paul was alive. Here. Older.
And . . .

Paul looked down at him. "I'm sorry, Jack. Tonight's events
were not to my taste. But they were to my orders." Cold words
uttered in a warm voice from a young friend now very much
Jack's elder.

Jack got to his feet. Paul turned, unconcerned, and strolled
closer to Will.

Jack couldn't accept it. What had happened to transform
the change-the-world idealist he had known into this?

"It was meant to be a two-minute hop to the future," Paul
said. "What I got was a ride to the end of the world. The world
I killed, when I activated the machine."

"The world doesn't look that killed, Paul."

Paul faced Jack, tucking his hands into the pockets of his
fatigues. The adolescent gesture took ten years off him for a
moment.

"When the end comes years of escalating horror will build

to a moment of perfect, unimaginable insanity and then . . . that moment never ends. Ever. That's what the end of time is. But I found a way out," Paul said gently. "I knew I had to do something, Jack. That's what kept me alive there."

He took an earnest step toward his friend.

"I traveled back as far as I could. To 1999."

"You told me the machine can't take a person back beyond the moment it was first activated."

"I just told you I found a way out. Now listen to me, and understand: I wanted as much time as possible to build something that would help us *defy* the end of the world—the end of time—by *surviving it*." His face lit up at this, clearly expecting a stronger reaction from Jack.

"Paul," Jack said. "It's good to see you. I was worried." Then, pointedly: "Can we have this conversation without an assault rifle pointed at my brother's head?"

Paul chose to ignore the request. "I've done seventeen years of living since I saw you last, Jack, but I still remember what you were like." Paul spoke with a warm smile, but taking no pleasure in what he said. "If you were a reasonable man, a level-headed man, my actions now would be very different." Paul held out a gloved hand to one of the troopers. Obediently the soldier unclipped a Taser from his belt and placed it in Paul's hand. "I can't take risks, Jack. I'm sorry."

Rage.

The world slammed forward, taking Jack with it as he shouldered into the trooper on the right. Fully armored, the yellow-faced killer flew across the length of the archives, met the wall hard, and dropped ten feet to the floor.

The air pressure pulsed as Paul manifested before Jack. "Stop."

Jack's boot came down hard for Paul's knee. Paul side-stepped it.

"Let us go," Jack hissed. "Whatever the fuck happened to you, let us go."

"I can't. Will knows too much, and now you're too dangerous."

Jack looped an arm for Paul's head. It didn't work.

"Will's too valuable, and you're my friend."

"Let us *go*!"

Paul dodged another punch with a flick of his head. "Jack."

"What's Monarch to you? Why are all those kids out there . . . why are they . . . why did you . . . ?"

Paul drew a line under this exchange with a short intake of breath. "Now's not the time. We can talk later." Paul smiled, a familiar detail. He had smiled like that at bad jokes, little victories, and *Team Outland*.

Déjà vu.

Paul's shoulder flinched, snapping his fist into Jack's face. Jack's senses had an argument. Nothing made sense. Then all was darkness.

Stone, cold and wet and flat against his face. Skull-ache, as if someone had taken a screwdriver to a bone suture and twisted. Blood in his mouth, like old dirt.

Somewhere in a hidden corner of the room Will was pleading in frustration. "We can't let this happen!"

Black tile. White tile. He raised his face from the lobby floor and the unpleasantly adhesive spill his cheek was resting in. He spat blood and dust and lifted his ringing head.

Jack was still in the library.

Forty feet away Will was frantic, desperate for understanding and out of ideas. Paul stood over him with no intention of engaging.

"I can stop this event! I have the data, I've done the research . . . !"

"No risks. No—"

Paul winced, abruptly and painfully, tight lips pulled back from white teeth. His face flushed red, every cord in his neck standing out, and then . . . the spasm passed. Faded. Paul breathed.

Whatever had happened inside him had hit hard—his voice was a rasp. "No chances," he said. "We both know what's coming, Will. We both know too well that it can't be changed, negotiated with, or avoided." He took a deep drink of air, tightly muscled chest expanding beneath the uniform. "Now, Will, for the final time, as your friend: come with me, help us to survive what's coming, or this has to end here."

Jack heaved himself upright. His inner ear was failing to distinguish up from down, left from right. Heavy headed, he watched the room slide sideways. He sensed Paul's hand as a brotherly weight on his shoulder, before it pushed him to his knees.

Will processed. "You're threatening me?"

"Would you risk the universe by leaving one problem unattended? I can't have you running loose, Will. Come with me. We need your expertise."

"You're wrong. This can be fixed. *I can fix it.*"

"William. You babysat me when I was eight. Please, don't make me—"

"*I can fix it!*"

Paul's silence communicated everything.

Jack shot to his feet, and this time Paul shoved him to the dirt without love or care. The exertion seemed to trigger something within him and Paul *screamed,* the space about his frame trembling for a second and then *snapping fractal*—a distortion field, glittering and crazed, sheathing him for half a moment. Then it was gone.

Paul gasped like a man with a perforated lung.

Jack had no clue what had just happened. The distortion was similar to the effect that had emanated from the time machine. The two had to be connected.

Paul appeared suddenly very old to Jack, very frail.

"I can't bring myself to shoot you, Will." Paul drew a reassuring breath, spine straightening. "It took me years to understand what has to be done. . . ." He was recovering quickly, far quicker than Jack was. "But we don't have years for you to come to the same conclusion. We have moments." Pressing a finger to his ear, Paul intoned, "Monarch Actual. This is your Consultant. Trigger."

And then to Will, "I never wanted this."

Something passed from Paul to Jack in single conscience-struck glance: an apology, and a futile hope for understanding.

The first charge detonated, flooding the archives with flame. Standing helpless and alone, Will understood that his time on Earth was over. Paul seized Jack, accelerated impossibly, and warped them both through the open front doors.

The last Jack Joyce saw of his brother was as the Riverport University Library folded into itself, corners and columns blown out by thunderclaps. Framed in the vacant doorway of a barren storehouse of knowledge, the inferno reached for William Joyce as the heavy, crashing curtain lowered on the story of his life.

Gone.

Paul skidded to a halt, using his body to shield Jack from the rolling cloud of dust and debris slammed out and across the yard.

"Easy," he said. "It's over." Jack snapped his arms up, broke Paul's grip, and drove his fist square into Paul's face. Staggered,

Paul shook his head and refocused only to find himself staring down the black eye of his own dully chromed .45-caliber pistol. He was disarmed. This close to the barrel, the degree of vibration in Jack's hand was pronounced. Paul looked away from the death dispenser to the face of the man who held it. The redness of his friend's streaming eyes made them seem twice as blue.

Jack snorted back a nose full of snot, but had no hope of keeping tears from flowing.

"Why?"

Paul's expression darkened. "No."

That was not an answer Jack could accept. He shoved the pistol closer to Paul's face. Closer again. He had to drag a hand across his flooding eyes. *"What have you done?"*

Paul repeated the word over and again: "No. No. No." And . . .

Paul Serene's body ignited, flashing bright, his form bursting into geometry at once impossible and humanoid, mirrored and reflective. Beneath it all, in glimpses, was Paul's screaming face.

The howl crashed and infiltrated and burst, colonizing the mind with doubt and fear. In that single moment, Jack felt both the impossible breadth and scope of Creation, and his own insignificance. Paul screamed a scream in a language beyond language, of an age older than God's.

And then he was Paul again, and his expression was as helpless and frightened as Will's had been moments earlier. The night was silent. Paul sank to his knees and toppled senseless to the lawn.

This was the tableau: by the light of his brother's burning tomb, Jack Joyce stood over Paul Serene, gun in hand. Jack was now in the role of executioner, as Paul had been moments before. It was hard not to feel Will's spirit watching over this, approving. The gun in Jack's hand felt heavy and correct, five feet from Paul's head.

The world had gone mad.

There came a tapping on Jack's shoulder. He turned his head. A familiar face smiled at him, ducking sideways to get a better look at him.

"Hey," she said.

This was it, Jack knew. This was the very last thing he could take. No more.

Her smile grew more beautiful.

"Zed?" he said.

She had let her natural hair color grow back. Red. Her tattoos were gone. But it was Zed. She even smelled right.

"Hey, Trouble," she said. "I'll see you in the morning."

He hadn't noticed her pressing something into his arm until she had done it.

A hiss, a sting, and the night ended.

7

From inside the Riverport University BearCat Gibson watched fire crews roll up and start arcing water and retardant into what was left of the library.

"Donny, you there? Get the others. That second target is chronon-active. We're going hunting."

"Uh, we can't, boss. Hatch's Priority One was to secure the lab. Chopper's inbound to extract the core from this thing. We've already changed into uniform."

A new voice came on the line: "Chronon-1 this is Monarch Actual. Standing orders are for radio silence. Clear the air."

"Chronon-1 to Monarch Actual, keep your shirt on. We're encrypted."

"Clear the air, Gibson. I won't say it again. Though, since you're on the line, you're wanted back at the Tower. Immediately. Monarch Actual, out."

Gibson took the elevator up to the top floor, back in his uniform, hands gripped behind his back to keep from punching the wall. That kid had escaped from him. That couldn't stand. Four years' hard training and fieldwork to get qualified with a chronon rig, top of his game, best in class, and some jack-off undergrad gets dosed right and . . . Gibson *strategically withdrew.*

Ran is what he did. From the first chronon-active target he'd encountered in the field.

Four years waiting for a chance to flex his material and *who the fuck was that kid to look at him like that?* Eye-fucking Gibson like Gibson wasn't the meanest motherfucker in the whole Valley of Death.

"We'll get him, Donny," he said to empty air, nodding. "Take him apart like a chicken dinner."

The elevator chimed and the doors hushed apart.

Mr. Hatch's place always blew his mind. Polished mahogany floors, and a view of the world that'd make anyone believe in God. Glass wall, glass ceiling. Helipad just outside. Someone waiting to fly Mr. Hatch wherever, whenever. Years of good decisions. Mr. Hatch knew the shit. Clear head. Crystal vision. Smarts. Knew how to direct the people under him. Best commander Gibson had ever had and the bastard had never been military.

"Mr. Gibson." Hatch smiled. "Thank you for seeing me so soon after the operation. Do you need to decompress?"

"No, sir. I'm energized, sir. Present and clear."

"Excellent." Hatch gestured to one of two Victorian leather club chairs positioned before his desk. "Sit."

Gibson did. Hatch didn't. Hatch didn't move from where he stood, behind his desk.

Hatch didn't say anything, just looked at Gibson, still smiling.

Gibson cleared his throat.

Nothing about Hatch changed.

"Sir, I—"

"We first met in 2003. One of Monarch Security's first recruitment drives. Your dossier caught my eye, and I traveled to meet you personally in Baghdad."

"April 3rd, 2003, yes, sir."

The smile. Hatch just let that hang for a moment. Gibson reflexively swallowed.

"You've done things for this company that you will never be allowed to speak of. You are in possession of privileged information at the highest level. You understand the terror we face, and you are one of the very few who know of this company's relationship with our Consultant. All these things you have earned. Your success rate is almost flawless, and you have a most peculiar gift for inspiring loyalty in those under your command. Of one hundred and twelve candidates for the Chronon-1 program, nine made it, and you were at the top of that list. You possess a unique psychology, Mr. Gibson, and a level of moral flexibility I find astounding. But I wonder, do you possess a holographic imagination?" Still the smile. "Are you able to construct a three-dimensional image of a future formed by actions you may choose to take in the present?"

"Sir, I—"

"It's one of the things that separates us from animals. The ability to delay gratification now for a likely greater reward later. The ability, for example, to choose to *not* pursue a grudge match against a total stranger, but instead follow orders and strive to keep alive a man critical to the ongoing survival of our species. But I interrupted you. Finish your thought."

"Sir." Gibson didn't like this. He had never imagined that one day Mr. Hatch might look at him like that. Now he was imagining all kinds of things. Like who he might be at the end of this interview, and suddenly he couldn't get one thought to connect to the next. Like a fucking chump. "With respect, Mr. Hatch, I was assigned to oversee Guardian squad's sweep-and-clear. I left Donny—"

"No mind on Earth grasped chronon theory so well as Dr. William Joyce." Hatch moved to the front of his desk. "You were tasked by me, explicitly, with keeping him alive. With keeping him out of the hands of our Consultant."

"Paul Serene, I understand, but—"

"*That*," Hatch emphasized, "is an excellent example of what I am talking about. Do you understand why we refer to Mr. Serene as 'our Consultant'? Paul Serene's primary role is to play the villain of our upcoming drama. In time Monarch's role will be to play the rescuing hero. Therefore Paul Serene being tied to Monarch will *destroy* our credibility with the governments of the world."

Hatch took a measured step toward Gibson.

"That *unquestioning trust* is the pillar most essential to the success of Project Lifeboat. Unheard-of technology must be delivered within a *very* short time frame. Technology requires development. That development will require unlimited funding, manpower, and intergovernmental cooperation, and it will have to happen very, very quickly. Time is quite literally running out, Mr. Gibson. Dr. Joyce's expertise would have bought us time. But now . . . now he is dead."

"Holographic. Right. I got it."

"I'm removing you from command of Chronon-1, Mr. Gibson. Henceforth you will be taking your orders from Donny."

"Sir—"

"This close to the end there's no room for second chances. You are in receipt of the last chance I will give you. Were you about to throw it in my face?"

Gibson said nothing.

Hatch turned to face Riverport, screwed in an earpiece, and got back to work.

Life escorted Randall Gibson to the door, and closed it.

Paul Serene was a man who lived in the space between moments, known to very few. In his too-long-seeming lifetime he had learned many truths. He had built a diverse, multinational corporation in secret, from hiding, using skills and gifts unique to himself. He had met many extraordinary people, many of them terrible to know.

That's how it had been for seventeen long years, from the moment he first stepped into the time machine until now.

All for this critical moment. For Project Lifeboat.

Chronon particles are critical to the functioning of causality. No particles, no causality. No causality, no flow of events—and what is time but a linear flow of events?

The activation of the Monarch-built time machine at Riverport University fractured the Meyer-Joyce field: the field of chronon energy essential to the functioning of causality. Eventually that fracture would cause chronon levels to drop disastrously low, the field would collapse, and time would end.

The universe would become locked in a single moment, dividing infinitely.

Because of him. Because of what he did.

For seventeen years Paul Serene had lived with this knowledge: Paul Serene had killed the universe.

He had but one chance to make amends for his great evil.

Project Lifeboat would enable areas of the Earth to be shielded from the collapse of the M-J field. It would enable operatives to move freely about the planet in their quest to repair the field, to reseed chronon levels and thereby restart the flow of time and causality—freeing humanity from its coma.

Then there was the issue of the Shifters: violent, non-Euclidean monstrosities indigenous to causality-free environments. Every single laboratory encounter with one had resulted

in violent fatalities. Paul knew well enough what they were capable of. At the age of twenty-eight he had spent what seemed
an eternity hiding from them, bunkered down beneath floor
panels, waiting for death at the end of time.

The technology—and the defensive capabilities required to
protect the last and best of humanity from the Shifters—would
require development. Only five years remained. Development
within that time frame was not possible without focus and
assistance on a planetary scale.

It required nothing less than humanity coming together,
united by a desire to survive.

That would require some doing.

The threat would need to be seen as formidable, the solution as clear and simple and singular.

All this spun through Paul Serene's head as he fought for
consciousness.

Many great people do not fear death or pain, but there is
not a person alive who does not dread aloneness without hope
or end.

One night terror differed from another. But however it began Paul was always choking on the acrid fumes of burning
insulation and superheated long-chain polymers: the atmosphere that had filled that failing airlock.

This thick mix coated his tongue, mucus membranes fla-
vored themselves toxic, the drug-taste dripping down the back
of his throat as he retched and fought for breath.

A knocking sound always accompanied the initial suffocation: a dull pounding against a wall Paul could never find, and
Jack's voice calling his name from very far away.

Paul always panicked. He would run for the voice but never
found a way out of the smoke and back to the real world. He
always knew what would happen next, and always wished that
the smoke would kill him first.

Paul knew what it was to be buried alive in a moment without end, to feel his psyche crushed like a shell of spun sugar. He knew the killing fear all humans are susceptible to, and yet his fear of the monstrous thing that knew his name, that had stalked him across time, dwarfed even that.

It was here now. He could hear it, in the smoke. Often there would be years between encounters, but each time they met the thing got closer. It howled from within Paul's head.

Infinite potential futures split and bloomed before him; endless corridors spraying in infinite directions. He chose one and fled down it as easily as a frightened child runs to their parents' bedroom.

The campus. The burned library. Jack had Paul's gun, the dull-chrome .45 Paul had picked up years before, a gift from the widow of a Russian warlord, one of Paul's zealots.

In this future Paul had no seizure. In this future he flicked the pistol from Jack's grip, sent it spinning into darkness. Jack's eyes widened with terror—a fear that had nothing to do with Paul.

The monstrosity was there, as always. The thing with the killing light in its palm. It strode from the flames of the library's ruin.

Panic rising, Paul focused on Jack as a means of escape, saw a hundred futures split off the man, chose one, and dived. The scene split, clone images separating, and then the present coalesced.

There was no escape. In this future Jack was gone, and Paul found the thing waiting, as always. It howled. Nothing living sounded like that. Nothing. It was a howl from within the head, not without.

Bestial, fractal, glittering, and hideous it swung for his face.

The palm of its killing paw shone like a star.

Saturday, 8 October 2016. 5:50 A.M. Riverport,
Massachusetts. Monarch Tower.

Paul woke, gasping, the straps of the breather biting into his
face.

"Paul."

The smoke was gone. He sat upright, in a narrow, steel-
framed bed, rubber straps straining as he pulled the mask
from his face.

Her hands were on his shoulders. The sharp taste of the
chronon-rich formulation filled his mouth, lungs, body, set-
tling the seizure. His cells felt intact and reliable. He was alive.

He knew this bright room. Her laboratory. He was home.

"*Paul.*" Sofia: kind, worried eyes and gentle-faced.

He relaxed; the panicked animal inside him receded.

They weren't alone. Martin Hatch was there, patient hands
clasped at his waist, dark-suited and unforthcoming, saying
nothing before it served a purpose. Martin had been with Paul
from the beginning. It was with this man, in this town, that the
idea of Monarch had been formulated.

Martin was the face and CEO of Monarch Solutions, the
umbrella company and global force that allowed Paul to quickly
and easily assemble the technology and talent to do what the
survival of the species required. A company rapidly built by
capitalizing on Paul's powers and knowledge of the future.

Martin received Paul's glance, and returned an acknowledg-
ing nod of the head. *You're fine,* the movement said. *We have
been here before. I am with you.*

Paul breathed out, the strap snapping free. "Jack. Where is
he?"

"When Talon squad located you, you were alone," Hatch
said, that voice as strong as the cornerstone of any parliament.
"A citywide be-on-the-lookout has been issued for Mr. Joyce."

"Regular police can't—"

"I know. I've put Chronon-1 on it."

"Paul," Sofia interjected. "The debrief can wait. How are you feeling?"

"How long was I gone?"

"Not long. Less than an hour this time."

These episodes were becoming more frequent. He examined his left hand, luminescence beneath the sleeve of his tunic. Sitting up and removing his shirt and gloves he examined the spread of the sickness Sofia was racing to understand, an illness that put Paul beyond the help of physical medicine. Six years ago the flesh of his left arm had been transformed, fractal and flickering—the first and most powerful sign of the spreading metamorphosis. Since then it had spread past his elbow, reaching for his vitals. Sofia told him of the inroads it was making, beneath the surface of his skin, fingers of bright corruption reaching upward to touch the underside of his brain.

He was shuddering. Thoughts of that *thing* were still in his head, its massive and distorted frame flickering between states. The hideous head-scream. The desire to make Paul one of them. To take away the mind he had jealously safeguarded for so long.

To claim him with the light of that shining palm.

The seizure he experienced at the library, while fighting Jack, was the illness's latest attempt to wrest control of Paul, once and for all. Paul's mind remained his own, for now, but the infection had claimed another inch of his arm.

"I don't have long." Saying it felt like an admission of death. "The visions, my reconnoitering of possible futures, they're narrowing."

Sofia took his hand, the sick one, without concern. "I've made good progress toward a cure. We will keep administering these treatments to keep the symptoms in check."

"The time frame of your visions has been growing shorter," Hatch said. "At a concerning rate."

"I've never been present in any vision beyond October tenth, 2016. We knew this would come."

Sofia's face grew dark; throwing an accusing look at Hatch. "I won't listen to this."

Paul had to stay alive long enough to see the world saved. If he died with Lifeboat's future uncertain then the world died with him.

Sofia's touch was the one real, selfish comfort he permitted himself in seventeen years, but only because it served a higher purpose. She healed, better than anyone was able to.

She healed, but she could not cure.

Paul swung his legs off the gurney. There was a chamber at the far side of this small lab. It resembled a glass cube, hairy with connections to banks of monitoring equipment, boxed in by a four-point stutter generation field. Inside the stutter contained within that glass box was one of the creatures Sofia had classified, in non-formal nomenclature, as Shifters. It was a being similar to the Shining Palm, but smaller in size.

The stutter chamber was powered by chronon energy flowing directly from the Regulator, the source of near-limitless energy at the heart of Monarch Tower. The Regulator was the very core of Project Lifeboat, housed in a sealed chamber adjacent to Paul's quarters on the forty-ninth floor.

What a boon to humanity the Regulator could be, if only they could understand how it worked. He cursed William for his pride, and turned his attention to the creature in the chamber.

At one time, not long ago, the thrashing thing in the glass box had been known as Dr. Kim.

Thing. Singular. Not strictly accurate.

Kim's role had been to unlock the Regulator's secrets, to

better harness its potential for Project Lifeboat, and the over-eager fool had gone too far. One mistake, a slip of the hand, and he had ceased to be Kim at all—transformed by the complex interaction of gravity, probability, and causality occurring within the heart of the Regulator.

Sofia had been told the device was the creation of Kim himself, a story the little man had been more than happy to play along with. But it was far from the truth.

Because of his error, Dr. Kim now existed in a state of quantum superposition. Moment to moment his form settled upon one configuration then manifested as another. The eye could not rest, detail could not be grasped.

The Kim-Shifter was a being of pure rage, thrashing against boundaries it could never escape.

Shifters manifested only within chronon-free areas—spaces in which probability and causality had ceased to function. Place a probability generator—such as a human—within their habitat and Shifters became incredibly violent. Sofia hypothesized that a Shifter's natural state was placid, but exposure to potential was agonizing, driving them to destroy the source of pain.

Dr. Kim had been human. Paul himself was being colonized by a condition similar to Dr. Kim's. Therefore, Sofia concluded, Shifters had once been human.

Examining Kim's state of superposition she believed he now existed not as *a* Dr. Kim, but as *all possible* Dr. Kims.

The Shifter in the chamber was form and reality at war with themselves.

This, she concluded, meant that Shifters were beings that existed outside and across all times, living in the spaces between moments, four-dimensionally. The Kim-Shifter existed. The Kim-Shifter would exist. The Kim-Shifter had always existed—even before the moment Dr. Kim became a Shifter.

The thing had long ago given up attempting to attack its cage. Now it existed in a state of perpetual, thrashing frenzy, a dozen versions of itself half-perceptible from moment to moment. Paul had come to think of its layered, multitudinous shrieks as the sound of utter hatred.

"Martin," Sofia said. "Cover that, please." She nodded to Paul and his clear distress.

"He has been like that from the moment he transformed," Hatch said, pulling a black cloth about the chamber. "Where does he get the energy?"

The cloth did nothing to keep the hate-sound from Paul's mind.

"He chose his fate," Paul said, more to comfort himself than anything else.

"One of him did," Sofia replied. "The multitude he has become did not, and I suspect they hate him for it."

Sofia went back to finishing her ministrations. "It is not a fitting fate for a man who may have saved all of humanity. The Regulator was his gift to us. Without it you have no way of sidestepping the end of all things. Lifeboat would be nothing."

Paul was just as important to the Project as the Regulator, and Kim knew it. That's why the man had locked himself inside the stutter chamber before the transformation had taken full hold: to provide a fully infected patient ready to be studied, and to help find a cure for Paul's condition.

Sofia may not have found a cure, but the treatments she had developed through studying the Kim-Shifter had bought Paul enough time to lay the groundwork for Project Lifeboat.

Paul crossed the room. One wall was entirely glass, looking down upon a glass-roofed farm of laboratories, each one staffed by men and women at the peak of their field. Many of them, in that moment, would be working to find ways to save Paul.

Pointless, but he couldn't tell Sofia that.

He need only survive a day or two more, that was all that mattered, then the process required to make Lifeboat a reality would succeed.

The flesh of his arm ached.

"I can't become like them," he said, as much to himself as anyone. "That kind of madness. Trapped between moments. Forever."

"Paul," she said. "That is not your fate."

"I'll kill myself first."

"That is not what I meant."

"They want me with them, Sofia. When they howl, it's a pull like nothing I've ever felt. When I dream of them it's like coming home."

"You make it sound like something you want."

"What if, as this sickness spreads, my mind becomes infirm? In a moment of weakness, I could surrender humanity's every future." Paul took her hand in his. "I need just a few more days. Give me that."

"I do not tend corpses," she said. "You will live. But, I will do as you ask. For the next few days." She laid one hand against his face. "In that time don't be stupid."

Hatch cleared his throat.

Paul glanced at him. "Yes, Martin."

"We need to debrief."

Paul gently touched Sofia's face, kissed her forehead. "Be rested for the gala tonight. Seduce the world for me, Sofia. I want you and Martin to leave them gasping. I'll be watching from my quarters."

"And afterward?"

"Just you and me." Then: "Martin, this way."

Paul directed his CEO into a free medical bay. Sofia's lab was secure on the top floor, close to Martin's office and away from the eyes of the rest of the Tower. Paul's association with

Monarch, despite being its unofficial founder, was strictly off the record. He'd never even walked the mezzanines.

"You said you've assigned Chronon-1 to bring in Jack," Paul said.

"That's right."

Paul dragged one palm down his sweating face, worked the ache out of his jaw. "Chronon-1 had him once."

"Randall Gibson had him once. I've demoted him and placed Donny in charge."

Paul was surprised. "Gibson's your boy, Martin. You've cleaned a lot of dirt from his kennel over the years. I expected rationales from you, not a spanking."

"In his defense, Randall was underequipped. Jack is chronon-active. That was unexpected." Martin let that hang for a moment, perhaps pointedly. "He informs me that Joyce woke and gave him the slip."

"You doubt the report."

"Randall's instinct for self-preservation is a primary trait."

"As is his unpredictability."

"It's the cost of an adaptable operative who possesses wide-spectrum moral flexibility, zero hesitation, and the mental fortitude for stutter operations. His success rate remains in the second percentile. In terms of cost-benefit the man remains an asset."

"So. Now that the university is done, what's the temperature outside?"

Hatch shifted his weight a touch, straightened his shoulders. "Almost everything went exactly as you said it would."

Paul took a second and slowed his subjective relationship to the moment. Focusing on Martin, he watched potential futures radiate off the man four-dimensionally. He isolated his awareness of these potential causality streams and focused instead on streams already expiring. Paul's awareness scanned through this fading back-catalog, located the inbound path that had led to the particular moment they now inhabited, and traced it backward.

This backward path was already weak and fading, becoming fainter as each passing second took Paul farther away from the present. Paul seized upon it, allowed his perception to inhabit that now-extinct possible past, and looked around as quickly as he could.

Martin, in his office, eighty-seven minutes prior. The black-glass surface of his smart desk channeled the voice of Talon Squad's senior operative.

"Stage One's complete, sir. All witnesses detained."

"How many?"

"Thirteen. They've seen what we needed them to see."

Martin digested this. "Thirteen is manageable."

"Sir?"

Martin Hatch radiated a sudden density of potential, a daisy-head of deeply consequential paths streaming from him. What he said next would determine the shape of the future—the success or failure, potentially, of everything Paul had worked for.

"Release three, then exercise the hard-line option immediately. Civilians and law enforcement are contained, but not for much longer. You have sixty seconds."

"Yes, sir. Talon out."

Hatch heard gunfire before the line had even cut.

The daisy-head withered, untaken paths already dusting out and being left behind as Martin Hatch walked Monarch into a future where they murdered ten college students, on campus. The flow of time dragged Paul away from other futures. Looking forward, Paul saw how the path Martin had taken them down would require cover-ups, raise questions, spawn suspicion, and require a retasking of manpower to smooth things over. Why had Monarch personnel cordoned the university? How could a private security outfit mandate to the Riverport Police Department who may and may not enter an active crime scene? Why was Monarch dealing with the shooters?

But it was all covered in their contract with the city, and events would progress fast enough that it would never go to court.

He saw the media explode with speculation about "Peace": who were they and why had they targeted the quantum physics building? He caught glimpses of Monarch revealing what had been inside that lab, the perfect way to prime the public for what Martin would reveal at tomorrow night's gala.

This had been the right move. Behind him Paul watched a dozen lesser causality-paths die.

Paul disengaged and rubber banded back into the present.

"We made an impression," Hatch was saying. "The correct witnesses escaped, the remainder were neutralized on-site. The narrative in the media is that it's an act of domestic terrorism. There's good footage of our helicopter airlifting the time core free of the Quantum Physics Building."

"Great. That primes the audience for our second-act involvement. We're in good shape."

"Your decision to prematurely demolish the library, however—"

"—was accounted for in pre-planning. It conforms to the narrative of an extremist attack on the Physics Building."

As an individual, Martin Hatch possessed minimal need for expression. The flex of thumb atop his clasped hands and his level gaze exuded tolerance. "Is it possible that you simply could not bring yourself to shoot a family friend?"

Martin knew him better than anyone, but even so . . . Paul found the thought of having lost a moment of control over his own transparency unsettling.

"Seventeen years and here we are, on the eve of our work coming to fruition, and you're questioning my capacity to place our mission first?"

"I never supported the elimination of William Joyce. Our best have striven for years to understand the Regulator. Dr. Joyce could have enlightened us in an afternoon."

"He resided on the correct side of your cost-benefit analysis, yes, I understand."

"Six years. That's how long I've debated Dr. Joyce with you. We could have brought him in, interrogated him, and learned. You and I will never know how far it could have taken this company."

"I helmed Project Promenade for three years before I finally went through the machine. In that time William was a consultant and troubleshooter only. He was never hauled off for questioning. It never happened, so it *could never happen*. Time is a closed loop. Nothing changes. I know. I've tried."

"The Regulator could have been our Rosetta Stone. It may have saved us, come the end." Hatch composed himself. This kind of outburst was out of character for him. "There is nothing more to be said. Kim is gone, and now so is Joyce."

These bullet points were recited, verbatim, from the last time they'd had a similar conversation. "Will had the knowledge and power to interfere. We're too close to zero hour. The risk he presented was unacceptable."

Hatch maintained his usual countenance. "Convince me that sentimentality will not play a role in your handling of Jack Joyce."

"We've tried and failed for years to replicate my abilities. Jack survived where we failed. He is valuable."

"That is irrelevant this late in the game."

"Replicating the powers Jack and I share, sans my . . . ailment . . . would lessen Lifeboat's dependence on chronon storage and rescue rigs, thereby increasing the viability of end-of-time survival."

"William's interferences would have been inconvenient. By contrast the actions of a chronon-active insurgent, such as Jack, in pursuit of a vendetta could derail—"

"Martin." Paul looked his friend in the eye. "You are Monarch. The blood of ten people is on your hands. Mine are plunged into an ocean of it. No single life is worth the life of all that has been, all that is, and all that might one day be. When it comes to Jack I won't hesitate, but for now he resides on the correct side of my own cost-benefit analysis." Martin held his gaze. That was enough. "I chose you to be the man to safeguard humanity through its most terrible hour. Your diligence now only reaffirms my confidence."

Martin inclined his head, an acceptance and leave-taking. He did not accept the rationale, or the flattery. Without another word he exited, the conversation over.

Paul's hand went to the talisman that hung around his neck on a thin, woven chain. Orrie "Trigger" Aberfoyle's bullet: a reminder that time cannot be taken for granted, and that eventually it runs out. For everyone.

8

Will was whistling while he worked, sitting at his wooden bench in the barn, an articulated lamp isolating him in a pool of warm light. Jack was outside the barn door, playing with action figures before bed. Will looked over, smiled, and kept on whistling tunelessly.

Jack looked up, saw the bomb drop. It punched through the barn's frail roof, scattering tiles, splintering wood. Then the flame: a wall of fire, bright and cold and . . .

It was dark. He was cold. He was in a car, moving, his head resting against the passenger-side window. Wind whistled off-key through two sharp-edged breaks in the glass. Bullet holes.

Christmas lights. The smell of coffee. Nick's cab.

Someone shared the backseat with him, curled into herself, the painted words on the back of her hoodie catching the moonlight: RESPECT EXISTENCE OR EXPECT RESISTANCE. Amy. She was alive.

Nick glanced at him in the rearview. "So," he inquired. "How was your evening?"

The radio was burbling. Some loudmouth Jack remembered from his high school years was still bellowing down the airwaves, except this time he sounded more alarmed than brash.

Nobody was talking about frozen time. Why would they?

They had all been frozen right along with it. Nobody would have noticed a thing.

"How'd you get off campus?" he said.

"Skin of teeth, friend," Nick replied. "We in trubbies."

"They killed everyone," Amy mumbled, turning her face toward him. "Like it was no big deal."

There were specks of blood on her face. She let him take that in, then turned away, pulling the hood tighter around her head as if she was trying to fall away to some other place.

"It's true," Nick said. "News is saying it looks like an act of domestic terrorism. Some anti-Monarch group."

"Those guys were Monarch."

Amy sat bolt upright, shot across the seat, and got in Nick's face. *"I fucking told you!"* She punched the back of Nick's seat, hard, then hurled herself back into her own. "We tried to get the others to the car," Amy added, voice close to breaking. "They didn't make it."

"Found you inside the cab," Nick said. "I must have left it unlocked." Then: "Monarch? Really?" Like someone had told him his mom had cancer.

Zed. Had Jack really seen her?

The water bottle Nick used to fill his little espresso gadget had taken a round and exploded. The front seat was soaked. "They must have made you as you left."

"A couple of goons, probably. We didn't hit the cordon. Amy had a way out. Blasted through a few hedges, trashed a fence, tore up the football field, and roared into the night." Nick's voice wasn't doing a good job of living up to the bravado of his words. He sounded far away. "Dad's gonna murder me. You can't get paint in this shade anymore."

"They'll be looking for this car."

"The cops," Amy said. "They have to be in on this. How can they not be? Was this all for a *library*?"

She had curled up again, vulnerable, shaking as the adrenaline wore off, so different from the rough-edged battler who had cornered him a few hours ago.

"No," Jack said. "This had nothing to do with you and your friends. Wrong place, wrong time, that's all."

"Sing it with me," she mumbled.

Library. Will's final moments looped for him, endlessly. Despair, farewell, flame, gone.

Then Paul. Jack wondered what he would have done with that gun, if Zed hadn't shown. Would he have used it on Paul? Killed the kid he grew up with?

"Nick? Where are we going?"

"Out of town, I figure. Wait and see what happens."

Amy sat upright. "I have to get home. My parents will be freaking out."

"I know, buddy. Jack, your phone work?"

Jack thumbed his on. Nothing but bars of rainbow scramble. "Nothing." Monarch comms had been working fine the whole time, though. "Most likely they remote-uploaded something to every cellular in the area. I watched a fifteen-year-old do it in a cafeteria once."

Amy was becoming agitated. "Just drop me off in my neighborhood, okay? I gotta get home."

"Are you hearing the radio? Everyone's losing their minds. If they're looking for us—"

"Then stop the car. I'm getting out."

"I don't think—"

"Stop the fucking car! Stop it! Stop it!"

"Hey hey, if you—"

Amy was already reaching for the door. Jack grabbed her. "Amy!"

She lashed out for his face, dug in, drew blood. Before she could swing again he locked her in a bear hug and did his best

not to move while she screamed every last thing she could think
of at the ceiling.

"Guys, guys, come on, man, we . . . !"

"Eyes on the road, Nick. Please."

Amy kept screaming, for what seemed like minutes. She
kicked the shit out of the back of those original seats, Nick's
head rocking back and forth with each strike. Eventually the
steam ran out, leaving her cold and vibrating. Jack loosened his
grip; she didn't push him away. Jack imagined that if she was
anything like him, right now she felt like she was falling down
a very deep well. A lot of people she cared about were gone.
Her entire world, for all he knew, and nobody could know what
that was like. She hadn't even begun to work that out. Neither
had he.

"They killed my brother," Jack said, quietly. The disclosure
dispelled the terrible isolation she felt, the being-alone with
friends who would forever be absences. It made their extin-
guishment all too real, a safety catch flipped, and it all poured
out of her. She gripped him hard, joints locked, her frame
bucking with each wracking sob.

Nick fished a box of Kleenex from the glove compartment,
eyes on the rearview mirror. "Jack," he whispered, as discreetly
as he could. "You might want one for your face."

Jack took the box, which was when Nick noticed that the
blood was still there but the cuts were not.

9

They dropped Amy off a block from her house, then Nick drove toward Jack's old place.

Jack had known only one home. It was several hectares of what had once been a turn-of-the-century horse farm, torn down, built up, and refurbished in the 1960s to serve as home to Jack and Will's newlywed parents. Warm old wood and airy rooms repainted every few years, with the exceptions of the kitchen doorframe. That the family kept for the notches carved there, each one bearing Jack or Will's name, and the date it was made, measuring their growth from children to loudmouthed teens to . . .

Jack was nine when the family routine ended. His mom and dad had died. As the eldest, Will had taken over the task of raising Jack, while continuing his scientific work.

Will had never been well. While their parents were alive a certain order had been maintained, allowing Will to function at high efficiency while focusing on what interested him. Maintained by medication and regular meals, Will did well. His scientific papers were received with interest, even acclaim. His future was bright. But the loss of their parents changed that.

Will couldn't look after himself, let alone someone as volatile and needful as a newly orphaned nine-year-old boy. Will replaced the organizational influence of their parents with a series of spreadsheets, allowing him to ensure Jack was maintained while maximizing the amount of time Will could spend in the barn, working.

For the first three years not an evening went by that Jack didn't hear the Dodge crackle up the driveway and feel his entire body leap with "Dad's home." This was followed by the immediate reminder that Dad was gone and Will was driving the truck.

Jack finished high school while working two or three jobs, managing the household, paying bills, and making sure they both ate regularly. Will's focus was on the world beyond Riverport, the span of history, the greater good. Jack's had been on the home.

Dates with girls were missed. Friends were few. Dances came and went. Neither Jack nor Will attended Jack's high school graduation: Will because he forgot, and Jack because he knew Will would forget. A glance at the kitchen corkboard told him that it hadn't even rated a mention on the spreadsheet.

The farm had been a great place for four people, a sad place for two.

Now, standing at the gate, headlights illuminating the family name on the gate plate, Jack couldn't bear the idea of returning to it as a family of one.

The smoke from the burning library was a faint blemish on a horizon turned morning-silver.

Jack had asked Nick to stop at the gate. He had been standing there for almost ten minutes, eyes on the roof of the old house, past the maple trees, past the barn. Nick wasn't in a rush, just leaned against the hood and smoked. The cabbie's eyes were closed, head back, not tired just—not running for his life.

"You want breakfast?" Jack asked.

Nick shrugged. "I don't feel like eating a damn thing, but sure. You think Amy'll be okay?"

"Not for a while."

"I'm sorry. About your brother. I'm sure he was solid."

"He was self-absorbed, unreliable, and way in love with the smell of all his burning bridges."

"But."

"But toward the end I think he was trying to do some good."

"Solid dude. Nobody's perfect." Nick closed his lighter, flicked his cigarette onto the asphalt. "What about Thailand? They might be watching the airports."

"They might be watching the house."

Nick shot a glance at the red-tiled roofline. Nothing suspicious.

"If they were," Jack said. "We'd know about it by now." Jack thought of his worn-out little apartment. The rusted key that fit the battered door. They may as well have belonged to someone else. "No," he said. "I'm staying."

Nick flipped his key ring in his hand, gunslinger-style, and got in the car. Jack found the white-painted latch flipped smoothly, but the gate stuck. He remembered the trick: lifted the gate, then pulled, and it swung just fine. Nick rolled the Charger over the hump and Jack got in.

The cab rolled in quiet and slow, lights off.

"Follow the drive." By the fence was a dilapidated toolshed, unused and kept for color, next to which a shallow wooden boat sat gathering age under an orange tarpaulin. That had been his father's, and something neither brother had wanted to be rid of. Grass grew wild and uncut around it, still green despite the fall weather.

The drive wound past a stand of four aged sycamore trees, each having dropped a flame-orange shadow of turned leaves, bringing the house and barn into full view. The last time Jack had seen the place it had been white-sided with dark-brown detailing. Since then Will had clearly decided it needed a paint job. Half of one side of the house was painted haphazardly sky blue; next to it a scissor-lift sat unattended and partially rusted.

"Jesus Christ, Will. Follow through man, or just hire someone."

It hurt his heart to see the place like this. Some windows were obscured with grime. Others had been soaped opaque or covered in newspaper.

"This place looks abandoned."

"No, pretty sure Will was living here."

"While time-sharing with bears?"

"Paul . . ." The name stuck in Jack's throat. "I was told Will may have gone off his meds."

Nick switched off the engine and the car rumbled to a stop.

"Come on," Jack said, getting out. "It'll be an adventure." He climbed out, booted feet touching down on home soil. The early morning air smelled like way back when.

An uncertain laugh made the hairs on his arms stand up.

Will spoke, attempting to make light of something. ". . . you can't just . . ."

And there he was, but not really, at the foot of the wooden porch steps. It was happening again. Will was younger, bearded, wearing glass frames Jack hadn't seen since Jack was, what, fourteen or fifteen?

"Hey! Hey! Shut it!" someone snapped, but Will didn't react. His nervous smile was still there, as if waiting for feedback he could interpret. This abuse didn't parse.

Someone else cut in, and Jack saw them now, two men who had been dead for six years, blown away at Bannerman's Overlook: Princess and Aberfoyle's second-in-charge. They were younger, too. Leaner. Better hair.

The second-in-charge cut in, more reasonable but no less intimidating. "You've had three months. No payment. No payment means we take the house."

Will wasn't making eye contact. "You . . . you don't get the house. I . . . I dealt with Mr. Aberfoyle." Will was talking to himself, the way he did when he worked, when teasing loose some complicated theoretical knot. He wasn't present. Those fuckers were totally taking advantage of him. "Mr. Aberfoyle is the one . . . the one . . . who . . ." Will twitched, blinked hard, once, twice, three times.

Jack knew that tic. He wiped his eyes. Whenever this was, Will had been in a deep hole.

Will shook his head, blinked hard, shook his head again. He used thumb and forefinger to readjust his glasses. He still wasn't looking at the men, his eyes on the steps or the trees. His tics were getting the better of him. Jack whispered his brother's name, to no effect.

Princess glanced at the second-in-charge, smiled that prehistoric fish smile, then scowled at Will. "We make you nervous?"

Something hit the gravel, grassy and clattering—groceries—and a kid twelve years away from where Jack stood barked, "Hey!"

Jack felt himself surrender, déjà vu dragging him around again.

Princess didn't even look at the new arrival. "Fuck off, kid."

The knees were gone from his jeans; those thrift-store sneakers had lasted four years. Jack had forgotten that he once had a T-shirt with NOT blasted across the chest and he had loved that jacket. He thought that jacket made him look like serious business: khaki canvas, two big pockets, plenty of zippers.

Jack knew those groceries in the drive were paid for by three hours of collecting cans after school. He remembered buying them from a supermarket owned by Orrie Aberfoyle.

Will was a caricature of good manners. "Jack. Welcome home." He swept his arm toward the door, a cartoon maître d', still not looking anyone in the eye. "Why don't you go up-stairs?" Will never had any real idea what he was doing when it came to the human race. He had gotten better as time went on, but it still beggared belief. The poor bastard.

Jack Joyce, aged fourteen, got between the two wide-bodies and his brother, hair hanging in his eyes. "What's the problem?" The size differential was shocking. The eye lines of Princess and the second-in-charge dropped toward this kid like two safes being lowered from a twelfth-floor window. The kid met their gaze unflinching. He raised his eyebrows helpfully—can I assist you?

Princess looked right at the kid, and said: "That smart mouth is gonna get your little brother hurt, Will."

The kid's eyebrows dropped. His voice was very level. "If I was being smart with you, dickhead, you'd never know it."

Jack laughed, his hand slapping over his mouth. His eyes prickled.

Princess snapped his fist skyward—intercepted by the second-in-charge. "Dude. He's a kid."

Princess hesitated, eyes beaming death. Then he lowered that broad fist. "We'll be back," he promised.

"I'll be here," the kid said.

You magnificent little shit, Jack thought.

The goons exited stage right and literally vanished. The kid watched them go.

Vibrations took hold of the kid's legs, and Jack watched as he hit the dirt—first those shredded knees, then his hands as well. They curled in the gravel, hard. The kid's breath was staccato. He was shaking.

Will said, "Foul language is unacceptable, young man. Mom and Dad would have been appalled." It sounded as if he were talking in his sleep.

The kid's head snapped toward Will, wild-eyed and furious. Will didn't move. He was doing that fiddly thing with his fingers, eyes on the gravel, or the trees. The kid's fury shaded to fearful, to outraged, then to disbelieving. Then contained. Then the kid was coping. Business as usual.

Will's tics were subsiding, but he still wasn't moving. "Appalled . . ."

The kid got to his feet and slapped white-dusted hands against his serious-business jacket. Looping Will's arm over his shoulder the kid turned his brother toward the house.

"Privileges revoked, mister," Will mumbled.

"You're right, Will. I'm sorry."

"Your grades are suffering. Bad grades are unacceptable. Your education—"

"Is my future. I know, Will. Steps."

The brothers climbed the steps to the porch.

"Let's get you to bed," the kid said.

"No, too much work."

"Let's get you to bed."

"All right."

The kid moved his brother to the front door and then opened it for him. "How much do we owe?"

"Owe?" Like he was talking in his sleep again.

"Mr. Aberfoyle."

"How do you know Mr. Aberfoyle?"

The kid escorted him into the house. "Let's get you to bed."

"All right."

The ghost door closed behind them, and the world came back into focus.

Nick was looking at Jack weird. Which was fair enough.

"I guess you're wondering . . ."

"Pretty much."

"A lot of memories."

"My grandmother used to do that. Talk to the air. God, specifically."

"Did she get answers?" Jack said it as a joke.

"The good Lord told her when she was gonna die, right down to the minute. Were you communing with something just then?"

Communing. Man, everybody in Massachusetts had some story about the life beyond. Jack had called an electrician out, years ago, to fix a light socket that wouldn't stop flickering. The guy hadn't been able to fix it and had advised Jack that it was most likely a spirit thing and to just make friends with it.

There was no point complicating things. "No. It's just been a bad night."

Jack climbed the bowed porch steps. He fished out his keys, looked for the one he never used. There it was, still stamped with the name of the shoe repair place on Ducayne where he'd gotten it cut when he was fifteen. "You know, Nick," Jack said. "Ghosts don't hang around because they can't let go of us. They hang around because we can't let go of them."

"You're a surprising man, Jack."

"That's not one of mine." Jack turned the key, the lock clacked. "Something an electrician told me."

The door opened, shoving aside a loose bank of uncollected mail. The cold air inside was stale, faintly rancid. Nick commented that it smelled like his old dorm room.

The date stamps on the mail were at least a week old, some dating further back. "The power might be off."

The door opened straight into the living area, staircase angling up and behind the fireplace. The kitchen was through an entry to the right, and before that was space for the dining table and china cabinet. A bay window looked onto the drive and sycamore trees.

When Jack lived here he had managed to keep back Will's piecemeal encroachment onto a house that was a memorial to his parents. So much of the interior character existed because of choices their mother and father had made; echoes Jack wanted to keep hearing for as long as he could. They were silent now. The place had changed.

Minor things remained as they had been: powder-blue walls, framed pastoral oils by some anonymous gas station artist, and homemade shelves where Jack had often set up action figures to be blasted down with dart guns. He smiled for a moment, before the memory of the previous few hours and the ghost-weight of a real gun in his hand fouled the recollection.

Atop that base layer Will had made the place his own. A whiteboard balanced on top of the mantle, gone smudge-blue from countless scrawlings and erasures. The china cabinet had been cleared and the dishware replaced with haphazard arrangements of scientific periodicals. The dining table was a work space, piled with papers and correspondence, the four chairs stacked in the corner, replaced by a single threadbare ergonomic saddle seat on four casters.

It hurt to see the place like this, faded and dusty and wrong.

"Your brother really believed in taking work home with him." Nick crossed to the plastic-sheathed sofa—moving with a pronounced limp—and rested there.

"Did you hurt yourself?"

"I'm fine. Busted my knee a few years back, is all."

"Hockey?"

"I was . . . in a car accident."

It clicked: the ignition in Nick's cab, slaved to a Breathalyzer. Nick "The Prez" Marsters. Jack knew this story. It had made the news a year or so before Jack left Riverport.

The realization must have been all over Jack's face because Nick rolled his eyes, laid his head back, and said to the ceiling: "It wasn't like the news reported it. I wasn't drunk." Shooting Jack a glance: "I wasn't. *Drinking,* yes. Drunk, no."

Jack went looking for coffee, found the kitchen had been used more often than cleaned. The fridge was empty, save for four small cartons of milk, a jar of pickled ginger, two bottles of sterilized water, and a decaying clutch of rubber-banded shallots. Coffee was in the cupboard, the milk was barely decent, and the sink held a stack of plates textured with outcroppings of dark green mold. That would have been the musty scent that Nick found so familiar.

The faucet juddered and spat. He rinsed the kettle, lit the burner, set the water to boil, then wandered back to ask Nick how he took his coffee.

"It was a pedestrian," Nick said. "They popped up in the middle of the road, I swerved and the car I was driving barrel-rolled through a fence and destroyed a gazebo."

Jack hooked a thumb back toward the kitchen. "Black?"

"A *judge's* gazebo."

Nick was asleep on the couch by the time the coffee was ready. Jack cleared a space among the papers on the dining table, set both cups down, and took a seat. Morning light brought out more color in the place. Coffee steam rose fragrant and pleasing from Jack's faded mug. Washed-away lettering advised never ever, ever, ever giving up. It was a Churchill quote. Jack's father had given him the mug when he started taking guitar lessons.

His high school yearbook lay open on a page of class photographs. The university security guard looked back at him in black and white, thirty pounds heavier and braces on his teeth.

Jack memorized his name.

10

At that moment, Paul was off-site in an operations room composed of a nine-rack of monitors and three operators handling six different hazmat drones—not so different from those used for exploring radioactive death zones, though these had finer motor control. Here, within the green zone of the area designated in official Monarch documentation as Ground Zero, Paul watched as tracked, claw-handed drones and lumbering quanton-insulated scientists worked the forsaken landscape within Warehouse 21B. The view these multiple screens offered was not always perfect. The crews at Ground Zero had to replace cameras frequently. Not much survived in the red zone.

"It pains me that Will is going to be remembered as a lunatic," he said to Sofia. "That his theories were never taken seriously."

Sofia leaned into one console, bending the thread-mic toward her. "Doctors Connor and Chang, please attend to remote unit C. One of the receivers has degraded. Thank you." She turned to Paul. "As will you, so you tell me." She snapped a penlight on, flicked the beam from his left eye to right and back again, snapped it off. "As will I, for all the work I've done here."

"The activation of the machine fractured the Meyer-Joyce

field. The Fracture will grow, universal chronon count will hit zero, and time itself will end." This was fact. "In that sense humanity is not going to remember anything: trapped, unaware, in a submoment self-dividing into infinity. Those of us chosen to go on will be tortured by more important things than a lack of recognition." He sighed. "But we have five more years. Time enough for Project Lifeboat to be properly developed and become operational."

Sofia pressed two fingers to his carotid. "About that," she said. "I have rechecked my calculations for a third time and can find no error." She checked his pulse against her watch.

"Sofia . . ."

She removed her hand. "You have been to this end-of-time event, yes, I understand. You saw clocks and calendars and papers. They provided you a date. But the data does not lie: we have mere days, not years. At the current rate of decay the Meyer-Joyce field *will* collapse—in two, perhaps three days at the most. You must take these findings seriously."

"The waveform—"

"Has collapsed, as you have said so often. The future is written because events in the past led you to witness the future. I understand. But you must consider the likelihood that the reason your visions do not extend beyond a few days from now is because *that* is when time ends. Not five years, not next month, but *this week*."

"*Enough!*"

Sofia flinched, stepped back.

"Please," he said. "Enough."

Another moment of lost control. This was becoming common. He was fighting to retain focus, to maintain his discipline and resolve. He had decided upon and built a protocol for his behavior when this final week arrived, knowing that raw programming may be the only thing to keep him on mission once his illness properly asserted itself. If he had to think too much, plan too much, adjust too much—it opened the gates to error, flawed thinking, damaged reasoning, and a lack of perspective. He had to trust to the plan laid out by his clearer-headed and less instinctual past self. He was a soldier now, taking orders from the more complete person he used to be. He could not tolerate anyone interfering with that coding.

"It is too late for a course correction. The future is locked."

Sofia's jaw was set. "I am not working night and day simply to pass the time between now and doomsday."

"Let's . . ." Paul glanced at the monitors. "Let's change the subject. The Tower's chronon stores, how are we doing?"

Warehouse 21B, nestled on the fringe of what had once been Riverport's thriving dockyards, had been a very respectable laboratory. In some ways the fingerprint of the original owner survived, despite the fickle entropic fluctuations that possessed the place. The work benches remained upright, though most of the original equipment had long since crumbled to dust. A bunk bed, neatly made, survived layered in the accreted powdery fallout of age and time. Resting atop a caved-in twelve-cup coffee maker, angled toward the camera, was a dusty photograph of a family of four: mother, father, two sons. Tape yellowed and withered and curled on three corners.

How Paul wished he had never activated that machine.

The scientists at Ground Zero clicked life back into the tracked claw-robot and gave a thumbs-up to the camera. In the operations room a controller leaned forward on a throttle and trundled the 'bot toward the room's centerpiece: a roiling and thumping time-space anomaly encapsulated and trapped within a twelve-billion-dollar contraption designed to harness and siphon off the rampant torrents of chronon energy it had been spraying out for the last six years.

Delicately, the operator manipulated the fine-work pincer to replace various burned-out components on the shell. Racked about the site an elaborate array of chronon batteries absorbed the anomaly's output as fast as they were able.

"Our chronon stores are holding level," Sofia said. "Containing Dr. Kim is our biggest drain, currently. But a necessary one. If we didn't have the Regulator I doubt we would be able to contain him at all."

"Lifeboat," Paul said. "Is it getting what it needs?"

"At this rate the Tower's capacitors will be fully charged in eighteen months. Well ahead of your schedule. However, *if* the end-of-time event occurs five years from now, as you say, and Ground Zero continues to generate chronon particles at the current rate, I estimate we'll have enough chronon energy stored in these batteries to maintain causality in a limited area for a number of years. Long enough to develop a solution to the crisis. If there is a solution."

"What if the M-J field were to collapse this week?"

Sofia glanced at him.

"Just answer the question."

"Less than a year. Eighteen months if we're extremely frugal. Less than a month if, for some reason, the Regulator ceases to function. I really do wish you would let me examine the research your people are doing on that. I feel confident I—"

Paul's phone began vibrating against his chest.

"I want you to have your people keep an eye on ambient chronon levels," he told her. "And look for any other fluctuations or deformations in the Meyer-Joyce field. If you detect anything—anything at all—let me know." Paul took out his phone. It was Martin Hatch. He knew what this was about. "Martin."

"Paul. We've held off, but I must insist we send in the troops now."

"Is Jack still at the farm?"

"Yes. And his accomplice."

"I'll be free in . . ." Paul checked his watch, glanced at Sofia.

"Ninety minutes," she said.

"I can be at the farm in one hour and forty-five."

"The team is quite capable of bringing Joyce in without your involvement."

"His brother is dead, Martin. He hasn't been home in six years. Right now he'll be going through grief and adrenaline crash. Two hours from now I'll be able to talk him in, not hogtie and drag him. Let me know if anything changes."

Hatch said nothing.

"Martin?"

"Yes, Paul. I'll keep you notified."

11

The morning light had shifted. Nick's untouched coffee cup had stopped steaming. Jack's never-give-up was half-empty, two fingers still looped through the handle. He had lost an hour flipping through the papers on the table. The stuff he could understand was bills, rejection letters from peer-reviewed journals, and several notes from a psychiatrist requesting Will come back for another appointment.

The stuff he couldn't decipher was 100 percent William Joyce moon language: calculations, scrawl, articles on Hawking radiation, footnotes on various isotopes, and—alarmingly—correspondence sourcing prices for a ten-thousand-terahertz laser. That had been slashed through with red. Through '97 and '98 he had been in contact with second- and third-tier universities around the globe—all of them about to come into possession of a nuclear research power plant. Beneath that stack of correspondence Jack found the fake credentials and airline stubs. Framed on the identity page of a forged U.S. passport, eight years expired, Dr. Howard Gordon Wells stared back at Jack with a distinctly unimpressed expression. Dr. H. G. Wells was a very young William Joyce.

A stupid, on-the-nose flourish like that was something a younger Will would have deemed delicious. Will had been like that, before their parents died. Funny. Excitable.

Lasers. Nuclear reactors. Isotopes. A ticket to Argentina. Fake passports. All that correspondence. H. G. Wells.

H. G. Wells. Jack released his coffee cup, turned in his seat to face the window, and looked at the barn.

The barn was the one place he had not been allowed to enter—the place where Will totally lost it one evening and frightened the life out of Jack and Paul.

The two boys had been maybe ten years old at the time. It had been a cool evening, Jack remembered, and Will had not yet returned home. Jack had made dinner, he and Paul had watched that *Team Outland* DVD for the thirty-seventh time, and then ran around the house with their action figures and, not for the first time, Paul had asked Jack why they were never allowed in the barn. What did Will do in there?

Jack had told Paul what Will always told him: "Work."

"What kind of work?"

With that one obvious question the barn had gone from being something matter-of-fact and as impenetrable as a concrete block, as taken for granted as the ground beneath his feet, to a locked door on a big secret.

Anything could be in there.

"Bombs!"

"Superstrength stuff!"

"A spaceship!"

It was a mission for Team Outland. Plotting the movements of imaginary guards, they sneaked downstairs, crossed the gravel path, waited, then leaped from bushes to press themselves against the barn's rough, red wood.

They quickly discovered Will kept the barn locked tight. Twenty frustrating minutes later Jack was about to call it quits when Paul realized the barn had a dirt floor: they could tunnel under the wall.

Eight minutes later they were in: dirt all over their fronts, grass strands sticking to their hair, action figures in hand.

"Whoa," Jack said with wonderment.

"Boring," Paul said with wonderment.

Jack rounded on him, hurt. "Seriously? Look at this stuff!"

The barn's interior had been crudely redesigned. The farm's previous owners had run a stable, taking care of horses for private owners who lacked the space to do it themselves. The barn had a broad entrance at either end, the northernmost sealed permanently with neatly arranged nailed planks. All of the stalls had been knocked out, clearing a great deal of space, which was filled with stainless steel equipment the likes of which Jack had never seen. Much of it had power cabling running to it from a padlocked room once used to store feed.

"Looks like a factory," Paul had said. "What's that?" He was pointing at the huge, flat, donut-like platform that took up the northern half of the space. A crude iron frame kept the walkway-ring off the dirt. Will had been building a frame around it. An oxy welder was off to the side, next to stacks of irregular steel and iron offcuts.

The centerpiece of the ring was a large cup-cradle of clean and shining metal, empty of whatever it was meant to hold.

Jack had been more interested in the benches and workspaces, all gleaming silver and perforated with neat rows of holes. Bits and pieces of equipment were bolted into the holes, keeping them steady. Black metal brackets secured lenses and cubes of glass. One long black tube pointed down a series of thick monocles.

"I think that's a laser," Paul said. "Your brother must have a lot of money."

"This is why our power keeps cutting out," Jack realized. "Like, every week, for a whole day. I wake up and nothing works."

Paul rapped his knuckle against a stack of boxes with a canvas sheet thrown over them: fuses. Hundreds of them. Paul had already moved on, was taking a closer look at a sequence of arcane objects of no identifiable shape and doing a lousy job of attempting to pronounce "interferometer."

Jack found a pair of dark safety goggles that made him look like the Terminator. Paul took the bait and a firefight erupted. Imaginary bullets bounced off Jack, so Paul grabbed one of the loose lenses, screwed it into his eye (painfully), and declared he was a cyborg. Jack fell on Paul. The lens fell into the dirt and a 'borg-on-'borg grapple-fest kicked off. This eventually segued into an unfair advantage to the Terminator when he resorted to tickling.

Paul got loose, bounded backward with a two-handed *blam blam blam* . . .

And then Will had been there, white as a sheet. What he beheld was Jack and Paul frozen mid-combat, like raccoons in a spotlight. Lenses and beam splitters scattered in the dirt, safety goggles hanging off Jack's left ear. The madness passed, and Jack realized just how much trouble they were in.

Will transformed. Shock transmuted to rage, a rage that made him unrecognizable. Jack had no words. Paul actually screamed. Paralyzed with fear they were easy pickings and within seconds Will had seized both of them by their collars.

Jack's voice evaporated. Paul whimpered and started to cry.

Will had dragged them bodily to the door, screaming like a demon. Jack said nothing, his shirt cutting into his armpits, sneakers scrabbling in the dirt. Paul kept whimpering, stammering excuses. At the threshold, Will tossed them both out into the night. Jack caught the fall on his bare hands, gravel tearing the skin of his palms. Paul rolled.

A heaving silhouette in the doorway, a nightmare made flesh. With a final animal shout Will slammed the doors,

banishing the boys to darkness. Then the thrashing of chains:
Will locking the barn, violently, from inside.

Paul was sobbing. Jack's heart was taking up too much space,
stopping his lungs from being able to do their job. Cries came
from inside the barn as Will discovered each new disaster.

"I wanna go home," Paul had said.

"Go. I'll . . . I'll . . ."

"You'll be okay?"

As Will discovered some new horror fresh cries reverberated
across the yard, echoed back from the treeline.

"I don't think so."

"I'm sorry. I'm sorry."

Back in the present, Jack stood outside the barn looking in.
The doors were cracked open, the dark interior illuminated by
morning light spearing through missing shingles and gaps in
the planking. Teasing the door open with one hand, he slipped
inside.

Empty.

The gear was gone. Every last bolt. The feed room on Jack's
left and the tack room on the right were unlocked. The floor
of the room on the left had been dug out and wooden covers
fashioned for the six-foot depression. The wooden covers had
half circles sawn out of them at the edges, presumably for cabling. Similar gaps were cut in both the interior and exterior
walls of the room.

"Generators," Jack mumbled. The interior of the hole and
the underside of the cover had been padded. Soundproofing.
He remembered crates of fuses, the mornings when nothing
worked. Whatever Will had been doing in here had required
juice. Lots of it. That wasn't a small hole.

The room on the right had been concrete-floored and air-
conditioned. A window was fitted to look out on the barn floor.
A control room, maybe.

" 'A spaceship,' " Jack said, in his best little-kid voice. "If only we'd known, huh Will?"

Something crashed on the porch. Nick cried out. Jack ran from the barn, skidding on the gravel and banking hard toward the house. He found Nick immobilized facedown on the boards, his left arm held painfully backward and aloft by someone in a jacket and baseball cap. A fireplace poker had skittered down the steps.

"Let him go!"

Nick's attacker complied, bouncing upright and straight backed. "He started it."

Jack hadn't been sure it was her he'd seen, and if it had been he mostly expected he'd never see her again. But here she was, and six years of anger, heartbreak, and unanswered questions all pressed tight in his throat, wanting out all at once.

Instead Jack marched up the steps, helped Nick to his feet. "You okay?"

"Peachy," he said, working his arm. "Who's this?"

"Zed," Jack said. "This is Nick. Nick, Zed. Zed, what the fuck?"

"He spooked me."

"I mean 'what the fuck' in a more all-encompassing sense."

"Wanna know how I found you?"

Jack closed his eyes. "The Breathalyzer. You tracked the camera and Breathalyzer."

"No. I asked myself what the worst place for you to go would be and went there."

Nick glanced nervously at the tree line.

"He gets it," she said.

It was uncomfortable, but Jack had to admit: he wanted Paul to come after him. "Things have changed."

"I know."

"Monarch can walk in here but they won't be walking out, I'll tell you that."

"You mean troopers."

"Yeah."

"And not snipers, who are a mile away and invisible."

Jack had no answer.

"Let's go inside."

Nick twirled his keys. "Not me. I'm outta here. Also: fuck you for not telling me about your death wish."

"Nick, wait. It's not like that. Monarch . . . they're not going to just let this go. They know you were there."

Zed agreed. "Monarch's been deeply preoccupied for the last few hours. Real pants-on-head behavior from management. Even so they're probably organized by now. I can't stop you going, but you need to know they could pick you up at some point."

"Dad needs his meds. I'm all he's got."

Jack understood. "Take care, Nick."

"Yeah." The cabbie twirled his keys—"frickin' namaste"—and headed for his car. Jack and Zed watched him pull out of the drive and disappear past the flaming sycamores.

"My name's not Zed," she said.

"And you work for Monarch."

"And I work for Monarch."

"So who am I speaking to?"

"Beth Wilder." She touched his arm, placed a brief kiss on his cheek. "And she's glad to see you."

Beth went inside. Jack followed.

Zed—"Beth"—took Nick's cold cup of coffee and locked it in the microwave. While she set it humming, Jack cataloged the changes: her drugstore-black hair was now a natural red. Her tattoos were gone, and the piercings. Seeing her changed left him desperately missing who she had been. The changes time had wrought on her told him how much history he had missed. She carried herself differently now, straight backed and crisp where once she had been both loose-limbed and economical with her posture and movement. "Beth" brought the cup to the table and sat. Zed would have had one booted foot on it.

He missed the glittering thread of her suicide chain running from nose ring to earring. Between the parkour, skateboarding, and general getting into trouble it could have ended badly. She hadn't cared. Fate had backed down and her twinkle-eyed fearlessness had left Jack no recourse but to lift his game. The world had gotten him down less and seemed brighter when she was around.

"Different hair," she said. "Different skin tone, bearing, vocabulary, hair color, hair style, no piercings, no tattoos, a breast reduction. Working out reshaped the bod a little. Dental work shaped the face just a touch. Lost the Jersey accent."

"So which one was real?" He pulled out a chair, turned it toward her, sat. "The Jersey accent or this one?"

She hitched that Bruce Willis smile he recognized so well, dental work or no. "This one."

"Why do all of this? Why did—"

"Jack." She leaned forward, her hand on his knee derailing him. "We can't do this here. We don't have time."

"You've got time for coffee."

"While you were overseas I've been here, working for Monarch. Making connections, getting inside their operation. I couldn't risk either Paul recognizing me—the young one or the older one."

"The older one's been here the whole time?"

"For over a decade, behind the scenes and off the books. He's got himself an apartment on the forty-ninth floor of the

Tower. Very few people can get to it. When he leaves the building it's always via helicopter to a private airfield. Never seen, never heard. All records say Paul Serene was the twenty-seven-year-old coordinator of Project Promenade, and that last night he died in an act of domestic terrorism. Killed by a group called the Peace Movement."

"If he's a ghost how do you know so much about him?"

"My buddy Horatio is deep in their system. He's high up in one of Monarch's side projects. Being where he's not wanted is one of Horatio's hobbies."

"I think he was a friend of Will's. Hacker, moustache, boutique muffins?"

She shifted uncomfortably. "That's him. Clearly Horatio and I need to have a conversation about security hygiene. Anyway, listen: this is the important part. What happened last night at the university was a disaster, and I'm not talking about the dead kids. The Monarch time machine initiated a small but lethal entropic feedback loop within the Meyer-Joyce field that will eventually result in a complete breakdown of causality."

"That explains a couple of things." Stutters, powers, and visions among them.

"Help me save the world. It'll take a day. Two, tops."

"Zed . . . "

"Beth."

"I spent four years looking for you." Jack said, shaking a little now. Seeing her again was becoming physiological, made it difficult to keep his voice steady. "I wasn't sure you were even *alive*. I thought . . . I thought Aberfoyle's . . ."

"I'll be blunt," she said. "I knew what my disappearing would do to you, and I did it anyway."

What a fucking day.

"You don't fully know it yet," she said. "But we're involved in something that's so much bigger than anything else." Then, again with that smile: "This might not mean anything any-more, Trouble, but I've *really* missed your stupid face."

"You . . ." The air felt a little thinner. He tried to breathe. "You have no *clue* how far I went, trying to find you."

"You got close, in Arizona. I was in the compound when you rocked up. I don't say this to torture you. I'm telling you because I appreciate your sticking by me. I don't take that for granted. You looked good on that bike."

"You *saw* me?"

"As I left. Then I was under the wire."

"I rode that thing across the entire country. Those fuckers trashed it and left me by the interstate."

"They had to. Couldn't risk you working out I was there and coming after me."

"You could have left a note and saved me four years."

"What did you find in the back garden of that house I was squatting in?"

"You know what I found. Everything you owned. Right down to the jewelry. ID. Clothes. I freaked the fuck out, Zed."

"Beth."

"I thought Aberfoyle's goons had murdered you."

"What made you decide they hadn't?"

"Nobody came after me, or Paul, or Will. Had to figure you'd just vanished like the ghost you always were."

"They say ghosts are the presence of an absence. I'm right here, Jack."

"And who are you?"

She was going to give one of her usual sleight-of-hand an-swers, he could tell. His expression said *don't*. Something like sadness flitted across her features. In the end, she just shrugged: *I don't know what to tell you.*

"A note wasn't an option. First rule of a good disappearance is take nothing with you, leave nothing behind." She leaned forward, probing his expression for some small understanding. "I've been preparing for this moment, right now, since I was eight years old."

"I don't understand."

"You will."

It should have been matter/antimatter having her there, at his family table, a piece of another world sitting real in this one. The whole planet should have exploded because she was drinking coffee in the house where he had grown up. Alive.

"Come on," she said, standing up. "Show me around. If there are answers here I want us to find them first."

They hang around because we can't let go of them.

Upstairs they stood outside the door to what had been Jack's bedroom for twenty-two years.

"If there was anything here Monarch would have it by now," he said. "They shot up a university. They're not going to think much of a little breaking and entering."

Jack had walked along this hall every morning at 5:00 A.M., then down the stairs, the low sun painfully bright through the windows as he padded to the kitchen, bare feet on cold floor. He'd fire up the stovetop, prep breakfast for two. Cereal. Coffee. Toast. Eggs. Will's would go in the microwave, to wait for when he woke up in a few hours.

"Jack?"

"Yeah?"

"Did you hear anything I just said?"

"Uh . . ." He blinked hard, smelling scrambled eggs. "Sorry. No."

"Monarch had Will under surveillance for a few years, but by then he had moved or destroyed most of his work. He kept nothing Monarch would be interested in."

"They got everything they wanted out of Will."

"Will designed more than a time machine. He pioneered an entire field of science."

"A field that was universally discredited, yeah, I know. It's how we almost lost the house."

"It was intentionally discredited. Your brother was an unusual dude, but he wasn't wrong about much. It's essential to Paul's plans that nobody else has this technology—or even gets curious about it. Monarch's very effective. Shit, they managed to get a constitutional amendment passed allowing their paramilitary to operate inside our *national border.* They've insinuated the company into the fabric of pretty much everything that's holding society together: medical, technology, weapons, charity, city planning, national policy. Freaking *child care.*"

Child care. "What do you mean you've been training for this since you were eight?"

She shook her head. "When Paul went through the machine last night, he went to the end of time, but not for good. Eventually he went back to 1999. That's seventeen years in the past. The young man you knew lived every one of those years, right up to this point. So understand: Paul has those seventeen years on you now. Seventeen years of getting good with the powers he has, plus foreknowledge of the future has gotta be how Monarch rose so quickly."

"And you knew all this six years ago. That's why you were here. But why get involved with me?"

"Was this your room?"

"Uh . . . " Oh shit. "Yeah, but there's nothing in there that—"

"You haven't been here in six years. You have no idea what could be in there."

"Wait, there's really nothing . . ."

Beth turned the handle and swung the door wide. It thunked

hollowly against the wall. "Well," she said. "This is a development."

"I liked that show. So did you."

"We both know that's not what I'm referring to."

The bedroom was a cozy affair, small, with a single picture-book window looking out over the back garden and the tree line beyond. A slim bookcase held novels, a lot of them with Dewey decimal system stickers on the spines. As a kid Jack had gotten a lot of his reading material from library clearances and secondhand stores. Leaning against the weathered spines were action figures of the two of the four main *Team Outland* characters, the plastic turning yellow with age. "September," the thin sniper guy, and the Team's cute pink-haired hacker.

Beneath the window was Jack's childhood bed, neatly made and topped with a *Team Outland* comforter. Pink, featuring Digit—the hacker—winking and giving an ostentatious two-handed "time out" signal. Time Out. T.O. *Team Outland*. There was always some message at the end of each episode about being true to yourself, taking time to think, or something.

"I still say she was the best member of the team," Jack said, defensively.

"How did I never see this room?"

"She had smarts. She was funny. The others just swaggered and got a free pass."

"So defensive. Gimme a skinny weirdo with a sniper rifle any day. September got all the best lines."

"She may be the reason I make bad decisions about redheads."

Beth cocked her hip and did a spot-on Digit impression: "Time out! Think before you act!" Wink.

"Gross," Jack said.

Will's old stuff had invaded corners of Jack's room. Cabinets, coffee cans full of receipts, Post-it notes rubber-banded together with dates and labels. Stacks of Carl Sagan VHS tapes. Abstract models of things that could have been molecules made out of toy store construction kits. A twelve-sided sphere weighing down a stack of handwritten papers. Polaroids of laboratories, labeled with the names of South American universities. Jack didn't remember any of that stuff.

He wandered over, picked up the sphere, turned it over in his hands. The papers beneath it had hand-drawn representations of it, and screeds of calculations.

"So you liked September," Jack said.

"Huh?"

"The skinny weirdo with the sniper rifle." Jack put down the sphere. Flipped through the photos.

"Oh, yeah, of course. He was lean, wore a lot of black, had that cool voice . . . "

A couple of photos looked like shots of a laser focusing on a tiny lead ball bearing. He put them back with the rest of the junk.

" . . . did things solo," Jack finished for her, "nobody knew where he came from, vanished all the time, turned up at the last minute . . . "

"Hey, don't be glum, chum. September may have been a loner oddball with a thin backstory but he got shit done, right? Pretty soon you're going to appreciate what a valuable character trait that is."

Jack wasn't having any of it. It had been six years. Twenty thousand road miles. Fear. Grief.

She touched his hand. The contact was shocking. "Hey. I was Zed. I am Beth. If I could have spared you pain I would have. In fact, more than a few times, I did."

Man, she had great eyes.

"C'mon, your brother was no ding-dong. There has to be

something Monarch didn't get a look at. Holy crap is that *you?*"
Beth made a beeline for a stack of boxes in the corner, on the
top of which was a framed black-and-white of the whole family.
All four of them. Jack must have been about eight when it was
taken. "Nice haircut."

"Mom had a thing for Paul McCartney."

She put the picture back where she found it. "Will went
through a real Manchester phase, huh?"

"He was different back then. Before our parents died. More
connected. Funny, even."

"Their deaths hit him hard?"

"I don't think it was the loss that snapped him. I think it
was knowing that he was going to take everything they had
built and spend it on his bullshit experiments. Like some sad
addict who couldn't help himself."

"And then you found out."

"A couple years later."

"And you left Riverport." She looked at him, choosing her
words. "But the experiments, they weren't bullshit, were they?"

This was difficult. He hated how well he thought he knew
her, while accepting that he knew her not at all. "Why are you
here?"

"The end of time is coming, Jack. The training, the travel,
the people in Arizona . . . meeting you . . . it was all so that I
could be here and do some good. I've said and done all the
right things. I'm inside Monarch. I'm in place. I'm ready."

The answer seemed foregone. "So, you're from the future?"

Again that tight Bruce Willis smile. "Not yet."

12

A few years back Will had claimed the attic as an office, the place he went to compose his articles and correspondence. Now it was mainly cardboard boxes full of nostalgic miscellanea that neither brother was able to discard.

Jack flipped one loose lid, peered inside: more papers. "There's more stuff here than I remember."

"Interesting." Beth forged a path farther into the confusion of plastic crates, garbage bags, and removal-company boxes.

"How long have you been with Monarch?"

"Four years. I'm a little below mid-level. Tried out for their chronon operative program. You met a few of them at the university. I got through all of the training then tanked at the end."

Jack frowned at this. "You . . . ?"

"On purpose. I wanted the training, but not to be locked down to a specialist unit. Better to be underestimated and filed as generic. More room to move without being noticed."

There was a single cot and a small writing desk with a cheap twelve-inch flat-screen bolted to the wall above it. An old-style Bakelite phone with a coiled cord hung on the wall. Maybe Will had started spending nights here.

"Ever done anything you . . . regret?"

"No. I'm very good at *not* being in the wrong place at the wrong time."

Jack thought of Aberfoyle's last moments. *I believe in cause and effect.*

"Which is why I'm not sweating Monarch's interest in you yet." Beth stepped around the rotting carcass of a recliner stacked with bundled printouts. "Does anything look out of place to you?"

Jack ran his eyes over ordered stacks of boxes, sloughing heaps of clothes-filled garbage bags. "Mr. Squishy."

"Pardon?"

Jack waded sideways past knee-high stacks of *Scientific American* to fetch a fading toy elephant from the top of a corner stack of boxes. "Dad won him at a county fair when I was, like, six? I carried him around the house for years. Will used to say, 'Squish knows all Jack's secrets.'"

Beth blinked, made her way back, and started rapping the boxes top to bottom. *Tap tap. Tap tap. Tap tap.* Nothing special. She booted the bottom one with her foot. It had all the give of a concrete block. "That one."

Together they tossed the top three boxes aside and tore open the lid of the fourth. Slotted neatly inside was what could only be the flat, hard, gunmetal-gray top of a . . .

"Safe." Beth tore the box away. Short, even-sided, manual combination lock. "B-rated. Less than three hundred bucks from Home Depot. Get me a drill and I think I can crack this."

"Seriously?"

"YouTube."

"We kept a lot of that stuff in the barn. Sit tight, I'll grab it."

Beth waved him off. She removed a bulky, palm-sized device from her pocket, checked the power on it. "I got it. Look around, see what else you can find."

Jack gestured to the hunk of black technology in her hand. "What's that?"

"Business. Be right back."

And, just like that, Jack found himself alone and outflanked by battalions of forgotten details in allegiance to a history he had tried to forget.

The muscles in Martin Hatch's jaw were flexing. "I must insist," he said once more. "Let me give the order. It can be done quickly and quietly."

Paul extended a leather-gloved hand. A waiting operative handed him his handgun and rig. "I saw many futures for William Joyce, most of them featured him doing harm to our cause. He had to die. The path we are on now does not feature Jack being an immediate concern. There is time."

Martin wasn't having it. "We both know that a motivated individual conditionally exempt from the laws of causality possesses enormous potential for harm to this company—on a timeline of any length. One word from you and that variable is forever removed."

Paul pulled on the remaining glove, concealing the light of his flesh and flexed his strange, aching hand.

Martin pressed his point. "Eliminating Joyce is an act of conscientious diligence, not only to our shareholders, but to our *species*. We are ten minutes from midnight, Paul Serene."

Paul slung the shoulder rig, zipped his light woolen sweater, and shrugged into a calfskin driving coat. "No. We have attempted time and again to replicate my condition. Time and again: failure. Dr. Kim—that poor howling bastard—represents what we have condemned each one of our test subjects to becoming. Yet here is Jack, intact, sound of mind and body, manipulating time as freely as I do. We cannot simply have him *killed*, Martin."

An operative pulled the van's door aside, letting in brisk morning air.

"Not before better options have been expended."

Inside the front door of the house Beth took a breath, focused, and moved briskly out and down the steps at a tripping gait, eyes scanning the tree line. The barn was unlocked. Once inside she double-checked the device in her hand. It was a two-inch-diameter polyurethane ball attached to a cell-phone-sized brick of tech with a one-inch monochrome display. She powered it up, cycled down the five-option menu to DISPLAY, and the screen flicked over to a white-on-black central dot. A single white-light clock-hand swung 360 degrees around the dot and vanished: the unit seemed calibrated.

She checked her watch, then scooted up the ladder to the hayloft. The hayloft doors that faced the house and the tree line beyond were closed. Sure enough the wall on either side of the hayloft doors held a few shelves, the shelves containing tools.

Beth ignored all of them and went for the hunting rifle.

Cross-legged in the dust, Jack stared at the safe. Then he looked at the towering stacks of his past. Then he looked at the stuffed elephant in his hand.

"You wanted me to find this," he said. "What combination would you have used? What combination would you have thought I'd know you'd use?" The elephant had no answers. Jack checked his watch. He had been here for two hours. He had to go. Then, halfway to rising, he chose to sit back down. Maybe the past had something to say. "If you want to show me, show me."

Nothing. Just dusty light and the smell of rat bait and moth-balls.

Then, just as he was about to leave, the light changed. The sun through the window sank below the eastern horizon, the attic interior cycling light-to-dark over and over, faster and faster, and then . . .

A man came into the attic, closing the hatch behind him. Jack heard something being placed on the writing desk, the sound of two latches popping. Papers. Two latches clicking shut.

A body pushed its way toward the safe and then Will was crouching beside Jack, peering at the tumbler, rubber-banded files in his hand. "Five left," he whispered. "Twenty-seven right . . ."

"Ninety left," Jack finished for him. "My birth date."

The safe cranked open and Will vanished.

Beth had a roll of black plastic tape in the pocket of her fatigues. Laying the rifle on the boards she placed the ball-and-box device as flush as possible against the rifle's frame—the device's LED screen facing toward the stock, the ball toward the barrel—and started looping the tape around the body. It held okay but the thing really needed a custom mount or a Picatinny rail. This was just messy.

Beth placed a can of nails on an old camp chair, moved it to just in front of the hayloft doors, and rested the rifle on it with the ball-sensor facing toward the closed wooden doors. She checked her watch and waited.

The file inside the safe was thin, unimpressive. It contained paperwork. Property. H. G. Wells owned a swimming hall. Inside the folder was taped a single key.

That wasn't what got Jack's attention. Jack put the property folder back in the safe and examined a two-page document with the alarming heading of PANIC BUTTONS.

Jack scanned it quickly.

Locations: Attic, kitchen, Jack's bedroom.

Maintenance: check the seals on the jugs at least once every six (6) months. They need to be airtight. If the seals degrade the ether will dissipate.

Attic goes first. Second-floor goes sixty (60) seconds later. If second floor fails expect the attic to collapse into the second floor after about twenty minutes.

Sensitive materials to be packed closest to the jugs in attic and Jack's room to ensure vaporization.

Jack sat with that for a while. Then he looked to the four corners of the attic. Crap and junk were piled into all the corners. He picked up Squish, got to his feet, and investigated the farthest corner, the one stacked with document boxes. He pulled them aside, made his way through a couple of layers, and was rewarded with the sight of something that made him take a step back.

Hiding beneath it all was a glass jug—just a gallon—sitting flush against the wall with what looked like a pipe bomb lashed to it with fraying old duct tape. The gallon was full to the brim with a clear liquid and stoppered with caulk. A thick green wire led from the bomb and down through a crack in the dusty floorboards.

On the wooden shelf above the device was a folder. On the cover was a hand-drawn rendering of the twelve-sided sphere Jack had seen in his bedroom.

Jack's phone bleeped, causing him to flinch violently. "Fuck me." The name on the screen was NICK (CAB).

He rested Squish on the topmost box and was about to take the call when something within him *pulsed*. The feeling was new yet familiar. He had felt it hours prior, before the first stutter had hit. "Nick?"

"Jack. Dude. Are you still at the house?"

Jack looked at the corner behind him. Glass glinted at him from between a couple of apple crates. There'd be one hidden in each corner. Will had wired the attic to become a fireball. "Why?"

"TV. Turn it on."

Christ. How had Will set this up without killing himself? The guy couldn't make cereal without setting fire to the curtains.

Jack navigated out of the mess, back to the desk, and turned on the crappy little flat-screen. Weather channel. "What am I looking for?"

"Channel twelve."

Jack flipped through. Kitchen appliances. *Who's The Boss?* Sharks. Nazis. His face. "What the f—?"

"Yeah. You mind explaining that?"

Jack reached for the volume. "Shut up for a second."

It was his face, but the voice he heard was deep, soothing, masculine: "*. . . reliably informed is Jack Joyce, the brother of a specialist Monarch Innovations fired some time ago. Monarch Security is working with the Riverport Police Department to determine if that is a relevant detail. We have multiple survivor reports which indicate that Joyce's stated intent was to detonate the library with the protestors inside. It would be irresponsible of me to speculate about motive at this stage but it is clear that he is associated with this so-called 'Peace Movement.'*"

Cut to a live broadcast, on-campus. The reporter was pretty,

Asian-American. Her interview subject was African-American, dark-skinned, bald, and a solid fifteen inches taller. The owner of that deep, soothing voice.

It was the lazy gaze and the unhurried speech; the way Hatch didn't look at the reporter but straight at the camera, no blinking. Standing thin inside that five-figure suit Martin Hatch radiated the threat potential of an apex predator.

The effect was smooth, and deep, and hypnotic, and made Jack dislike him immediately.

"Jack Joyce is a career itinerant with a preference for world hotspots: Afghanistan, Syria, Thailand. He has the interest of the RPD, FBI, NSA, DHS, and Monarch Security. If you see this man do not approach. Call 911 immediately. Thank you."

The report cut to a live feed from the site of the library's smoking ruins. Early morning sunlight flashed off wet, black timber. Arcs from fire hoses cast rainbows. Jack's throat closed. His brother's remains were somewhere under that.

The reporter's expression was stern, standard-issue, her features pleasant. His gut kicked again. "Jack Joyce, who has had numerous prior run-ins with the law, is suspected of attempted murder and the premature demolition of the Riverport University library. His accompliii . . ."

The moment dragged out for what felt like seconds, the image on the screen crawling, deinterlacing. Nausea rose in his gut as the second stretched and divided, stretched and then . . . snapped back into shape.

". . . iiiice and brother, William Joyce, who had directed threats at university staff after being fired, died in the library explosion. The Riverport Police Department urgently requests that any information regarding Jack Joyce's whereabouts be directed to them immediately."

A stutter was coming. And soon.

Nick cleared his throat.

"Monarch's outside my house, Jack. Do I go in?"

"I wouldn't."

"What about my dad?"

"I'm sorry. I don't know."

The volume on the phone dipped then spiked. "Hang on. Someone's calling. Shit, I think it's . . . they're calling from my dad's phone."

"Don't answer."

"They've got my dad."

"They can't threaten you if you don't answer." Jack's phone trilled in his ear. Fuck. Unknown number.

"They calling you now?"

"Nick, I take it back. Go in, tell them I abducted you. Do what's best for yourself and your dad. Whatever happens I don't blame you for it."

Jack ended both calls and then flinched as a nearby bell complained: heavy, shrill, and loud. The thirty-five-year-old Bakelite phone on the wall was vibrating. Jack's nostrils flared; he made a decision and picked up—angry. "Call my cell." And hung up. His cell phone rang. "So what do we do?"

"Jack."

Paul. A thousand words couldn't release everything that fought to get out, so Jack lowballed it. "Explain." Walking to the window he could see the barn, but no sign of Beth.

"I'm sorry about Will."

Fury came out matter-of-fact chipper. "You will be."

Paul didn't acknowledge the threat. "I thought a long time about Will. I didn't want that. But he forced my hand, Jack."

"Hey, no worries, Paul. We're still solid, yeah?" Jack experienced an anger so profound it messed with his vision. His phone's casing surrendered a meek little *pop*.

"What I did will haunt me till I die."

"So less than a day, then."

"Listen to me!" Paul's breathing was suddenly spasmodic, tremulous. "I'm trying to help you. To help us."

"Y'know, I'm lousy on phones," Jack said, all charm. "What say we talk this over face-to-face?"

Paul sighed. "Sure," he said. "Come downstairs. I'm in the kitchen."

Gibson had gone from his meeting with Hatch straight to the squad room. When he'd walked in he knew straight away that everyone knew. Donny had been a man about it, walked straight up and let Gibson crack him in the face.

"No worries, boss," the kid had said, checking his nose, wiping away blood with a thumb. "It was a bullshit decision. None of us here buy it."

Irene nodded. They all did.

Gibson said to Donny, "What are our orders?"

"Sit tight. Cool down."

"Nah, that ain't right. They'd be going after Joyce. They need us."

Donny shook his head. "Hatch sent Technicians and Strikers. After last night, he wants us taking a half day."

"To 'decompress,'" Mully said.

"They want us fresh to run security on the gala tonight," Voss put in.

Technicians and Strikers. Chronon-active standard troops, and bulked-up show ponies using first-gen chronon tech in an attempt to mimic a couple of Serene's powers. All of them more in love with their gear than their creed.

"Donny, get me a spot on one of the Technician units on the Joyce farm detail."

And that's how Gibson wound up in the woods surrounding the Joyce place.

It was a nice morning. Clear, fresh. His daughter, Lorelei, would have appreciated it. Maybe he'd buy the place when this was all over. He could pick out one of those big trees over there, build the kid a house. Sit on that porch and watch Tamiko push Lorelei on a tire swing. Listen to the kid's laughter carry across the garden.

He was lying on his belly, draped in ghillie netting, next to one of the ding-dongs from Talon squad, about a half mile from the Joyce spread. He tapped the side of the long-nosed sniper rifle the guy was resting his face on. "That one of ours?"

The sniper lifted one leafy paw, tapped the Monarch stamp on the rifle's breach. That was poor discipline right there. An operative worth the name would have grunted an affirmative and kept his eye screwed to the scope. "Linux-based targeting system. Weather conditions, wind speed, target speed."

"Got Netflix on there?"

The wookiee snorted. "Might as well. Once the scope tags the target I can put a round up the ass of a moving june bug at eighteen hundred yards while jerking off."

"Sounds like you're one innovation away from unemployment."

The goon coughed up a less-convincing chuckle.

Fuck Gibson was bored. He'd gotten on this detail because he knew Mr. Hatch wanted that Joyce kid dead and Serene didn't. If Randall could hand Mr. Hatch that little fuck's head *and* plausible deniability, then the boss gets what he wants minus any fallout. Gibson could just say he was defending himself.

Fuck he was bored. He'd been there with his dick in the dirt for the last hour and nothing was happening.

"Ever had to shit yourself on the job?" No response. "Is that still part of the training? Shitting in a bag? Lying in a ditch for four days waiting for a target. I mean if you gotta go you gotta go, right?"

The shooter mumbled something about it being a small price to pay for freedom.

What an asshole. He was probably wearing one now.

Fuck he was bored.

Then: "Target spotted. Barn. Upper floor. Female."

Gibson wrestled the binoculars to his face. The hayloft doors had been opened. Some broad in a baseball cap, fatigues. Looking good in a T-shirt but couldn't make out her face. "Well hello there, punkin' butter." Cap pulled low, head always dipped. One hell of a hardbody, though. "Name's Randall. And you are?"

The stud beside the trigger clicked. "Target locked." Then: "Lost visual. Target stepped away from the window."

A voice, deep and comforting, murmured over comms: "Highground One." It was Hatch. Gibson kept his mouth shut. "Please describe the target."

"Caucasian female. Mid-twenties. Five ten. Baseball cap. Appears unarmed," the sniper mumbled.

"Our Consultant hasn't emerged?"

"All units report no exit as yet, sir."

Silence on the line. Then: "You have the green light. Proceed."

Jack came down the stairs, gun in hand.

Someone coughed in the kitchen, took a reassuring breath.

Jack stepped off the stairs, moved left toward the kitchen, the interior coming into view.

Far wall, framed pictures, fridge, bench, and cabinets . . . someone that looked like Paul.

"Hi," Paul said.

Paul didn't appear to be offended at having a gun pointed at his face—that familiar-but-different face.

"Except for last night it's been almost twenty years since I've seen you, Jack. And here I am with no idea of what to say." Paul smiled and Jack wanted to do something he wasn't sure he'd regret. "Seeing you here, the young man I remember, in this house . . . it's eerie." Paul jerked his thumb toward the drying rack. "Will kept every Ziploc bag you used for lunches. After dinner every Friday night we'd wash and hang them on the rack there. He made a box of those bags last for years."

"Will's dead. You killed him."

"Jack—"

Jack cocked the automatic's hammer, uselessly. "Shut up and start talking."

"The person you grew up with is gone, Jack. It's for the best. But I still remember. That counts for something." Paul pulled the silver chain around his neck, drew out what it secured: his silver bullet. "I remember it all."

The sight of the bullet made Jack think of the gun in his hand; the gun in his hand made him think of Paul holding a gun on Will. Thinking of Will dispelled pity. "I don't think you do."

"Will was right: something was wrong with the machine's calibration. Time will end. I've seen it. In fact time will end *because* I've seen it. The waveform of that particular potential future has now collapsed and become an unavoidable certainty."

"Except . . ." Jack had to believe there was an answer here. "The time machine. I go back, I find us, I tell us not to use the machine, this never happens, Will never dies, and I spend the rest of my life trying to forget how badly I wanted to shoot you."

Paul shook his head, sadly. "Has that happened?"

"When I do go back it will have happened. And then . . . I guess we won't ever remember having this conversation."

"So if the events of the present we currently inhabit never occurred . . . what would motivate you to go back in time and warn us?"

Hearing that was like watching Will die all over again. Jack shook his head. "There's a way."

"You can't change the past. I'm sorry."

Hate pulled Jack forward. "You're lying."

"If changing the past were possible I would locate Will's prototype—the first machine, older than Monarch's, the one he built in the barn out there—and do my damnedest to make that work. Then I would use it to travel back and prevent the Monarch machine being made. That would prevent the Fracture from occurring and spare me a terrible life. But it is not possible."

Jack's mind wheeled. There was no answer to this.

"Do you know where Will's machine is, Jack?"

"If this is true, then why do any of this? Why kill my brother? Why kill all the people at the university?"

Paul weighed his words carefully. "There are reasons why last night was necessary. First, we took the core from the lab and installed it into a secondary Promenade within Monarch Tower. We made it known that this was done as a safety precaution by Monarch personnel. Now the world knows a sensitive Monarch project was targeted by a terrorist group. Second, I need the mood of the nation to be primed. The public and the administration want a simple target for their anger. Soon I will provide that target in a manner that is advantageous to the objectives of the company. For that to work the events at the university had to be . . . mediapathic. Showy."

There was a time, Jack remembered, when Paul couldn't bring himself to use a mousetrap.

Paul looked Jack in the eye, earnestly. No guile. "Monarch doesn't exist to change the future—it exists to help us *survive it*. We have a plan," he said. "We call it Lifeboat."

"If you hand me a brochure, Paul, I swear to God—"

"We can't stop the Fracture, Jack. We can't stop the arrival of the end of time. That waveform has collapsed. But Lifeboat will assure—*does* assure—that our best and brightest remain able to repair and reseed the flow of causality *after* the Meyer-Joyce field collapses and time ends."

It took a second for Jack to fully understand that his rage was becoming dilute with horror. Horror at the realization that he understood Paul's decisions . . . and maybe sympathized with them.

"And Will?"

"Will was unique. A pioneer. He was given every opportunity to play a key role in the success of Lifeboat. But you know Will. No one can do his thinking for him. The knowledge and expertise that he had, and the *powerful* desire to use it against us, made him a very real threat to the future of humanity. I loved Will like a brother, Jack. You know that."

It became harder to keep the gun straight, vision threatening to blur.

Paul took one step toward him and said, as gently as he could, "You are faced with the same choice."

Standing as far from the open hayloft doors as she could Beth went through her breathing exercises, focused on what she was about to do. She shook the tension out of her hands, checked her watch again; and then she fished for the notes in her fatigues. They were a couple of crumpled pages torn from a Moleskine, written in blue ink, meticulous and neat for maximum legibility. No fuckups permitted.

She knew them back to front but checked the times again anyway, ran through her checklist, checked her watch. Closed her eyes and breathed.

Fifty-seven seconds.

Inside the house, Paul Serene said, "Six years ago I was exposed to a near-lethal burst of chronon radiation. I became ill, and my relationship with time changed even further. I can, with effort, stand at the junction between myriad possible futures—and choose which one to take." The flesh of his arm ached, phased minutely from one state to another. Paul shuddered, discreetly.

"You want to tell me how this scene ends?"

"I use the ability sparingly, Jack. It costs me. I use it to save nations, not win the lottery. I'm here now because I trust you not to kill me, to hear me out."

"I don't trust me not to do that."

Paul persevered. "This selective foreknowledge I have has allowed me to subtly exert a profound influence over government at local, state, and national levels, and consequently the world. Oncoming history is a slalom, Jack. The extinctions and conflagrations that I have navigated our idiot species past, my God. The atrocities I have had to facilitate in order to avoid a greater catastrophe down the road." Paul couldn't look at Jack as he said it, his left hand flexing uncomfortably. He cleared his head, got back to business. "Discreet teams of lobbyists, the manipulation of favor economies, deniable personnel, and leveraging the specialties of divisions within Monarch . . . all form a scalpel that can cut into deep tissue, remove, remodel, and leave no scar. It has been the work of sixteen years to reach this point."

"And?"

"We call it Project Lifeboat. Monarch has been exploiting Will's innovations and Dr. Kim's advancements to allow ordinary people to operate freely in a chronon-devoid environment—the end of time itself."

"So you can have a dozen people wandering around a frozen world, waiting to die. That's a shitty use of sixteen years, Paul."

"A few hundred people actually, all at the top of their field, all carefully selected." Paul sighed. "If we have mobility then we have a chance to restart causality. It is our only chance." Paul straightened. "Come with me. Come to Monarch Tower. You need to see what we've been building."

Jack shook his head. "I need to think. Call off your goons."

"With respect, Jack—"

"Thinking's not my strong suit, yeah, I get it. Do it, Paul, or the next time you see me I'll be waving at you as Monarch Tower falls into the Mystic River."

Paul held up his hands. "All right. All right. Please don't make me regret this." Paul touched a finger to his ear. "Monarch Actual, this is your Consultant."

Ten seconds. "Everything works, everything works," Beth told herself. Five seconds. Four. One breath in for the road. Two. And out.

Go.

Two steps, turn, face the woods, and . . .

Beth jerked her head left as the .338 slug trilled past to blow a fresh-wood crater in the aging timber of the barn's back wall. She translated the movement into a full-body turn, swept up the hunting rifle, and let the ShotSpotter tell her exactly where that bullet had come from.

———

A gunshot rang out across the front garden.

Disbelief. "You bastard."

"Monarch Actual!"

Paul warped across the room, away from Jack's gun. *"Monarch Actual!"* Then zipped from the kitchen and up the stairs.

Jack warped after him, overdid it, slammed into the back of the sofa, and flipped over it. Paul was shouting from the bedroom upstairs, which was when Jack realized he'd left the attic ladder down.

Gibson was over it. "You fucking *missed?*" This was bullshit. Up at sparrow-fart to lie in the dirt with some overequipped self-shitting paramilitary neckbeard only to have him completely fuck up the one thing he was here for.

There was a short *zip* and the shooter's head snapped back. He slumped, lifeless, over his expensive rifle.

Gibson shouted, "Yes!," tossed off his netting, grabbed his rifle, and threw himself down the slope toward the farm. Maybe the morning wasn't a dead loss after all.

From outside: a second gunshot from the barn. Beth was still alive and armed, evidently.

Zipping and angling up the stairs Jack stopped short of the bedroom door, then swung in with weapon raised. No Paul. "Fuck." He could feel his capacity for folding into the moment diminishing like a kind of soul-breathlessness. He moved into the hall, took a moment, and summoned enough energy to flash up the ladder, to the attic.

He found Paul in the middle of Will's life, waiting. A slapping sting in Jack's gun hand and, suddenly, the gun was in Paul's. "Let's talk about this."

———

Back behind cover, Beth unzipped her jacket and checked the charge on her rescue rig: a lightweight belt-and-braces-style harness made of segmented plates attached to a power source distributed about her waist. A quick click revealed the chronon pack on the back of the belt was at full charge.

Slipping out of her jacket she took a mesh drawstring pouch from her leg pocket, unrolled it, and drew out a neatly tied roll of wires. Two sets. One end had a rudimentary series of plugs, the other a series of five cups: four for fingertips, one for the thumb.

Slipping the cups over her digits, Beth Velcro-strapped the thin cord to her forearm and bicep, and then slotted the five plugs into five jacks on her shoulder harness. She repeated for her other arm.

The rescue rig was good to go.

"You could have searched this place anytime you liked. Why now?"

"We did. There was nothing here at the time, but this"—Paul glanced about—"much of this is new." He opened the nearest box, dug deep, pulling aside papers and folders. "Have you seen any diagrams or schematics of a device like a twelve-sided sphere? I need you to think: this is very important."

Jack let himself rest against the desk. "Sure," he said. "Yeah. In the corner over there."

"Where?"

"Far corner. Near the stuffed elephant."

Jack had loved that house. It wasn't much without a family in it, though. "Y'know, Paul," Jack said. "You dropped a building on my brother." Reaching behind the flat-screen, he found the panic button: a palm-sized metal box with a plastic idiot shield covering a fat red detonator. He flipped it up.

Paul shifted sideways, peered deep into the stacks of magazines and papers.

Saw the gallon jug. Knew immediately what it was. Reacted accordingly.

"Seems fair that he return the favor."

The detonator went *click*.

There were two hearts in that attic. Both stopped for an instant. From behind a stack of plastic storage tubs something popped, then hissed. Concealed wiring along the ceiling join blackened and fritzed. That was it.

Jack rolled back his head, exasperated. "For Christ's sake, Will."

Paul went for his sidearm, Jack reacted. . . .

Then the attic exploded.

Gibson vaulted the fence in time to see the attic window spit glass, unrolling a tongue of thick flame across the yard.

Then the stutter hit and the whole of the Lord's Creation . . . stopped: sounds Randall Gibson hadn't even noticed—the rasp of leaves in a morning breeze, the distant hush of traffic, the trill of a lonely bird trying to get laid—all drew out, alien and discordant, beneath a boom turned to a roar turned to a whine turned to nought but the tinnitus pinging in his ears.

That rolling column of glass-speckled flame hung absurdly, like a mistake, across a bright-blue sky.

The chronon gauge on his rescue rig read a full charge, all good. Designed by the Merlins at Monarch, the rig was a brace across his waist and shoulders that fit neatly beneath his jacket. It afforded him a discreet profile, better than the 'roidy NASA-looking crap the Strikers wore. Downside: the charge sucked.

If Paul Serene was still alive in there he'd be mobile; moving unassisted through a stutter was just one of the things that cold-eyed freak could do.

Nah, the Consultant would be fine. Best check on that little hardbody in the barn.

A God-clap vanished Jack's past beneath an all-consuming tidal wave of flame. It lunged from all corners, the attic filled and gone in a roaring instant. From within his bubble of suspended time Jack watched as all that was left of his former life died in less time than it took to blink.

The flames hesitated, paused, backtracked, resumed.

Within a thermosphere of frozen time even the dust on the boards beneath his feet remained undisturbed, as was the section of wall caught in the bubble.

All else: Hades.

On the far side of an immobile wall of flame something shimmered through the suspended smoke and haze.

A man-sized dome of suspended time.

Within it, shaken and furious, Paul Serene stood up.

Gibson slipped into the barn, strolled to the ladder, and climbed on up. What a dump: cans, shelves, crap. All of it older than he was.

There she was: back pressed to the rusty shelf by the hayloft doors, rifle in hand, still as a statue.

"Hey there. You waitin' for me?" He liked the way her T-shirt hugged her, beneath that canvas jacket that was spoiling the view. Her head was down, focused on the rifle, red hair tied back in a ponytail. He ducked his head, angling for a peek of her face beneath that cap.

He noted the ShotSpotter taped to her weapon. An unusual piece of equipment. That told Gibson she knew what she was getting into, but taped to a cheap old deer rifle? Couldn't be civilian, the way she zeroed in on the Guardian squad shooter. So who was this warm little slice of pie?

Examining the rifle meant Gibson noticed her hands—specifically her fingers, which were capped with rubberized thimbles.

Like the ones he wore, attached to his rescue rig.

The hardbody glanced at him from beneath the rim of her cap.

She put her shoulder into a swing straight at the bridge of his nose, but Gibson was ready, shifting his weight and angling away. That put a big old smile on his face. She spun with the wasted momentum and he leaped on her for the split second her back was to him. He grabbed the rifle and yanked it like a crossbar for her throat.

She surprised him. She let go immediately and dropped. Weight displaced, Gibson lurched backward, rebounding off a rack of flimsy yet unmoving iron shelves.

Turned out she had a pistol. That figured. He—

Holy shit. It was Washout Wilder.

"Drop the rifle," she said.

"You have got to be fucking kidding me."

"Drop it!"

"You have fucked your life up masterfully, Wilder. I stand before you in awe."

He tossed it away. Ten feet out the rifle lost whatever chronon charge it had picked up from either of them and froze, suspended in mid-air.

"Spare me. I know all about you, Gibson."

"Want me to sign your tits?"

"I want you to deactivate your rig."

"Yeah, and I want you to s—"

She cut him off with a barely tolerant, "Don't." And a very slow shake of the head.

Gibson racked up a checklist of things to work through once he got that gun off her.

"Deactivate it," she said.

"Why? You on a clock?"

"You have a kid."

"So? You just shot Larry, his sister's got diabetes."

"Lorelei doesn't have to grow up without her dad. Three."

"Or what? You'll *murder* me?"

"Killed Larry. Two."

"Okay. Okay." He took that moment to catalog her: height, weight, complexion, hair, eyes, build, accent, distinctive features. "You should have shot me." Gibson slapped release plates on both hips, the power supply disconnected. Gibson froze.

She lowered her weapon, hands shaking.

Gibson was frozen, no longer a threat, rig deactivated. Even immobile, locked into that self-dividing moment, his expression told her this wasn't over.

This was a mistake. Once the stutter broke Gibson would radio in and blow her cover. Or kill her. Or worse. If he could.

She should kill him. He wouldn't be the first, or the last, but killing him meant killing the love and joy she had seen in Lorelei's eyes. Beth knew it meant condemning that little girl to becoming someone too much like herself: wounded and robbed, full of questions that would never be answered.

"You shouldn't have done that," Paul said.

The stutter rolled forward, slowly, excruciatingly, seething.

"It was worth a shot."

Paul looked at the stolen gun in his hand, like he had never seen it before. Then he checked the mag. "We recover quite quickly, don't we? From injuries. Our relationship to the chronon field constitutes a kind of secondary immune system— one that keeps us alive, protected not from infection but misadventure. But it still allows us to feel the pain of our mistakes; permits them to scar us. I myself have many scars." The bullet impacted against Jack's stutter shield before he registered that Paul had raised the gun. "Some injuries our privilege cannot save us from." The bullet hovered, impatient, two feet away from Jack's head. "Do not confuse your new state of being with being invulnerable, Jack. You are anything but."

Jack's shield quivered and expired. He jagged left, the bullet snapping past his ear to spark off the time-locked wall behind him.

Oxygen vanished, shockingly—chewed up to feed the slow-motion flames. Mouth working uselessly, Jack felt his chest tighten—fast and painfully.

The stutter lost its grip, heat kicked off, Jack's chest burned from the inside, and then, downstairs, the secondary charges blew.

Jack's ankles bit as the floorboard punched upward. He was airborne—and then causality quit. The stutter kicked back in, guillotining the roar to silence. He and Paul crashed back to earth on floorboards halted in the moment of splintering and heaving upward, gouts of flame spitting up through gaps in wood right across the attic. Jack's hand came down through one such gap, hand and forearm disappearing into flame. With a yelp he snatched it back, just before the stutter rewound and the splintered jaws of the floor snapped shut, resealing. He toppled, and then the boards reerupted a second time, knocking him sideways. With a yell he rolled with it, batting the side of his face as his hair briefly caught fire.

Time lost track of itself again, slowed abruptly . . . then froze.

Paul didn't hesitate: he warped across the room and out of the attic—down into whatever was left of the second floor.

Gulping uselessly, vision dimming, Jack folded into a moment—floor and attic and flames slipping past him in an instant. His hip connected with the desk, spinning him past the flaming ruin of the trapdoor and almost flipping him through the blown-out window. He spied movement at the gate to the property, out by the road.

Impossibly, Monarch troops were moving through the stutter, onto the property, where they divided into two large groups: one continuing down the drive, the second breaking off to loop around the rear side of the barn. No sign of Beth anywhere.

The floor and walls pounded, expanding and retracting, rupturing and resealing. His home had become a superheated heart in the grip of complete arrhythmia.

Paul flashed to the trapdoor and leaped down, transferring his weight and movement into a roll that was intended to propel him down the hall and toward the staircase. He hit the boards hard, ducked, tucked his shoulder, and came up running just as the door to Jack's bedroom blew off its hinges on a super-heated cloud. With a yell he transferred the run into a slide, getting under the twirling blade of the door, but too late to avoid singed skin and hair—just before the explosion had sec-ond thoughts and took it all back.

Pause.

Paul scrambled to his feet, batting at his clothes—nothing was burning. Whether it was luck or nostalgia, either way Paul spent a second glancing into a room he hadn't visited since he was a child. Through the open door, on a desk, waiting for him, was the answer to an obsession.

A small wire-framed replica of a twelve-sided geodesic. This was a shape, a design, that had resided inside Paul's brain for the last six years. This was the shape of the thing he had tasked the greatest scientific brains with unraveling, understanding, replicating, implementing.

This was the shape of the thing that rested at the heart of Monarch Tower. The thing upon which all of their discoveries had been based, yet was so poorly understood. A masterpiece of arcane design, created by the genius Paul had to kill.

"The Regulator."

A 3-D model, perched atop a stack of yellowing documentation.

He lunged forward, channeling his chronon flow to influence the door, allowing him to release it from the stutter, shoving it open. Paul flung his hands forward to protect the model, clutching. . . .

Play.

The bomb in the wall behind the desk redetonated, catching Paul in the face just before the shield erected, the shock wave slamming him into—and through—the frail door. Yellowed papers flew like burning birds as he crashed into the opposite wall, face in agony, his clothes aflame.

Shrieking and screaming, he flipped over and rolled to suffocate the flames, narrowly avoiding being killed as the safe in the attic above fell through the weakened ceiling and cannoned through the floor two feet from his thrashing head.

And pause.

Time struggled against that constraint, tumbling forward slowly as hesitant causality continued to tear the place apart—with agonizing fussiness: erupting boards, wallpaper blackening and curling and flaming. Framed photographs tumbled as the cords that held them incinerated, the glass snapping and crazing with thermal shock as the images they contained turned dark and died.

Scrambling upright he wheeled toward the bedroom—the smashed door suspended in mid-air, the interior an inferno. Everything in the room was lost.

The Regulator model was destroyed, but Paul held something that gave him hope.

Scorched and torn papers were bunched into his balled fist: remnants of Will's design for the Regulator, charred and half-destroyed, but it was something.

The stutter would collapse any moment. Half-blind and agonized, Paul Serene propelled down the stairs, through the kitchen, and out the back door.

In the attic, Jack spun away from the window as the far side of the roof collapsed in a thick rain of burning beams, shingles, and insulation. Ceiling had parted from wall, kindling shrapnel spraying wide across the property. A blown-back flap of roofing allowed the sky to peer through the ceiling's rib cage.

Directly ahead of him the floor bottomed out completely as the weight of the safe killed the boards, sending it plummeting down to the hallway below, punching through the floor and shattering a downward runnel through kitchen cabinets.

A searing plume of flame jetted upward through the trapdoor—then froze. Somewhere below Paul screamed in pain. The conflagration paused and juddered, partially rewound, then leaped forward, repeat, as though undecided about what should happen next.

The scene abruptly leaped into a rapidly escalating shudder. Things could burst back into real time at any moment.

Against his better judgment, Jack let his feet propel him toward the massive hole in the floor. The lips of the wound vibrated steadily upward, closing, before trembling downward again. The cycle accelerated, up and down, flame and sparks and debris jetting in and out, jabbing at eyes and skin.

Forearm across his face, the floor trembling and snapping, Jack slipped—skidded—and tumbled through with a yell.

Pause.

He tumbled through a cloud of time-locked debris. Shreds of unmoving ash, wallpaper, shrapnel slashed at his hands and clothes as he plummeted downward, hit the second-floor hallway and tumbled backward through the wound in the floor which the falling safe had left behind. Shoulder blades clipped shattered kitchen cabinets as he tumbled feet first to the debris-laden kitchen floor—where the safe lay facedown in the wreckage.

The kitchen ceiling was a crumbling mess, wreathed in rolls of static fire. Curtains, blackened and blazing, framed a snapshot of the front garden on an otherwise perfect autumn morning.

Groaning he rolled to his hands and knees, scanning for any way out. The back door out of the kitchen had collapsed. In the opposite direction flaming debris was filling the living area as it rained from the conflagration in the attic. Vacillating between falling and rising, curling one way or another, it was a raising and lowering curtain of death. He ran for it. Palming away skipping sparks and cinders, diving under a crossbeam that rose and fell like an axe blade, Jack sped through the living area, shielding his face. Leaping across the flaming dining-room table he tripped on the back of a time-locked chair, hit the ground, rolled with it, and—shoulder aching from impact—belted through the screen door on the far side of the house and into the greenhouse.

Dull heat gave way to muted cold. Jack skidded to a stop, hip banging hard into a rusted planter rack. Aching all over, he took a second to assess the next course of action. Once this place had been full of life. His mother had made of it a verdant womb, a place that had once brought her happiness. Jack had loved it in winter, when the world was ankle-deep in frost and this sweating glasshouse had been close and warm and alive. Orchids had been her passion.

Jack Joyce, twenty-eight years old now, sprinted through the fragile mausoleum to his dead mother, feet pounding across mold-encrusted concrete, past racks and beds gone to rust and ruin, and shoved wide the frail, grime-darkened glass door to stumble, gasping, into morning sunlight.

The black eyes of a dozen assault rifles awaited him.

Without pausing, he translated himself into speed and flew forward as the Technician squad unloaded—missing by a wide margin, bullets sparking off the time-locked greenhouse. The delicate bones in his hand cracked as his fist met the face of the first trooper square below his nose, spun, and booted his compatriot in the back of his knee. He didn't bother with the assault rifle, which was strapped to the man, but went for the sidearm while the rest of the team oriented and reacted. The first trooper punched the gravel, back first. Jack snatched the weapon and warped back toward the momentarily bullet-proof greenhouse as the squad opened up and the second trooper hit the dirt, covering his head.

Jack popped back to regular speed behind a row of moldering planters stacked flush next to the greenhouse wall, the bones in his hand already mending. He popped up fast, and his healing hand lost grip, and the pistol flew from his fist.

Jack had enough time to belch out a disbelieving, "For fuck's—!" when Beth opened fire from the hayloft.

Caught in the open, the rescue-rigged Technicians scattered

fast. Chronon tech, just like the art-killers at the university but far less polished.

Retrieving his weapon as the Technicians scrambled for cover, he noticed the second unit: a crew flanking the barn. They had put together what was happening and were looking to kick into the barn from the rear, taking Beth by surprise. Jack blatted off three shots, catching one man on the hip and causing the rest to rethink their plan. Jack fell back to the rusted planters as a swarm of shots sought him out, every round sparking off—rather than penetrating—time-locked earth and glass.

The house was in a terrible state, rolling slowly outward in pieces from the attic and second floor, stopping, winding back a little, only to roll forward again toward the inevitable.

It was hard to focus. The light-headedness was back. Warping and shifting was costing him. He needed to regroup.

Four troopers clustered together behind the garage across from the house. Jack popped up and blasted out a stutter shield. The localized self-dividing moment popped to life around the four grunts, locking them into place—"Ha!"—for about a second before the tech they wore to keep them mobile tore the shield apart. "Crap." Jack zapped forward, closing the distance . . . and his abilities ended there.

The ground seesawed. Jack forgot where he was.

A trooper fired a blind spray around the corner of the garage. Slugs zip-fanned above Jack's head. He flinched, translating his forward momentum into a knee-skid across the drive's white gravel. Righting himself as fast as he could, instinct then sent him scrambling—not for the blind side of the garage, but onto the porch and into the front door of the dying house.

Literally into the front door. In his panic he didn't extend his chronon field, to make the door active, and Jack rebounded off it as if it were concrete.

The garage squad regrouped, crept along the south-side wall. Beth kept them back by kicking up a wall of dirt in front of them with a three-round burst.

Jack got to his feet, eyeballed Beth. Framed by the upper hayloft doors she pointed to herself and then at the crew behind the garage. Then she pointed to Jack and jerked a thumb toward the crew circling the barn. Jack gave the thumbs-up, took a deep breath, and rabbited toward the barn—gun up and firing. From her elevated position Beth opened fire with Gibson's carbine.

Paul had crashed out the kitchen door, half-blinded, onto the porch that curved around the north and east sides of the house. The occasional clap of gunfire made him jump, reflexively dropping a stutter shield. No bullets came; the threat was not to him.

He sped from the shield, west, into the forest-fringed back garden, jagged south to put the house between him and the firefight that was taking place in the front. His chronon field was already working to restore his vision, the lacerating caustic sting of his facial injuries fading to a livid mottling of his flesh.

The gunfire at the front of the house escalated from a smattering of pops to a full-on multipointed fusillade. Jack was still alive. Paul wheeled, prepared to translate himself at speed around the southern side of the house to attack and apprehend his unskilled friend—to put an end to this madness.

But stopped. What he saw made the strength flee from his legs.

They existed. Five of them, south of the house, near the tree line. Flickering, hulking, twitching.

Then it was there, in the morning light, dark and glittering and monstrous, as though it had a right to be in a world that held Paul's happiest memories. That thing of . . .

It moved.

The ground belted him in the ass before his inner ear had the chance to realize he had toppled. The Shifter with the shining palm came for him, unhurried, like every button-pushing nightmare because it *could,* because he couldn't get away. Because the universe itself knew Paul Serene was so much worse than *dead.*

The thing raised its black, shifting hand to display the killing star at its palm.

He froze; he was an animal trapped in the barrow of his own skull, with death at the entrance.

Chanting. The same syllable, repetitious, forever. In time it penetrated and the sound became a word.

Paul listened as his throat coughed up the word "go," over and over and over.

His boots kicked against the cold ground, carved runnels in damp soil. His body twisted, fingers clawing at grass, and he was stumbling, chest grinding into the sod. Paul picked himself up and then he was running—straight for the woods.

Jack let the tree trunk take his weight, slid to the ground, jacket biting into his armpits as he found the ground. The emptied and open pistol smoked, cradled loose in his slack fingers. Eight men dead. One of them kneeling beside him, face resting against the selfsame tree, lost to his wounds. Others were scattered about the area, frozen, like this one, at the moment they died: some in mid-pirouette, some on their backs, one in mid-air.

Misted blood hung like a spray of rubies. As the stutter slowly inched forward every dead man engaged in the last dance of his life.

Jack couldn't look at it.

Throat raw and gasping, his head swimming and kill-sick, Jack's brain tapped out. Beth called his name from the barn. He heard her clack in a fresh magazine.

"Yeah," he called back. It took all he had.

"Get up, Jack. Right now."

His tree was east of the barn. It was a perfectly pleasant place to sit on this sunny morning and watch the family home die. Will's desk had flown out of the shattered attic on a tongue of flame, smashing into the gravel drive. Flaming papers trailed its descent.

It came to him then, the cause of Beth's alarm: the sound. It made its way across the garden, skipping schizophrenically through sliced-up and compartmentalized submoments. It was the sound of a combustion engine. A big one. Jack had first heard it early that morning, outside Zed's—Beth's—empty house, in the dark: the grumbling blat of a Monarch BearCat's 300-horsepower diesel engine.

Survival instinct got him upright. Extending his chronon field to the dead trooper beside him almost exhausted Jack to the point of blackout, but he managed to snare the dead man's rifle and two magazines before the stutter rebuked him. The toppling corpse refroze halfway to the ground.

Even before it had cleared the trees the BearCat opened up, livid streams of fire *chunk-chunk-chunk-chunk*-ing from something patient and furious and roof-mounted. Large-caliber rounds exploded like cherry bombs across the time-locked and invulnerable planking of the hayloft exterior.

Jack shouted Beth's name and that drew the needle-nosed attention of the double-gripped machine gun on the BearCat.

Without breaking fire it swung the flashing stream toward Jack, who had no choice but to cut south toward the cover of the garage—no powers available. Boiling red lines of tracer fire stitched the air, rebounded in curling spirals from an environment that wouldn't budge.

The BearCat gunner tried to lead the fleeing figure but couldn't rotate fast enough. Fire swept toward and rebounded off the garage, rounds ricocheting madly. Someone cried out, "Whoa whoa *whoa*! Watch what you're fuckin' doing!"

A risky three-round burst from Beth got their attention and the BearCat threw into reverse, angling to net both Jack and Beth inside its firing arc.

Jack caught a glimpse of the vehicle, noting the roof gunner protected on all sides by shoulder-high plating. Something else caught his attention: the bracing applied to the BearCat's chassis. Segmented, it followed the X and Y axis of the vehicle. The design was similar to the rigs worn by the Peace Movement and Monarch chronon troopers.

That frame was keeping the BearCat active inside the stutter.

Jack shouldered the rifle and squeezed. Recoil sent the first shot high, sparking off the hood. The second shot hit one of the rig's polished segments square on. The panel took the hit, buckling, to no effect.

The gunner opened up. A .50-caliber round struck the garage, fragmenting. A needle of molten lead slashed across Jack's forehead.

He threw himself behind cover and fell back, clutching his face.

Paul's hands were scraped from tumbles, and from slapping bark to suddenly course-correct. His path had been chosen thoughtlessly and yet, he soon realized, he had always known where he was going.

The mound was easy to miss, constructed as it was with craft and guile. Built into a gentle-sloped hill and masked with deadfall the shelter looked like part of the environment—more so now than when Jack and Paul had played there as kids. The forest had incorporated it into itself. Drifts of pine needles had built up against it, while moss had prospered across the roof of mud and daub.

It was a sign.

No. He was panicking. He . . .

They were everywhere: on the far side of the shelter, flush between two trees, *there*!

He ran for the tumbledown shelter, kicked away drifts of soft deadfall, and clawed at the primitive hewn-log door. He wrenched the door, strained it toward himself on fused hinges, rotting wood tearing along the frame, troweling up soft earth in which knots of earthworms writhed furiously, and swung into a foul-smelling twilight. The frail door clattered, warped with damp, into the handmade frame. What light made it in here fell through the gaps in the rough planking. The floor was cold, moist earth.

Eye pressed to a gap in the door's planking Paul saw two Shifters, monstrosities like Dr. Kim, side by side, not fifty feet away. Fritzing, flashing, snapping, tortured as different versions of their form fought for dominance, staggering for him as though he were the cause of their pain.

A rotten foam mattress decomposed on a raised earthen platform against the wall. Opposite this, a rudimentary wooden shelf had collapsed, just below the shelter's single long window—someplace to eat and watch the woods, maybe. A heavy wattle-and-daub cover swung down to close it off. Paul approached,

peered through the slats, and whimpered. Control was slipping.

Three more Shifters, arrayed unevenly, between thirty and
fifty feet distant.

He was surrounded.

As soon as people stop shooting, Jack told himself, *I'm getting on
a plane.*

Then he remembered that since stepping off his last flight
he had rocketed onto the Most Wanted list.

All because Paul wanted to do good. "These people trust
me, he said. I'm responsible for their livelihood, he said. They
promise this massive unlicensed black-hole-driven motherfucker is perfectly safe, he said. . . ."

Beth risked a shot, the round snapping harmlessly past the
BearCat gunner's helmeted head, but keeping him low.

Will knew the machine was defective. Said it was *obviously*
defective. The miscalibration had got by everyone on Paul's
team. Was it sabotage? And if it was, who did the work?

Who in Monarch had the expertise to tweak a time machine
to cause this kind of damage, and conceal it from a team of
experts?

Jack needed an elevated position if he was going to get a shot
over the gunner's shielding. The garage was too low. If he went
for the barn that'd put both he and Beth exactly where those
Monarch goons wanted them: dead center. He needed another
option.

Jack felt the stutter change. Blinking blood out of his eyes,
he saw every slow-motion thing stop. There was a different tide
within the energy of his body now; and an opposite, subtle momentum to the energy of the world.

The stutter was rewinding, slowly, and picking up speed.

On the driveway, Will's desk reassembled. Flames fed their own reduction, seeming to fuel the house's slow reconstruction. Cinders turned to sheaves of paper. Disturbed gravel tidied up as the desk left the ground.

Jack waved to Beth, frantically. He pointed to the BearCat, then to him and her, counted three on his fingers, then mimed firing. She nodded agreement.

The desk was airborne, two feet off the ground and accelerating as the stutter gained momentum. The house began to suck the exploding ether back into itself, planks eagerly flying home. Window frames reassembled as they traveled back to their housings, preparing to self-socket.

Jack swung out blasting as Beth streamed a fusillade overhead. The gunner responded by going full auto even as he ducked behind his shield. Jack kicked in his somewhat replenished reserves and flashed across the gravel, twisted, landing butt first on the unstable desk. Beth scored a few close hits, the gunner yelped, and the machine gun stopped barking for one crucial moment.

The desk angled steeply, quickly. Jack dropped the carbine to keep his grip on his ride, but the desk hadn't just fallen out the front of the house; it had been blown out. It had come out flipping.

As it rotated beneath him Jack tucked his legs, grabbed the lip of the desk—its four legs now skyward—and scrambled to get his feet onto the underside.

The BearCat driver was screaming, "Shoot, you fuck! He's right there!" Beth exhausted her mag, which bought a few more seconds, and then the gunner was back at his station.

Jack mantled onto the underside of the desk as it climbed to eye level with the second floor, which was when a reverse-burning 1997 phone book shot up from beneath the desk and smashed Jack in the face.

His head snapped back. His center of gravity held for a moment . . . but the desk kept rotating. A steel leg came down, jammed hard in his chest, doubling Jack forward as pain exploded below his collarbone. He threw his arms forward as the desk leg shoved him down. His fingertips strained for the desk's edge, but there was no reaching it. Instead, desperately, his fingers closed on the leg, like an impaled man might grab the spear that was killing him. The rotation was slow enough that he could grasp it with both hands, hanging free, hands over his head and feeling his grip slip.

The desk was the right way up, two floors above the gravel, on its journey to the attic, when the machine gun swung toward Jack.

Hosing tracer fire—aimed too high—swept toward him like a killing whip.

Shrapnel and wreckage flew toward him from below.

"Fuck it."

Jack leaped off the desk and let the storm take him. A cardboard box full of novels slammed into his chest as a hose of tracer fire slashed downward, angry fireworks pinging and whining among the storm of wreckage. The box abandoned Jack at its parabola, continuing on its way as Jack sailed free, punched around the legs and spine by trash and memorabilia before tumbling through the shattered wall to hit the attic floor.

He gasped, rolling aside as the desk scythed overhead and stopped.

The stutter froze. The attic wall was a half-bloomed flower.

Silence and a dimness. That dead-thing reek of earth and rotting bedding.

Someone laughed and Paul spun.

Two kids were in the shelter with him, standing on tiptoes,

elbows resting on the ghost of the bench that had collapsed, watching the woods, though the window was closed to all light.

"No such thing as witches," the first kid said. His dark hair was fresh-cut and parent-approved. Even here his shirt was tucked into his trousers, his hair neatly combed. The boy next to him, fair haired, was a different story: thrift-store khaki jacket with some big pockets, unwashed blue jeans, and that Riverport Raptors shirt he'd worn to death.

The voices of the things outside used Paul's own brain as an amplifier. As one, they *howled* for him—long and broken.

"Who'd live in a place like this if they weren't a witch," ten-year-old Jack asked Paul's younger self. "Look at this place."

"The disenfranchised," the neatly dressed Paul responded.

He had always repeated the big words his mother used, had tried so hard to sound much older than he was.

"The wh—?"

And they were gone. The howling ceased.

Something strained at the door, yanked it, the thin shield of it wobbling.

Paul's gun was up the second the door opened. A single round blasted through the head of the swaddled woman who stood there. She turned, pushed the door wide to let in the air, and lowered her backpack onto the rotted mattress.

The gunshot faded and fluxed, echoing, distorted through the time-locked woods.

Her hands were weathered, and she hummed to herself, pulling earphones free. Unzipping her bag she laid out two dented bean cans, a half loaf of bread, a cold cheeseburger.

This was the Witch in the Woods, the figure Paul and Jack had mythologized. And then she was gone.

Howls. Paul's hands slammed to his ears, hard, pistol-whipping himself in the process. Crying out, the cry turned to a scream. One breath and the scream turned to a roar.

"What? What do you want?" He slammed his face to the cracks in the door, wide eyes scanning.

Oh God, they were twenty feet away. Five of them.

Paul looked at the loaded gun in his hand. Better he end it here than let them get him. Better he die by his own hand than become like Dr. Kim. Better he kill himself than live to see the world turn to a colorless and unending purgatory, stalked by monsters and tortured by memory.

Better, kinder, that he cease to be.

The machine gun stopped firing. Jack figured it had to be reloading.

He gasped like a landed fish. His chest was one massive bruise where the desk leg had punched him, his cough wet and red.

The roll across the attic floor had cost him. The snapped halves of a rib or two scraped together, spearing him with brightest pain. The jagged ends found each other as his body rapidly healed; the snapped rib-halves kissed, then fused, seamlessly. His skin crawled at the fingers-inside feeling of his chest unbruising. Back arched against it all he saw the safe was back upstairs, twenty feet away from his head, one corner half-submerged into the crumbling floor, ready to repeat its fall through the first-floor hall and into the kitchen below.

Will's file was inside the open safe: the property deed. The key. The only real lead Jack had left inside this burning building.

Body healed but mind still flailing, he propelled himself forward and skidded across the hot floor on his unbruised chest, plunging his hand into the safe.

The stutter broke. The safe dropped through the floorboards, just as Jack snatched his arm free and popped a shield.

The room reexploded, flame billowing out from four corners, papers flying from the folder, out of the shield, to be vaporized. "No!" He scrambled, saved a few, and jammed them into his jacket.

Paul had prepared himself for moments of doubt, for trials such as this. Seventeen years preparing to overcome more than any man had ever endured in order to purchase a future for the human race. He had taken lives, manipulated nations and economies. The soul of the man he once was had long been forfeit to a greater cause. It was his duty to undo what he had done.

He took his emotions out of the equation, broke the situation down into what needed doing.

He had to live.

If he did not see his plans to the end then all of Creation would stop.

To live he had to get away from what was outside the shelter. What was outside the shelter was . . .

Blackness flooded the corners of his vision. He shook his head, reduced himself to an equation, a piece on the board.

What was outside the shelter was a threat. The only way out was that door. If he waited they would enter. If he allowed the enemy to dictate terms he was doomed.

Without a second's hesitation, Paul Serene kicked the door off the hinges and came out shooting. It was the only option he had left.

The Monarch teams were coming to terms with the playfield suddenly changing. The stutter juddered, rewound further. Behind her, as Beth reloaded, Gibson's hand rewound far enough to unslap the deactivation plates on his rescue rig.

As she swung out to take an opportunity shot at one of the team leaders, Gibson locked her from behind, combat knife pressed to her neck.

"All righty punkin' butter, drop it."

Beth let the rifle hit the boards.

"See, Wilder, this is why you didn't make the cut. Stupid." His breath was hot in her ear. "And now . . . now you go from being a soldier to being something I do in my spare time."

At that moment the second Technician team swept into the rear of the barn as the BearCat gunner opened up on the hayloft from the front. Heavy-hitting tracer rounds curled and spat, ricocheting off time-locked surfaces, sending high-velocity rebounds spraying down onto the barn floor to pinball about the space, tearing men to shreds.

Gibson yelped and leaped sideways, freeing Beth to snatch her stolen rifle and roll away from him. She wheeled, dropped to one knee, and brought the sights up level with Gibson.

Gibson threw himself off the edge, into the barn below.

The BearCat was ripping into the hayloft. From the attic inside the house Jack could see Beth hunkering down, making herself as small as possible, but it was only a matter of time before a ricochet found her.

He had no weapon, and the BearCat was armored. He had a stupid idea, so he ran with it.

He ran at the blown-open attic wall, folded into the moment, and threw himself out—aiming for the BearCat. The warp negated the impact, and Jack landed boots first on the hood. The driver had time to shout a warning before Jack clamped both hands to one section of the chronon-mobility lattice that sheathed the vehicle, and channeled everything he had into it.

Chronon energy flowed from him to the vehicle's battery.

Keeping his head under the roof-gun Jack poured everything he had into the BearCat's mobility rig.

Somewhere inside the cabin things caught fire. Jack let go, scrambled over the windshield, grabbing the barrel of the weapon for leverage.

The chronon battery erupted. Then the fuel tank kicked off.

As Jack leaped clear, the BearCat exploded, the rear of the vehicle leaping skyward.

Everything went black.

Paul came out shooting, keeping the faces of those he loved— Sofia, the Jack he remembered, his own mother—at the forefront of his mind. These talismans would keep the darkness, the fear and horror, at bay. These—

The first shot took the nearest Shifter in the head. Paul caught a glimpse of a human face beneath the distortion, the spray of blood, but it made no difference. In less than a second the creature had phased through half a dozen versions of itself—all of them alive and furious.

He fired again and again, each death rendered meaningless by each Shifter's infinite litany of potential selves.

There were not enough bullets in the world to kill even one of them.

They did not seem to mind his attempted murder. The assembled Shifters didn't react; they didn't move. Paul jagged right and altered course, aiming for the house, just beyond the thinning tree line ahead.

They did not pursue, but he knew they would not let him go.

Most of the barn team was dead. Those who survived were getting their shit together. Beth saw Gibson book it out the back

of the barn, headed for the house. She presumed he'd be looking for Serene, looking to confirm for his boss, Hatch, that Paul
was either alive or dead.

Her big problem was that Gibson had positively ID'd her.
Once the stutter broke comms would be working again, and
Gibson would immediately blow her cover. She should have
killed him, she knew that, but she'd met his daughter. She was
a sweet kid and she loved her dad. She deserved a family.

The thought flashed: *Who are we really talking about here,
Beth?*

She had to kill him. Grabbing the lower lip of the hayloft
door she bounced out, braked her boots against the outside
wall, and dropped to the ground, glancing only once at the frozen, semi-exploded BearCat in front of her—Jack static, unconscious, in mid-air, at the top of that flame plume. Several
men behind the garage were in the same state. The rest were
falling back toward the woods.

"I'll be right back," she promised Jack, and ran for the house.

She came in through the front door, pushing past falling and
burning debris suspended in space. That's how Gibson got the
drop on her, leaping at her through the chaos to her left with
a knife in his hand.

Beth feinted left, swung the rifle right, and both combat-
ants missed each other. Gibson landed low, pivoted, and leaped
again before Beth could swing her rifle around.

The stutter vibrated, the death-thunder of the house a blast
of deafening, stop-start sound. Beth shielded her head; Gibson
didn't hesitate. He got close, slashed, as a chunk of burning
plaster dropped hard on the back of his head. The blade was
off-target but still opened a small cut in her bicep. Beth danced
out of the way.

The stutter shuddered again, harder. She had to save Jack
before the BearCat exploded properly, killing him.

"Consultant! Are you here, sir?"

"You had a family, Gibson," she said. "Instead you wanted this."

Gibson spun, jabbed. Beth avoided the attack easily, closed in. "It's over."

A rabbit-punch to the jaw sent him staggering backward, the back of his leg connecting with the couch. With one move she slapped both hip-plates—locking him solid. The ceiling overhead bulged under the weight of its own burning collapse. In about four relative seconds the room would be an inferno.

Beth got the hell out of there, cleared the distance between stoop and BearCat. The truck was balancing on its front-left tire, the rear underside of the vehicle cracked open and exploding. Jack had been hit by the blast wave as he leaped off, knocking him out and deactivating his powers, leaving him frozen.

Beth managed to get a toehold near the windshield, then leaped for Jack's ankle. Grabbing it, she pulled herself up onto the angled roof of the vehicle, hanging on to Jack the whole while. Hoping this was going to work, she double-pumped her hands and channeled her rescue rig's charge into him. The bars on her belt ticked off one by one, and—

Jack reanimated, all dead weight, and crashed onto her. They tumbled back over the hood and hit the dirt, hard. Beth rolled over, got herself upright. The rig had a single bar left out of five.

Jack lay insensible on the ground, barely conscious. She grabbed his jacket with both hands, dragging him toward the cover of the barn. The stutter pulsed, the house exploding outward a fraction, double-time, before retracting, then rolling out again in excruciating slow motion.

She needed to get them both behind the barn before the house gas mains went up, but Jack was a lot of dead weight. She dropped him, then got around front and hauled him upright.

"You . . ." Jack managed to take in enough to make an assessment. "You . . . saved me?"

"Not yet." She said, pulling him off the ground. "C'mon, Trouble, get up or we're dead."

Jack focused. He saw the house suck itself back in, and tremble. He felt the same motion in his own bloodstream; the motion that told him the stutter was about to break. That was all he needed.

On his feet now and stumbling they cleared the barn and garage and kept sprinting, straight through the sycamores. Once they got close to the fence line Jack grabbed her arm. "Wait, wait." Jack had stopped, was looking back at the house.

The facade of the building continued to roll outward, then stopped. Juddered. Then, all at once, drew itself right back in, in one disconcerting move. Exploded wood and shattered windows rewound perfectly, peacefully and completely, closing behind a final belch of spark and flame. Sealed.

Leaving the Joyce family home intact.

The place where he had grown up, whole and complete, for the last time.

The stutter broke. The house erupted upward and outward as the brakes released and causality leaped forward. The shock wave knocked Jack and Beth to the ground, the detonation of ether, C-4, and the gas mains blasting the building to kindling— kindling that rained down around them.

The barn had taken a fatal blow and, after a moment, it creaked and collapsed away from them.

Sycamores burned. It was all gone.

The other Shifters moved aside, flashing to new locations throughout the woods, allowing Shining Palm to come forward. To close in. To claim the man it had been stalking for so long.

Paul stared into the oncoming glare of something worse than death, his legs and mind betraying him instantly, clinging to those last moments of *himness*, of being Paul. These were his last breaths, his last thoughts. All he was, all he had built, was about to be turned on himself, corrupted and inverted and perverted. His was an eternity of chaos and loss. An eternity.

It flashed to forty feet closer. To twenty.

Paul couldn't move. He couldn't look.

He could feel it, radiating, mere feet from him now.

It roared, demanding to be seen.

He couldn't open his eyes. His teeth, crushed against each other, strangled a scream.

The ground shuddered with a terrible roar as the Joyce house detonated. Birds shrieked to life, flying free from the forest canopy. Paul felt the wave of heat push through the trees to wash across his face.

Chronon-flow normal. Causality returned. The stutter broke.

The stutter broke, and he was alone.

Alive.

Weakly, gratefully, Paul Serene collapsed to the wet earth and wept.

13

"It's really quiet out there."

Nick was driving slow and steady, sitting low behind the wheel, staring ahead from behind his sunglasses. Riverport at nine thirty on a Saturday morning should have been livelier—even in autumn and with most of the college crowd still away on vacation. People should have been lining up for coffee. There should have been traffic. Buskers along the Main Street area should have been laying out hats and guitar cases for the day. Not today. This morning everyone's attention was on the university. If they weren't laying wreaths, pinning photographs to memorial boards at the site, or just paying their respects, they were moving at half speed, processing what it meant to be the news.

"You sure they can't track me?" The Breathalyzer's vitals were laid out on the front seat, next to the webcam and Nick's smashed coffee machine.

Beth was in the backseat, Jack lying out of sight with his head on her lap. "You're good, though the cops and Monarch will be looking for your license plate." She glanced at Jack: the face of Riverport's tragedy—Massachusetts's bin Laden—thanks to Hatch's evocative on-air summary that morning. "We should ditch the cab as soon as we can." She had gone over Jack, checking for injuries, found nothing save for a little mottling where cuts and scrapes had quickly healed over.

"They were supposed to be the solution," Nick said.

"Who was?"

"You were. Monarch. Jobs. A future. Hope. You told us you'd save us."

Beth felt that, wanted to rebuke it. She wasn't Monarch. She was never Monarch. She was inside Monarch to bring Monarch down. But Nick was right: she hadn't succeeded in preventing anything. "What's your favorite movie, Nick?"

"Happy Gilmore."

"Do me a favor and say *Star Wars.*"

"I don't like art films."

"You know that bit in *The Matrix* when Neo works out how to glitch it? He games the system, gets superpowers, rewrites reality?"

"Sure."

"In this story Neo is Monarch. The Matrix is planet Earth. The hack is money, influence, shamelessness, lies, entitlement, not giving a fuck, and an overwhelming lack of critical thought on our part."

"And actual superpowers."

So there it was. "What tipped you off?"

"Monarch were waiting at my house. Figured they had to be watching Jack's. So I watched his place for a while before coming in. You know what I saw?"

"The moment Jack's house blew up a dozen Monarch goons popped into existence and dropped dead simultaneously. At the same time a BearCat materialized out of thin air and exploded on his front drive."

"Also your boyfriend looked like ground beef when you rolled him onto the backseat. Now he looks just fine." The cab rolled to a stop at a red light. Nick glanced at Beth in the rearview. "Is this some deep-black bullshit? *X-Files*, Alex Jones, Area 51, something like that?"

Beth glanced away from the traffic to look Nick in the eye. "It is a conspiracy. It does go all the way up. It involves other dimensions. It was all planned."

He glanced at her again, then back to the road, saying nothing.

Jack risked lifting his head, peering out at the street. "Looks like the end of the world out there." Outside was the wide expanse of river on one side and rows of uncared-for warehouses on the other.

Nick had navigated them carefully around Main Street's periphery, sticking to back roads when he could, eventually taking them down a rutted service track by the river. "Who builds a swimming hall out here?"

"This was residential back in the day," Beth said. A three-legged dog skipped across the busted curb in front of them, glancing self-consciously at them before disappearing in the weeds. "Way, way back in the day."

Jack sat upright. Beth's hand—still thimble-clipped into her rig—slipped from his shoulder.

"Will didn't buy this place for the view." Jack looked at her hands, traced a finger along the rubberized thimble covering her thumb to the first joint, then the insulated wiring that led to a wrist clip of the same color and material.

"Zero State Mobility Rig," she said. "The exo carries its own chronon charge, maintaining my personal M-J field, even in a complete causality vacuum. It means I can walk around in a stutter, as long as the charge lasts."

The bridge was ahead. The address put the swimming hall directly beneath it.

"Before we do this," Jack said, "I need a few answers. That morning on Bannerman's Overlook. That show with Aberfoyle—the chop shop, the yachts, what happened to Aberfoyle and his men, the *timing*. The way nobody came to ask us questions. How . . . ?"

"Do you like Douglas Adams?" she said.

"The writer?"

"He wrote that the knack to flying lies in learning how to throw yourself at the ground, and miss."

"And?"

"Same thing."

Jack thought about that. "No it isn't."

"Here we are!" Beth was pointing at a decrepit building shoved snug beneath the bridge. It was completely unremarkable. The faded signage, half-lost to gravity and vegetation, read BR BURY SWI MING HALL. Beth was out of the cab, making a line for the place.

Jack followed. Colonies of seagulls and pigeons populated the underside ribbing of that third-rate bridge. Thin-stalked greenery reached up against stanchions supported by crumbling brickwork. Even the graffiti hadn't been updated since the nineties. The hall was as broad as the bridge itself, and built from the same brickwork. Two levels, all of the windows barred and boarded-over. Double doors of steel-banded wood sat square in the middle of the construction, falling-apart sign overhead. Steps led up to the door, a concrete wheelchair ramp swerving up from the side. Grass and vegetation had spent a decade or two undermining the concrete and brickwork, splitting it, green explosions reaching for the bridged-over sky.

Beth turned back to the cab. "Nick, you got a crowbar, tire iron, something . . . ?"

Nick, out of the car, clicked his tongue and gave her pistol-fingers in the affirmative before jogging around to the trunk.

"So," Jack said, trying to be casual. "Did you . . . see . . . anyone while you were away? A guy?"

"Not really."

"Oh?"

"I had a lot to get done in that time. Well, there was one guy, I guess."

"One guy who?"

Nick jogged over. "Here ya go!"

Beth took the tire iron, tested the heft, moved for the door.

Jack sidled over, dropped his voice to a whisper. "Was it serious?"

Beth was busy trying to wedge the iron between the two doors.

"Are you . . . in touch?"

Beth stopped what she was doing, looked him in the eye, and said his name in the most well-meaning tone she could manage. "Jack." He got the hint.

She got the tire iron in there, started sawing the other end of it to and fro.

Jack found it oddly uncomfortable to watch, looked away.

Metal and wood complained, splintered, finally popped. "I think I got it."

Jack grabbed the handle on one of the doors; she got the other. Sure enough the lock had fallen apart as it separated from the housing. The doors shrieked across the concrete.

Beth surveyed what this revealed. "Oh, get bent." A proper, actual security door. Thick, metal, heavy, with a code lock.

Nick whistled. "He wasn't screwing around."

Beth gestured at it. "Where'd your brother get that? NORAD?"

"Wait a sec." Jack stepped up to it. The code lock looked like it still had power. He punched in six digits. Waited.

From deep within the door's body came a weighty triple-*thunk* and, just like that, the half-ton iron door popped loose—opening an inch.

Beth examined it, looked at Jack.

"My birth date," he said.

"Huh." Beth pushed the door open easily. "After you."

"Hey!" Nick was waiting, twenty feet back, shifting uncertainly on his feet. "Your brother, uh, he wouldn't . . . there's not like shotguns on trip wires, or claymores . . . he wouldn't have stuff like that set up, right? He wasn't that kind of dude? That's a serious door, is all I'm sayin'."

Beth glanced at Jack. Jack shrugged. Beth went in first. Slowly. Jack followed, stepping into the twilight foyer of the swimming hall. Light struggled through soaped-up ceiling-level windows, revealing a cold, thickly aired time capsule to the mid-nineties lit by what light filtered through. There was signage for the 1996 Riverport Swim Meet ("Fun in the Sun!"), a wetly disintegrating corkboard that still held rainbow push-pins and handwritten ads for second-hand flippers and puppies that needed good homes. A dusty arcade cabinet stood in the corner, its colorful cartoon siding peeling away and the particleboard beneath coming out in leprous chunks.

Jack faux-retched. "Tastes like the inside of an air conditioner in here."

The counter faced turnstiles, which led to floor-to-ceiling swinging doors—the kind that made Jack think of a hospital.

A laminated sign announced the pool would be shutting down for good on March 1, and the staff thanked everyone who had been swimming there—some of them for fifty years. A few photographs curled on the floor beneath the sign, sticky tape yellowed and withered on the corners. Jack examined one—three old guys, holding up a black-and-white of their

younger selves at the same pool, not long after the end of the
Second World War.

He let it go.

Nick stuck his head in. "Smells like feet." He tentatively
stepped inside. "And not the good kind."

Whatever that meant.

Jack opened a cardboard box, dug through report cards (all
grades declining over time) and shrink-wrapped comics, and
came up with a framed color photograph of a white mouse in
a cage next to—

"That looks like Monarch's machine," Beth said. "A model
version of it."

Nick wandered over. "Monarch has a machine? What kind
of machine?"

The device in the photograph was small—mouse-sized—
and certainly not built with aesthetics in mind: all exposed ribbing and loose wires. Written neatly in Sharpie were the words:
"In Memory of Schrodinger, the world's first time traveler."

Beneath that was a twelve-thousand-dollar bill from a
moving company

"Pickup address was from home," Jack said. "Dated 1999.
Delivery address here."

Jack put down the bill, smoothed it thoughtfully on the two-
tone boomerang-patterned Formica countertop, and then
took the turnstiles at a vault. Booming through the push-doors
granted a deep vista of dim light and deep shadows. The doors
banged against the tiled walls, echoed off the opposite end of
the hall, then back again.

He wheeled around to Beth and Nick. "Can we get power
in here?"

Beth took the more civilized route through the turnstiles.
"You think there's gonna be power? After all these years?"

Jack couldn't see much of anything. Anemic light filtered

through filthy glass that lined a raised middle section of the
roof, but it was still pretty murky in there. He could make out
the doubly dark depression of the Olympic-sized pool, and a
few things covered in canvas against the walls on either side.

Nick came in, working his phone.

"No calls," Beth reminded him.

"Chill, sister." He held up his glowing phone. "Just making
light of the situation." He thumbed an icon and the LED flashlight kicked in. Nick strolled around, playing the light across
the walls. "You seeing all this cabling? Industrial. Well hel-*lo*."
Nick's phone lit up a large yellow metal prism, about eight feet
high and maybe fifteen long. Stacked next to it were four forty-
four-gallon drums, one of them fitted with a worn metal hand
pump.

Jack took a closer look. "What is that?"

"Generator," Beth said, her own phone-light up and probing.
"Diesel, judging by the drums."

"This thing's hefty," Nick observed. "The enclosure keeps
it quiet. You were saying something about your brother having
a machine?"

Jack glanced at Beth. She swung her light down to the base
of the generator, followed the mass of cabling across the floor
to where it dropped down into the dry pool. Jack and Nick followed suit. As one, the three pools of light tracked the path of
the insulated lines across mold-encrusted tiles, over workstations set up on folding tables, to the textured steel of an
access ramp, to the massive circular construction that dominated the deep end.

Silence, until Nick said what nobody was thinking: "Your
brother found a fuckin' *UFO*?"

Beth snorted.

"No, Nick, that's crazy." Jack jumped into the pool. "It's a
time machine."

"We gotta get the lights on," Beth said. "Nick, you seem to know something about this. Can you get the generator to run?"

"Time machine?"

"Nick?"

"Uh . . . yeah, sure, sure."

Jack was exploring the benighted guts of the swimming pool, scanning the contents of various workstations that Will had set up. "Computers, diagnostic equipment. A lot of this is stuff I remember from when I was a kid. He had all this set up in the barn. Except the laptops, those are new."

Nick called out. "Hey guys?" The generator thudded to life. "I think someone's been here."

Beth checked the drums against the wall, near the generator housing. "Jerry cans here. Not as dusty as the forty-fours. Nick might be right."

Nick found the breaker box, flipped it, and long racks of fluorescent overheads sputtered and snapped discordantly, laying Will's laboratory bare.

Hunkered in the deep end of the swimming pool, taking up the whole space, was a kit-bashed-looking version of the machine he had seen in the university lab. Ring corridor, airlock, and at the center of it a geometric sphere connected to the rest of it by knots of heavy gauge cabling. Monarch's project was neat and clean and tooled. This thing looked like it could have been powered by an old Buick. It was scrap metal and solder, with occasional touches of tungsten and titanium where it counted; around the core, for instance.

By the ramp was an old laptop on a burnished trolley. The laptop was open, a fluorescent green flash drive jutting from a side connector. Taped to the top of the screen was a note in Will's handwriting. It read: Message for September on flash drive.

Jack pressed the laptop's power stud. The computer pieced

its thoughts together and booted the OS. "You think he wanted someone to find this?"

Beth dropped into the pool, checked the laptop. "So he and someone else used this place as a monthly drop point, a way to stay in touch off the grid. September was the last one. I wonder what year."

Jack checked the flash drive's directory. Just one video file. "Let's see who he's talking to."

His finger hovered above the mouse button.

"Jack? You okay?"

This might be the last time Jack heard his brother's voice say something new. The last time he would see his brother alive.

He clicked the file. The player popped open. The view seesawed as Will got the angle right.

"July fourth," Will said. "2010." He had recorded the message here, on this laptop. The background was the workstations, the shallow end of the dry pool, the swinging exit doors. "September, I hope you receive this."

A chill in his chest. "September's a—"

"—person," Beth concluded.

The video continued. "I . . . I've come back here because I'm left no choice. It's happened. The Countermeasure is—was—finished, completed. Ready to use. I went to my workshop by the docks. It's a disaster. The Countermeasure, it's gone. Taken. I'm hoping to God you have it, because . . . whoever took it . . . " Will shuddered, both hands now gripping his head. "The workshop was destroyed. Utterly destroyed. I need to know for sure. If what you said is true then someday our lives may depend on my knowing the truth about what has happened. Contact me. Find me. Please."

The video ended. Jack closed the laptop. "Countermeasure?"

"I don't know."

"I think you do."

"I don't!"

Nick was watching from the far end of the hall, wondering why Mom and Dad were fighting.

Jack let it go. "I say we get this thing fired up."

Beth wasn't convinced. "Safe cracking I can wing my way through, but kick-starting a time machine is one of the few things not covered on the Internet."

"Paul walked me through it. I think I can do it again. How different can it be?"

"That's not my concern. My concern is that this is a *time machine*, Jack. As a student of popular culture, I have no desire to go the full Bradbury."

"Think about it: we fire this up, we go back to *before* the university incident. We get in there, we *stop it*, and then this never happens."

Beth shook her head. "I know you know that's not possible."

"Of course it's possible! We have a—"

Her hands came up, T for time-out. "Stop. It isn't about going back earlier. It's about causality. We are here having this conversation *because* the university happened. If we could go back and prevent the university event from happening—and we can't—then causality would fall apart."

Jack's expression was stage-one grief. She felt like she'd kicked a dog. "We go back, Jack. Of that I'm certain. But it doesn't play out the way you'd like."

"You want to explain that?"

"We're in your brother's hidden lab. He left a message for someone he's collaborated with about something called a 'Countermeasure'—a measure that counters. The only time-machine-related thing that needs countering right now is the Fracture. He just said that the Countermeasure was taken on

July 4, 2010. It sounds to me like there's a chance that we're the ones who took it. Maybe that's what we do. Take it, bring it back to our time, and fix the Fracture."

"And you just pieced that all together."

"It's a theory."

"And you think I didn't notice who that message was addressed to? September?"

Beth's heart sank.

" 'Go Team Outland'? Skinny weirdo with a—"

"With a sniper rifle, I get it."

"You want to tell me what's really going on here? Zed?"

"I honestly don't know if Will's message was meant for me, Jack. I don't know if 'September' is a name I give him at some point. That's the truth. I'm more interested in the date of that recording. You remember July 4, 2010?"

How could he forget? Sixteen years ago. Paul, Zed, himself at the Overlook. "Aberfoyle."

"Coinkydink, you think?"

"Coincidence that you disappeared the same day the Countermeasure did?"

"Now wait a minute, that's not—"

"It's not what? Paul and I got woken up at four A.M. by three goons who then decided not to kill us because *you* called their boss. They drive us across town and you pull that magic trick on top of the Overlook. Will—who was being held at *gunpoint across town*—is suddenly released without question, and later that day his workshop is trashed. Then both you and the Countermeasure disappear on the same day. But hey, now you're back. And you work for Monarch."

Beth chewed her lip. "That does look bad doesn't it?"

"Yeah, Zed, it looks pretty fuckin' bad."

"What do you need me to do?"

"If you work for the other side then I can't stop you doing

whatever you're going to do next. All I can do is ask you not to do it."

"I've always been on your side, even when I left."

He didn't want his emotions to dictate what he said next, so he looked at the machine.

"Here's what I know, " he said, trying to sound confident. "A machine can only take me back as far as the moment of its activation. This machine was activated long before Monarch's. If it can get me back to just before Monarch's university machine was activated, then I can find Will. I can save him and he can help us fix this." Complex arguments weren't his strength, but he did his best. "Wait, hear me out: just because right now says I didn't go back and save Will doesn't mean I can't make a present in which I did. *Proving* that I can or can't change the past is impossible, right? Because whatever the *present* is it's connected to a past built on a causality that has denied all attempts at changing it. That doesn't mean creating one of those alternates is impossible. It just means *proving* that it's possible is impossible. Right? All I can do is try and see what happens."

Nick piped up from the back of the room: "What?"

"You really are Will's brother," she said. "I had a few conversations like that, back in the day. Maybe that's why I like you so much."

Jack shrugged. "So maybe stick around this time."

"Maybe I will."

Saturday, 8 October 2016. 3:43 P.M. Outside Riverport Swimming Hall. Five hours and thirty-seven minutes later.

Beth snapped off a piece of grass, adjusted her sunglasses. Amber light bounced intensely off the water. "They say the river's coming back to life these days, since the docks shut down." Beneath the bridge, on the other side of the broad support across from the swimming hall, reeds poked out of an artificial peninsula of accumulated trash. The ducks didn't seem to mind.

Jack's eyes were on the one building that dominated Riverport's new skyline: Monarch Tower. "The news is saying the gala's tonight, and it's going to be huge. Their CEO is launching a whole range of promise-the-world bullshit." The building was an asymmetrical black obelisk fifty floors high. The Monarch logo—a fragmented, geometric butterfly—glowed incarnadine against that surface of glossy black glass.

"We call it Mordor," Beth said.

" 'We'?"

"Not everyone in that building is a reptile, Jack. Monarch does well because it delivers on most of its promises. Look around. Remember what Riverport was like when you left? It was devolving into *this*." She jerked a thumb toward the discarded neighborhood around them. "Massachusetts flyover country. Not even a second-rate cousin to Worcester. Six years later and look at it: dog walkers and artisanal coffee and people who couldn't afford a trailer are now bitching about their McMansion not having a Ping-Pong table."

"I'm going to use that machine, Beth. I have to."

"I know."

"I could go back early enough to stop Paul going through, y'know. Stop him turning into whatever he is now."

"You can try, you're right about that."

"You're not going to stop me?"

"I don't need to, Jack."

"You're very relaxed about this."

"Want to see a trick?"

"Sure."

Beth reached into her pocket, pulled out two sets of soft foam earplugs. Handed one to Jack and put hers in. Jack did the same, skeptically. Then Beth pulled out a revolver.

"Uh, you got that where?"

"Nick's glove compartment." She snapped the cylinder open, popped out all six shells, put one back in. The barrel chittered when she spun it, then she snapped it shut.

"I've seen this movie. Knock it off."

Beth pressed the barrel to her head—

"No!"

—and fired.

Click.

Jack made a grab; she sidestepped.

Click.

He grabbed again. She deflected.

"Stop it!"

Click.

"Zed!"

The gun was still to her head. "If I stop, you won't get it."

Click.

Jack punched her in the face. Her head jerked back. The gun discharged, the bullet flying at a forty-five-degree angle past her head. It ate a piece of brickwork with a short, sharp shriek.

"Knock it off!" he yelled, uselessly, having gone sheet white. "Fuck. I'm sorry. Fuck. Are you . . . you were . . . "

She looked him in the eye, pissed off, jammed the barrel to her temple, and pulled.

Click.

When she took it away there was a circular brand where the muzzle had kissed her. Then she threw it away. "I can't die," she said, yanking the plugs out of her ears. "I can't die because when I was eight years old I met my older self. I can't die because I haven't done that yet, I haven't gone back and met my younger self, you understand? I've always done whatever I've wanted, knowing that at worst I'm looking at a hospital stay. Parkour, martial arts, hang gliding, skydiving, bungee jumping, hitchhiking, roof surfing, hanging out with pirates and reprobates, staying up too late, not looking before I cross the street, everything that just went down at your old house . . . free pass. Makes me a very, very good operative. Nobody gets to kill me, nobody gets to take me down. The laws of causality won't permit it." She pointed back toward the swimming hall. "I go through that machine? Meet myself? I'm done. All bets are off. After that I could develop an allergy to fabric softener and drop dead. Choke on a fucking kiwi." The adrenaline was washing out of her, bumming her out. She leaned heavily against the brickwork. "You wanted to know how I pulled off that magic trick on Bannerman's Overlook? It has something to do with that. Same reason I'm not dead on the ground right now with Nick's gun in my hand." She stared at the reeds, tossed the plugs into them along with all the other trash.

Jack had taken his out, was staring at her. "You could have just *fucking said so*."

"It wouldn't have sunk in. You'll come to rely on me being capable, but what if I go through that machine, meet myself, and from then on I'm second-guessing every move I make? You need to step up. No matter what it costs. If we fail, everything dies."

"And not meeting your younger self isn't an option. Right."

"Right. If I don't then I'm not here, we're not talking, and nobody is trying to stop Monarch. If my older self doesn't spirit my younger self away to a string of West Coast and South American training camps I don't become me and there's nobody here to save the day. But it's not just me. You need to do the right thing, even if that means abandoning your brother, killing your friend, anything at all that means we succeed. Be prepared to do things you never thought you'd have to, because the alternative is so much worse."

"Paul said something similar."

"We're both right, but he's going about it the wrong way. That's all I know." She'd said her piece. Done. "So the mission is this: we go back, we find the Countermeasure, find out what it does, and then—most likely—we get it back here. That done, we fix the Fracture and save the world."

"Beth."

"Yes, Jack."

"We don't know what the Countermeasure is, or even what it looks like."

"No. But we know who had it last, and where. The rest we improvise."

Saturday, 8 October 2016. 4:37 P.M. Riverport Swimming Hall.

Nick patched up the coffee maker, found a few plastic cups in the cafe overlooking the pool, and made a passable espresso with what was left of his pods. The three of them sat on camp chairs in the pool, next to Will's workstations. The sunlight through the filthy vertical skylights was blazing amber as it approached sunset.

"What do you remember about 2010?" Beth asked.

Nick shrugged. "Best of times, worst of times. Played center position on the ice and everyone knew my name. My face was on coffee mugs. I had my college ride, and then I blew it. You?"

Jack shrugged, sipped his coffee. "Spent the first six months getting sick of my brother, the last six months looking for her." He jerked a thumb at Beth.

"What about you, Beth?"

"First six months hanging out with this guy, last six months in a compound in Arizona. Ran a lot."

"What kind of compound? Like—"

"Just a bunch of guys waiting for the end of the world. Ex-special forces. Thought they'd seen the writing on the wall and made a few decisions. I was just there to learn."

"Guns and stuff?"

"Mainly cognitive, mental, and physical. Resolve. Team-work. Judgment and adaptability. Discipline. Stress control. Multitasking." She finished her coffee, surveyed Will's battered old machine.

"So you're really doing this," Nick said.

Beth stood. Jack took her by the arm. "If we do this we're only going back six years. That's more than fifteen years *after* you met yourself. You don't need to come along. Stay here. If I don't come back—"

"I've made my peace. Don't psych me out now, Jack, okay? Let's do this."

Her eyes were sharp and her voice certain. Jack let it go, but he didn't like it.

Jack went to refamiliarize himself with the instrumentation—Will's device being far more primitive than Monarch's. Beth didn't follow. She walked up the ramp.

"Paul said something similar." That's what Jack had said to Beth earlier. She stood at the machine's airlock, palm against the hand-riveted metal frame. Paul had entered Monarch's machine and been reborn as something altogether different. Beth was on the same path. Both of them were attempting to save the world, in their own way; both of them thought they were right; both of them knew the past couldn't be changed, were dedicated to their cause and, she knew, both of them would be reshaped by traveling through these machines.

The machine shouldn't have smelled like anything more than age and industrial grease, but not so. It had a scent of its own, the lingering, meaty heaviness of . . .

"Death."

She stepped inside the airlock, a heavy, ten-foot square iron chamber reminiscent of something submersible. It was clear just how heavily Monarch had based their design on Will's work—it was functionally identical: clockwise for future travel, counter-clockwise for past. Unlike the Monarch machine, this corridor was rigid, not self-assembling, and midnight dark in both directions. The stink grew more intense as she stood in the chamber.

She exited.

"I think something might have died in there," she called out, hoping for an obvious answer.

Jack was moving from console to console. "Will wasted a lot of money on that security system if a raccoon can get in here. It's just old. All right Nick, can you get us some juice?"

Jack's reasoning didn't make her feel any better. She glanced back into that darkened airlock, interior details half-formed in the shadows. Beth suppressed a chill.

Nick redirected power from the gennie. There was a deep *thunk* and the airlock interior illuminated under the power of an old-school filament bulb, which promptly popped. The corridor trembled as behind the scenes the contraption's innards shifted and the core came online. Beth took a few careful steps backward down the ramp.

The vibration joined forces with a secondary instability, their crashing and separating rhythms beginning to shake components loose from the Promenade. A distortion wave struggled into existence around the corridor-ring but was failing to become substantial.

The shaking and thrashing built in strength as systems

beneath the machine began to emit desperate, high-pitched alarms. This wasn't working.

"Goddamn it, no. Nick! Reset the power!" Wheeling away from the destination console, Jack moved to reboot the core when Beth got in his way.

"No."

"What do you mean 'no'? I'm trying again."

"The hell you are. Clearly something is wrong with this thing, and none of us have any idea what it is. If you damage it, we're boned."

"We can't stop trying. Will's notes are all over this place. Maybe we can—"

"We'd have as much luck trying to repair the Large Hadron Collider." She sighed. "And I've seen your brother's hand-writing. We need an expert. Fortunately, I know where to get one. Dr. Sofia Amaral. Head of Monarch's Chronon Research Division and one of the handful of authorities on your brother's research worldwide. One of the few who risked their careers to give Will any credibility at all. She's a believer, and she built the Monarch machine. Well, she and Dr. Kim."

"Which means she works in the Tower."

"Works there, lives there, almost never leaves there. She's one of their highest value assets."

"What about this Dr. Kim?"

"Dead," Beth said. "Car accident. So they say. Sofia is pretty much it. Every tech-head under her is working in compartmen-talized divisions on a need-to-know."

"What about the people working with Paul at the university?"

"There were a few people who had an operational under-standing that we might have been able to exploit."

" 'Were'?"

"I kept tabs on them in case they became useful, but three weeks ago they vanished. One from the university and three

from the chronon division. Which leaves Sofia, and probably
Paul, and it's not like you can invite Paul over for beers."

"No," Jack agreed. "But he did invite me to the gala."

"When? Before you tried to explode him to death?"

"Even then he seemed pretty certain he wanted me to come
up and check the place out."

"That's as good as giving yourself up. If it's just me I can—"

"Guys," Nick interjected. "Listen, how about we relax tonight, okay? Wait until everyone's good and hungover tomorrow morning, then we just pick her up when she ducks out for
a post-bender hamburger. Yeah?"

Beth shook her head. "If I was Paul in this situation, what
with the university and Jack on the loose and *knowing* Jack as
well as I do? I'd keep her under lock and key, trot her out for
tonight's performance, and then make her vanish till I needed
her again. If we don't grab her tonight we may not get another
chance." This was going to be a hard sell. "My cover is still
good. The only person who ID'd me at the farm was Gibson,
and he was in the house when it blew. I can get inside Monarch Tower, get close to Sofia, and get her out."

"You don't have any kind of powers."

"I can't die. How's that for power?"

Nick blinked. "Excuse me?"

"Sure," Jack retorted, "but you can be *detained*. You can still
fail. You can't get her out of there alone."

"Her offices are on the top level. Just off the top level is a
helipad."

"You can fly?"

"I was told I'd need it. Seriously, Jack, me alone is our best
chance."

He put his hands up, walked away. "Fine. Whatever, Zed.
You're the boss."

Nick and Beth sat in awkward, simmering silence as Jack

climbed out of the pool and left the building. The slam of the security door echoed through every chamber in the place.

"He still wants to save his brother," she said. "Thought he could pass on some message in 2010 that might save Will's life in 2016. He's frustrated, but he'll be okay. Science isn't his thing, really."

Nick nodded. "Yeah, that's gotta be hard for a guy." Twiddled his fingers. "So," Nick said. "You're *Zed*, huh?"

14

The glass wall afforded Paul an angel's view of Riverport. The town was nothing special, but neither had Alamogordo been before Oppenheimer, or Sarajevo before Gavrilo Princip, or, for that matter, Bethlehem if he wanted to be grandiose.

On official blueprints his rooms were listed as office space. When Paul had reason to leave the building he came and went via private helicopter, his existence a company secret.

Paul had never wanted for anything material. Wise investments had furnished his parents with a pleasant home and their son with the freedom to pursue a life of his choosing. The world had always been open to Paul. But it was Riverport, Massachusetts—not the universities of Europe or the Machiavellian war zones of world finance—that had shaped him. This town, of all the places on Earth, had been his crucible. Riverport had birthed him, raised him, changed him. Compressed and bound by fate, it had all happened here.

Urban camouflage fatigues lay pressed and ready, draped across the chair beside him; props to lend authenticity to the press release he was soon to be filming. He had the chair commissioned, carved from a single piece of a *Fitzroya cupressoides* taken from the Chilean rain forest. The tree had been over thirty-six hundred years old when Paul had it felled and turned into something he might sit upon. It was older than the Americas, than Christianity, older even than mathematics.

It was Paul's favorite chair.

Time would end. But, perhaps, by using every part of his wealth, talent, determination, and intellect, he might liberate humanity's fate from the end he had written for it.

"You're doing it again."

If he had died today there would be no one to undo what was coming. He had risked it all to save Jack, for friendship. He could not be so irresponsible again.

"Paul."

Sofia had entered, dressed for the evening in something tight, floor-length, and Italian. Tablet in hand, mind forever on the project.

"I'm sorry, what?"

"Grinding your teeth," Sofia said.

Paul felt something stir in the waters of his body, a pulse of nausea behind his eyes. He braced.

"I could hear them popping in the hallway. You'll need a dentist more than you need me if you don't learn to relaaaaaaaaaa . . . "

Sofia slowed and froze as time hesitated, foreshadowing an incoming stutter. They were becoming more frequent now, that was undeniable. Paul kept his composure, waited for the elongated moment to play out, and snap.

" . . . aaaaax. The ground-floor atrium looks beautiful, and the demonstration space is perfect. Now, there was something you wanted to show me?"

"You are about to woo the world with the wonder of chronon technology, and all of our efforts are about to conjoin. Lifeboat has a fighting chance. You're here with me. That's all I need." She had noticed nothing. That brief stutter was more severe than the last instance. A sizeable one was due.

"Nervous?" he asked.

"Not at all." She moved closer to him. "Once the world sees with their own eyes what we have achieved, how foolish our critics will seem. The reputations of Doctors Joyce and Kim will be restored, the value of Monarch stock will ascend toward Heaven, and I will finally have you to myself. Even if we have to live in the shadows for the rest of our days."

The timing was right. God had nodded his head.

He reached inside his jacket and withdrew a slender sheaf of fire-damaged paper. "But if you could find the time to give an opinion on this, I'd be grateful."

She gave him a curious look, lay her tablet on his ancient chair and took the filthy collection of papers with both hands. Her eyes grew wide. "The Regulator."

"Take your time," he said. "They're only partial, but perhaps you . . ."

"Dr. Kim's notes. Are there more?"

He wanted to tell her: *Kim was a fraud. William Joyce created the Regulator.* But that would be a mistake. If she knew that then she would question other truths, and force herself to analyze William's fractured reasonings and paranoid convictions . . . and he needed her focused; on tonight, and on the research. If anyone could learn something new about the device at the heart of the Tower, it was Sofia. There was no one else.

She fixed him with an expression of such need. "Paul, are there more papers like these?"

He shook his head. "William Joyce stole them during his time with us. Kept them at his house. Those were all I could save."

She seemed to forget him almost immediately, returning to the printouts and diagrams. "I . . . I will need some time."

Then she surprised him by grasping his hand, fixing him again. "I love you. Do you accept that?"

He laid his hand atop hers. "I do."

His heart hurt for her, for his Sofia.

She didn't know, couldn't know, that once the endgame began, she would never see him again.

Saturday, 8 October 2016. 7:58 P.M. Riverport Swimming Hall.

The acoustics in the swimming hall were fantastic.

"Beth! You need to see this!"

Nick was in the dry pool, in one of the castor chairs. The portable TV was on. She came in from a back room, sleeves rolled up. She'd been running maintenance on her gear while she had a moment.

As Beth climbed down the three-step ladder and dropped to the bottom near the deep end, Nick turned up the volume.

". . . *details again: The state's most wanted man, Jack Joyce, was apprehended here, on the sidewalk outside Sullivan's Deli, about a half hour ago. According to witnesses Joyce, age twenty-eight, approached a uniformed patrolman, hands raised. What happened next remains unclear. Shots were fired, and evidence at the scene suggests Joyce was wounded. However we're told he was soon after wrestled to the ground and handcuffed. WSRP-TV understands he was taken to Riverport Police Department where . . .*"

"Turn it off."

Nick clicked the remote.

"I thought he was upstairs."

"He was! He said he was gonna catch a few hours' sleep. I don't get it."

"The cops'll hand him over to Monarch. The idiot thinks once he's inside the building he'll be able to bust out and save the day."

"Too many of them?" Nick asked.

"That and he's not that good, is completely unprepared, has no security clearance, no clue what Sofia Amaral looks like, and no idea what the layout of the building is."

"Ah."

Beth checked her watch. A few hours until the gala kicked off. Guests would be arriving soon.

"Plus they've got the means to suppress chronon levels, which will almost certainly impact his ability to recover from whatever horrible shit they're about to do to him. You need to drive me to Monarch Tower. Right now."

Saturday, 8 October 2016. 8:10 P.M. Floor 49, Monarch Tower. Paul Serene's Quarters.

The axe was about to fall on the only life Paul had known for almost two decades. Gone would be his protection from the unknown. In twenty minutes he would record a statement. When the time was right that statement would be released.

From that moment the world would change forever.

Every day was déjà vu. The closer he got to the end, the more rapidly the unknown gave way to memories of a future he had not yet lived. He expected that, in the days before his death, he would be a man walking through nothing but memory until he found himself enacting the recollection of his own death.

And then there would be nothing.

He glanced behind himself. Sofia, at his desk, the singed remains of William Joyce's research spread across the black glass, going over each page one at a time, dictating notes into her phone in a low murmur.

Footsteps in the hall. The urgency of their beat told Paul there would be no knock at the door.

The door opened. Martin Hatch entered, one hand resting on the brass knob.

"Jack's here," Paul said.

Martin stopped. "He's been transferred from holding, to this building."

"Sofia." Paul took her hand. "I have to go. Would you meet me after? For a toast."

She smiled, nodded assent.

"I'll see you then." He released her hand, swept his uniform from the lacquered arm of thirty-six hundred years of history, and went to meet his future.

Saturday, 8 October 2016. 8:15 P.M. Outside Monarch Tower.

Nick pulled the cab up three blocks from Monarch Tower. Spotlights were on early, panning across the midnight surface. The lights of the forecourt and lobby could be seen from here: limousines and armored town cars, a Monarch Security detail in two-piece formal wear opening doors while scanning sidewalks and streets. Camera flash, camera flash.

"They're bringing him here tonight?" he asked Beth.

"They'll want to get Jack inside a dampening field as fast as possible, before he realizes he's made a mistake and makes a move. This is the best and only location. Okay listen up: Serene will evacuate Dr. Amaral as soon as she makes her presentation.

So I'm going to have to get her out of there via helicopter before she takes the stage. What I need you to do is park close and keep your phone handy. If something goes wrong, you're our backup escape. Got it?"

"I'm going to trust you've at least sketched this plan on a napkin."

"Go Team Outland."

"What?"

Beth got out, shutting the door behind.

Saturday, 8 October 2016. 8:17 P.M. Floor 35, Monarch Tower.

The elevator carriage lowered toward the thirty-fifth floor.

"The studio is set up for you on forty-nine," Martin said. "Adjacent to your quarters. They're ready to go, once we're done with Joyce."

"And the Peace Movement teams?"

"In place, as per your visions. They know what to do, once the stutter hits."

"Good."

"Paul," Martin said. "You and I have worked toward this for half our lives. We're at ten minutes to midnight, and even so I have to ask: is there no alternative to your sacrificing yourself in this way?"

"None," Paul said. "Everything is at risk. Just promise me Sofia will be cared for, after I'm gone. Helicopter and pilot are on standby. Have her out of here and secured off-site as soon as the formalities have ended."

"If you feel it's necessary. We have Joyce."

"And he may at some point use a time machine. Infinite variables. Secure her off-site."

"As you say."

They walked into a plain hallway, glass-walled on one side, strip lighting along floor and ceiling. Armed guards flanked a door on the right at the far end. "I'm doomed, Martin. Always have been. From the moment I stepped into that machine." Paul stopped, glanced at his compatriot. "The stutter's close. Have the Peace teams activate their rigs now. I'll feel better. No mistakes."

Martin's face was somber, almost mournful. "That's it, then."

Paul clasped Martin's arm. "Knowing my fate has been a gift. It has allowed me to make decisions that made Monarch the force for salvation that it is. But that will count for nothing if the company does not emerge heroically from the coming chaos. For that to happen, we must have a villain."

Saturday, 8 October 2016. 8:20 P.M. Outside Monarch Tower.

Red carpet, velvet rope, and camera crews choked the sidewalk outside the Monarch Solutions Visitor Center: the entryway to the Tower's atrium. Security, plainclothes and otherwise, ringed the block. Locals had turned out hoping to get a look at some of those big West Coast names they'd heard were flying in for the bash. The reporter Beth had seen on TV back at the hall was there, noting that Monarch had chosen to go ahead with the gala despite the all-too-recent tragedy at the university, and that Martin Hatch was expected to make a statement.

Beth crossed the street, headed for the western entrance, away from the crowds. A couple of guys were on duty, all groomed, tuxedoed and bored.

"Hey, Davis. You look pretty."

"Hey, Wilder. Still in uniform?"

"They got me upstairs. Bradley Cooper showing up? I heard he was in town."

"Anyone whose manicurist makes more than I do can blow me. You have a good night."

"Roger that." Beth marched between the two guards, toward the security entrance, then turned back. "Hey, Davis. I heard they caught Joyce."

Davis glanced over his shoulder at her. "Gibson's people took custody about an hour ago. Got him on thirty-five. Doesn't look like much of a terrorist, but who does?"

Beth waved herself through security and into the atrium.

Beth entered the lobby from the west. The lobby floor was divided into three sections, from left to right: the main event area, the reception, and the displays. The central south-facing doors led to the security corridor. Through that was the Visitor Center, where guests were now being received. Within minutes guards would open the security doors and let everyone in.

The display area was intended to prime the audience for the main event: lots of information on chronon research, projections for its applications, but nothing too specific. Hatch was saving that for the big reveal. The main event platform was an elevated stage with full lighting rig and Marshall stacks. A two-story-tall videoboard was the backdrop. Light and sound techs were scuttling about, squaring away the final bits of unevenness, getting out of sight, running final checks.

In the wings, out of sight of the main floor, she caught sight of a pilot being assisted into his Juggernaut, arms reaching into the oversized chronon-powered exoskeleton. The pilot angled his legs into the frames of the Juggernaut's legs. Techs consulted with tablets and diagnostics, asked the pilot to run through a few simple routines to confirm the suit was in working order.

The Juggernauts were prototypes, a side project that had been brought under the umbrella of Monarch's Chronon Research Division. The torso was a simple, blind, geometric half shell. Each facet of the trunk had a couple of hi-res optics nested at the center. From inside the pilot navigated through a standard eyes-and-ears headset.

The prototypes were pretty much for show, which is why the rear of the thing was a naked frame and completely exposed. Beth guessed the techs wanted visibility on the innards, and to be able to get a pilot in and out quickly if needed. Nonetheless, it didn't stop them being highly functional. The frame had enough hydraulic power to flip a station wagon, and came armed. A multimissile pod hovered above the thing's headless body on a thin articulated arm, and a light auto-cannon replaced the suit's left fist.

Looked like Hatch planned to go all out with the display.

Mezzanines ribbed one side of the lobby from the second floor right up to forty-eight. Forty-nine and fifty, she knew, were off-limits.

Saturday, 8 October 2016. 8:20 P.M. Floor 35, Monarch Tower.

A guard tapped an access plate. The door to the room that held Jack Joyce slid aside. It was a typical meeting room, save for the four pieces of abstract technology in each corner. It was nothing elaborate, but it didn't need to be. Potted plants and AV cabinets had been moved aside to ensure maximum coverage for the chronon dampeners. The floor-to-ceiling blinds had been lowered.

Paul sensed the room had been nullified before he'd set foot inside; the familiar leadenness palpable even from the hall.

Chronon-1's new senior operative was here, his fist in his palm. Donny took his eyes from the figure handcuffed to the stainless steel designer chair in front of him, nodding an acknowledgment to his employer.

Jack was slumped in the chair, chin on chest, the fabric of his jeans spattered with fresh blood. He was the only thing at the center of the room.

Noting Donny's mood, Paul glanced at Hatch. "No word on Gibson's remains?"

Hatch gave the smallest shake of the head.

Clearly Donny was still processing whatever passed for grief. In Paul's experience this breed of man had long ago replaced all secondary emotions with primary ones. "Donald, is it?"

"Yep."

Paul heard his teeth grind at this dismissive familiarity. Hatch cleared his throat.

Chronon-1 was exceptional only in that its elite members were the first and the only group to have fully passed muster in Hatch's cost-benefit-calibrated viewpoint. Technicians operated in a similarly lightweight fashion, but functioned only as soldiers. C-1 were, to an operative, multifaceted specialists able to adapt, survive, infiltrate, and succeed in almost any environment. Highly trained, highly valuable.

Nonetheless, Paul very much wanted to drive two fingers through the man's clavicle.

Donny noticed. "I mean . . . yes, sir, Consultant."

Martin stepped aside, gesturing with an upturned palm toward the door. "Would you mind stepping outside? We'd like some time with Mr. Joyce."

Donny took a last, longing glance at Jack and exited the room crisply.

Jack turned his head, spat blood onto the carpet. Groaned.

Paul crouched in front of his friend. "Jack."

Jack said "Wait," and slackly spat again. A gobbet of syrupy black adhered a tooth to the fabric of his jeans. "Put that in my pocket?"

Paul sighed, collected the tooth between thumb and forefinger—it might have been a molar—and cleaned it on the arm of his fatigues before zipping it into the pocket of his friend's leather jacket. "I can't debate this further." Paul sat on the carpet in a half lotus. "Martin's mind is very clear—we should kill you. I don't want to, but I know Martin is right. What are we going to do? Tell me."

Jack appeared to be forming a response, and then he blacked out.

"Paul," Martin said, checking his wristwatch. "I have to go. I'm expected downstairs."

"Of course. I'll be watching from my quarters. Let's return here after we have both done what we need to do . . . and come to a decision about Jack." Paul got to his feet, took a last look at his friend, and marched for the door.

Martin did not follow. He remained in the room, bent at the waist now, peering, as if committing Jack's face to memory. Head tilted, like a curious animal.

"Martin."

Martin Hatch straightened, adjusted his jacket, and joined Paul in the corridor.

Saturday, 8 October 2016. 8:27 P.M. Parking garage.

Finding a parking spot on a Saturday afternoon was a bitch, even with the city in shock. Nick supposed some people needed escape, and others wanted to give a Massachusetts fuck you to the group they thought had shot up the university by going out unafraid and spending. Maybe that's why, despite the fear and the anger, there was a block's worth of star spotters pressed to the front of Monarch Tower.

If only they knew that the people they were ogling were the people who had terrorized them. Monarch had made a big deal out of this gala. The publicity promised that tonight would be an unveiling of the future. The new revelation would reinvent society—just as the printing press and the Internet had done in former times—to change life on planet Earth forever.

Big claims from a corporation with form got a lot of interest from people that mattered.

From the third level of the parking building Nick had a good view of the crowd on the street. Every now and then, as a new foreign-made sedan rolled up, the crowd surged forward a little and phone cameras flashed. Sometimes people exclaimed and whoever had gotten out would turn and smile and wave. Nick couldn't make out anyone down there. He supposed he could have checked the live coverage on his phone, but he was down to 25 percent. Couldn't risk a dead phone in case Beth called.

Then someone turned up whom Nick did recognize, though not straightaway. The man didn't step out of a polished Mercedes. His arrival started as a disturbance in the crowd on the other side of the street. First a few turned heads, then exclamations, and then space opened up as this person moved through the crowd. From above it was like watching a shark glide through a shoal of fish.

The last time Nick had seen this man he had been walking across the Monarch campus—the only gunman with his smiley mask off, like he didn't care—shooting people. The others were rounding people up, herding them together, but that guy was smiling and shooting anyone who ran.

Randall Gibson looked like hell. If people weren't looking

at the Tower they were looking at Gibson's ruined clothes, his bleeding arms, his fucked-up face. Randall Gibson looked like every inch a man who had somehow survived an exploding building.

He hurt, that was clear. He was favoring one leg and the set of his jaw said he was gritting his teeth as much out of pain as fury. His eyes were set dead ahead as he moved for the cross-walk. When he reached the traffic lights he tapped the Walk button, and waited.

Under the blood and dirt Nick could tell there'd been some real damage done there.

The light turned green. Gibson crossed the road, shouldered through the crowd, and made for the western entrance to Monarch Tower.

Nick and Beth had talked, back at the pool. She'd told him about Gibson, about how he had been inside Jack's place when it blew.

She said he had identified her. Knew she worked for Monarch.

Down there, that was a man looking for blood.

He'd come looking for her.

Nick checked his phone. "I should text her. I'll text her."

Then he stopped. He didn't have her number. He didn't have her goddamned number.

Saturday, 8 October 2016. 8:27 P.M. Ground-Floor Atrium, Monarch Tower.

Jack was on floor thirty-five. Martin Hatch's office and heli-pad were on fifty. There were a couple of other pads to choose from, but a bird on fifty could be guaranteed. Beth hadn't lied to Davis: her unit was meant to be part of the security on the mezzanines, but she was early. That gave her time to roam before anyone wised up to what she was doing.

Door security announced they were opening up the atrium. The attendants in the middle third of the atrium collected their trays from the temporary bar, adjusted their smiles, and got into position.

There were two elevator bays on either side of the bar, which had temporarily replaced the receptionist station. The bays were three-sided glass tubes built into the glossy black wall, door in the middle plane. That's when she saw seven of the eight remaining members of Chronon-1 hanging out on floor five, leaning on the rail, looking down on all the fuss. Beth could imagine Irene wanting to spit on heads.

C-1's attention swiveled to their right as Donny stormed out of an elevator. The conversation was animated, heated. There was excitement, and then they all headed for the elevators. Beth jogged to the opposite bay, heading up as they headed down.

Saturday, 8 October 2016. 8:39 P.M. Outside Monarch Tower.

Nick had only ever had two jobs: ushering at a Cineplex and driving a cab. With both these jobs each night ended with wiping down seats and collecting lost property.

The trunk of the cab looked like it had been stocked by raccoons. Underwear, shoes, wallets, ID, false teeth, burner phones, cheap jewelry, medical results, toys, glasses, handbags, and a laptop. There were also two full suits, still in dry cleaner's plastic.

The first one floated on him. The second one, while not perfect, was passable.

Two minutes later he'd changed out of his jeans and hoodie and was failing to complete a tie. Fuck it.

He did his hair in the rearview mirror, then rummaged in the driver's side footwell. He found a red plastic traveler cup. In the glove compartment was a small bottle of bourbon and a discarded pack of cigarettes. Nick poured a couple of fingers into the cup, stuck an unlit smoke between his teeth, locked the cab, grabbed the coat from the roof of the cab, and got down to street level as quickly as he could.

People were still arriving and the crowd was still straining for a look. Guards by the rope were yessing and no-ing to randoms, making sure they had invites. Nick had to go through the main entrance. The guards on the western entrance weren't distracted enough. He insinuated himself into the crowd, jacket off, cup in hand, keeping it steady as he could within the press of backs and shoulders.

His eyes were on the guards, looking for the one who was busiest. Heavyset dude, shades, and an ear mic, fending off a fifty-something blonde who felt she had a right to be in there.

"No invite, no entry."

"What's your name?"

"My security number is . . ."

A dance as old as time.

Nick used a few bodies to stay on the guard's blind side, and then, as though this had only just occurred to him, asked, "Oh, hey buddy. Sorry to interrupt." Nick held up the cup. "I'm on break. Is it cool if I take this outside?"

The guard held a hand up to the woman, silencing her for a second. To Nick: "Say what?"

Nick took the cigarette out of his mouth. "I said I'm on break. Ten minutes. Is it cool if I take this outside?"

"You drinkin'?"

"Steve said it was cool. We've been in there all day."

"Get the f— 'scuse me, ma'am." More civil. "Get back inside. And put your jacket back on."

"But—"

"Before I report you."

Nick sighed, saluted, and stepped over the rope.

Saturday, 8 October 2016. 8:53 P.M. Outside Monarch Tower.

It was about to get ugly for Davis and his partner when Gibson's squad came out of the security door behind them. Donny shouldered Davis out of the way as Chronon-1 pulled up before the scarred, fucked-up wreck of their former senior operative.

"Boss?"

Gibson's left eye was swollen and fused shut. Hair had been seared away in patches. He was missing a tooth. His skin and fatigues were black with impacted soot, ash, and blood, slashed along the arms and knees. Keeping the weight off his left leg gave him the posture of something that had crawled out of a crater.

"Hey, Donny. You want to get these nun fuckers away from me?"

"Sure, boss."

Davis and his partner backed off, herded away by bloodless glances from Voss and Irene.

"Seen Beth Wilder around?"

"The washout? Her unit's doing internal for sure. Why?"

"Get me inside."

"Sure thing. Voss, scramble a medic."

"Fuck that. Get me inside. Davis, you say nothing. Donny: let's go."

Saturday, 8 October 2016. 9:00 P.M. Monarch Tower. Atrium.

The two-story videoboard faded out from images of foreign lands, laboratories, workers, children, and innovations, cross-faded to the company logo, the word MONARCH fading in peacefully atop it.

Martin Hatch took the stage. The crowd applauded.

"Invited guests, thank you for being with us here this evening. You all know me. I'm Martin Hatch, CEO of Monarch Solutions. I know a few of you have noticed the four strange-looking objects arrayed about us."

Hatch pointed to the four stutter-field pylons delineating the western third of the atrium, bracketing the audience. Chrome and hazard-striped, each had a small chronon battery affixed to its base. Each one was manned by a chronon technician.

"I overheard my good friend Harold Ashworth, CEO of Exxa, wonder to his lovely wife if perhaps Monarch's big announcement would be that we are branching out into the production of avant-garde furniture."

The crowd laughed.

"No, Howard, we are not."

A few chuckles.

"For tonight's demonstration to truly impress I request that you all ensure you are within the yellow border marked out on the floor for you."

Beth double-checked her notebook, filled with dates and times and scraps of future information. Beth's future self had written in that notebook that the Monarch gala was about to get hit with a stutter.

The elevator came to a stop. Getting off at thirty-five she turned on her rescue rig. Her skin tingled, sharp, and subsided.

Monarch Tower was a hell of an operation. Within five years it'd be a fully functioning arcology: a city within a building within Riverport. Entirely self-sufficient: apartments, a small school, gardens, water, recycling—the lot. The perfect place to hide out come the end of time.

Assuming Project Lifeboat was on its feet by then. Still only in the blueprint phase Horatio hadn't been able to fathom how they'd get chronon efficiency to the required levels in time. Despite the size of the company, Monarch didn't have the capital, resources, or personnel to pull it off within five years. Lifeboat didn't just want to shield the Tower; it required operatives that could survive for months in the wild. The energy reserves required to do that were monstrous. Unthinkable.

Her ear mic patched her into Monarch comms. A couple of people in her unit were already on duty, lower down, updating over Monarch frequencies. Questions were asked about the fate of Jack Joyce. Through this Beth knew exactly where they were keeping him.

Beth carded herself through the first security door and into the warren of corridors on thirty-five. She accepted that her progress would be tracked, questions would be asked, but it didn't matter. By the time tonight was over Monarch would know she had given notice. Abducting their key scientist would make that pretty clear. She would find Jack, free him, and incorporate him into the plan. Assuming the idiot was still breathing.

She rounded the corner, was heading for the room where Jack was being held when the first pre-stutter hit. It was unexpected but she seized the opportunity, broke into a run, double-pumped her left hand to get the chronon-flow going, got between the two frozen guards at the end of the hall, and used her live left hand to swing the time-locked door open.

She skidded to a halt, stopping in time to avoid crossing into the stutter field which would have nullified her rescue rig and rendered her immobile.

Jack was in his chair, frozen.

Beth closed the door behind her. The stutter broke.

"What'd you say?" one guard said.

"I didn't say anything," replied the other.

Jack was reanimated. Beth held a finger to her lips. Quietly as she could she deactivated the stutter pylons.

"Hey," he whispered.

She unfolded her knife, snipped the zip ties holding him to the chair, looked him in the eye, and explained in detail how she intended to hammer his balls flat on a stump.

The lights dimmed by half and Hatch waited as the music swelled. The videoboard lit up with an on-message color-and-movement mélange: orchestral segueing to dubstep as family-values imagery cut to forest-fringed highways, gear-shifting vehicles, rapelling troopers. Sweat, strain, sharp eyes, and bared teeth, all coming to an explosive halt on the Monarch logo.

In exchange for six figures a Mayfair agency had provided forty-five seconds of idiocy.

Hatch waited respectfully as the applause faded.

"Friends," he said. "Let's talk about death."

The videoboard behind him flared white: a scene in a hospital ward. A mourning family gathers at the bedside of a fading grandmother.

"No matter your demographic," Hatch said. "The number one killer is time."

The scene cross-faded to a desert battlefield, a lieutenant calling for backup, and a pall of orange dust providing fantastic depth of field.

"At Monarch Solutions we have elected to remove time from death's equation."

Back in the hospital now. The lieutenant lay on a gurney. Recognizing the pylons that surround the fallen lieutenant's bed, the crowd aahed, intrigued.

"Imagine if we could pause time for the terminally ill. Imagine a mortally wounded soldier, or a gravely ill loved one, suspended perfectly for as long as is needed, at the flick of a switch."

Hatch snapped his fingers, and a gently luminous canopy enveloped the bedridden lieutenant onscreen.

"Chronon-stasis technology keeps the patient safe within a moment that will continue to self-divide for as long as a medical technician deems it necessary. The person's condition will never deteriorate, and they will never age. If need be they can remain in that localized zero state for years, even decades, until a cure for their condition, or a donor organ, is found or can be grown."

The crowd applauded.

"But there are so many more applications."

Spotlights sprang to life, swept to darkened corners at the back of the stage. Exclamations from the audience as two Juggernauts cycled to life, stood erect, and strode to the front of the stage—laser targeters panning across the assembled crowd.

In the wings, Sofia Amaral tapped her foot and checked her watch. Her cue was coming up, but her mind was elsewhere. She couldn't stop thinking about the notes Paul had salvaged from the Joyce house: Dr. Kim's plans for the Regulator.

How had Joyce purloined those documents? Joyce and Kim had been colleagues at one point, years ago, that much she knew. William Joyce must have acquired the documents during his time as a consultant on Project Promenade, and then studied Kim's designs in secret. What scraps that remained were littered with parenthetical notes and observations. Had Joyce been an early collaborator on the Regulator project? Had he felt sidelined? Had there been bad blood between the two?

No matter now. Her crucial finding was this: it was now clear that the device was *not* intended to function as a power source, but had been designed to release its massive charge in one focused burst. But why? Why had Kim built such a device? And why his charade of attempting to plumb the device's secrets, as though its creation had been little more than a quirk of fate?

She shook her head. She hadn't been trusted with the details. There was more going on and clearly it had been deemed above her security level. The man she loved had been keeping her ignorant; her expertise and professionalism had not been trusted. That hurt her, deeply.

This had driven her to reassess her own calculations, and try as she might she still could find no error of process, calculation, or reasoning. The end of time *was* approaching. It *was* going to hit, and far sooner than Paul believed. She had to speak to him. He may not have trusted her with the true nature of the Regulator project or her role in it, but Sofia's pride demanded that Paul hear her on this. The life of the universe itself was at stake.

"Handing yourself in was a dick move, Jack."

Jack kept his voice low. "I got arrested so you wouldn't have to risk yourself." He stood, rubbing his wrists.

"You can worry once I go back and meet my younger self.

Until then I'm protected by a chain of causality connected to a collapsed waveform. Take this." She handed him her gun.

"What about you?"

"I'll grab one when the next ministutter rolls in. I need you to tell me when you sense one about to hit. We use those to leapfrog from concealment to concealment until we get to the ground floor. Once the main stutter lands, we take Sofia, get to the roof, steal Paul's helicopter. With luck we can be back at the pool before the stutter breaks."

"I overheard Paul saying he was watching the gala from upstairs. Security's supertight up there."

"Okay, fine. I've got Nick outside on standby. We can book it out the western exit, take our chances on the road."

The screen behind Hatch shifted to a collage of ten faces: the ten students killed early that morning at Riverport University. Standing at the back, watching, Nick recognized two people he had tried to save: a man and a woman, gunned down on Founders' Walk as they ran for his cab.

They faded out as Martin Hatch, the man who had ordered them killed, concluded his homily.

Nick kept his fists jammed in the pockets of his borrowed suit, sweating.

"Friends, here is where I think chronon technology shows its worth. Take a scene like the one that terrorized this town this morning, then bracket the location with four high-strength zero-state pylons. Everyone within that bracket freezes. Time stops."

Hatch stood aside, swept an arm toward a person standing at the back of the stage.

"Our chronon Technician." A jumpsuited Monarch employee stepped forward. Running the zip down her front she revealed the lightweight chrome-and-wire frame that followed the lines of her torso and limbs. "Our lightweight model, built for the basics. Operative Wilson here is wearing a 'rescue rig.' This enables her to move freely in a zero state and to release items and people from that state at will. Next . . ."

A larger figure strode in from stage left, carrying an assault rifle. In profile he was a man in modern white armor fitted with a black gas mask. On his back was a broad dome, studded with what looked like soda-can-sized fuses. Each of the fuses glowed with a pulsing amber heat. The figure pivoted and walked downstage, into the light.

"Our Striker. Fully mobile within a zero state, he is armored for combat operations. As an added extra he is also able to manipulate his relationship to his personal Meyer-Joyce envelope, folding deeper into the stutter, briefly inhabiting a smaller subdividing moment within a larger one—but with no loss of mobility. What this means," Hatch said, "is that within a zero state the Striker has the capacity for superspeed, crossing short distances in quick bursts. Useful for rapid response and flanking maneuvers."

Hatch spread his arms and two spots found the oversized, seemingly headless, blank-surfaced exoskeletons stationed at either end of the stage.

"And finally, our large friends: the Juggernauts."

The crowd went nuts. They couldn't get enough of the big guys.

"Gentlemen, if you'd be kind enough." Hatch made circling motions with both hands.

The Juggernauts rotated in an ungainly fashion, displaying their open backs. There was a *clack* and a soft whine as the two pilots released from their harnesses and stepped free.

"We've left off the back half of the Juggernauts' signature clamshell design to give you a better look at how these fellows work on the inside."

The stuff they were showing off was pure eye candy. Nick wanted to see more of the show, especially all the detail on the Juggernaut prototypes, but he couldn't. He had to find Beth, and a nearby elevator pinged open. As its passengers exited Nick stepped inside.

An infoscreen opened up on one glass wall. "Welcome, visitor. How can I help you?"

"Uh . . ."

Nick realized he had no idea where to go, and also that most of the building was locked off without a security pass.

Out of nowhere a rush of bodies and hardware filled the elevator carriage: big dudes and one serious-looking woman in Monarch fatigues, all packing sidearms.

"Floor thirty-five," one of them said.

Someone swiped a card and hit the button.

The last one in was Randall Gibson.

Nick's spine snapped rigid. He didn't move, pretending to be deeply interested in the wall map.

"Nobody touches her," Gibson said, low. "We find her, we do her, we report it."

Busted, messed-up Gibson. He filled the elevator with the thick smell of old sweat and smoke. One of his eyes was actually fused shut.

Any one of these people could kill Nick as easy as turning off a TV. The elevator began to rise. Nick watched the atrium fall away beneath him.

"How'd you make it, boss? I heard—"

"Triangle of life," Gibson muttered. "I hit the dirt alongside a couch. Beams and shit hit the couch, left me a tight shelter next to it. Debris hit the shelter, left me in a pocket." He coughed. Sounded wet. "I'm good."

"Rigs on," one of them said. "Stutters."

Thirty seconds later the elevator shushed to a stop on thirty-five, pulling level with its glass-walled neighbor—as two people filed into it.

Nick looked through the glass walls that separated the two elevators and instantly recognized the two people inside the one opposite.

Jack and Beth.

"Boss!"

Beth's head snapped toward them, recognized Gibson's squad—then clocked Nick.

Nick shook his head tightly, terrified. *Do not acknowledge me in this elevator full of killers.*

Nick's elevator emptied in a heartbeat as the doors to Beth and Jack's hissed shut. She glared at him, mouthed *What the fuck?*

And then they descended.

"Senior Operative Gibson, sir!" Two Monarch regulars came to a halt before the squad. "Sir, Jack Joyce . . . he's . . ."

Nick stepped out of the elevator just as Gibson's squad rushed back in to pursue Jack and Beth. The elevator chimed shut and departed.

The two Monarch guards, looking as though their careers were flashing before their eyes, disappeared through the security door they'd appeared from, barking into ear mics.

"Right," Nick mumbled, trapped. "Now what?"

Martin Hatch accepted the applause. "Now, friends, if you would be kind enough to stay within the yellow zone we would like to conclude with a practical demonstration of this world-changing technology. We'll need all of you to space out evenly, and marks have been provided."

People shuffled, each choosing a mark for themselves, taking position.

Hatch got a thumbs-up from the four chronon techs.

"Three. Two. One." Hatch snapped his fingers.

The techs activated the pylons, the chronon levels within that sectioned-off piece of the M-J field dropped, and the entire crowd froze.

The operatives onstage got into new positions. The pylons shut off, the crowd reanimated, exclaimed as the operatives "teleported" before them, and burst into applause.

Hatch snapped his fingers. The crowd froze. The operatives rearranged. The pylons shut off. The crowd came to life. Their laughter and applause turned to an ecstatic roar.

Repeat.

Disbelief. Delirium. Dollar signs.

From the audience's perspective each time Hatch clicked his fingers everything changed in a moment.

Hatch's smile was wide, but there was no joy in his eyes.

He clicked again.

Paul, in his quarters on the forty-ninth floor, sipped a small glass of champagne, dressed for operations in underarmor and urban camouflage.

Martin's demonstration was playing out on a closed-circuit feed displayed on a laptop. It all seemed to be going well.

Then the call came in over a Monarch secure channel: Jack was loose.

Paul immediately switched the feed to elevator cams—and

there was Jack in the company of a Monarch employee, headed for the ground floor. For Martin's demonstration.

Sofia. She was down there with Martin, waiting to give her presentation.

The elevator identified the employee accompanying Jack as Beth Wilder. Paul called up her file. Her face looked back at him, and he felt, viscerally, a lost part of his own story click into place. "I know you. Beth."

He tapped the desk, contacted the on-duty security chief. The voice on the end of the phone demanded identification.

Paul Serene had effectively founded Monarch, and yet he'd be stopped at reception if he walked in unaccompanied.

"I'm placing an alert on Beth Wilder, employee mike-romeo-one-zero-one-four with Martin Hatch's authority, code mike-romeo . . ." What was it? What was the blasted number? "One-one-niner-four-golf-sierra. Do you copy?" Choosing one thought above all others hurt *so much*. His hand throbbed. He needed another treatment, and soon.

"Who is this?" the idiot on the line demanded again.

Lifeboat's success required him to be a non-entity, but it never ceased to be an indignity.

"Do you copy?"

A pause on the line. "The code checks out."

"Twenty Technicians, chronon enabled. Ground floor. Extreme prejudice. You will have stutter cover. Double time."

"Whoever this is, we're not gonna need twenty men to stop one girl."

That neatly put-together redhead was a woman Paul had met once, a very long time ago, a long time from now.

"They won't be able to stop her," Paul told the security chief, getting out of his seat. "But they might slow her down."

Cutting the line he ran for the elevator.

The elevator hushed open, parallel to the main stage. The crowd was loving it, freezing and unfreezing. This was entertainment to them, a show, not cutting-edge science that could change the world. The elevators were outside the pylons' bracket and remained unaffected by the demonstration.

"Beth, we've got ten, maybe fifteen seconds before the stutter hits."

The second elevator with Gibson's goons was right behind them.

Beth exited. "Get Sofia. She's Brazilian. Five eight, about a buck twenty. Dark hair, cut in a bob. Carrying a tablet. She'll be backstage. Check the wings. I'll draw them off."

She ducked into the assembly before Jack could protest.

The second elevator opened and Chronon-1 fanned out, by which time Jack had warped toward the cover of side-stage: scaffolding, black cloth drapes, security barricades.

He was over and up the aluminum stairs in a blink, backstage.

The stutter slammed into being, disorienting. The entire world went still.

The area for the demonstration had been boxed out in yellow, with audience members asked to space out evenly. The Monarch performers were getting off the stage and taking up positions next to audience members, intending to wow them once the stutter broke.

Gibson silently signaled his crew to hold up. Hatch was onstage, waiting for the stutter to break before he could wrap up the performance. Gibson didn't want him tipped off that something was up.

"No shooting," Gibson said. "Mr. Hatch needs this to go well."

"She's got a gun, boss. You really want to bring blades to a gunfight?" Irene said.

"She won't shoot. She knows as well as we do: these people are bulletproof while immobile, but once that stutter breaks and the bullets start flying . . . heads pop."

Irene sighed, unclipped her knife.

The elevator came to sudden life, heading back up to retrieve a passenger. Someone upstairs had channeled chronon flow from the Regulator to the elevator's rig—part of the Tower's emergency system. That took authority. The elevator headed back up.

"Emergency system. Someone with clout's coming down." Gibson drew his knife. "Work fast."

From the wings Jack could tell the stage was clear. The operatives were in position in the crowd, ready to surprise a few randomly selected guests by materializing in front of them.

Jack saw Sofia in the wings, frozen in the act of checking her watch.

Folding into a submoment he jetted across the space, unseen, right up next to her.

"All right, Doctor. I'm gonna need you to work with me here." Jack stepped behind her, placed one hand around her waist and one over her mouth—everything about her as hard as stone. "I'm really sorry about this."

With a little concentration he extended his chronon field across her and felt her begin to cohere into the frozen moment.

Sofia came to with a hand over her mouth and freaked out.

"Ssh! I'm not gonna hurt you, but I can't let you go. You gotta listen to me."

That didn't work. She elbowed Jack hard in the ribs, driving one stilettoed heel hard into his foot. Jack bit down on the pain.

"*I'm a friend!*" he hissed. "My name is Jack Joyce. William Joyce was my brother."

Beth moved low through the forest of still bodies, stealing glances toward the stage. Hatch was immobile. She couldn't see Jack. Chronon-1 was entirely focused on her.

"We need you to help us," Jack continued.

Sofia twisted in his grip—"I do not *care*!"—then stopped. It dawned on her that the world about her had stopped moving entirely. The demonstration was to encapsulate the audience— not the entire building.

"You admired Will. Believed in his work. He mentioned you in his notes."

Sofia wasn't listening. She was taking it all in, like a kid in their first snowfall. "Zero state," she breathed. "We exist within a deformation in the Meyer-Joyce field. Yet we see. We hear. We breathe. Move." She wheeled on him, twisting round in his arms. "You must come with me. Paul needs you."

Sofia glanced behind herself, at Hatch, as static as all those gleeful faces before him.

"Paul's mistaken. Will had a Countermeasure, you understand? We can stop the end before it happens."

"Countermeasure," Sofia cut him off. "To repair the fracture in the Meyer-Joyce field. To—"

"To save us," Jack said. "From the end of time."

"*You!*" It was Paul—a portrait of fury at the far side of the stage.

Every chronon operative in the audience turned reflexively—

with no idea what to make of the scene onstage. Performers to soldiers: weapons up.

The jumpsuited Technician barked, *"On your knees!"*

Weapons were pointed at all of them—Paul included.

Paul had no time for them, stalked across the stage toward Jack. *"Get away from her!"*

Jack realized they had no idea who Paul was.

"On your knees!" the Tech shouted. Weapons tensed in all hands. *"Final warning!"*

Gibson risked a glance and saw the morons from the stage show pointing assault weapons at the Consultant.

"Hold fire! Hold fire! Target: male, left! All others high-value friendlies! Strikers, go!"

The two armored Strikers—soda can fuses flaring sun-hot—flashed up from the audience, boiling energy tracing from their back units. Sofia shrieked as they tore past. Jack let go of Sofia and dashed fifteen feet out onto the stage as the Strikers snapped to a halt. A lucky swing saw a rifle butt glance across his forehead.

Paul darted across the stage, driving his shoulder into Jack's back and continuing on his way to stop in front of Sofia.

Jack spun with Paul's passing blow, the pistol slipping from his hand to skid across the stage, his back on fire.

Paul took Sofia's hand. "Come with me."

The Strikers flashed forward, each one taking a lock hold on one of Jack's arms, jetting him across the stage, headfirst, toward a Marshall stack.

Jack warped backward—just a nudge—the reverse momentum swinging the two Strikers into each other's faces. There

was a crack of shattering faceplates and Jack's arms were almost ripped off in the process.

He turned to see Paul spiriting Sofia into the shadows of
the wings.

Beth saw Paul take Sofia through stage right—Beth's left. She
moved fast and low, aiming to circle around the back of the
stage and intercept.

The jumpsuited Technician had her handgun out, while the
Juggernauts awkwardly angled for a shot that wouldn't endan-
ger Hatch—still frozen onstage as the satisfied host. But they
were having trouble navigating through a sea of smiling people
who might as well have been made of concrete.

The Strikers recovered as Jack went for his gun. They split
his focus by zipping left and right. He tracked one and popped
a localized substutter over him. The Striker slowed fraction-
ally, then escaped the field—his mobility rig rendering him
largely immune.

While Jack was diverted, the other Striker flashed in from
behind and smashed his rifle like a club into the back of Jack's
legs. Which was when Jack realized the weapons were
unloaded—show models.

Jack went down hard as the Technician closed in with cuffs.
Jack warped forward, cannonballing her legs out from under
her, rolling into the stutter shield he just dropped as she
snapped a shot off after him.

Okay, her firearm was loaded.

The bullet impacted the shield, caught. Jack stood, his
knees feeling cracked, side by side with unmoving Martin
Hatch.

Jack's energy levels were low, running out of zip. The Strikers didn't seem to be having the same problem.

They were wearing him down.

Beth exited the crowd and looped around the left side of the stage.

Irene was waiting for her. "Hey there, chicken." Knife out, combat-gripped.

There were no innocents behind Irene, so Beth drew her gun.

Irene leaped right, under the stage.

Jack stayed under the shield, played up his difficulty standing, and let them come to him: one Striker to the left and another to the right. The Technician dead ahead with her gun leveled. Two Juggernauts behind, but he had to assume the auto-cannons were for show.

The Strikers communicated something to each other, then one warped in hard, slowing a little as he hit the shield. Enough time for Jack to fold into a submoment, blip backward, grab the Striker's back unit as he passed, and pull. There was an alarming crack of energy, and reflexively Jack blip-kicked the Striker out of the shield where he crashed into the back of his partner. The first detonated almost instantly in a corona of yellow-hot energy, setting off the chronon pack on the second— an eruption that sent him rocketing over the audience, where he exploded and locked. The Technician got caught in that first blast, was thrown backward by the eruption . . . leaving all three actors frozen in a catastrophic ballet, mid-air, as their rigs shorted.

Jack ran out of charge. His shield flickered and vanished.

Beth cornered around the rear of the stage in time to see Paul Serene drag Sofia toward one of the two western elevators. The second elevator opened and twenty heavily armed and rigged goons poured out.

Paul glared at his security and shouted, "*Stop her!*"

Beth dove under the stage as two of them opened fire, three-round bursts chipping craters out of black Italian marble.

"Hey chicken." Irene was back.

The blade came out of nowhere, sliced the top of Beth's right shoulder—a line of white pain dangerously close to her carotid. The space was tight and low under the stage, interlaced with diagonal supports. Irene went for a second strike, Beth reflexively fired—no target, but the sound was enough to make her opponent flinch.

Beth twisted away from Irene's messed-up second strike, aiming her left shoulder toward the floor, firing twice as she went over. But Irene had followed through on the momentum of her aborted strike and used it to roll clear and vanish into the mass of shadow, half-formed shapes, and scaffolding. Beth sent two more shots after her, hoping for the best.

Adrenalized and breathing hard Beth rolled back to her knees, ignoring the blood on her hands and legs and headed for the audience side of the platform. Slipping out from under the black cloth, she kept low and got back among the statue-crowd—equidistant between the two Juggernauts who were now moving into the open space on either side of the stage.

Hatch was still frozen onstage. A Striker was paused behind him, mid-explosion, as was the Technician he had slammed into. Above Beth's head a second Striker was airborne above the first row of the crowd, his back unit rupturing. Jack was on-stage, breathing heavily.

"Jack!"

He saw her. She motioned: *get after Paul,* then ran deeper into the unmoving crowd, firing her pistol twice into the air. Every unit present, save the Juggernauts, went after her like it was their mission.

Jack ran into the wings, headed for the elevators.

Beth bolted through the reception area—open bar, servers, trays of champagne—and beyond that into the far third of the atrium. It was all business here. The area was divided into nine islands, each island showing off a subsidiary or two of Monarch Solutions: Innovations, Industrial, Pharmaceutical, Multimedia, Technology, Business, Energy, Financial, Security, Childcare, Aerospace, Agricultural, Human Resources, Protective Services, Automotive, L&T, Consumer, Construction, Entertainment, and Communications.

Even passing the displays at a run it was easy for Beth to see how Monarch was becoming ubiquitous. Hatch and Serene had a finger in every pie going. Superpowers and foreknowledge went a long way.

Her pursuers entered the reception area as she jagged behind a giant display for a gaming console Monarch Entertainment was releasing next fall. They opened fire on her, rounds fragmenting and sparking off frozen bystanders and objects. Those bullets that sailed past eventually slowed to a halt. When the stutter broke they would continue on their deadly course.

"These people are *investors,* assholes!" she shouted.

Thankfully Hatch's demo had pulled almost every person in the atrium toward it. The display area was mostly people-free and she was running away from bystanders.

Her pursuers weren't listening. She caught glimpses of

twenty Technicians fanning out, Chronon-1 bringing up the rear—monster-faced Gibson super pissed.

Gibson knew what Wilder was up to. She was falling back to the eastern elevator bays, pulling attention from Joyce's pursuit of Mr. Serene and Dr. Amaral.

He rounded on C-1, headed double-time back the way they'd come.

"Top floor. Now."

The reinforcements fired at Beth with little fear of hurting anyone, but Beth's firing line included the demo crowd on the other side of the atrium—directly behind every asshole that was coming after her.

Fuck it. She'd been telling Jack she couldn't die. Time to put her money where her mouth was.

Three five-man squads crept down an aisle a piece while the fourth hung back covering. Beth waited behind the Medical display at the far end, leftmost aisle. In moments fifteen armed men would be in her firing line as they passed the final displays.

She swung out when she heard the nearest squad just around the corner.

The stutter broke.

A Striker in front of the stage arced out over the audience, back unit exploding, before flailing heavily to smash through tables and glassware. Onstage, a Striker detonated as he flew into that nice Technician lady in the jumpsuit. Gunshots rang out simultaneously onstage and beneath it. Reanimated bullets whipped to life in the display section and blew a Monarch GMO display to pieces.

Hatch, however, was gone.

People freaked the fuck out.

Beth shot five goons in the legs and ran for the nearby eastern elevator bays. The middle squad moved to assist their injured comrades while the third and most distant squad opened up, perforating a 3-D-printed concept car as she fled.

Jack felt the stutter quit as his elevator arrived on the fiftieth floor.

The elevator purred: "Good night, Dr. Amaral."

Jack pocketed Sofia's ID. "I've had better."

A security door was pneumatically swinging shut as he exited. A short dash and he was through, the door clicking behind him.

Down a corridor to his left he heard Sofia cry out.

Paul booted through a security door into Martin's thousand-square-foot private garden: an open-air platform, green and pathed, with a bird's-eye view of the city. A series of stone steps led to Martin's office dead ahead. The branching path also led right, toward the chronon operations for the building. When the Tower was designed Martin had been clear: he wanted to be close to the most critical elements of Project Lifeboat.

"Faster," he said. "We've got to make it to the helicopter before—"

His hand tore from Sofia's grasp as her soft flesh turned to stone. The stutter had kicked in again. Sofia stood, static, movement captured in her pose, the expression on her face perplexed and anxious.

Behind her: monsters.

Shifters. The ones from the Joyce farm, the same ones he

always saw. He was sure of that now. Ahead, foremost and advancing, came the Shining Palm.

Jack caught sight of them as Paul open the door to a rooftop garden at the end of a long enameled wood hallway. Jack folded, propelled forward, but not fast enough.

He felt the stutter kick back in, a pulse throughout his entire body.

With a desperate surge he wedged a hand in the door, tore it open, and got through.

The tight, enclosed hallway led to a green expanse open to a night sky, slashed by the slow beams of spotlights positioned on every corner of the Monarch Tower block. A Y-shaped path divided flat green lawn, one path branching left toward the pillared, glass-fronted façade of what had to be Martin Hatch's apartment. The other cut right, toward a doorway in the building proper. Had to be the chronon labs, like Beth said.

The apartment was fronted with a pillared open-air deck. An L-shaped gantry led from that, over a fifty-floor drop, to a suspended helipad where a helicopter waited, lit bright—polished and sharklike. Paul had stopped running, Sofia having deanimated for a second time as she stopped cold and the stutter settled in.

A wall of Shifters stood between himself and Paul. Paul was pinned, terrified. That was the kid he remembered from Bannerman's Overlook.

The phalanx of Shifters recoiled, shrieking with something like rage—or pain?—as Jack had thrown the door open. As if his very appearance had sent a wave of fire rolling through them all.

As one they forgot poor, terrified Paul, and rounded on Jack.

Jack was a closer potential-generator than Paul and, because he was making this up as he went along, generated more Shifter-agonizing variables. He was an excruciating presence to these monsters and, as such, a thing to be destroyed.

The only one who did not turn was Shining Palm.

Sofia remained between Jack and Paul—as potential- and causality-dead as stone. Safe, invisible to the Shifters, and unable to be harmed.

The Shifters roared, fritzing and flashing, and Jack bailed, running hard, back the way he came. They were too close, there were too many, and he had nowhere to lose them.

Paul backed away. Shining Palm hesitated, head whipping from Paul to the pursuing horde and back. With a final glance at its sweating prey the Shining Palm turned and bounded after its hunting kin.

Paul remained, stunned into disbelief by his continued survival. The creature had him right there. Why had it chosen to . . . ?

Run, you idiot.

Paul fled toward the security door, and into the Tower. The chronon research labs would have stutter generators. He would be safe there until the stutter broke. When it was over, when Jack was dead, he would return for Sofia.

Monarch Tower's chronon response had kicked in, channeling particles to the elevators and keeping them active. Beth was grateful for that.

As she stepped out onto floor fifty, an overeager fusillade of automatic gunfire sparked and flashed off the time-locked glass wall opposite the elevator.

"Fight back, bitch!"

Gibson. He'd circled back and cut her off.

Another spray came her way, angled for the door frame. Beth threw her hands up, shielding her face from hot fragment sprays.

She didn't think. Double-pumping her free hand she pushed off against the elevator's wall, and leaped across the space between the elevator and the glass wall in front of her.

Christ, did the high-pitched *vip* of incoming rounds always have to sound so goddamn *happy*? None of them connected. In a single fluid move she hit the carpet, rolled, pressed her free hand to the glass, unlocking it into vulnerability, and put two rounds through it. The wall dropped in a single, sparkling sheet of cubed safety glass and Beth leaped inside, clear of Gibson's line of sight.

Meeting room. Glass wall with door opposite her. Hallway outside—cube farm beyond another glass wall.

Horatio had walked her through this level. Helipad outside Hatch's office. Office on opposite side of garden. Garden was . . . *that way.*

She double-pumped her hands, opened the door, and took off left down the hall.

At the four-way corridor junction fifty feet ahead, Gibson rounded the corner—assault rifle leveled at the hip.

"Hold up, punkin' butter."

One barking shot lanced across the space between them. *Pain.* Beth's legs went out from under her.

She hit the floor, face-first, hard. The pain took her breath away.

"That's more like it."

A piece of her outer left thigh had been blown away. With one hand clamped to the wound she grabbed for her lost weapon.

Gibson opened up. Rounds sparked and fragged inches from her fingers. She whipped her hand back.

"Leave the hand there, darlin'." Gibson walked forward. C-1 brought up the rear—all eight of them. "I'm gonna shoot that fucking thing right off." He spat to the side. "For starters."

"Boss," Donny piped up.

"Not now, Donny."

"Boss."

"I said *not* . . . !" Gibson stopped.

Howls.

"Shit."

Jack Joyce came sprinting around the corner, bringing a shrieking, tumbling wall of clawed, fractured madness with him.

"Shifters!"

Gibson, Donny, and Reeves saw them coming and split back the way they came, to the mezzanine. Irene and Voss jagged opposite, heading deeper into the warren of cubicles—toward the fortified chronon labs behind that.

Mully had been covering the curving wooden hall leading toward Hatch's private garden—and had the most ground to cover to make an escape. Bristol watched as reactive thinking short-circuited Mully's ability to adapt. He could have blasted the glass wall, as Beth had done, and sidestepped the tide. But he didn't.

A paw, flickering and phasing and hooked, swept up and through Mully's shoulder from behind. Without slowing, the Shifter lifted the screaming trooper over its shoulder, tossing him back into the pack. Bristol saw a roiling, fractal head rise from the back of the surge, along with two crackling arms, to pile drive Mully out of sight.

Bristol saw all of this—when he should have been running.

A prone Beth saw two Shifters do things to Bristol's geometry as the screaming trooper was smashed underfoot—things that would stay in her head forever.

Jack skidded to a halt and hauled her up, the horde thirty feet behind. "Up up up!"

No hope. The Shifters were already on them.

Beth closed her eyes.

Howls.

Jack turned, shielding her, and—

One Shifter flew left, through the shattered office wall. Another was grabbed by the head and pulled backward to the ground. A third Shifter—the largest—drove a crackling foot into the creature's chest, pinning it to the floor. Chronon flow arced off the flailing body, played off the walls.

Jack saw flashes of the same hallway, decorated and designed a dozen different ways as the slowly collapsing M-J field sliced the place up along different timelines. Sometimes it wasn't decorated so much as destroyed. Alternate hallways, alternate outcomes, alternate presents.

With his own eyes Jack watched reality inch closer to falling apart completely.

The big Shifter threw its arms wide and *screamscreamscreamed*.

Eyes wide, hands wide. Shining Palm.

The pack held back behind it, cowed. The Shifter on the floor thrashed infinitely, simultaneously.

Jack stumbled backward.

Beth was on her feet, hauling him now, hobbling heavily on one good leg. "This way. Run." Blood flowed thick between the fingers clamped to her wound.

"Beth, what's happening?"

Without warning the stutter collapsed, every still bullet

flew free, glass walls shattered and the Shifters abruptly . . . vanished.

"This won't last. *Run.*"

Paul made it into the chronon research wing as causality kicked back in. Was it over? No . . . just another temporary cessation. He could feel this event was not yet spent.

This exertion was costing him. The lack of focus was taking hold again, the feeling of becoming unmoored from his body, from the world. The desire to surrender to care, to allow the release to course through his entire body and take him. The voice of his sickness, his chronon syndrome, was growing louder, more seductive, within the chamber of his mind. Taking up space once occupied by his own counsel.

Treatment. He required treatment. Sofia's lab. He would administer a treatment to himself, within the safety of an artificial pylon-generated bubble of causality, and soothe this madness. Once the chaos had passed, there would be work to do. Damage to contain. Steps to take. The final steps.

He pushed through secondary lab spaces, past coldly lit glass infoboards and the warm hum of sterile machinery.

Sofia's laboratory was at the far end of this array, from which she could oversee all of the work being done in her name, to her guidance. It was elevated above the broad glass boxes in which the labs were contained. Moving through the secondary labs, Sofia's quarters were always visible through clear plexiglass ceilings.

Of modern design, Sofia's quarters were configured for living as much as working—a flat oblong with a long observation window suspended above the glass-roofed lab-farm. It had been designed to her specifications, on Paul's orders.

Moving at speed toward these quarters, and the relief they

contained, Paul watched a wide tongue of flame shoot from the observation window, spitting glass.

Secondary explosions took the roof and walls off Sofia's laboratory quarters completely. Heavy debris blew outward and upward to crash down through the glass ceilings of the secondary laboratories.

Paul watched his only hope of forestalling the progress of his condition literally vanish in flames.

Overwhelmed, Paul blacked out.

When he came to, his hands were bloody and a nearby workstation was trashed, a desk snapped in half. His left arm was on fire, as was his chest. A coppery taste filled his mouth. His chest was alight with starlight and his mind full of *howling*.

Remembering himself was like struggling to remember a dream. Muscle memory took his hand to his chest, fingers closed around Aberfoyle's bullet. He was Paul Serene. The future of humanity. And he must live.

Monitors above the workstation flashed meaningless information. He found a laptop, shakily entered his credentials and switched to secure feeds. Called up the feed for floor fifty. Scanned.

Found the corridors. Smashed walls, shattered glass, two members of Chronon-1 who had ended their lives horribly as complex stains on expensive carpet.

Scanned.

Jack and Beth, running for the garden. There she was: Beth. Hobbling on a wounded leg.

Closing on Sofia—who was now reanimated and discovering herself completely alone.

Paul fumbled for his earpiece, switched frequencies, contacted the helicopter pilot.

"*Leave!*"

"Sir?"

"Get that bird away from this building, pilot, or I'll kill you myself. *Go!*"

Jack approached Sofia quickly, hands up and open. She was not receptive.

"No! Not again!" She was close to hyperventilating. "The . . . the mind is . . . not meant to take such shocks! Where is Paul? Paul was here. Where is . . . ?"

Beth grabbed Sofia's hand in her own bloody one.

Sofia recoiled "Oh my God, you're hurt!"

"Hurt," Beth said. "Short on time and low on patience so, please, rediscover the ol' internal monologue." Beth hobbled toward the stone steps leading up to Martin's office, dragging Sofia with her.

The stairs led to a Roman-style atrium, floored in red-and-white check: a place for Martin to sit and look out across the greenery, or to meet with fellow businesspeople. His office was on the far side of this atrium, locked and sealed. Fortunately, an L-shaped gantry led from the right, straight to a square helipad that hung off the side of the building.

Their ride was already cycling its blades, building to a muted turbine shriek. The pilot glanced between them and his over-heads, willing the machine to get airborne.

"Jack! That chopper's leaving without us!"

Jack zipped down the gantry, banked left around the curve, headed for the pad—just as the helicopter lifted off the pad.

The pilot caught sight of Jack and went defensive, banking hard and low over the side of the building.

"Jack!" Beth could see what he was doing. "Don't be stupid!"

Beth needed a medic, and that chopper was their only way out of here.

Jack threw himself toward the lip, throwing his arms forward in an attempt to localize a stutter around the chopper.

He ended facedown on the pad, two feet from a fifty-story drop. He came to as Beth grabbed him by the collar, hauling him to his feet, and laughed out loud: the helicopter floated below the platform, angled slightly, blades immobile, hanging in space. Sofia gasped at the sight of it.

Jack smiled, satisfied with himself. "If it's stupid and it works, it ain't stupid. Right?"

"Eurocopter Airbus AS365," Beth muttered. "Just like she ordered."

The bubble wasn't large enough to have trapped the entire bird, just the midsection and blades. Jack could see the pilot, still animated, frantically strangling the controls but going nowhere.

"Can you make the jump on that leg?"

"We got a bigger problem." Beth pointed back the way they came. Chronon-1 had stormed the garden, moving at speed toward the helipad.

"They lost two of their guys," Jack said. "They're pissed."

"Keep Sofia safe, I'll—"

Jack took Sofia's hand. "Trust me."

And Jack shoved Sofia Amaral off the edge of Monarch Tower.

The doctor fell without a sound, shocked into silence that her life could end so suddenly. She fell toward the helicopter, but wide of it, connecting with the stutter bubble Jack had thrown around the chopper.

Sofia Amaral froze, suspended in space, five feet from the open passenger door of the trapped helicopter.

"*Woo!*"

Beth's look was either confusion or murderous intent.

Jack gestured, success self-evident. "What?"

"Your balls," she said. "On a stump." Beth backed up, and took a running leap toward the edge as Chronon-1 started blasting. She bounded off the lip, the pain of it forcing a cry from her throat, launching herself into space. She aimed her still-cycling boots for the chopper's open side door and hoped for the best.

She fell feetfirst through the bubble, through the door and hit the carpeted floor inside, slamming into the closed starboard-side passenger door. White pain flooded from leg to brain and Beth skimmed right across the surface of a total blackout. *Back in the game, Wilder; back in the game.* "Get the doctor!"

Jack dumped a chronon burst as Chronon-1 hit Hatch's Romanesque atrium, catching the incoming fire. He took the lip of the platform at a run, leaping across the space—"Sorry, Doctor"—landing boots-first onto the chest of Dr. Sofia Amaral. She didn't move a micron and Jack's feet went out from under him. His back connected with her sternum and he bounced off. One flailing hand seized onto Sofia's outstretched forearm, leaving Jack's feet flailing fifty stories above Riverport's streets.

Beth had already scrambled halfway over the cream-colored calf leather passenger seats, dealing with the inconvenience of having to do so with a gun taking up one hand while screaming at the pilot.

Dangling, Jack reached out for the upper rim of the helicopter door, grabbed it, and began to will Sofia loose from the hold of the stutter bubble. As her stasis softened he pulled in farther, one foot finding purchase inside the door. He drew her forward, grabbing on to a more secure safety loop bolted into the ceiling.

Sofia found her voice—a sound that went from silence to bass-syrup to a human scream—and suddenly she was so much deadweight, falling straight down.

Jack held her hand in a tight monkey-grip, shoulder wrenching as he caught her full weight. From the helipad Gibson was shouting for blood. Chronon-1 was almost to the edge of the pad.

Beth glanced back over her shoulder. "Get her inside!"

Jack hauled her up, Sofia clawing at the carpet, panicking as her sheer evening gown kept her leg from swinging up and in to the chopper. Someone started shooting, slugs *vip-vip*-ing into the shield. Donny, red faced and furious, glared down at them, then vanished from the edge of the pad.

Beth buckled herself in one-handed. To the pilot: "All right, asshole. Sit tight and you'll be home in time for Kimmel." She put her gun away and took the second stick.

Jack heard Gibson call Donny's name, just as he hauled Sofia inside the chopper. Sofia fumbled her way into a jump seat, wrestling with the safety belt.

"Beth! Take the stick!"

Donny vaulted off the edge of the helipad, his trajectory taking him straight for the open passenger door, handgun pointed square at Jack's face.

Jack threw his arms wide and nullified the field.

The helicopter sprang to sudden life and Jack was flipped off his feet as the blades threw Donny in two directions at once.

Gibson saw it all, his face a disfigured mess, contorted by an obliterating rage at the loss of his best friend and second-in-command. His weapon unloaded right at them, without a second thought.

The stick had bucked suddenly in Beth's hand as the helicopter kicked back to life, but she wasn't letting it win. Jack scuttled back from the open door as the chopper's frame swerved and tilted, grabbing hard onto a jumpseat support as Beth sent the bird into a dive.

Beth had a death grip on the stick. Keeping the bird low, she swung it out over the Mystic River. Once their flight was stable and level Beth thumbed a contact on her phone, piped it to her earpiece.

"Horatio. You in the Tower? I need a favor."

Inside Monarch Tower, on the thirty-fifth-floor mezzanine, Nick watched a gathering of the world's wealthiest and brightest freak the hell out.

Everything needed a security card, and he didn't have one. He was trapped.

"Hey. You."

A man marched toward Nick along the curve of the mezzanine.

Handlebar moustache, loud bowling shirt under which was something about theater sports.

"Horatio," he said. "Friend of Beth's. Looks like today's my last day. Let's get out of here."

"Sir, yes, sir," Nick said.

"One stop first. Super important. Floor fifty."

15

News reports started coming in less than thirty minutes after the stutter broke.

Simultaneously, at locations across the globe, impossibilities occurred. All of them were captured on video. Intentionally.

9:12:42 P.M. Pier 14, San Francisco.

Civilian witnesses filmed two police officers closing in on a suspect, their Tasers drawn. The suspect, a man in his thirties of African descent, offers no resistance.

In the space of a single frame the entire scene changes: two strangers have materialized. They are dressed head to toe in black, save for Smiley masks. The white letters on their shirts read PEACE. They wave, friendly.

The strangers, somehow, are suddenly in possession of the police officers' Tasers. The officers' faces are painted with clown makeup, their belts have been loosened, their pants are around their ankles. Still moving forward at a brisk pace the cops trip and crash to the pavement.

The suspect shouts, "Oh my God! Oh my God!" repeatedly.

The strangers mime laughter, then Taser the two cops.
In the space of a frame, they are gone.
The incident was filmed by three separate witnesses.

**9:12:42 P.M. Outside Melisse Restaurant,
Santa Monica.**

Security footage captured a celebrity socialite exiting the restaurant with a male companion. Their gunmetal Infiniti Q60
pulls up. The valet exits the car, holding the passenger-side door
open for the socialite, as her companion walks around the rear
of the vehicle to enter the driver side.

In the span of a single frame the vehicle, and the socialite,
are gone. Footage shows the male companion accosting the
valet. Footage ends.

**9:12:42 P.M. The Viper Room, West Hollywood. Eight
miles from Melisse Restaurant.**

The venue was playing host to a well-known heavy metal act.

Security footage and handheld recordings uploaded by a
dozen attendees at the concert show the headline act onstage,
mid-performance. In the span of a single frame the disappearing socialite appears onstage—flanked by two black-clad figures
in PEACE shirts and Smiley masks. The cartoonish figures
wave animatedly at the crowd. After a moment the socialite
collapses in high distress.

The band, now realizing what is occurring, summons security. The two masked suspects run to the edge of the stage,
leap toward the crowd . . . and vanish in midair.

7:12:42 A.M. Al-Salamiyah, Syria.

Footage from a single stationary camera.

Twenty bound men kneel, facing away from ten hooded men carrying automatic weapons. One hooded man delivers a short, curt speech to the camera. The ten men then level their weapons at the back of their captives' heads.

A figure appears mid-frame, wearing the now-distinctive PEACE garb. She waves happily at the camera. Within a second she is gone. The captors are given a second to react to this intrusion, before, in the space of a single frame, the weapons they were holding vanish from their hands.

At the same time their kneecaps simultaneously explode and all ten hooded men collapse, screaming, to the ground.

Notably the captives' hands are now freed, and the missing automatic weapons have been laid before them.

This scene was uploaded to a wide spectrum of sites across the Middle East. By the time Western media picked it up the file had been viewed an estimated 489,000 times.

12:12:42 A.M. Washington, D.C.

The simplest incident of them all.

The United States President, in the final months of his administration, calls a late-night press conference to address the mass shooting at Riverport University and now the attack on Monarch Tower itself.

Beyond letting the nation know what's being done, he expresses the hope that his successor will have better fortune in curbing this uniquely American illness than he had. He concludes by assuring the press and the public that solid leads have been gained on this so-called "Peace Movement," that a terrorist is a terrorist no matter their nationality, and that strong and decisive action could be expected shortly. The events of the night were startling, and upsetting, but Americans should not be intimidated. They would continue forward as they have always done.

Smiley appears behind him and to the right, a large-caliber handgun leveled at the back of the President's head. In the time it takes a secret service agent to yell "Gun!" the trigger is pulled.

There is a pop, the President flinches, and a flag unfurls from the weapon's barrel.

It reads: TIME'S UP.

Smiley vanishes before anyone can touch him.

The President is rushed out.

Saturday, 8 October 2016. 9:45 P.M. Monarch Tower.
Martin Hatch's Apartment.

Martin Hatch splashed a finger of fifty-year-old Dalmore into a tumbler of Tuscany crystal. At that moment the walls of his office were transparent, providing a soothing view of the atrium and garden. Shell casings had been swept away. Tomorrow workers with appropriate clearance would repair the bullet holes. Window cleaners were, at that very moment, squeegeeing streaks of Donny from floors forty-nine through forty-six.

"Our final chapter begins with a non sequitur," he assured Paul. "That's all this is. The future is written; we both know that. The events of the gala, the destruction of Sofia's lab, her abduction . . . this changes nothing."

Paul was pacing, shaking his head, clearly wanting to rub and soothe his infected hand yet fearing to touch it. "No. The gala: a disaster. The lab: destroyed and the Kim specimen gone with it. The treatments, the research: ash. How did Jack know? How did I not foresee that? In all my explorations, deepening with each foray, *how did I not see this happening?*"

"Your agitation gains us nothing."

"Something works against me here. This is wrong."

"Paul."

"It's wrong."

"*Paul.*"

Paul's head flicked up, wild.

"You are prepared. Failing mental cohesion was always going to jeopardize Lifeboat. You laid down clear steps for moving forward. You don't have to think anymore, or worry. Trust those steps." Martin sipped, letting the liquor mellow in his mouth before tracing a warm line down his throat. "Let's get on with laying a strong foundation for the development of Project Lifeboat. Let's get on with saving the world."

Rage boiled at the underside of Paul's skin, but Martin's words filtered in. Soothed the part of him that was still most like his old self. "Yes."

"Let's debrief."

Martin moved behind his broad desk, the heavy crystal tumbler clinking on the surface of black glass. He tapped a virtual key, transforming the eastern-facing wall from clear to opaque before coming to life as a videoboard, dividing and subdividing into multiple newsfeeds. Dozens of talking heads covered the events at Monarch Tower.

"Our people in Washington have contrived to keep the FBI from our door for a few more hours," Martin said. "It will be all we need."

"Sofia," Paul uttered.

"They took her to the swimming hall, naturally. The helicopter was abandoned and a car stolen. It'll be a relief to finally take possession of Will's rusting prototype when this is over."

"Jack thinks he can change things. . . ."

"I've taken steps to bring Sofia back safely and claim that machine for ourselves. I respect the structure of causality as much as you, Paul, but I do wonder if we should have just seized the machine years ago and been done with it."

Paul was raving. "She was shot in the leg."

"Sofia?"

Paul shook his head. "No, the woman with Jack. Beth Wilder. When I first met her she told me her name was Beth. She had the same wound. It was fresh. I bandaged it for God's sake." He thought of Will's machine gathering dust at the bottom of that dry pool across town. Monarch had known about it for years, all part of keeping tabs on Will. "She goes through the machine. Everything that happens, happens. It doesn't matter."

"Paul? Look." Martin flicked through the various newsfeeds. All of them reporting a second Peace Movement strike on a Monarch target within twenty-four hours: the Tower itself. First, the university lab, and now the grand unveiling of Monarch's new innovation: chronon technology.

Martin flipped through the feeds.

". . . *what is 'chronon technology'? . . .*"

". . . *said the hardware demonstrated an ability to be anywhere, at any time . . .*"

". . . *patient in perfect suspension, and a great advance in medical . . .*"

". . . *despite the attacks share prices have skyrocketed in the wake of documents and footage released . . .*"

". . . *terrorist groups interested in the technology . . .*"

". . . *Hatch was unavailable for comment . . .*"

"*. . . Chronos, of course, being the Greek god of time . . .*"

"*. . . a field of study once widely derided, now seems to be vindicating itself with a vengeance . . .*"

"*. . . States military is said to be interested in exploring applications of the . . .*"

"*. . . this technology renders borders useless . . .*"

"*. . . threat to global peace, some say the survival of our species . . .*"

"*. . . wearing Smiley masks as a joke. Authorities urge people to not . . .*"

"The stage is set," Martin said, turning to face Paul. "The world knows what Monarch can do."

He flicked to a different set of feeds and recordings.

"*. . . hard put to explain the 'Peace' events, or who this enigmatic group is, but we are assured the footage and the events are authentic . . .*"

"*. . . footage verified by experts. Washington has refused comment . . .*"

"*. . . fear and paranoia across the country tonight, with many still convinced the events are an elaborate hoax . . .*"

"*. . . First Family to an undisclosed location . . .*"

"*. . . speculation that the 'Peace' events are a viral campaign to promote Monarch's new tech . . .*"

"*. . . what is stopping Peace Movement terrorists from appearing anywhere, anytime, with guns or, God forbid, with nuclear weapons?*"

"*. . . are our leaders safe? Can anywhere be secured from hostile forces with this technology? With us now is . . .*"

"The audience is groomed, and ready," Martin continued. "Speculation is rampant. Sidebar: we expect gun sales to spike sharply as a result of this."

"How are the events of the gala being framed?"

"To our advantage. It's been married seamlessly to the narrative of the university attack, linking it to the Peace Movement. It's proving helpful in directing sympathy toward Monarch. So: our two key objectives are achieved: the world knows Monarch is the only organization pursuing chronon development, and the ruthless terrorist group that murdered their way into our university lab is now taking liberties with the laws of the universe."

Martin finished his drink at a swallow and stood, adjusting his jacket.

"Phase One: the university event successfully framed us as a target and the Peace Movement as the easily recognizable villain. Phase Two: with the aid of your explorations and foreknowledge we were able to choreograph the Peace Movement's baffling, simultaneous events immaculately. Result: Peace's every meaningless detail is subject to rampant media speculation: the targets, locations, timing, masks . . . the name. Showmanship and confusion are performing the vital task of drawing bandwidth away from reason, building alarm and metastasizing public panic. A terrorist—foreign or domestic— could materialize anywhere at any moment. We have taken the first steps toward creating a world in which nowhere and no one can ever feel secure again. All eyes are now on the Peace Movement and Monarch Solutions."

"A good start," Paul agreed. "We're close now."

"Now we escalate further. Your announcement was released minutes ago to all the major news agencies from an anonymized address."

The wall switched, this time to a single image: Paul Serene, behind him two men in the black garb and smiley masks of the ghostly Peace Movement.

"I am speaking to you.

"I am Paul Serene. I am listed among the dead.

"My life ended last night, along with many others, on the campus

of Riverport University. Murdered by men and women like those standing behind me. Or so it was reported."

Subwindows flashed open, showing a collage of newsfeeds and Web sites sourcing information on Paul Serene, recent photos of a younger man compared to the older one doing the talking.

"The Meyer-Joyce field. Familiarize yourself with that name. It will soon become the focus of what little remains of your life.

"The Meyer-Joyce field maintains causality, the flow of cause and effect and the linear passage of time. Early yesterday morning, on Saturday, October eighth, at four twenty-two a.m., I modified an experimental Monarch Solutions device . . . and mortally wounded the Meyer-Joyce field.

"Some of you have already witnessed the early effects of this: power fluctuations, visual anomalies, lost time.

"Before long you will all experience the consequences of M-J field degradation. Reality, causality, probability . . . all these things will soon begin to forget their own rules.

"Close to the end will come escalating horror the likes of which you are ill-equipped to imagine. Trapped and isolated within a shrinking, schizophrenic reality—a reality just for you—lovers will forget you. Mothers and fathers will not know their children. The dead will return as if they had never left. Legions of the living will vanish. That which was will have never been. Your tiny souls will unmoor, to drift and drown upon a sea of Everything.

"Die alone in perfect lunacy—or live forever within a horrifying final moment that never, ever stops. The choice is yours.

"This is the cessation of all things. The dying of time.

"We are Peace, and Peace we bring you.

"It is time for suffering to end.

"The universe has five years to live.

"You will not hear from us again."

Martin clicked the wall to silence.

"The terror will amplify as events play out. The world will not be able to deny that reality is slowly unraveling. When the public learns that there is no solution—"

"Monarch appears at the gate carrying the Grail."

"Project Lifeboat: the only viable way to survive—and undo—time's end."

"But only with the combined and unquestioning support of governments worldwide." Paul took a deep-chested breath. "I'm ready."

Martin crossed to his friend, laid both hands on his shoulders. "You are performing the greatest kindness, Paul. You are saving all that was, is, and shall be. And these people"—Hatch pointed to the wall screen and its two dozen talking heads—"will live to revile you for it."

Paul smiled, but not with joy. "Only if I succeed."

"I'll leave you to prepare."

"You're going?"

"Not for long, old friend. Never for long."

Saturday, 8 October 2016. 9:56 P.M. Monarch Tower. Chronon Labs, Floor 50.

Horatio had taken Nick to a bank of elevators away from the chaos of the atrium, straight up to floor fifty. They stepped out into what Horatio called the chronon labs. The place was a mess. Glass everywhere, the cross-hatch frame of the utterly destroyed false ceiling empty within a larger, vaulted chamber of ceramic white. At the far end of the chamber that contained the labs, above the frame of the false ceiling, the smoking wreck of an expensive demountable was being picked over by yellow-suited technicians. Nick kicked a flimsy mound of fire retardant foam, watched it scatter and drift.

"I've been inside Monarch's system for months," Horatio was saying. "Installed a rootkit back when the Tower's systems were still being finalized. Even so I haven't been able to get a lot of dirt on the chronon division or Hatch."

"Why did you think there was dirt?"

"Beth made a convincing case." Horatio headed left, away from the burning demountable and fire crew. "Beth and I both know Hatch and the chronon division are up to hinky shit, but I've never found anything really mediapathic, anything Reuters would pull a muscle to grab."

Aside from the thick frosting of busted glass, the lab seemed intact. Horatio was fumbling in his pockets as he walked, pulled out a crumpled note, checked it.

"Stuff related to C division and Hatch exist on a separate server that I'm not privy to, that exists only on floor fifty, but I do have the big man's password. This has been my only chance to get onto fifty, and it took the whole tower shitting itself to make that happen. The meeting room up ahead was reserved for daily powwows between Hatch, Sofia, and C division. Daily updates, daily course corrections. Any terminal there would have access to the C div server."

Nick caught up to him. "You think there's stuff on there that might . . . bring Monarch down?"

Horatio shrugged. "Been here a few years. It'd be shitty timing to find something now, don't you think? But . . . yeah, I think so."

Nick glanced around, not liking this at all. "How long you need? We get caught we're goin' out a window."

Horatio pushed open the meeting room door. "After today I'm out of here. This is my last chance."

Long mahogany table. Whiteboards on two walls. Central teleconference dome. Five-thousand-dollar seats. Vid-screen.

Terminal. Built into the flat of the table, right in front of the door.

Horatio sat and got to work.

"Listen, Horatio—"

Horatio slapped his security card on the desk, kept typing. "Five minutes." He took a thumb drive, jacked it into a slot in the table's polished surface. Smoothed his note, typed.

Waited.

The screen lit up with Monarch's geometric logo.

"Yes." Horatio dived in, keyboard clattering.

Nick took the card. "I'll keep the elevator ready. Five minutes."

If Horatio heard, he didn't respond. Nick was just out the door when Horatio said, "Jesus H. Macy."

Nick came back, peered over his shoulder. "What?"

"Wait. I need to . . . I need to copy this. And . . . fuck me. Wait." Keys clattered. Files were copied to the thumb drive. "So Hatch has been pushing for the development of Project Lifeboat—this grand plan that's already racking up cost over-runs and has a five-year dev schedule it is *never* going to meet. The Lifeboat team is talking chronon harvesting and storage technology orders of magnitudes more efficient than what we currently have, technology to allow whole teams of specialists to move through chronon-free zones for months or years on end and pylon technology to preserve causality within a much wider radius than what we're currently—"

Nick twiddled the security card. "And?"

"And there's a second group involved with the project. From *outside* Monarch that nobody but Hatch seems to know about. Hatch has been corresponding with them since day one. Project Lifeboat is above top secret, but this other crew—and it looks like they're scattered all over the planet—are getting regular updates. From what I can tell nobody in Monarch knows these guys exist. What the fuck is Hatch up to?"

"Copy it and let's go."

"There's also reference to a second time machine. In a . . . swimming pool?"

Nick craned in. "Say that again."

"A swim—"

"Fuck. We have to go. We have to go right now."

"I'm mailing this to Beth."

"Now, Horatio."

Horatio held up one hand, still typing with the other. "I'll be right there. Thirty seconds."

Nick jogged out, got to the elevator, swiped it open.

If Horatio had found something that could cause some damage . . . yeah. Nick was all for using it to give it to Monarch in the neck. But it wouldn't mean anything if they were too dead to use it.

Nick glanced at his watch. "Horatio! Come on, we—whoa!"

Horatio was no longer typing. He was in his seat, shuddering, arms slack by his sides.

Martin Hatch stood next to him, four fingers and thumb locked deep into Horatio's throat, gazing at Nick as Horatio's life ran out of him.

Nick swung into the elevator and hammered the Door Close button.

Martin Hatch watched him go.

Saturday, 8 October 2016. 10:05 P.M. Monarch Tower.
Paul Serene's Apartment, Floor 49.

If Monarch's success and hypersonic rise could be attributed to one thing it would be Paul Serene's explorations of possible futures and his identification of key junction moments that led to the choicest outcomes.

He had not always been sick, and he had not always possessed the ability to fly down the branching corridors of future probability. The gift was a trait of the sickness. The chronon syndrome.

In the early days his vision had been tight and nearsighted. A day ahead at most, with no control. In time he had learned to focus on moments that led to moments. He called them junctions. These almost always manifested in the instant, allowing him to make a choice *now* that would elicit an outcome later. This was fine for short-term gain, but there was a blindness to it, an element of chance. The choices he made were best guesses based on what shadowy perceptions he could grasp at the end of what probability branches were at hand—and he always had to choose quickly, before the moment passed.

But that would not do. It was not enough.

Paul did not want choice forced on him. He wanted knowledge, awareness, and control. In time, with great effort, he learned to identify junction moments before they arrived. This enabled choices that were more considered and better informed.

In this manner Monarch Solutions had first begun to shape the life of every person on Earth.

With greater effort and diligence Paul began to explore a larger selection of possible futures. And then to explore the possible futures that branched from those.

Greater exploration came with greater effort. Especially deep forays came at a cost: the giving of himself to the sickness, and the sacrificing of his flesh.

The dreams were terrible after such journeys. Not just *a* dream, but dreams about dreams. Dozens of iterations of surreal scenarios played out atop one another yet all of them, somehow, simultaneously comprehensible. Parallel timelines, near-identical causalities, each with small variations blooming into sometimes vastly different outcomes.

In the moment it felt like joy; on waking it felt like madness. He was never right for days after such deep journeys. But the company profited. Armed with detailed foreknowledge, Martin Hatch's captaincy had been immaculate.

The sicker Paul got, the easier it became. The farther he went, the sicker he got.

Paul's instincts honed. His efficiency sharpened.

Now, as Paul's time on Earth grew short, he centered himself for his greatest and most complex voyage to date. His mission was to chart the most detailed probability map that he could, covering the coming days. This would be especially difficult as, given the events of the last twenty-four hours, the skein of cause and effect was in a state of high agitation.

The journeys he had taken previously would be as garden pathways compared to the seething jungle tangle that awaited him.

This final foray would cost him greatly.

Paul Serene sat comfortably on his magnificent chair of thirty-six-hundred-year-old *Fitzroya cupressoides*. At each compass point an articulated stand directed a microphone toward him.

His final operation as a surgeon of causality—his final voyage as a cartographer of future history—began in this instant.

The map he would leave behind would allow Monarch to navigate the coming storm, to survive the inevitable scrutiny, and to win the loyalty of those who could assure the company's future as the savior of mankind.

It would assure the development and success of Project Lifeboat, which, without immediate and unconditional global governmental cooperation, would fail. Humanity, this universe, this timeline would cease to be.

Paul closed his eyes.

And began.

His consciousness became four-dimensional. He rose above the weave entirely and allowed his consciousness to point—compass-like—toward the future he desired most.

He had never perceived the skein of probability so completely, so vastly, as he did now. Vast enough to crush a mind, perfect enough that the changing part of Paul Serene wanted to dwell there forever.

His mind found its direction as though it were the most instinctive thing on Earth. Paul Serene's awareness found the future where Martin Hatch stood before those who control the world . . . and those who control the world said:

Yes.

Paul Serene started there, examining in detail the threads of cause and effect that led each and every person in that room to that singular and most-desired outcome, and worked his way backward.

Only then did he begin dictating to the microphones.

His flesh burned with starlight.

Saturday, 8 October 2016. 10:07 P.M. Monarch Tower.
Martin Hatch's Apartment, Floor 50.

When Randall Gibson entered Martin Hatch's office the great man was cleaning one hand with a dark handkerchief, meticulously working the spaces between his fingers.

"Mr. Gibson," Mr. Hatch said, without looking up from his work. "The tragedy in your unit has returned you to command. Welcome back, Senior Operative. They were good soldiers. Let's not have you tarnish their memory, hmm?"

"Sir?"

"You and the remainder of C-1 are to head to the Riverport Swimming Hall. A time machine is inside. You are to enter the swimming hall, enter the machine, and go back as far as you can—to 1999—and kill Jack Joyce. Do you understand?"

"And . . . the Consultant? Mr. Serene? He's gone and changed his opinion on the science? Last I heard messing with collapsed waveforms was verboten."

"Mr. Serene has not been well. Leave the laws of the universe to me."

"Y-yes sir."

"Doubt, Mr. Gibson?"

"Sir, no, sir! I look forward to executing the mission with the utmost aggression, sir!"

"And I look forward to you and I renewing our friendship. Now go forth, and deliver a mighty suffering."

Gibson felt his chest light up like a ball of phosphorous on a dark night. "Sir, yes, sir!" *With the utmost fucking aggression. Oo-fuckin'-RAH!*

"Dismissed, Senior Operative."

Gibson saluted, pivoted, and marched on out, head high.

Hatch sighed, folded his handkerchief, and tucked it into his pocket. Today was a day for housecleaning, and setting things in motion.

Saturday, 8 October 2016. 10:17 P.M. Riverport Swimming Hall.

Beth had left Sofia in Jack's care while she shut herself in the locker rooms to tend her savaged leg and change out of her Monarch uniform. Jack had some first aid training and figured she'd be okay in the short term. There would be a scar, but the slug had done no damage to bone or arteries. He had offered to stitch her up, but Beth wanted to take care of it herself and retreated to the change rooms.

So he was stuck with Sofia.

"You don't need to convince me," Sofia snapped. "I'll help you. My own calculations are very clear: the Meyer-Joyce field *will* collapse. Well in advance of Paul's five-year prediction. We have a day. Two at most. Now please let me work."

Sofia was already examining the console of Will's machine, looking up occasionally to compare what she was seeing onscreen to some detail of the machine's structure.

"So you do think the world's about to end."

"Yes, I do."

Jack leaped on that. "Paul's been to the end of time. He has the date. If a collapsed waveform can't be altered, if things can't be changed, how can he be wrong?"

"It's his word against my expertise and a model supported by verifiable data," she scowled. "I can only conclude his recollection is flawed."

Beth reappeared from the locker rooms out back. "He wants you to tell him it's possible to influence a collapsed waveform, to change events." Gone were the monogrammed Monarch jacket and fatigues. She had prepared an outfit that was fashion agnostic: blue jeans, plain black T-shirt, mid-range leather jacket of classic cut. An outfit that wouldn't look out of place anytime in the last twenty years. "Jack," she said. "You have to let go of the idea that you can save Will. Focus on what's possible."

Jack let it go, but wouldn't be giving up. Will was alive in 2010. There had to be something he could do.

Beth turned to Sofia. "Are we good?" She was favoring her good leg pretty heavily, but otherwise looked okay, all things considered.

They could both have used some sleep.

Sofia stepped away from the keyboard. Gathering her thoughts she said, "Before I do this, I have a question for you: your brother built something he called a Countermeasure." Being here, looking at Will's machine, and piecing together her own experiences with Paul Serene and Monarch, it was now clear to her that Dr. Kim had little, if anything, to do with the pioneering of chronon research. That, quite possibly, she had made a grave error in helping Monarch to achieve their goals. "'Countermeasure.' That is a very specific word."

"Will built it to repair the fracture in the M-J field," Jack said.

Sofia's face broke into a sudden smile. It suited her. "Then it exists."

"It existed on July 4, 2010, we know that much."

"And that is your destination?"

Beth stepped in. "We go back, retrieve it, return here, fix all this. How soon can you get the machine working?"

"It's ready now, if you are."

Irene Rose was in a top-down position on the pool, her rifle's barrel nosing through a gap in a thin and grimy window, waiting for go.

"Count all three. Joyce, Wilder, Amaral. They're focused on the machine, seem pretty excited about it."

Gibson was hanging out on the corrugated eave, outside the cafeteria-level window. He had just finished laying a sheet of black plastic adhesive across the pane. "Team, report in."

"IR, roof," Irene responded.

"Voss, rear door, ground level."

"Chaffey, Reeves, Dominguez, rear door."

"Gibson . . ." Gibson took out his knife, tapped the plastic hard. The glass pane beneath it snapped, came away clean. He laid it down carefully. "Cafeteria, top floor." He ducked inside, unslung his carbine as a car pulled up outside, braking loudly.

Irene piped up. "Boss."

"I got it. Count one: Caucasian male. Limp. Voss, how you coming with that door?"

"Already in."

Shouting from the lobby bounced around the swimming hall. "Jack! Beth! You here?"

Nick ran into the hall, heavily favoring one leg. He and Beth were a matching pair.

"Thank God. Guys, Monarch knows you're here. They've always known. They're probably on their way right now."

Jack and Beth were on the ramp to the time machine's airlock, waiting for Sofia to give them the go-ahead to depart.

"Horatio got you out?" Beth asked. "Is he with you?"

Nick's expression said it all. "He . . ." Nick struggled. "Horatio . . . he was trying to e-mail you something. Martin Hatch . . . he . . . he's got something going on. Something's not right with that company, man. Or that dude. Way, way not right."

Beth nodded, pushed the grief down. Horatio was a good guy. "Tell me about it when I get back. Sofia?" Beth entered the airlock. "We're going to fix this. Nick, you should get out of here. Jack?"

Sofia brought the power online, chronon particles flooding the Promenade. The bare-bones frame of the old machine clunked hard, picking up a rattle like loose change in a dryer.

"Go now," Sofia said.

Jack moved up the ramp.

"Breach," Gibson said.

At the back of the swimming hall, thirty feet behind the time machine, the door to the locker rooms blew off its hinges.

Jack threw a stutter bubble at his feet out of pure reflex, as the cafeteria window shattered. Bullets impacted the shield, thudding dully. Sofia shrieked, going rigid, shoulders hunched, an upright target.

Irene opened up from above. Gibson kept up fire from one end of the cafeteria as Voss swept in doing likewise from the locker rooms. The bubble protected Jack from multiple kill shots, torn between entering the machine or protecting Sofia.

A shot from above blew a crater out of the tiles at Sofia's feet, there was a spray of blood and Sofia fell forward across the controls. Collapsed, she vanished behind the instrument panel.

"Voss! Stay wide of the machine!" Gibson shouted. "Wide of the machine! We need that."

The airlock sucked shut.

"Beth!"

Nick fell back into the lobby, wide-eyed.

Jack ran to the airlock, but he had been here before: it wasn't opening. Beth had her notebook out, scribbled, tore off a page, pressed it to the viewport:

CHARGE MUST EXPEND. NOT SAFE TO OPEN.
SEE YOU THERE.

He was shaking his head no. Beth pressed her hand to the viewport, and stopped.

Jack angled his view, knew immediately why she wasn't going through. Something had gone wrong: the left hatch— the door to the past, the one they were meant to take—was closed. The right one was open. The past was locked, the future waiting.

Something must have happened when Sofia went down. Had the controls taken a hit? It was impossible to tell.

The machine began to tremble violently. From somewhere in the back of the Promenade a riveted steel plate detached and crashed to the tiles.

Voss didn't risk getting into Jack's line of sight. Irene and Gibson held fire, waiting for the shield to drop—at least fifty bullets waiting for permission to splash right through Jack.

Jack took a chance. He stepped out of the bubble, spraying three-round bursts toward the ceiling-line windows. Dirty glass shattered as military rounds punched through rusted iron paneling, sending Irene flinching back from the edge.

Gibson took a shot, but not before Jack manifested a second shield in his line of sight that took the hits. Jack cleared the short distance between ramp and console, throwing down a third bubble as Voss opened up.

Three rounds pounded dully into the bubble, eye level with Jack.

"Boss," Chaffey piped up in Gibson's earpiece. "You want us in there?"

"Negative. Stand by."

Sofia was at Jack's feet, facedown and unmoving. The dark fabric of her evening gown made it tough to tell where she had been hit. Blood pooled into antiseptically shaded tiles.

There was blood on the console, one thick line pawed diagonally across the screen and keyboard, ending at Sofia's fall. The destination date had changed. The trip to the past was now the trip to the future, the destination committed and locked. And the date was blank.

Through the airlock's grimy viewport Beth pressed a hand to the glass. She tried for an "oh well" kind of smile. Pointed at her watch, then at Jack—*Don't be late*—gave a single wave and, just like that, walked into the future.

No date, headed forward. The end of time.

"Beth! Wait!"

The machine screamed and threw off a pounding beat of energy.

Jack didn't notice Irene drop through the ceiling—a fast rappel—timed to coincide with the machine's flash and noise. He leaped the console and went after Voss, who immediately booked it beneath the machine.

"Boss! I need cover!"

Gibson pressed a finger to his ear mic. "Nice goin', Voss! Keep him busy!"

"I ain't playin', boss!"

Irene glanced over her shoulder. Nick was still at the entrance, framed and petrified in the doorway. "Don't sweat it, Voss. I got you." She blasted a few random shots in Nick's direction, sent him hobbling. "Gonna play with your little friend, Joyce! Hope you don't mind!"

She set off after her target with an easy, loping grace.

Jack gave up on Voss, changed course, and jetted after Irene. Nick retreated to the lobby. Irene used gunfire to herd him up the stairs to the cafeteria and chased along behind.

Gibson waited until Jack had pursued far enough to take him beneath the cafeteria, then hopped out the window. "Chaffey. Time to bug out." He landed on the roof of the prefab housing the diesel generator, then down to the ground floor. He went straight for the machine's bloodied controls.

Subvocalized into his mic. "Voss, come on out. You're first up."

Voss rolled up from the maintenance recess as Chaffey, Reeves, and Dominguez flowed in from the locker rooms.

"Wilder went through, Voss."

Realization dawned. "She knows the mission. You think . . . she went back to protect Joyce?"

"Get into the airlock. I'll scatter us all wide, different dates. Chaffey's boys as a crew, the rest of us solo. She won't be able to pick us all off."

Jack zipped to the base of the cafeteria stairs. As Irene ducked out of sight Jack heard the machine crescendo. Dust punched off the walls and ceiling as the core fired. A framed black-and-white from a 1940s swim meet crashed to the floor.

Irene called out, "You're looking tired, sweets. Is all the fun taking it out of you?"

Then, behind Jack, the front door kicked open and a Monarch Security team flowed in.

A shot took Jack through the side, spinning him. Shouting, Jack encapsulated the first four members of the squad in a sphere of frozen time, blocking the door with it, and fell to the ground.

Prone and gasping, he fired bursts at the first two, six rounds suspended on a trajectory for their targets' helmeted heads.

The round had blown a hole the size of a golf ball just below Jack's ribs. Manifesting a handful of stutter bubbles, and flying after Irene, had expended almost everything he had. He felt the cells of his body thirstily draw in every scrap of chronon energy they could get, shock and instinct repurposing and localizing it to the wound. His body was pulling itself back together, but it was going to take time.

Upstairs Nick threw himself out the cafeteria window as Irene closed in from behind. He hit the tiles hard, yelped, and hobbled to his feet, limping hard.

———

Irene pulled her sidearm as the time machine shrieked and flashed.

"Voss is clear! Irene, get down here! Chaffey, Reeves, Dominguez, you're up! Go go go!"

She didn't hesitate. This was everything they had trained for. She hopped down, bounced neatly off the roof of the generator prefab, just as Chaffey's crew went through. Crossing the distance to the machine's ramp in no time flat she sprinted—straight to the airlock, no hesitation.

Gibson closed it down, gave her a new date, and sent her through.

Nick limped to Jack—his hockey injury now kicking his ass. That fall hadn't treated him kindly. He found Jack on his back in a pool of blood, a bloodied hole shot through his side and pale as a sheet. "Jack . . . Jesus man don't be dead."

"I'm . . . okay. Irene went through didn't she?"

"The machine? Yeah. I think they all did."

"Fuck." Jack got to his feet.

Gibson changed the date again. Four different dates meant anyone who came after C-1 had no chance of stopping them, or knowing when they would emerge from the machine.

The airlock door opened. Gibson keyed the machine to activate. The airlock door hissed, preparing to lever itself shut.

He quickly changed the onscreen date but did not commit it—just covering his tracks, making sure nobody could pick when he had gone to—then leaped the console, pounded up the ramp, and slid inside the airlock just before it sealed.

Atmosphere vented, internals pressurized, the airlock and Promenade flooding with chronon particles.

Mission accomplished. *Ha-ha fuck you.*

The door to the past opened, and Gibson was history.

So.

Jack felt the fight go out of him.

That was that then.

Nick leaped backward as Jack turned and emptied a full magazine into the stutter bubble behind him.

Nick looked away as the stutter bubble collapsed and freed rounds tossed the Monarch Security squad like dolls.

"Okay," Jack said. "Let's go."

He ran to the controls, kneeled, examined Sofia. The hit was to her left arm. She was cold, and her breathing was shallow, but she was alive.

He glanced at Nick. "Can you get her to a hospital?"

Nick nodded toward the television. It had been running on silent the whole time, tuned to coverage of the Riverport situation. It was clearly getting worse. It wasn't just the attack on Monarch Tower; things were beginning to go wrong across the city. The Riverport power grid was fluctuating, brownouts traveling across neighborhoods.

"The Riverport Emergency Facebook group has a conversation going at the moment. People are seeing ghosts, reporting lost time. Not a lot, but a few. Checked it on my way over here."

"Sofia said the end was coming soon." Jack got to his feet and tried to make sense of what Gibson had done. He didn't know where to begin. The date field was blank. Sofia wasn't going to be able to help with this. There was only one date that he knew for certain would get him somewhere he needed to be: the date he tried to send Beth to. The date she would head for, if she could.

Jack set the controls for July 4, 2010. The day of Bannerman's Overlook. The day Will's Countermeasure went missing.

"I'm going to catch up to Beth. It doesn't matter if the city's losing its mind, Sofia needs a doctor."

"I'll get her there."

"See you soon."

Jack slapped the button, activating the machine. He ran up the ramp and swung into the airlock. Earlier Beth had noticed an odor to the machine. She wasn't wrong. He smelled it now. It was the odor of rot and decay.

The airlock smooched shut. Chronon particles flooded the chamber. The door to the past opened, and Jack ran.

16

The hatch between airlock and the bulb-lit Promenade hissed and smooched shut behind her, the homemade corridor curving away ahead. In that moment some higher power hit Stop on the player. Abruptly, cruelly, every sound and movement ceased. Stillness. The follicles on her arms and scalp puckered closed. This world was separate and apart from the one she had just left.

Her wounded leg ached, powerfully.

Ninety-eight percent of chronon trainees washed out once they hit their first laboratory stutter. Finding themselves isolated in a death-calm reality, a world in which they had no agency whatsoever, flipped most trainees out. They couldn't open doors, move objects, eat or drink anything. They couldn't be heard. Monarch psychologists concluded this triggered base-level lizard-brain fears of entrapment, inflaming terrors of suffocation, dying alone, being forgotten, and nullification of self.

Twenty percent of candidates who washed out in the stutter training phase left the company, followed by institutional stays at Monarch's expense.

Something about it disassembled people on a code level.

Something about being in that tight curving corridor, the air thick with the hot nasal tang of superheated metal and the world gone voiceless, she understood why so many couldn't handle it. It was as close as Beth had come to being buried alive.

She marched forward, fast, cleaned out her thoughts with improvised ritual: handgun, loaded. Hair, tied and out of the way. Figured she must have been halfway around the loop. It was getting harder to breathe. She tried not to think about the possibility of the door not being open at the other end. Cricked her neck, rolled her shoulders. Three quarters. Breathe, Zed. Ashleigh. Starr. Wilder. Whatever. Breathe.

The exit hatch, dead ahead. Punched the release plate.

Fuck. Come ON.

She felt the charge bleed from the air. The Promenade de-activated, causality kicked back in.

The Promenade transformed *completely*.

Lighting flicked from warm to cold, amber to white. The sterile chill of environmentally friendly fluorescents, half of which didn't work, replaced the warm filament bulbs.

As the floor beneath her feet snapped from waffle-treaded insulation to cheap and heavy iron grillwork she almost lost her balance.

Will's pentagonal corridor was gone. She was now in a four-sided corridor, the construction of which made Will's look like a masterwork of thoughtful craftsmanship.

Will's Promenade was gone, Beth laying at the doorstep of what could have been the entrance to a moonbase's methadone clinic.

Get it together, Wilder. This is just the load screen.

Beth leaned against the new wall. Her leg didn't want to take the weight, but she made it. Ignored the pain, put it in a room, locked the door.

She glanced at the overheads. That type of fluorescent hadn't existed when Will made the machine. The machine had grown older.

Gun held in a double-handed grip, Beth peered into the airlock.

Whatever this is, she told herself, *it doesn't end here. Whatever this is it can't possibly hurt you.* She still had an appointment to keep with herself.

Get out, reconnoiter, set a new destination, bug out. Simple plan's a good plan.

The airlock had also changed. It could have been an old-school diving bell. Beth stepped inside, stiff-legged, the sound of the rusted grating a short squeal underfoot. The exit hatch was as heavy and submarinal as the rest of the machine's new construction. There was a single circular viewplate bolted into the exit hatch. Through its grimy cataract she could tell the machine had moved. It was now in a very wide, open space. There were . . . arches? Just outside. Beyond them: light. Was the machine in some kind of pit?

A four-spoked iron wheel was affixed to the center of the hatch. Leaning against the hatch was a crowbar. Holstering her pistol, she wedged the bar into the wheel, got leverage on it, and pushed downward. Two attempts and it gave. Beth cycled the wheel, released the hatch, and swung it wide.

Thank fuck.

The air outside was little better than the stale, static atmosphere inside the machine, but she disembarked gratefully. Wherever she was, whenever she was, this place was almost certainly a basement. She descended a short stepladder onto a floor of reclaimed brick. The roof was wood-reinforced plaster. The basement was divided by a plaster wall, itself broken into three brick-reinforced archways.

Beth thumbed the light on her phone and looked back at the

machine: it was a different beast now. Cruder, crappier, like a weekend survivalist's attempt at creating a submersible bunker. The only familiar thing about it was the core—that was Will's—wired into an odd new housing.

By the stepladder was a wooden workbench, scored from decades of use. Its undershelf housed the cabling and innards of what Beth recognized as some kind of chronon battery—but it was markedly different from the models Monarch was iterating upon. Fundamentals were all in place though: plus-sized chronon aggregator, some kind of capacitor, shitloads of insulation and cabling. One strand of the tech-spaghetti led up to a rubberized mat on which rested a thin plate of glass. The glass was illuminated with diagnostics—a viewscreen. The diagnostics told her the machine had a chronon charge of zero.

Her way home had gone out of business.

If she didn't find a source of chronon energy someplace, the mission was a bust. Beyond the basement arches a curtain of blue-white light dropped straight down from a smashed-out ceiling. Cautiously she moved toward the light, noting banks of old freezers left and right, and wooden shelves stacked one atop the other, pressed to the sides of the pit. It was freezing in here. A wheeled scissor lift stood against the left wall. Construction lighting—halogen lamps on thin telescoping yellow stands—were arranged in four corners, dead-eyed. Looking up it was clear what had happened. The ragged lip of the pit was about twelve feet up, accessible by a metal ladder or the lift. Up there she could see what remained of what had once been a kitchen. Someone had knocked out the floor, without grace or care. They had also knocked out at least one of the kitchen walls. Someone had gotten a hold of William's time machine core, had chosen this place to set up operations, and used this house as a cover—a shell over their subterranean base of operations.

All this she could deal with. What bothered her was her hearing. The sound down here had a strange quality to it, super-crisp. Her footsteps, an experimental cough, all began and ended very sharply. No resonance.

The atmosphere was thick with dust; she felt it against her face as she moved. Resisting.

She stopped by the ladder and gazed at the light that fell down from the upstairs world. She reached up, sweeping her hand gently through the day-lit particles suspended there. The motion of her hand carved a track, the motes moving aside obligingly, but nothing swirled to fill the space her hand cleared.

Stasis.

She shone her phone-light back the way she had come. Her passage from the machine to the ladder had carved a tunnel in the dusty air. She wiped a hand across her face. It came back thick with dust.

Holstering her weapon and pocketing the phone, she climbed the stepladder up to the surface.

Hands gripped to a floor paved in cracked red-and-white tiling, she emerged into what could have been either construction or destruction. The wall between kitchen and living area was gone; the jagged remnants of the wall-that-was remained at ceiling level, trailing scraps of flower print paper from the fifties. Seven or eight tables were stacked atop each other and pushed to the walls. A few were kept as surfaces on which to array tools and supplies. This had been a home converted to a sandwich shop. Chalkboards remained nailed to one wall, offering basic food and soup at steep prices. Four bucks for a glass of water.

There was a pile of mail gathered inside the front door. Beth walked through the clutter, shielding her mouth from the dust, and scrutinized the luridly enveloped junk letter at the top of the pile. The date stamp was enough to flush her heart with cold water. *2021.*

She knew what this was, when she was.

A stutter was a hiccup, a moment temporarily self-dividing. Eventually it ends and time continues. As such the odds of her emerging directly into a specific split second that had been affected by a stutter were statistically impossible. The only way the machine could have delivered her into the heart of a frozen moment is if the machine's destination parameters had been thrown forward so far into the future that there was no-where—*no when*—farther to go.

She reached for the faux-brass door handle, stopped, caught by the sight of her rig-thimbled fingers, the wires tracking up her sleeve.

Beth rapidly squeezed her right hand together twice, felt her fingertips tingle. Quickly she touched the door, freed it from the stutter, opened it, and double-squeezed again to kill the flow. She was going to need to conserve all the energy she could.

The street was the same as the sandwich shop, which was the same as the basement: uniform temperature, no resonance to sound. Muted colors, as though life had bled from the world.

Beth knew immediately where she was. The treelined street led straight to Riverport University campus several blocks away.

The library was gone. A forest of twenty-foot-tall crystal prisms stood in its place—a memorial, she supposed. The dome of the Quantum Physics Building was still there. No doubt repaired and refurbished after Gibson had gotten through with it.

The skyline wasn't so different. A few more skyscrapers, a few more apartment complexes. She turned and looked the other way. There it was.

Monarch Tower. Still the biggest bastard on the block five years into the future, but not unscathed. Something had taken a swing at that misshapen obelisk, and snapped a bite out of its top third. Black glass and reinforced concrete had been swept away, the rectilinear honeycomb of its innards now open to the air. The familiar distortion-flicker of a chronon field enveloped the top of the building.

Someone was alive up there, and keeping the lights on.

It had been a brisk winter's day when everything had stopped for the final time.

Riverport. The world. The planets in their rotations. Galaxies, even.

Every last thing in Creation's inventory accounted for, and stopped.

2021 was when it happened. All her efforts would come to nothing. The Countermeasure would not work.

She sniffed, ran the heel of her palm across one eye, and checked the charge on the buckle of her rescue rig. She had three hours before she became one with the universe.

17

The man's legs were tense, angled, frozen in a position of struggle. He had stepped off the hood of his car, which he had parked next to the tree for this purpose. The noose about his neck was electrical cable. If Beth looked at the tree from one angle it was burning. If she looked at it from another it was dead, the branches caked with ice. From another . . . there was no tree, the man and noose hanging from nothing at all.

Not everywhere was as torn between timelines as this tree; almost everywhere, thankfully, was consistent. The upsetting product of conflicting realities coming to a bizarre settlement, yes, but blessedly concrete.

The man had failed to kill himself in time. The terror in his eyes told Beth he had known that.

Paul had said time would end in five years, and he had been right. The evidence bore that out: the changes to Riverport, headlines, dates on phones. Despite the evidence of their eyes and Sofia's calculations, the rising chaos of 2016 hadn't stopped the world.

How?

Her rig had two hours left in it. She had been wandering for an hour. Walking, and trying to piece together how her universe had died. The best place for answers was probably Monarch Tower, but she had no interest in spending her final moments anywhere near that place. If things ended with her never having to see that deconstructed butterfly logo again that'd be just fine, thanks. Instead her feet had taken her around the familiar, through parks and down side streets, taking the scenic route toward the university.

Almost every block had men and women bearing tracts and alarmist sandwich boards: SELF-ANNIHILATION LEADS TO THE FIRES OF DAMNATION!

Riverport was a jumbled toy box, the panicked mingling with the sanguine; men and women walked hand in hand past parents and children rigid in the act of fleeing from something that no longer existed in this settled-upon waveform. On the sidewalk outside the park Beth almost tripped over the head and arms of a man protruding from the sidewalk—his reality betraying him to some facet of another reality—one in which the sidewalk was a hole in the ground, probably—delivering the grim fate of materializing inside earth and concrete.

There was a pattern to the evangelists: they were all preaching the same platform. Not Jesus, not redemption, but "suicide is sin." Every single one of them, from ecstatic to miserable, railed at the world: meet the fate God had intended for them. Do not rob the Lord by meting out death at your own hand.

She scanned what she could from the static, windblown, and weeks-old pages of *Metro* in parks and bus shelters. She spent an iota of her rescue rig's energy to release a fairly intact issue from where it had been tucked beneath the wipers of a parked electric car. Garbage was everywhere, the papers were out-of-date, windows were smashed. Everything pointed to a society where people just stopped going to work—including cops.

The dateline on the papers read January 12, 2021—and those papers didn't seem fresh. Newspaper distribution would have broken down days or weeks earlier. Birthrates were way down, attendances at religious services way up . . . even as the number of self-proclaimed faithful in developed nations had plunged. There was a recession, China was capitalizing on that, and it looked like many First World police forces were now so heavily militarized they were indistinguishable from the actual military. Beth noticed American cops wore the Monarch logo somewhere on their uniform. All of which was by the by. The paper she held was stained and stiff and fading. Things would have gotten a lot worse since it had been printed.

The main headline told her everything: in the week preceding the catastrophe suicides had spiked by more than 5,000 percent globally. People were ending their lives in droves. Governments the world over had been using Monarch as a means to comfort and calm the populace with assurances of progress being made to correct the instabilities triggered in 2016. Clearly, at some point, people stopped buying it and the wheels began to fall off civilization as everyone chose between dying or not living. The conversation among Christians circled around the issue of "can you get to Heaven if you never die" and the counterargument that the end of time was the end of the world as we know it and was the herald of the Lord's return. Secular sources urged people to remain calm, illustrating that the subjective experience of the end of time would be unremarkable. One moment chaos, the next the M-J field may have repaired and all would be well.

Beth knew that was wrong. This was the end. If the M-J field ever repaired then the "end of time" would have been a sub-second pause in the flow of causality. The odds of the machine threading that needle and landing her in it were statistically impossible. But if the end of time is the end of the line . . . then getting here was as easy as hitting a brick wall.

The police had stopped being police, for the most part. Economies had begun to collapse. Death, mourning, and fear had become a global pandemic. Looting had become par for the course.

The universe ended. Her machine's progress—or non-progress—was a testimony to that. And it never, ever recovered.

She tossed the paper into the street. It flew open, joyfully, fluttered, slowed, barely touching the icy blacktop before halting altogether.

These people, the ones who had stuck around for the end, had seen their world lose its mind on every conceivable level. The end hadn't come neatly and cleanly; it hadn't been a quiet cessation that had claimed them unawares.

The Meyer-Joyce field had broken down unevenly as it lost the charge to sustain itself. At first one galaxy moved out of synch with another. Then planets. Looking up at the sky the people in Riverport would have seen the stars become jumbled. That would have been when they realized—knew—that their reality was caving in on them, redesigning itself in ways that couldn't possibly work.

Continuity errors between nations would have come next. The first aircraft disasters would have occurred then. Shortly after, cracks and fuckups and discord would have shocked the country . . . and then, in no time at all, ships would be stuttering into bridges that didn't have time to rise, traffic would be smearing through crosswalks, mechanisms would have broken down, planes would have fallen into oceans, mountains, fields, and streets. Time would have been carved along strange new borders that shifted and shrank. "A" would no longer fit "B" as well as it once had. As electric wiring disagreed with itself, families would have slept soundly in houses that burned to the ground around them . . . while others would have burned to death in houses that hadn't yet become bonfires. The dead would have come back to life, wondered what had happened, and frozen mid-sentence to never move again.

Animals would have turned on owners. Minds would have
snapped.

The world around Beth wasn't easily understood. As apoc-
alypses went it wasn't as mercifully comprehensible as hordes
fleeing the killing flash of a mushroom cloud. Every single stage
of The End was represented here, before her eyes, pulled and
pushed in ways that made no connective sense. The world had
been blanketed in a kaleidoscopic Venn diagram of fluctuating stutters as the universe's chronon field fought for its final
breaths. The spaces in between stutters—the places where causality still worked—would have been places of high madness.
One by one these oases of time and causality would have dried
up, myriad on/off stutters vanishing completely as the M-J field
died and everything finally stopped.

Here, at The End, the Earth was a planet-sized diorama,
staged by a child who had grown bored with his tiny toys.

On a sidewalk, a humanities student played guitar for coins,
while a portly Mexican in a Captain America T-shirt shielded
an arguing couple from a Molotov cocktail thrown by a gleeful old woman who had retrieved it from an array of such weapons set up next to an academic bookstore, bearing the
spray-painted words: "Embassy of the End Times—All Welcome."

Beth had seen every vehicle in a dealer's lot set alight, while
across the street people wandered out of a warm café sipping
cocoa.

Another anomaly, like the hanged man and his tree. A helicopter had attempted an emergency landing on the Riverport
University campus, and failed. Forty feet above it the same helicopter was attempting the same emergency landing: same
markings, same horrified expressions on identical occupants,
doppelgangers all.

She found these places difficult to look at. It strained the

mind in ways it was not built for, and she quickened her pace
past such sites.

When the end came, it would have gone from business as
usual to bedlam very quickly. Every one of these people would
have seen something different, depending on where they stood.
Completely alone they would have been locked in their own
version of universal death by madness. Step to the left and it
would have been something else entirely. Step to the right,
something else again.

By then the total collapse of the M-J field would have been
a mercy, locking everything into a final agreed-upon tableau.

The existence of this tomb planet told her that she would
fail. She would not save the world. Nobody would. Look
around. This is where we end up.

But it wasn't where she ended, she knew that. At some point
Beth was destined to meet her younger self, and would ensure
that girl was trained. That meant Beth was getting out of here,
and it meant that when Beth met her past self she still believed
enough in the mission to ensure that young girl was taken and
trained.

That meant there was hope: It meant her future self had reason to believe it was still worth trying to save the world.

This world may be still, but she had agency. She could retrieve the Countermeasure and, if not activate it in 2016 . . .
she could activate it here. That'd work, right?

Didn't matter. It was a direction. That was all she needed
right now.

She needed to find chronon energy, stat.

She turned toward the university.

A copse of twelve-foot-high polycarbonate stelae occupied the
site of the old library. Each of the four-sided columns bore a

plaque memorializing a student who had died on the morning of October 8, 2016. A piece of the destroyed library was entombed inside each stela: a fragment of scarred, charred wood suspended two feet from the ground.

Fifty feet away from this small crystalline forest stood another monument: a piece of rough black stone. Bolted into it was a plaque of textured, blackened brass, with these words:

> *Land of Heart's Desire,*
> *Where beauty has no ebb, decay no flood,*
> *But joy is wisdom, time an endless song.*
> —W. B. Yeats

New buildings had been erected over the years, designed to pair with the older construction on the western side of the campus. They swept eastward from the crystalline hump of the Quantum Physics Building to curve south. To Beth it looked as if the bulk of the university buildings were like a top-down view of a pair of arms encircling the campus, the Quantum Physics Building as its bejeweled head. The monument to the dead students was in the southeast corner, separated from the street by frosted hedgerows.

Across the way from the memorial a young woman, collar turned up against the cold, had walked southwest along a companion path to Founders' Walk. Beth made her way toward her—a little tricky as it turned out. The pathways were covered in stutter-locked snow that didn't yield to her tread, making the ground uneven; but, surprisingly, because the ice wasn't melting beneath her steps, not slippery.

Whoever the girl was she had been strolling alone, her earphones in, a smile forming on her lips. Beth wondered what she had been listening to as the world ended.

Beth pumped her fingers twice and touched the girl's arm.

The charge on the rescue rig dipped significantly, the smile bloomed on the girl's face, and as momentum kicked in, she spilled forward. Arms pinwheeling backward she righted herself, saw Beth suddenly there, and reflexively panicked. With a scream she pitched backward, her boot concreted within an inch of stutter-locked snow. She hit the ground hard, breath punching out of her with a dull, human sound. Stunned, blinking, she struggled to her elbows.

"Hey hey!" Beth said. "I'm friendly. Here." She extended a hand. "Hand up."

The girl swatted the hand away, eyes wide with outrage, and turned her attention to her trapped foot.

A voice echoed across the expanse, like a gunshot: *"No!"*

At the northeastern fork in the path, where it carried on north toward the Quantum Physics Building, stood a lone, desperate figure. Male. Mid-twenties. Lean beneath a scavenged weather-rated jacket and jeans gone faded and worn along the knees and thighs. Even from that distance Beth made out the shadows under his eyes, the frantic hair, anxious and fretting.

Beth immediately recognized Paul Serene. Early twenties, filthier, but undeniably him. The Paul Serene who had first traveled through Monarch's machine, that night at Riverport University.

In that moment all she felt was the weight of the gun in her armpit.

"Leave her," Paul shouted. "She'll draw them in! Leave her!"

Draw them in. She knew exactly what he was referring to. The campus seemed clear. No movement other than herself, the girl and young Paul Serene—still waving urgently.

She wasn't leaving anybody. "She's coming with us!"

"Leave! Her!" Then: the howls. Fractured, broken; ten

voices, each as if shrieking from three different directions at once. A sound felt, received, but not heard. A sound that resonated in the oldest chambers of Beth's mind, heirloom fears disinterred from dark primordial soil.

The girl on the snow began screaming.

"Wait . . . just hold still." Beth said, trying to keep the quaver from her voice. The girl at her feet was thrashing, wrenching at her ankle. Beth kneeled, double-pumped her fingers.

Beth released the snow around the girl's boot, and the girl scrambled free. Paul was already running—north. Then Beth saw them, suddenly present, coming for them from the southern streets and from behind the shrine to the east.

Shifters.

"I'm sorry," Beth said, but the girl had already taken off, slipping, collapsing, scrambling. "I'm sorry!" Beth got to her feet and ran, stiff-legged, each heavy landing on her wounded leg like a knife twisting in her flesh.

South and east weren't options. To her left was a building and she didn't have time to be releasing doors—plus anything could be in there. She ran north, following the girl, following Paul Serene, headed for the fork in the path. "Bank left," she called out. "Make for the Quant—"

The girl stopped so abruptly Beth had no alternative but to turn her shoulder and take the impact.

It was like running into a wall.

Beth spun with the impact, cycling around the girl's right-hand side. In slow motion Beth saw that the girl's flight had been arrested mid-run, both her feet off the ground, hair thrown forward over her face by the force of a fractal fist slamming between her breasts, passing through her chest, ending her instantly—immobilizing her in the microsecond of her death. The monstrosity's phasing face tracked Beth as she stumbled, her steepled fingers pressed to the cobbles to keep her from going over completely. For a horrifying second pain bloomed bright and she was certain her bad leg would betray her, but then, like a runner at the blocks, she propelled herself north toward the Quantum Physics Building.

Behind her the thing howled again. Its siblings answered the call, and they were *everywhere*.

Her leg was stiffening, seizing. She wasn't going to make it.

"Move!" Paul was at the end of the path. It terminated at a paved walkway that ran east–west. "Follow!" He ran west, alongside the crystalline Quantum Physics Building, making for the entrance.

Behind Beth were at least a half dozen of the shifting, flickering, howling things, converging fast, lurching weird, grasping and spasming, as if each one was having a violent argument with infinite versions of itself. She couldn't die like this.

She hit the walkway, used hands-on-wall to arrest her momentum and shift it forty-five left, powering after Paul.

"What are they? What are those things?"

He didn't answer. He was at the door, disappearing inside. *Don't you lock it, fucker. Don't you lock it.*

She slammed through.

"Leave the door open," he yelled. "Over here!"

The atrium was no longer an open reception area with a wealth of superfluous space: the interior of the dome was now crowded with a maze of smaller buildings and construction. Beth ran into the narrow lobby just as Paul toppled a heavy drum onto its side in front of the doorway, and—

"Is that a grenade?"

"Door 3 behind me, get inside"—and he pulled the pin, held the spoon, released a safety seal on the drum.

A wall of flickering, roaring black forced its way through the door.

She heard the spoon *ting* as she leaped into the room. The

room was a techno-hive, but she'd worked at Monarch long enough to know a chronon aggregation setup when she saw it: racks of charging chronon batteries, sterile surfaces, monitoring stations.

Batteries. Aggregators. Chronon energy: exactly what she needed.

Paul crashed in behind her. "Floor!" he cried, gesturing frantically. "Floor!"

A panel of flooring had been lifted aside, down which he leaped. The roars were deafening. They'd overrun . . .

"Floor!"

Beth leaped into darkness. Paul appeared out of nowhere and yanked the hatch shut.

The grenade detonated. Most of the howls ceased entirely. Outside, from what Beth could hear, the stragglers reluctantly, resentfully retreated.

"That," she said, "was a chronon battery. You blew up a chronon battery."

The crawl space beneath the aggregator was intended for maintenance. It was tight, airless, crammed with the underguts of an apparatus that might have been giving them lymphoma if it weren't as stutter-locked as everything else. The crawl space led away from the hatch, opening into what looked like a small service area. Beth saw a wax candle, immobile as anything else: a source of perpetual yet strangely static light.

"They . . . we . . ." Paul seemed to be having trouble with language. "They don't like . . . the chronon burst restarts causality for a brief time in a limited area. They can't manifest outside of chronon-free areas, so . . . they're my safeguard. Potential. It . . . they find it . . . painful." He turned on all fours and crept toward a dim light past neat knots of fat cabling. "Hurts them. When you're alive, you can be anything," he was murmuring. "When you're dead . . . you're just one thing. I keep batteries up there. They . . . only exist in stutters."

Beth looked to the light ahead, hand to her gun, out of a need for security.

There was a reason her Zed persona had been so extreme. It was to make her Beth persona unrecognizable by contrast. In this moment it paid off: Paul didn't recognize her at all.

Checking her gun again she crawled toward the light.

"Cost me a week's sleep," he was saying. "What you made me do. When you made me waste all that chronon. A week's sleep."

"A week's . . . ?" She emerged into his hidey-hole. Ambient light from underfloor diagnostics lit the place midnight blue and shadow. He had enough space for a thin, closed-cell foam sleeping pad—with a jacket for a pillow. By this was a hunk of technology Beth recognized as being a refined, miniaturized version of the stutter shield generators Monarch used to run Strikers and Juggernauts through their paces. This was smaller, though, redesigned. "Hey," she said. "Nice place. How long have you been sleeping here?"

Paul closed his eyes, shook his head. "Don't know. Meaningless question. Don't know." He tapped the device. "Slept . . . a lot." She leaned forward to get a closer look, minding her head against the low ceiling. "Don't . . . ," Paul said. "Don't touch it."

"I won't. Is it . . . it's a stutter generator?"

Paul shook his head. "Causality."

She took a closer look. Science really wasn't her thing, but . . . "This generates a causality bubble?"

Lifeboat. Of course. Its directive was to ensure people would remain mobile and aware once time stopped flowing. Just like the bubble she had seen around the top floors of the Tower.

"Can't sleep without it. Fall asleep, I'll become like . . ." He gestured toward the hatch.

"The monsters?"

Paul shook his head. "The other people. I'll . . . never wake up."

Beth remembered: the Joyce farm. Jack knocked out by the erupting BearCat—freezing at the moment he lost consciousness. If Paul lost consciousness in a chronon-free zone he'd become as immobile as anyone else.

She imagined him, living here, under the floor, for months— maybe years—scavenging not only food but *time*, living in fear of Shifters, in an effort to stave off oblivion.

"My name's Beth," she said. "Who are you?"

He trembled. "Paul," he said and, just like that, that pathetic figure of a man burst into tears. When was the last time someone had asked him his name? Asked him anything? "Please," he said. "Take me back inside."

"Inside? You mean upstairs? The lab?"

"No," he said, hurt by her obvious cruelty. "The Tower."

The flickering shield around the top floors of the Monarch building. Someone keeping the lights on.

Beth calmed him, distracted him, decided they needed to eat. Paul showed her how he had been surviving: canned goods, a propane cooker, bottled water, stored in the staff kitchenette upstairs.

She had about forty minutes left in her rescue rig. After that she'd be as stiff as every other poor bastard.

Out from under the floor Paul had noticed her wounded leg immediately. With all the care of a small boy tending a fallen bird he had cut away a portion of her fatigues, enough to expose the wound, and tended it as best he could with antiseptic, fresh gauze, and a tight binding.

She told him she had gashed herself running from the Shifters.

"You have to be more careful here," he told her. "When everyday things don't yield, they become dangerous. You could slash yourself on a falling leaf, you hit it right."

"Thank you," she said. "You tie a pretty competent bandage."

"Boy Scout," he said, closing the kit.

Paul's kitchenette was spartan: steel benchtops, small microwave (useless, no power), fridge (redundant, food lasts forever), one table, and four chairs. He chatted as he heated a pan on a propane camp stove, cracked eggs, mixed flour, chocolate, and maple syrup. And cinnamon.

Paul told her his story, about the university shooting, going through the machine and expecting to emerge back into the Riverport University time lab. Instead he found the airlock packed with passengers: men in Monarch armor. They had been nervous, Paul's sudden presence in the machine with them unexpected. One had almost shot him but the soldier in charge said (and this was confusing), "Don't shoot, it's him." Then the main airlock had opened.

From outside the machine someone had said "Welcome." The Monarch troopers were asked to come forward and relinquish their weapons. There had been some back-and-forth, but the troopers eventually exited, hands open.

Then someone had called Paul by name, asked him to come out of the machine.

Terrified, Paul had stepped off the Promenade, into the airlock, and surveyed what awaited.

Outside the airlock was a glossy-floored expanse of polished black ceramic, the ceiling vast above. A glassed-in observation deck looked down upon him from one side. Swaddled figures stood motionless there, faces obscured behind safety goggles. He saw the Monarch soldiers being led away by a group of men and women wrapped head to toe in protective layers of dark material, weapons held loosely in hand. Paul didn't know what had happened to the soldiers after that. He never saw them again.

At the foot of the steel ramp people in sand-colored floor-length robes waited for him, attended by personnel in black military-style uniforms.

Behind them the far wall of the lab was gone, torn away and with it part of the glossy black floor. Riverport was laid out through a flickering violet energy haze. Smack in the middle of the view was the university. The sky above it was a thick mass of black cloud punched through with pale eddies, bolts of terrible energy leaping from earth to sky. There was flame and there was smoke—none of it moving—with great gouges slashed perpendicular to Main Street.

"Come out," the tallest figure had coaxed, gently. "You're expected."

"Wait," Beth held up a hand. "How did they know you were arriving?"

Paul was getting frustrated with what he was cooking, sighing, watching it fall to bits atop the plastic spatula. The gas cooker froze every now and then and Paul had to make contact with it for a half second to reanimate it. "The people in the Tower, they're always working, up there."

Project Lifeboat. Had to be.

"Sometimes they come out in BearCats, hauling trailers. Sometimes monsters come for them, and they do what I do: drop chronon charges and run."

They did it, then. Lifeboat happened. The world ended, and Hatch got what he wanted.

"They've even got planes," he said. "I've seen them taking

off from the airport. Why go anywhere? The entire world is like this, right?"

"I really don't know, Paul. I . . . woke up," she lied. "Someone put this gadget on me, told me how to use it, then left me to it. Told me to come here and look for a chronon supply before the charge runs out."

She watched as he reached for a plate and moved it to the stove. He scraped the mess onto it.

"Are they . . . good people, do you think? In the Tower?"

"I don't know," he said, sullenly. "They gave me supplies, led me from the Tower, and that was that. Sounds like you got the same treatment. Maybe it's an experiment."

"Thank you," she said as he handed her a plate. It smelled like something a kid would make for breakfast. If she was going to eat she had to make it quick—before the charge dissipated. Taking bits and pieces between her fingers she transferred it to her mouth. Lumpy, sweet, dry, and powdery . . . but who knew where her next meal was coming from? She noticed him watching her hands—specifically her thimbled fingers. "The people up there wear these?" She waggled her digits.

"Only when they go outside. I've seen you around, haven't I?"

Beth swallowed. "This is good."

"I've seen you around."

"Gotta get out sometime," she said, hoping that'd be the last of it.

"You know who I am."

Her bones flashed glass-cold. "Sure," she said, dutifully taking another mouthful, buying a few moments to think. "You're Paul."

"I'm not wearing a rig," he said. "You weren't surprised by that at all." The cooker's blue flames became rigid, Paul forgetting his own meal. "Why are you here?"

She swallowed, the clumped lump sticking in her throat. "I figured that was normal for some people."

Paul had nothing to say. He just looked at her, working her out.

She couldn't tell what he was thinking, but if he was half as skilled as the Paul Serene she knew in 2016 he could kill her here and now. All she could taste was chocolate and cinnamon and . . .

She knew who he would become. The things he would done. She had to shoot him. Right here, right now, with the taste of that child's meal in her mouth.

"I'll help you," he said. "I have plenty of chronon batteries. I don't need a rig so we can make them last a long time. The chronon umbrella only fits one, but we can sleep in shifts. You'll be okay."

Ah . . . shit.

He had shown her how to tap the current-model chronon containers to recharge her rig, and then they had retreated beneath the flooring. Shifters were howling in the city, but it was distant. Paul was right: it was safer here on campus. She figured the concentration of chronon energy—stored as it was—may have been enough to keep them away.

He wanted to double-check the dressing on her leg, but she had insisted it was fine. She had told Paul she'd take first watch, and to get some sleep.

Paul had crawled on to his little mat, pulled his sleeping bag over him like a blanket, and curled up fetal. "I'm sorry I was suspicious," he said. "There hasn't been anyone else. Not for . . ." He stopped talking when his voice cracked.

"It's okay." She gave his hand a reassuring little shake. "It's—"

Paul's fingers clasped her hand and he looked right at her. "Would you . . . would you just hold my hand till I fall asleep?"

God, she needed to backpedal. She was off mission. She was way, way off mission. "Sure," she said, knowing there was a special room in Hell for her, for what she was about to do. "Sleep. I'll be here when you wake up."

Paul nodded, buried his head into his bunched-up jacket, his hand vise-tight on hers, and shuddered, grateful to no longer be alone.

A room, just for her.

Paul had a gym bag he used to store cans of beans, sachets of meal replacement powder, and bags of old T-shirts. The chronon canister fit neatly into it. She left it by the dome's main door, then went back into the chronon accumulator lab and climbed through the open floor panel. Paul was still asleep, fingers curling and uncurling in his sleeping bag blanket.

She couldn't kill him. She couldn't. Beth remembered the look of terror and betrayal on that girl's face as she had woken up to the end of the world. The terrible sadness that had flooded her face as she died.

Beth had done that. She didn't have it in her to kill another innocent.

So she did what she could do. She kneeled beside him and, deeply ashamed of herself, turned off the chronon umbrella. The light faded from inside the tiny hidey-hole. And in no time at all Paul's breathing stopped. It was just Beth now, kneeling in the twilight.

"I'm sorry," she said, wiping the back of her hand across her eyes. "I promise we'll do everything we can to fix this."

She got up, bending beneath the low ceiling, wiping her hand on the legs of her fatigues. Hoisting herself aboveground, she double-pumped her fingers and moved the floor panel into place—sealing Paul Serene into his sad little refuge for the rest of lightless, self-dividing eternity.

She snatched the bag from beside the dome's doorway and got out of there, the canister feeling heavier than it should.

It took a relative hour to get from the campus to the gutted building that housed Will's machine. Exhaustion weighed her down by the time she got there. She hadn't slept since before the university shooting and her leg still wasn't taking weight as well as it used to.

She took a direct route to Will's machine, an almost straight line between campus and Monarch Tower. Company vehicles, hardware, and troops were thick on the main streets, making for the Tower at speed as causality fell to pieces around them. A BearCat had swerved, two wheels lifted off the ground. A Monarch operative hung out the side, carbine loosing a final spray before the vehicle surely flipped. Beth noticed the damage to the vehicle's antiballistic surfacing—deep tears, ripping whole panels free in places. The killing blow had ripped along the passenger section, killed the gunner, and took out the vehicle's chronon rig. They'd been running from Shifters.

A Juggernaut was caught in a pose of alarm and distress, most of the front plating torn from the protective suit, the shoulder-mounted micromissile pod hanging by a single joint. The pilot had been killed halfway through jettisoning himself out the back of the rig, like a skeleton stepping backward out of its own skin.

A four-way intersection was where two thick conical sprays of destroyed vehicles and dead people had plowed into each other, disintegrated at high impact, got airborne, and sprayed killing debris in two fat directions simultaneously.

Causality had fallen into a disagreement with itself here. The flow of traffic both ways had stuttered, machine-gunning twin rivers of vehicles into each other at speeds that should have been impossible. It was as if hours of traffic from two directions had fed into each other in an instant. Cars, shrapnel, and bodies hung in a wide spherical radius centered on the intersection, debris so heavy that the site was like an imperfect, damaged dome of steel studded with contorted bodies.

Car frames reduced to ugly blasts of metal, human bodies ruined and unidentifiable. In those last moments every rule had gone out the window.

This would have been happening the world over.

With all her heart Beth hoped her parents hadn't lived to see it.

She released the front door and entered. "Get to July fourth, grab the Countermeasure, and split." She slung the bag across her shoulder and climbed down into the excavated basement, doing her best to compartmentalize everything she had seen at the intersection—next to the compartment set aside for what she had just done to Paul. "See you there, Jack. Don't stand me up."

Not Monarch Paul, Jack's friend Paul. The kid who couldn't operate solo at parties; the kid she and Jack had relied on to keep an eye out for the cops when they were up to no good, much as Paul had hated it; the kid who had sat through a couple of episodes of *Team Outland* one night, defending the character of the show's dork-genius.

The place gave her the screaming heebies. Not just the basement but the whole tomb-like silent world. She had to get the fuck gone, as a matter of priority.

Cricking her neck, she began piecing together what had to happen next.

The corridor needed a conventional charge as well as a chronon load. The core would also be brought online electrically. Whoever had relocated Will's machine down here had provided a generator, and it seemed to be in good shape. All she needed was for the chronon charge in each critical component to hold long enough in this chronon-free world for her to run the fastest lap of her life.

She double-pumped her hand and reanimated the clear-screened laptop. The charge she imparted lasted long enough for her to lock in her destination date: 4 July 2010. She unzipped the bag and hauled out the canister. It was a standard Monarch capacitor design, sealed and insulated. The socket design was unfamiliar; she hoped it was standard to 2021. If Monarch tech and Will's kit-bashed jalopy weren't compatible she was going to have to make a run at the Tower for another way out of this time zone. Fuck that.

She just wanted out of this grave to someplace where she could breathe life for a few more years. This place was too final, too sad, too . . . meaningless. Too nothing. She had never realized how much she depended on ambient sounds and smells and surprises to know she was alive. Voices. The way snow didn't crunch under her feet, the way streets didn't smell like carbon monoxide cut through with the occasional sharp line of perfume or aftershave, the *silence* . . . were killing her by degrees. It was claustrophobia by way of agoraphobia. It was like falling off a cliff, flailing and helpless. Surely it must be what astronauts felt in deep space. To be the only living thing in a void is to be both dead and forgotten, but alive enough to know it.

A blade of paper she had adhered to the canister's shell by

some latent static charge, slid to the benchtop: a printed screen cap. Wikipedia. The subject was Paul Serene.

She skimmed the article. It was all there. Everything she needed to know between then and now. A thought occurred and she opened the gym bag. The bottom of the bag was floored with a nest of similar clippings. She gripped the printout, read it all from start to finish in a rush.

Humanity knew it had been killed by Paul Serene. The narrative was simple: on the morning of October 8, 2016, he had sabotaged and activated a device—a time machine—that Monarch Solutions had decommissioned for ethical reasons. Twenty-four hours later, Paul Serene issued his one and only communique to the world, detailing what he had done and why: the M-J field had been dealt a fatal blow. The universe had a few years of life left. In that time the chronon levels would drop, causality would become increasingly schizophrenic, and then—finally—time would cease to flow altogether.

In the days after Martin Hatch had come forward with a proposal: Project Lifeboat. He spelled it out very plainly: the end of time was inevitable, but humanity could survive it *if* Lifeboat was operational. Humanity's best and brightest could work beyond the end of time to engineer a solution.

Paul Serene was known and remembered as a monster: the man who had erased the universe.

Martin Hatch was known as the man who may have saved it.

The frozen world outside was waiting for him to succeed.

The Paul Serene asleep on campus now had known this. Saving her, making pancakes, holding her hand . . . he had known all this.

"Shit." Dropping some charge, she reefed out a fat coil of textured cabling from the tray beneath the workbench. "Shit shit shit." It ended in what looked like a compatible plug:

multipronged with a threaded safety collar. It took a little force but eventually the connector snapped into the battery and she screwed the collar down tight. *He had known.*

Transferring a c-charge to the laptop she dumped half her rig's power into the machine, releasing it from stasis. She checked the ladder, listened. Nothing.

A few keystrokes and the power gauge on the canister lit violet, the laptop registering a steady flow of c-particles from the canister to the corridor.

"One point two one gigawatts," she muttered to herself, wandering over to the generator. "One point two one gigawatts . . . Here we go." She double-pumped her fingers, pressed her palm to the flat casing of the diesel generator parked on bricks by the wall. "First you get sentimental over Gibson's kid, now you do this." Quickly she pulled off an access panel, hoped for the best, and kicked it off. "You're too soft for this, Starr. I should have chosen someone else." The generator sparked to life with a furious complaint, shuddering violently. Closing the hatch muffled the sound quite well.

She moved back to the laptop and tried not think about having just buried someone alive at the end of the world. "One point . . ." Oh God. ". . . twenty-one gigawatts . . ."

She had a choice.

"You're weak, Starr." Her voice resonated briefly, died suddenly, in stasis. "Go back."

Events can't be changed. We're slaves to cause and effect. Paul Serene lives. Paul Serene founds Monarch. Paul Serene causes the Fracture. *You're weak. You're weak. You've fucked up.* "I've got to kill him." *But you can't kill him.* "I've got to kill him." *It's not possible.*

"You told me your name was Beth."

In the reflection of the laptop's screen she saw him: at the foot of the ladder, daylit.

She wasn't afraid. She was ashamed. "Paul."

She double-pumped her fingers, brought the terminal online, remembered she'd already done that.

"You know who I am," he said.

"I know you're a good person, and a sweet kid." Locked it in. "And I know that you'd never want to hurt anyone."

You're the reason I am who I am. My whole life was authored by yours.

He was bare chested, in his worn-out jeans, standing at the foot of the ladder . . . a look of utter betrayal on his face.

"You weren't asleep," she said.

"Martin Hatch told me our machine was the only one. No previous working prototypes." He took a few hesitant barefoot steps toward her, through the dust-mote tunnel she had carved out of the basement air. "You were going to kill me?"

She'd only ever heard stories about the powers Paul Serene was meant to have. If Jack's fumbling around was a comparison, this may not end well for her.

She reminded herself: *you can't die.* Not yet. By the same rule Paul couldn't either. So where did this leave them?

Somewhere beyond the walls, Shifters howled.

Paul's limbs locked, his breathing caught in his thin chest.

"Why do they make that sound?" she asked.

"We hurt them. . . ." He choked on the words, swallowed. "Causality . . . potential . . . possibility . . . it all fountains off living people. It's excruciating to Shifters."

"That's why they don't bother the people frozen outside."

"It's why they kill," Paul snapped. "To take you from being *anything* to being *a thing.*" His eyes settled on the machine. "Is this why they wouldn't let me stay in the Tower?"

So that part of his story was true?

Paul's eyes fell on the machine. "Am I supposed to go through that? Does it work?"

She felt the weight of it at her back, like a threat. "Paul. You have to be brave enough for an entire world here, man."

He wasn't listening, walking closer, halfway to her now. "What does that mean?"

"You know what happens if you leave here." Paul wasn't listening. He moved closer still, eagerly, his eyes tracing from the machine to the generator, back to the laptop. "Paul, back up."

"Fundamentally, it's almost identical to our model."

Shifter shrieks shotgunned through her every cell. Beth and Paul shocked away from the direction of the sound, the front door, the world outside.

He spun on her, eyes bracketing nothing but animal violence. *"Get out of my way."*

Six months learning to speed-draw paid off in that moment, side-drawing from inside her jacket and locking him square . . . but only for a moment. Paul vanished, her fingers wrenched, and the weapon swept away. She cried out in pain, clutching her hand.

He was at the laptop, her gun next to the keyboard. The dates were already changed.

She rushed him from behind, pointlessly. He was gone before she even got close.

As her world vanished in a blast of pain and light her inner ear lost all sense of vertical and horizontal. A bed of cold stone crashed into her spine, and the only sensible thing that penetrated her undoing was something someone had told her a long time ago in Arizona: "It's the hits you don't see coming that get you."

She was bone and pain, a small mess of connections and associations that didn't fit together. Something pneumatic engaged, and she heard something vent with a deep hiss. She blood-felt the discordant rage of Shifters, skipping and phasing toward them from the outside world, homing in faster as their excruciation escalated.

Paul was talking to her, panicked, moving about. He stepped over her legs to get to the laptop. ". . . this'll never happen. You'll be someone else. I'll be someone else. I'll never, *never* . . . "

The shattering cries of Shifters had become deafening.

"Paul . . ." She almost drowned on his name. Rolling sideways was like having her head stepped on. She cough-cleared her mouth of blood, watched sprayed droplets catch on suspended dust particles. Her voice was a croak. "Change is impossible—"

"It's a time machine, you idiot! I helped build this thing!" He was white with fear.

"No . . ." Her hands pressed to the stone floor, trying to keep her gorge down. "You didn't."

He was moving again, backing for the entry ramp.

"I know the science. If we made this happen we can . . . I can unmake this."

She wasn't having this conversation again. Her hand slapped down onto the benchtop, grasped for the gun. It wasn't there.

Paul had it. He pointed it at her. His voice was fragile. "Please don't." He had never hurt anyone before. He had never hit a woman. Now he had a gun pointed at one. She could see Paul was collapsing from the inside, knowing already what he was becoming.

He wasn't looking at her, though.

Roiling humanoid non-shapes, barely coherent, stood at the far end of the basement. Snapping. Jigging. Agonized.

The gun wavered in Paul's hand. "Please . . . don't let them get me."

She laughed. It hurt. "You can't go back, Paul. You can't

change things." She pointed to the laptop. "Because you haven't primed the machine."

Onscreen an amber text box requested: ACTIVATE?

Shifters rounded in their direction, caught sight of their infinite potentials, their fountaining causality. Their hatred and madness hit them like a physical thing.

Metal screeched as the corridor's locking mechanism cycled. The airlock seal cracked, the lock auto-spinning as atmosphere vented and external hydraulics levered the door aside.

With a cry of relief Paul spun for his escape.

Waiting inside was the biggest Shifter either of them had ever seen: broad across distorted shoulders, its thrashing head snaking three ways through space. One distorted flashing shadow of a paw grabbed the lip of the airlock, levering itself forward as its second hand reached out, into the room, for Paul's face.

The center of that hand shone with light.

Backing away Paul let it all go and screamed—because it was going to be the last thing he would ever do.

The Shifters rushed forward, half their frames missing as they flick-vaulted through space, over workbenches.

Beth hit ACTIVATE.

The chronon distortion wave kicked off the Promenade, hit the Shifters, and for a moment—as when Paul had saved Beth from them a few hours ago—they vanished.

It was all Paul needed. He was gone, in a blink, through the airlock. Beth swore and vaulted after him. She barreled up the two-step ladder and into the airlock as the distortion wave subsided and the Shifters phased back in. The big Shifter, Shining Palm, half out the airlock door, had time to roar once before Beth was through the right-hand door behind it. It locked behind her and . . .

Silence.

As fast as she could she ran—not to 2010, but toward the date Paul had set.

She ran to 1999.

18

William Joyce, twenty years old, finished his celebratory cocoa, rinsed the ceramic Riverport Raptors mug, and returned it to the cupboard above the sink. The house was dark, silent. He had taken Jack, his younger brother, over to the house of the Serene family. He'd be staying for the night.

Tonight solitude was imperative. Tonight Will would undertake a journey of great risk. One he had worked toward since he was a boy of fifteen. Utilizing grant money, academic connections, and a falsified passport he had secured through—of all places—a local biker bar, William Joyce had financed the construction of a device that learned men and women many years his senior had laughed off as ridiculous, impossible.

Screw those guys.

William zipped his jumpsuit to the neck, ensured his canvas utility belt was securely fastened. Clipped to it was everything a chrononaut might possibly need: penlight, cell phone, a roll of elastic tubing, alligator clips, pens, waterproof notebook, a digital multilanguage translator he had bought from a magazine, a canvas pouch containing aspirin and iodine and anti-malaria medication. Around his neck were binoculars and a Brownie camera. Beneath the jumpsuit was a secondhand bulletproof vest.

The pack on the kitchen table contained a change of clothes, a bottle of water, three cans of spiced ham, seven novels, an edition of that day's *New York Times,* and an untested chronon storage device—painstakingly charged over a period of years that he was fairly sure had been adequately shielded.

A note rested on the kitchen table beneath a thin vase. It read:

Dear Reader,

If you have found this letter, then I am gone. Grieve not for me, but make proper use of the gift I have left mankind. In the old barn, sitting stately outside the casement of this very kitchen, is a time machine.

Yes! You read that correctly! A time machine!

I bequeath now to the government of the United States, who are best equipped to plumb the secrets and discoveries I have made, catalogued extensively in the notes I have left behind, the right to license my work for the betterment of mankind. I leave the negotiations to Mrs. Serene of 94 Chestnut Avenue, who has more experience in these things than I.

As to my brother, Jack, I bequeath to him all the proceeds and royalties from all goods and services based upon my research, discoveries, inventions, and intellectual property. Additionally, this shall cover all costs of his being cared for by the Serene family of 94 Chestnut Avenue, as they continue to foster and care for him up until the age of 21.

All I ask is that great care be taken with the Chronon Core™ for as long as it remains active and connected to my beautiful Promenade™. I may yet—someday—return.

Look for me in the year 2019.

Ad futura, ad astra.

—Dr. William Joyce (qual. pending)

William read the note one more time, nodded with satisfaction, hoisted his travel pack, and marched for the barn—stopping only for one last backward glance. How he wished his parents had lived to see this moment.

He opened the front door and, hunching against the icy winter air, closed that chapter of his life with the *thunk* of a lock.

An inch and a half of snow had fallen the night before, and several inches that month. William was pleased that he had invested his few remaining dollars in the sturdy utility boots he had found at the thrift store on River Street. They kept the moisture out well, the snow crunching satisfyingly beneath their worn tread. Warm light fell in subtly fanning lines from between the boards of the barn across the garden: amber illumination sparkling white, glowing moonlight blue. With shaking hands, he unclipped his key rings and snapped loose the three padlocked chains from the flimsy barn door. Gravity snaked them eagerly through their iron loops, sending them clinking heavily into the freshly packed snow.

Stepping into his barn laboratory he pulled the door closed behind him. It was only a few degrees warmer inside, made so by the grumbling generator and the ambient temperature of his beautiful Promenade and its stout, multifaceted heart.

William surveyed his kingdom, nodding as he found each essential piece as it should be. The generator: jouncing and thrumming. The chronon capacitor: running a little hot, but the charge at 100 percent. The departure station, created from a dozen PCs running in tandem, the date prominently onscreen in satisfyingly retro font: November 1, 2019. The systems monitoring station: online, all gauges reading nominal. That would change once his creation was brought to life. Which left the core.

The core was offline. Utilizing a 10,000-terahertz laser, small quantities of multiple isotopes, a small reaction chamber

within a nuclear research lab at a South American university, a homemade carbon launcher, and a supercomputer,
William had fabricated within a magnetically sealed geometric
sphere one stable and relatively safe microscopic black hole.

That's what was resting at the center of the machine, within
that sphere, waiting to be brought online.

No time like the present.

He crossed to systems monitoring. A socket rested at the
center of every facet of the core's geometric casing. Resting
half-inserted into each socket was a fat eight-inch connector.
Running from each connector was a wide-gauge length of cabling, connecting directly to one segment of the Promenade.

Triple-checking all settings and conditions, William deemed
all things to be optimal. Five years, great risk, and all of his
grant money and professional earnings had gone toward this:
his moment of truth.

"Make it so."

He clicked a single key. Masses of black cabling jumping
once as electromagnets charged and plugs slammed into sock-
ets. Will's eyes flicked from the core, down to the diagnostics
screen, and back to the core.

A bass thump kicked pleasingly through his ribs as a single
distortion wave pulsed off the Promenade. Electricity plugs
sparked and burned out. Lightbulbs exploded, dropping the
barn into freezing half-light. The generator screamed and
black smoke poured from all the wrong places. Will's eyes
scanned information feverishly as it poured down the line,
filling pulsing onscreen gauges, numerals skittering as they
extended.

The Promenade lit up from within, a solid bar of white light
blasting thickly from the airlock, through winter air grown
pungent with diesel fumes and burning insulation. Diagnostics informed him that the Promenade had flooded itself,

momentarily, with chronon particles. That wasn't meant to happen. Not yet. He hadn't yet primed the Promenade for departure.

AIRLOCK: DISENGAGING.

Deadbolts thunked back within the Promenade's housing. Chronon levels were now at normal levels within. Hydraulics engaged. Atmosphere vented.

William forgot the diagnostics. He stepped away from the bench to stand before the airlock.

The hatch levered aside, and someone appeared inside the Promenade's airlock, lurching into sight from the left. A visitor?

The translator! He fumbled on his utility belt. He may need the translator. . . .

"Wel-welcome, traveler," William said, stammering. "Damn it. I am—"

What the stranger had to say needed no translation. From the ramp of the airlock the figure raised one arm and shot William in the head.

Paul popped into existence the second Beth stepped out of the corridor, into the airlock. She caught him leaning heavily on the door, pointing the gun he had stolen from her at whatever was outside the machine.

She didn't stop to think but barreled right into the little fucker, snapping one elbow into the side of his head. Paul's skull rebounded off the heavy iron door frame. The bounce-back pitched him slack-bodied down the exit ramp.

It's the hits you don't see coming that get you.

She swept up the sidearm as it hit the ground and came up level with Paul's head.

Paul's face was a mess of tears as he rose weakly up off his knees. "No." He put his hands up. "Please." Backed away, half-naked, stumbling. "No. No no . . ."

Oh fucking hell. She gritted her teeth. Steadied her arm. "Shut up."

"Please. Please . . . *please* . . . no . . . no."

It was freezing but Beth felt nothing but sick. "Stop saying that. Shut up." Their frantic breaths misted in clouds before them. She advanced, he backed away—off the ramp, onto a dirt floor.

She recognized this place. They were in the Joyce barn; the same barn in which she'd have her altercation with Gibson seventeen years from now.

There was a body on the floor, dressed like a cut-price Ghostbuster. It was Jack's brother, Will.

Paul chose that moment to turn and run.

"Stop!"

She fired. The round caught him above the hip, splashed right through him, impact turning him around. He was looking at her as he stumbled backward to one knee, tears streaking his quivering face. Staring down at himself in disbelief, seeing what had been done to him, he screamed in a ruined voice wet with despair. Even then he was still trying to get to his feet, still trying to get away.

Paul looked back up at her, as Beth shut her eyes and fired again.

It took him through the shoulder, wrenching him around and down again. He coughed, scrambled weakly, trying to buy a few inches closer to an escape from this nightmare.

"Don't," Beth said, trying to see clearly.

She shuddered, trading a little piece of herself to aim at the back of Paul's head.

Then, just like that, he was gone—the barn door smashing wide open in his wake and all the cold in the world rush-
ing in.

Shock.

He was gone. Paul Serene was out there, in the world.
Loose.

"Fuck!"

She flew to the door, liking her chances of being able to find
him quick in the snow. The tracks were there all right, stretching all the way to the woods. Paul had covered hundreds of
feet in no time. In this weather, wearing nothing but jeans, she
wanted to believe he wouldn't make it.

She needed confirmation. She needed a body.

The one on the floor behind her groaned. Will was alive.

Paul was out there, but Will was in here—wounded.

She couldn't give chase, so she just screamed at the trees.
Her own rage echoed back twice. Seconds later she was at
Will's side, telling him to remain still. Will's response was to
shout something incomprehensible and utterly fail to follow instructions.

"Calm down!"

Will froze. She could see the livid tear across the left side of
his skull, the flowered bruise, the free-flowing blood.

"I didn't do this to you. That was—"

"Chut!" Will barked. "Nothing!"

"What?"

"Don't! Just . . . !" He panted, eyes ranging back and forth
across nothing in particular. "Have I been shot?"

"Yes."

Will fainted.

If she was honest with herself she was tempted to leave him
there. The adrenaline was draining and a freezing cold was
working its way to her bones. He had a canteen clipped to an

overloaded belt. She unscrewed it, poured ice water across her fingers, and flicked it at his face. Will snapped to, barking.

"Agh! Agh!"

"You were grazed, that's all. But you need to get to a hospital."

"Stop," he snapped, totally confused. "Talking." Then: "Don't tell me any—"

"Don't tell you anything about the future, got it, I saw the same movie. Can you stand?"

That took the wind out of his sails, and Beth felt a little bad about it. She imagined he might have been preparing that speech for years. He righted himself, got to his feet. "I should have expected this. Why didn't I expect this?"

"Getting shot?"

Will looked pale, like he might throw up. "Please stop saying that. It's very . . . just, please stop saying that." He took a couple of steadying breaths. "Visitors. I should have expected it once I activated the core. It stands to reason that future users would want to go back as far as they could."

Beth looked around. "Looks like it's just us, though."

"Yes," Will said. "My thoughts on that are undecided."

"Will," she said, hugging herself. "I need to get out of this cold. And . . . there are some things you *need* to know. That's just how it is."

"Wait," he said. "Just . . . wait. What do I call you? And, please, no real names. I don't want to know anything about you."

Beth remembered Will's video message from the swimming pool. The vast universe felt suddenly like a small, tightly-arranged room with everything in its place. They had always been in their place.

"September," she said, feeling very far from home. "Call me September."

Sunday, 28 February 1999. 9:49 P.M. Riverport, Massachusetts. Forty-six minutes later.

The kitchen table was an oasis of light. Beth's mug was empty; William had no interest in his tea. She was silent as he processed all that she had told him.

He hadn't looked at her for twenty minutes, eyes scanning left and right, processing.

Eventually she broke the quiet by asking if he understood what had to be done.

"You will not find his body," Will said. "The man you pursued here."

"I know."

The index and middle fingers of Will's hands wiggled nervously. Processing. "All the events of the future world of which you are a citizen will come to pass. In a sense they have already happened, and cannot be avoided or undone. You must understand that, September."

"Dr. Joyce, you know all you need to know: a machine based on your design damages the M-J field. We need to repair the field. Can you design something that we can use, in my time, to repair it?"

"It will take ten years."

"2009. Perfect. I'll jump ahead ten years, meet you and . . ."

Will was shaking his head. "It took five years for the Promenade to accumulate enough of a chronon charge for one journey, and your arrival depleted most of that."

Beth put her mug down, carefully. "You haven't perfected chronon aggregation."

"I've barely begun. Most of my funds went into the creation of the machine's core."

She felt panic rise. She didn't like it. She barely recognized it. She took the fear and compartmentalized it. Moved on.

"Tell me how we're going to fix the fracture in the M-J field."

"It will be a broad-spectrum solution—a carpet bombing—but it's the best I can do with the resources available. It will be my life's work. It's also a long shot."

"When can you start?"

He still hadn't looked at her, his eyes still ranging over nothing in particular. "I started twenty minutes ago."

Wednesday, 24 May 2000. 6:11 P.M. Fifteen months, twenty-five days after time core activation.

Point of view tilts sharply up, then down, then centers. Camera appears to be positioned on a writing desk. Location appears to be an attic—mostly empty.

William Joyce enters frame, sits, adjusts his glasses.

"I was averaging ten entries per three-hour videotape, resulting in a collection of over sixty cassettes. It became apparent to me after a . . . passionate . . . entreaty from my visitor that this posed a significant security risk. As you can tell from the empty bookshelves behind me that collection has now been sanitized. I will be restricting myself to a single videotape for the purposes of ordering my thoughts henceforth." He gathers his thoughts. "I . . ."

Joyce reaches off-camera, retrieves a mug, drinks from it, winces.

"I ran the numbers again today. My initial ten-year projection holds firm, but the cost has not—as expected. I . . . have had to take the extraordinary measure of . . ." His voice fails, momentarily. "Without funds the Countermeasure I am creating cannot be completed. It follows, then, that if I fail in this task the universe itself will . . ." He becomes angry at himself. "Today I extinguished my parents, with the stroke of a pen, *by taking what money they had set aside for my younger brother and funneling it toward my work.* I took their final gift to Jack, the boy who is all that remains of my family . . . to correct my mistake." He hit himself, in the chest, hard. "William Joyce! William Joyce . . . killed . . . everyone." William's formerly guileless expression has flushed, teeth locked. "I am the terrible thing at the end of the world. The figure poets and mystics foretold. And it is not great. It is not proud. It is not mighty." He howls and then claps his hand over his mouth—as if afraid of being discovered. He listens, hears nothing, resumes in a lowered voice—trembling. "Buffoon. Simpleton. Idiot. I did not stride toward Armageddon, I stepped in it—like shit in the street. How does a person survive this kind of self-knowledge? I killed the universe. I killed . . . *everything*. It is destroying me . . . and I can tell no one. *No one*."

He drains the mug. "I will require materials similar to those I used in the initial construction of the time core—and then some. I am tempted to neutralize the core I have but the sick truth of it is I need a working model for reference and observations. At present I believe I can refine my work on the chronon aggregator, allowing for the devising of a kind of . . . it's a stupid term but 'chronon bomb.' 'Bomb' in the sense of an intense, localized hypersaturation of chronon energy calibrated to trigger particle propagation at a rate faster than I would expect an M-J fracture to foster dissipation. However, more research needs to be done in a range of areas—I can't just make the fucking thing go boom. Propagation is one thing, but the damage to the field is another. If the device doesn't attend to the problem at the very heart of the disaster—then causality will be left to bleed out once more. At best."

He reaches for his mug, finds it empty, sets it down. Looks off camera. "She remains in the woods, in the shelter she built for herself. Residing in the town isn't possible as she has no paperwork and can't very well take a job. She's let her appearance go, looking very little like the woman who stepped off the Promenade last year, and she avoids Jack like he's contagious. And his little friend Paul. If I'm honest I fear we're both losing our minds."

Wednesday, 16 August 2000. 7:00 P.M. Riverport, Massachusetts. Seventeen months, seventeen days after time core activation.

She had to wait until spring before starting work on the shelter. Before then she had slept in the barn. Staying in the house was not an option. Things were complicated enough as it was without letting young Jack see her before he was due to actually meet her as Zed in ten years' time. The first time she caught a glimpse of him from the barn, two feet shorter and seventeen years younger, was like vertigo. And anyway, Will wanted to limit contact with her for fear of learning more about the future than he needed. That was fine by her. So she got some bedding and set it up in the control room in the barn. The ground was freezing, but it was a small room, easy to warm with a space heater.

So she had killed time, watched actual music videos on MTV, and managed to avoid the final reactions to Clinton being acquitted, all while being quietly grateful that she wouldn't have to witness and live through everything that was coming after in New York the following year. She had always known she would be here, and had always imagined the experience to be . . . cute? Fun? Instead, interacting with so many things that she knew to be dead—the news, the culture, a CRT TV, dial phones, newspapers, the music, the lingo—left her feeling ghostly.

Her time here had ended long ago. She didn't belong.

Both she and Will agreed that once a potential future was

witnessed that future then became inevitable. With that in mind she supposed they could have spoken candidly about everything that would occur between now and 2016 . . . but they didn't. It made Will exceedingly nervous and it made her homesick as hell.

Friday, 18 August 2000. 7:10 P.M. The Joyce farm.

Irene Rose had been with the company for almost ten years. Working under Randall Gibson had been some of the most fun she had ever known. He was the one who gave her the handle "IR." As in Irene Rose. As in infrared. As in she was very good at murder-in-the-dark.

Gibson, IR, Donny, and the other muscle were the closest thing any of them had to a family. That fit Monarch's selection criteria for their particular role. A couple years ago, Gibson had told Irene Monarch had been trawling her background for eighteen months before she'd even heard the name "Martin Hatch." This was when Monarch had been half the size it was in the present day. She'd been running combat operations through Iraq and Afghanistan for years when the call came in.

No family, flexible morality, battlefield experience, top third percentile success rate, psych profile configured for uncommon resilience—that was the starting criteria. What it boiled down to, really, and everyone in the family knew it, was that Hatch wanted highly skilled, mentally reinforced, intelligent, and self-aware sociopaths who were perfectly loyal to a paycheck if not a person. Loyal without fault.

Monarch had her pulled back Stateside, then kept her waiting six months. She took a job in Vegas, analyzing poststrike drone footage of funerals in Afghanistan. A big burial turnout meant the target had a lot of support, so IR spent hours and days going over hi-res RPA footage and matching attendees against available intelligence. Before she clocked out each day she filed recommendations for future targets. She hated the job. She was a doer, not a giver.

IR had trouble breathing the same air as civilians, with their dumb concerns and cartoonish ideas of masculinity. She had no idea what Gibson got out of being married to one.

She had been one week away from heading back to the Middle East when Martin Hatch had called her in personally, and flown her first class to Massachusetts.

The non-disclosure agreements surrounding her employment with Monarch had been dense, with the ink-and-paper termination clause being standard and the verbal one being quite literal.

She was cool with that. They all were.

A bunch of people just like her had been recruited, run through the program. Standard boot camp, double the pay. Pretty much nobody flaked out. The academic stuff weeded out about 30 percent. The stress tests zipped up another 50. The remaining 20 percent, herself included, had been black-bagged and shipped off to someplace anonymous. The usual shell game of trucks and planes and trucks and planes until they took the hood off and she was in the cell she'd occupy for the next six months, in between being groomed for Monarch's fledgling Lifeboat program. That had been her first experience with laboratory-induced stutters and her rescue rig.

They started small, and brief: one cubicle, sterile, stuttered for a minute. Before long it was larger rooms, more complex environments, airborne detritus. Then came rescue scenarios, liberating frozen subjects and the like. Then came live fire, understanding how far a projectile travels and using the suit's capabilities to best advantage against a hostile, chronon-active target.

Then came, one day, mankind's first encounter with a Shifter—and it all went to shit. They were going to be in a sealed-and-stuttered environment for fifteen relative minutes. The environment would be in flux, posing a threat to life and limb.

The Shifter had phased in. The eager students calmly identified what they assumed was a new challenge—some engaged, others intended to evade en route to the exit zone. The blackly flickering thing had just stood there, immobile, taking a ton of punishment. IR remembered rounds pinging off it, squirreling away through space and freezing, before, finally, it activated. No, not activated: reacted. It came to life with such shocking ferocity she realized it hadn't been patient, or biding its time: it was pain. The thing had been immobilized by the sudden, shocking agony of its arrival. It identified the operatives in the room as the sources of that pain, and it turned on them like a living thing no longer capable of reasonable thought.

It blitzed them. A combine harvester had a better grasp of foreplay. It put them down like a burning man tries to put himself out: frantically, furiously, blindly, desperately. In seconds a dozen operatives—men and women IR had come to know by name—were standing around, positioned like performance art, weapons half-lost from grips, spent shells glittering the air like rain, all of them dead before any blood could escape them.

It had been really interesting.

IR hadn't moved from her starting position. Typically, she waited to see how the pattern of the room was going to play out before committing herself. It had paid off. Everyone else had died, she stayed put, the thing seemed to appreciate that. It stood there for minutes and minutes. So did IR—as still as she could. Finally, the thing was just gone.

Then the stutter broke and all her little friends hit the floor and started gushing blood. Ninety percent of the graduating class washed out in less than a second, leaving just her and everyone else in Gibson's squad. The longest serving and the best. A-grade. Hatch's favorites.

Paul Serene didn't like Shifters. That was a well-known secret. He really didn't like them. Tough man, but there were gaps in his armor, that's for sure. Didn't feel to her like he was meant for the life. But he was a big deal, a secret that had to be kept, and she liked that she and Gibson's crew were in on that. Their little secret. She got to see the world, got presented with fun and complex tasks, and she usually got to kill someone at the end of it. She, Gibson, their family, were a big part of Monarch's success: the strategic elimination of obstacles on the way to 2016. Paul Serene had some kind of foresight, told them who would be a problem and when . . . knew how things would Tetris out if a block here and there were removed. She and her crew removed those blocks. It was a great way to make a living.

And now here she was: time traveling.

IR let the airlock smooch and hiss, watched it open. She popped her head out and back, then committed to a slow pan of the barn down the barrel of her assault carbine. Clear, but the two rooms at the back were question marks.

She advanced down the ramp, carbine pressed to her shoulder, cleared both rooms: one crappy control room and the other storage for tech stuff. She let the carbine hang and turned up her left wrist. The Velcroed gauntlet had a clear window on the underside. In that window was a printed portrait of a ten-year-old kid. Jack Joyce. Target of the evening. Her orders were to kill the kid and no one else: especially not William Joyce, and especially not any other child in the house.

IR could do that. She was down with games.

She'd been given the rundown on how to operate one of these machines. Entering the control booth at the back of the barn she checked the date on the clock: Wednesday, August 16, 2000.

7:12 P.M. Neat. Weird. She unclipped one vest pouch, unwrapped a small piece of gum with one hand and her teeth, popped it in her mouth, and then reshouldered the carbine, chewing.

House.

Nice night outside. Nice and warm. About to get ugly.

Strawberry bubblegum.

Gravel drive. She progressed heel-toe, foot over foot, nice and quiet, scanning windows and doors. Got to the steps. Tested each one with her boot. Stepped over the creaky ones.

Front door unlocked. Big property like this, nice little town, traditional values. She couldn't respect that. Nudged it open, crept on in.

Big room. Nine-to-three she clocked dining room, stairs, sofa, fireplace, kitchen entrance. Clear.

Dossier cited second floor as being where she'd find the kid's bedroom. Stairs. Carefully as she goes.

Floorboard creaked. Spins to kitchen entrance—someone there. Finger almost hits the sweet spot and then she remembers: just the kid.

"Identify yourself."

Female. Knife in hand. Big one.

"What's up, IR."

Recognition. "Wilder." Guessing it was cool to smoke this one, but what about leaving blood all over the house? Probably not cool. Training said leave no tracks. "Outside." Easier to conceal.

"I already fucked up one of your squad in this living room," Beth Wilder said. "That tastefully eggshell loveseat is what saved Gibson's life."

"Won't say it again."

"How many more are coming? Randall? Voss? All of them?"

Safety clicked off.

Beth sighed, understanding. "All of them. Fuck's sake,

Irene, didn't they teach you anything about the immutability of collapsed waveforms?"

Wilder took a step for the door, complying. A nervous lick of the lips, a half glance to the stairs behind.

IR's instincts said: *target*. She glanced.

There was no one on the stairs. The new information, all of a sudden, was that she couldn't breathe. Or feel her arms. Or legs. She watched the room tilt upward and rush to smash her in the face.

The flat blade of the carving knife caught moonlight just below her chin. Wilder's bare feet padded over to her, careful to stay out of the dark lake spreading across the boards.

One disappointed sigh. "Goddamn it, Irene. I wanted more time."

IR spat her gum onto the wet floorboards.

And that was that.

Thursday, 17 August 2000. 3:23 P.M. Riverport, Massachusetts—Northside.

Starr Donovan walked home from school, same as every day. She didn't much want to be there, but getting solid grades was one of the things that made her mother happy. That was pretty important these days.

She had her earphones on, the Discman looping that one Chumbawamba song. It was one of those songs that made her happy. That was pretty important as well. It got her to and from school, made sure there was a smile on her face when she walked in. She learned early that this was important as well. People reacted differently depending on what she did with her face, and how she felt seemed to affect that.

Starr's family had lived in Riverport for two years by this

time. Her folks had said Dad was moving where the work was. But almost as soon as they moved to Riverport the work dried up, the docks closed, and now Dad was away as much as he had been when they lived in Phoenix. It was cool though; if he'd been home all the time it would have felt weird.

Their home was a little two-bedroom place from the fifties, on a corner block. High wooden fence, big back garden. She had her bus pass and house key on a loop around her neck. Fishing it out she let herself in, dropped her bag by the door, closed it behind her. She fished the Discman out of her jacket pocket . . .

. . . *knocked down, but I get up again* . . .

. . . and clicked it off. Looped the cords around the steel-gray plastic body, put it on the kitchen counter. Made herself a sandwich. Raspberry jelly and cheese. Held it on one hand, walked to the TV. Stopped. Noticed the door to the back porch was open. Someone's shadow stretched on the wooden decking, someone on the porch.

Starr padded over and peered up at the person leaning on the wooden railing. Dressed in dirty jeans, a pocketed old canvas jacket. Made her think the lady did the same work her Dad did: construction. Concreting. The railing's flaking paint pressed beneath her palms, the sun on her face.

The lady smiled at Starr, but Starr could tell she had been crying. Starr guessed the lady was doing that to her face— smiling—to make her feel better. Just like Starr did with other people. The lady had red hair, like Starr, and looked like family.

"Hello?" Starr said, because she couldn't think of anything else to say.

The stranger turned around properly and got down on her haunches—eye to eye with Starr—and her smile felt more real now. She wiped the tears from her eyes with the swipe of a thumb. Laughed at how silly she was being.

Starr reached out and touched her arm, and tears fell from the lady's eyes anyway.

"Hey, me," the lady said. "It's you."

Friday, 18 August 2000. 6:07 A.M. The following morning.

Will woke up every morning at 5:55 A.M. The paper was deposited in the mailbox by the road at 6:00 A.M. Will walked to collect it, with his coffee, at 6:05 A.M, while oatmeal warmed on the stove.

That morning's edition of the newspaper ran with the story of a local girl—Starr Donovan—missing from her home, believed abducted. Her mother was frantic and her father was believed to be flying back from the Gulf where he had been working on an oil rig. The girl had been missing less than twenty-four hours.

Will snorted, sipped his coffee. That passed for news in a flyover town.

There was something extra with that morning's edition: a handwritten note.

Will,

I unplugged the core. Don't know if I did it right, don't care. I'll be back in two weeks. Strip the Promenade, the whole thing. We're moving it. No more arguments.

The bleach stain at the bottom of the stairs was me. Don't blame Jack.

September.

PS: I've wired the house to explode. Instructions on your desk.

The missing girl looked back at Will from the front page, redheaded and blue eyed. It felt awfully cold for that time of year.

Thursday, 18 June 2009. 10:00 A.M. Nine years later.

Randall Gibson had wondered what it'd be like to go back in time. What it'd feel like to be inside that corridor once it charged up. Turned out he had been well prepared: it didn't feel so different from a stutter. Over the years he'd racked up about two hundred hours in simulated zero states, but this week he found there was something about the real thing he liked a whole lot more. Everything got real quiet. He could go anywhere, do anything. It was a powerful feeling, being the only person in town with agency and will—maybe the only person in the entire world.

Inside the time machine, he kept his assault carbine tucked tight into his shoulder as he moved steadily around the loop. Nothing and nobody in here except him. Wherever his team was, that wasn't where he was going. They were gonna find that Joyce kid, and they were gonna kill him, just like Mr. Hatch ordered. But the thing Gibson wanted more than anything else was to find Beth Wilder and hurt her till she died. He hoped Voss or IR hadn't beaten him to it.

His face hurt. His face never stopped hurting. The Monarch medics said he could keep his eye, but it wasn't what it was. In his pockets were enough high-grade painkillers to keep him going for weeks.

He wanted—needed—Wilder dead; the bug in his brain wouldn't stop wriggling unless he knew she'd died scream-ing . . . but he had a family to think about. So he sent himself through last, made sure he came out later than his crew. 2009. If one of his squaddies managed to smoke her, he'd just have to live with that.

The exit door came into view around the corner. Gibson slapped the release plate and stood back as the hatch opened. Then he crossed the threshold from zero state to causality, moving into the airlock, scanning left to right, up and down. Clear.

He slung the carbine, snatched a quick look out the grimy viewplate. Looked like the machine was set up inside a concrete room, basement maybe. Some kind of signage was sprayed on the opposite wall. Standing lights provided stark illumination. Gibson worked out how to release the hatch and crank it open.

The stench hit him like a physical blow: stale and rich and sweet. His wife's huevos rancheros belted up and out of him in a single wave. He recognized that smell: it was the stench of pits, execution chambers, and abattoirs.

With one arm pressed tight against his nose and mouth, Gibson moved down the ramp, carbine slung, sidearm in hand.

The standing lamps were bright in his face, so bright that he almost tripped over Voss's body, gone black and leathery, curled up on the ramp, recognizable only from insignia and name tag.

Gibson's vision adjusted and the rest of the cramped room came into focus. The room had been built up around the machine, built to enclose it. There was barely enough room for the machine, the ramp and the lights.

There was a body on the ramp. From the haircut he knew it was Chaffey. Half his head was missing, his sidearm still clutched in one bony black hand.

What was left of Dominguez sat on its knees, lonely behind

a standing lamp, head pushed into a corner. MRE and candy bar wrappers lay scattered here and there.

Leave the laws of the universe to me, Hatch had said. Bullshit. His plan was rolling and C-1 knew all about it. They'd been sent here because they were now on the wrong side of Hatch's cost-benefit analysis. Gibson gave the tiniest laugh, because this wasn't real. But just the one.

There was another body, this one at the foot of the ramp.

Propped against the wall, at the base of the ramp, was what had to be IR: half-skeletonized and collapsing into her blood-stained uniform, carbine resting across her lap.

They were all dead. He was the last of Chronon-1. Gibson wheeled around, frantically scanning the machine. The controls had been removed. He spun back looking for any advantage, anything he could use, any—

Behind him the airlock hissed—Gibson threw himself at the door—and it smooched shut.

He bellowed, red with fury and frustration, knowing beyond doubt he and his crew had been set up. Wilder had gotten there early and sealed the machine inside a fucking sarcophagus. They had all landed here, greeted by IR's corpse, and slowly starved to death. How long had they sat here, making their rations last, with corpses for company and knowing they was looking at their own future?

This would not be his fate! He would not die here. *Not like this.*

The words spray painted on the wall at the base of the ramp said otherwise.

YOU LOSE, PUMPKIN BUTTER

Gibson read them, and roared till he tasted blood.

When that was done, the security camera adjusted focus,

giving itself away with a tiny *whirr*. Gibson looked up into the lens that looked at him, knowing who was on the other end.

"You know I'm getting' outta here, don'tcha? You know. And when I—"

There was a loud snap and a descending whine as power to the machine cut off.

Gibson noticed, wouldn't be intimidated. "—and *when I do*—"

Power to the left bank of lights cut abruptly, throwing the coffin-room into bleak twilight.

"—I'm comin' for you, ya little bitch! For Donny! And . . . and . . . for *Irene!*" He knew what was coming, and he met it. But the remaining lights didn't switch off. He glanced back at them, then back at the camera.

The camera *whirr-whirr*-ed, shaking its head left to right. *No.*

Half-mad with rage and terror, he screamed, put all he had into it, as though volume might save him, or kill her.

Light vanished, and blackness devoured Randall Gibson.

Sunday, 4 July 2010. 00:01 A.M. Riverport Swimming Hall. One year later.

Jack stepped out of the time machine onto the ramp, armed and scanning.

He recognized the swimming hall. Pretty much everything was the way he remembered it from 2016, but with one difference: someone had built a concrete enclosure around the machine, and had then tore it down. The jagged track across the empty pool's width remained.

The air smelled different, too. Like fresh laundry, and cooking. Hot, frying smells. Bacon.

Someone was living here.

The workbenches in front of the machine were still there, one now cleared of Will's clutter. Laid across it was a neatly arranged kit: Kevlar vest, assault carbine, handgun, three magazines for each—all Monarch-issue.

Someone appeared in the doorway at the far end of the pool, equipped with the same kit that rested in front of Jack, her red hair tied in a ponytail.

She stepped into the light. It was her: Beth. But changed.

The years had left their imprint, the line of her jaw a little softer, care around her eyes etched more deeply than she deserved. She looked tired, but it was still Beth, still strong, still unbowed.

"Hey, Trouble," she said, quavering. "Want breakfast? I got an early start."

Jack dropped his gun and ran to her.

Half an hour later.

He had a hundred questions and she did her best to answer what she could. She walked Jack through her eleven years here—living from 1999 to 2010, the present day: the almost perpetual déjà vu, distracting herself from everything she knew by obsessively searching for things she didn't in an effort to remain engaged with the world, to not think of it as a video game she had played before. To think of lives and events as happening to real people, and not simulations of history. She told him about Gibson and his crew, and how they had ended. She told him how she had lived for years in a hideout in the woods, keeping an eye on Jack's younger self and Will, ensuring no threat from the present or future interfered with Will's work. If enemy action resulted in the Countermeasure being somehow flawed, it was all over.

"Hey," she said. "Remember what goes down this morning?"

Jack nodded. "Aberfoyle. Bannerman's Overlook."

"My younger self's all grown up. She's Zed now. Got in touch a few weeks ago, asked for some help. I obliged."

Jack looked at her. To him, forty minutes ago, in another world, everything had been as it was. Now . . . forty minutes later, the woman he loved had spent eleven years without him. Had grown eleven years older than he.

Was a different person than the one he had known.

That, at least, he was used to.

His hands closed tight on hers, and he kissed her. She was still Beth.

She rested her forehead against his.

"Let's take a drive," he said.

Sunday, 4 July 2010. 4:52 A.M. Riverport, Massachusetts.

Bright morning light pushed through the pines and birches that blanketed the hillside sloping gently toward Riverport. Jack and Beth stood on a slanting boulder, squinting toward a channel in the woods that framed an excellent view of Bannerman's Overlook two miles away.

"Funny thing," Beth said. "I'm history's only Scorpio with a birthday in March."

Jack took a pair of binoculars from their backpack. "Say what?"

"I was born October 30. I went through the machine October 9—twenty-one days before my birthday. I came out

February 28, 1999, a leap year. February 28 plus twenty-one days is March 20. So now the day that I age a year is March 20."

Jack slung the binoculars' strap around his neck. "And I thought what I disliked about time travel was the jetlag."

Beth checked her watch, clicked her pen, made a note in her Moleskine pad. Jack focused the binoculars, bringing the Bannerman's Overlook platform into sharp focus. Their twenty-two-year-old selves and Aberfoyle came into focus: Jack and Paul looking over the rail toward Riverport, Aberfoyle and Zed talking thirty feet behind them. Jack panned. Three goons, waiting with the car. Panned back to himself and Paul.

"You okay?" Beth asked.

"Sure."

"Really? 'Cause for a second you sounded like a dog having a nightmare."

He couldn't look away. "I didn't know how this would make me feel. Being back here."

"So . . . how do you feel?"

"Mortal." He lowered the binoculars. "Did you talk to her then?"

"Zed? Sure. I practically raised her. Well, I left her in the care of friends. I checked in a few times a year."

Jack shook his head. "You abducted yourself. Gave yourself to strangers. Couldn't you have trained her while she was still living with her folks? Your folks, I mean?"

"No, Jack. Because that's not what happened. I also don't have the resources or facilities to raise a child here, and how exactly do you imagine I'd go about negotiating with her parents? I've lived with this whole deal, every detail, my entire life. You just got here. Believe me, I'm across it."

Jack was still twenty-eight. Yesterday she had been, too. Now, a day later to him, she was thirty-nine.

Jack reached out and took her hand, wanted to say something, but didn't know where to begin.

"Gonna need you to keep an eye on the Overlook," she said, taking her hand from his. "Need exact times for the detonations."

He let it go, glanced back through the trees. Their younger selves were still in the same places; nothing had escalated yet. "But you set the explosives a week ago, right?"

"After Zed got in touch, yeah."

"So, that trick you pulled . . . Zed pulled . . . *pulls* . . . pointing and having things explode. How do the two of you expect to get the timing exactly right? That's a hell of a needle to be threading."

"It's impossible for the timing to be anything *but* exactly right." Beth held up her notepad. "The timers on the explosives have been set to detonate at the exact moments required."

"Yeah . . . but . . . that's some really fine choreography. I don't see how you're gonna get it to—"

"It breaks down like this. You ready?"

"Sure."

"Think of Zed as my Younger Self, and me as my Older Self. My Younger Self gives my Older Self the detonation times."

"Yeah, but how did she get—"

"Hut!" Beth cut him off with a waved finger. "Hear me out. My Younger Self gives my Older Self the detonation times. My Older Self sets the bombs to those times. The bombs detonate. As they detonate my Older Self notes the exact timing of the explosions and writes them down in a new book." Beth held that new book up. "My Older Self then gives my Younger Self this new book. My Younger Self transcribes those times into her own new book—the one that is a precise copy of the *old book* her Older Self gave her *when she was eleven,* so that she can in turn give it to her Younger Self, in 1999, when she becomes her Older Self. Then that eleven-year-old Younger Self grows and becomes that same Older Self . . . and here we are."

Jack wasn't blinking.

"So," she continued, "to boil it down: the buildings explode at exactly the right moment because I'm sitting here noting the exact time when Zed gestures and then, when she becomes me, that information is used to set the timers on the charges."

Jack wasn't saying anything.

"I know. I had the same problems. Will was very patient with me on that front, actually."

"If I'm understanding this . . . that doesn't make sense. I mean, there has to be a point somewhere in there when that happens for the first time, right? When you don't have any of that information? When you *can't* set the bombs for the right times?"

"Yes and no. Yes, and this *is* the first time, right now. And no, there is never a moment when I don't have the information. How much do you know about this stuff?"

"I skimmed a *Terminator* argument on Reddit once."

"No. The bottom line is: it works. The paradox is accounted for or factored out, because the behavior of fundamental particles on the quantum scale under certain conditions aren't strictly deterministic. They follow 'fuzzy rules.' "

"What?"

"General relativity works just fine for predicting paradoxes, but once those paradoxes are considered in, or subjected to,

quantum mechanical terms they pretty much vanish—
provided causality is maintained."

"Says Will."

"The dude built a time machine. I'll take his opinion over
Reddit's. Also"—she waved the book again—"I *have* the
times."

"Jesus."

"You should have been there when I explained this to Will.
He was really upset. He said this observation could be critical
in formulating a theory that unifies general relativity with
quantum mechanics but, ironically, he didn't have time to look
into it. He was too busy building the Countermeasure and trying to save the future."

"I thought science wasn't your thing."

He took each of her hands in his. She was still Beth. Still
Zed. Still the person he fell for.

"Jack, how much do you remember about being sixteen?"

Weird question. "Not a lot, it was twelve years ago."

"Jack," she said. "You remember being sixteen the way I
remember you. I haven't seen you in that long." Beth steeled
herself and said, as gently as she could, "If it wasn't for me
watching you grow up I probably wouldn't remember what you
looked like. It's been eleven years of living off the grid, staying
out of the way of the future, and trying to keep both you and
Will alive. I don't need love, I don't need romance, I don't need
drama. I just want to go home."

Jack let go of her hands, stepped away, and turned back
toward the Overlook. Paul was standing alone. Zed had led
Aberfoyle away from Jack. Aberfoyle raised his gun, level with
Zed's head.

"I know you have feelings for that girl over there, but she's
gone. Love the memory. Okay?"

He really did.

Beth's phone chirruped. Onscreen was a message. It was from William Joyce. It read: COMPLETED.

Jack said, "It's happening."

At Bannerman's Overlook, Zed pointed to the horizon.

The first building went up in flames.

19

Beth drove, her notebook propped on the dash, her phone nestled in the crook of her shoulder.

"I'd like to report a suspicious vehicle. Bannerman's Overlook. I heard gunshots, and then a black town car tore right past me. Well, I believe I saw bullet holes in it. Yes, ma'am. As a matter of fact I did, yes. Do you have a pen?" Beth rattled off the license plate of Aberfoyle's town car, and then hung up before the operator could ask for her details.

"I could murder for a frozen lemonade and a stuffie."

"It's seven A.M., for Christ's sake."

"Can't get 'em in Future Riverport."

"If your cash was printed after 2010 it's effectively counterfeit."

"It's 2010, they don't check."

"What we're doing is heading back to my place, sanitizing it, and then we're going home to 2016."

"Beth, we're clear. Let's take one last look around—enjoy it."

"This might be novel for you, kiddo, but I'm done."

The woods embraced the Joyce family home, the eastern fence line being the only side open to the world. Beth drove them to the southern perimeter, the side facing away from Riverport. The mesh fence on that side had a section that could be pulled aside. She drove the car through the gap, swept the grass upright behind her, and rolled the mesh back in place, clipping it shut.

There was a dip in the land into which she nestled the car, and a mess of camouflage netting that she threw over the top.

"Come on, this way."

This was all Joyce land. Back in '99 she had identified the best place for her to build a place to live while still being able to keep an eye on the house: a spot deep in the woods, but on enough of a rise that she had a good view of the property, and close enough that she could get there in a minute or two at a dead run.

A few trees had been felled strategically, and she'd limited her construction hours to when young Jack wasn't home.

"Welcome to where the magic happens."

At first glance he didn't know what Beth meant. Then he realized he was looking at a shelter so well camouflaged it was almost invisible against the side of the small outcrop against which it was built. The shelter had a wide-but-narrow frontage made of pine logs, wattle, and daub. Beth flipped a latch and pulled open a handmade door camouflaged with greenery, scraping up earth and needles as it opened.

The interior was beautiful, dug into the side of the hill. The room was about thirty feet long, paved with stones that had been carefully selected for their flatness. The left wall had a long bench before a window that ran the full length of the room. Beth propped the window upward and open with a length of timber. Against the right wall was a raised stone shelf, insulated with foam matting, atop which was her bed: a good mattress, thick with covers. She had fashioned a simple four-cornered frame that she could drape mosquito netting over for the summer months.

"Paul and I used to play here," he said. "Well, we never came in. We were scared shitless."

"The witch in the woods," she said. "I know. You two weren't as quiet as you thought you were."

"Will warned me off. Grounded me once because I wouldn't stop poking around here." His chest ached. "The whole time it was you."

The sight of her bed and the earthy, floral scents of the place made his heart hurt. How many thousands of nights had she lain down here, waiting to catch up to the future? What had life meant for her here, day after day?

"Come on," she said. "I need this place stripped and burned. Tools and such in the drawer under the bed." Beth opened the door on the right and stepped inside. He heard gear being moved around.

A long recess was dug into the wall, home to books, a glass of water, candles. The walls were wooden on all sides. Jack noticed electricity outlets, a space heater, and against the far wall was a small fireplace and opening. A couple of colorful rugs lined the floor, a broom by the door. On the right wall, adjacent to the fireplace, was a door—leading farther into the earth.

Through the now-open window hatch on his left he had a panoramic view of the woods, sloping downward toward the south side of the house: greenhouse, garage, barn. He wondered if Will was there now.

Crouching by the bed he lifted the soft, floral covers, finding the large drawer built into the base of the shelf. Inside was a red metal tool chest, which he hefted out. Something hanging from the bed frame caught his eye as he prepared to lift the chest onto the bench behind him.

Hanging from the canopy, above the pillow, was a silver bullet on a long, thin chain. Leaving the tool kit on the rug, Jack stood up and cupped the bullet in one hand. She had inscribed it with a collection of scratches: two sets of four vertical strokes and one cross-stroke, and one single vertical stroke. Eleven. Marking off the years as she did her time here.

He rotated the bullet. She had inscribed the casing again, beneath the marks, with a single word: "Trouble."

"I borrowed a metal detector." She was standing by the fireplace with a gym bag in one hand. "You weren't supposed to see that."

He didn't know if he was feeling joy or grief. "Why not?"

"Because it'll make what happens next harder than it needs to be." She put the bag down, crossed the room, and took the bullet from him, unlooping it from the frame.

It had been quick work to dismantle her home. All of the wood, rugs, curtains, netting, sacking, anything flammable they piled in a nearby clearing. Jack doused the collection in gasoline. Beth tossed the match. As they watched it burn, she reached and took his hand in hers.

"Is this what you did the first time? In 2010?" he asked.

"First rule of a good disappearance," she said. "Zed's burning her gear right now, at her place, which your past self will discover in about an hour."

"Why didn't you want me to see the bullet?"

She looked him in the eye. "When I was Zed . . . I never saw my future self after today. So—"

"So it means everything goes to plan. We get the Countermeasure and leave."

"Maybe. But we need your head squarely in the game. The Countermeasure makes it to 2016. Nothing else matters."

"Not to me."

"Jack . . ."

"Knowing you changed my life. You showed me what life could be. That I could change things. I loved you for that." He shrugged. "Take that away, that's when nothing matters."

Sunday, 4 July 2010. 10:10 A.M. Riverport dockyard.

"Are you sure this is all just 'playing safe'?" Jack wore Kevlar beneath his shirt and jacket, a 2016-era Monarch-issued assault carbine slung from his shoulder. Beth was decked out paramilitary; also Monarch-issued.

A tanked shipbuilding industry meant 2010 prices for dockside real estate were mighty low. That's how Will was able to buy and outfit a workshop for himself, away from the house and without Jack's knowledge.

Jack and Beth were two doors down from that workshop. Parked between two large warehouses, Jack had heard his past self tear up on his motorcycle, throw open the workshop door, and immediately start shouting at Will. Accusations of stupidity, irresponsibility, neglect. Theft.

This was happening in the hour before past Jack found Zed gone and pointed his motorcycle toward the nearest Greyhound station, in the futile hope of finding her again: the beginning of a meandering four-year quest for answers.

Now Beth was beside him, leaning against the cooling hood of the car with a carbine in her hand, waiting for the final moments of that quest to run out.

Jack could hear his brother feebly defending himself, caught red-handed, surrounded by everything family money had bought.

There came sounds of violence: Jack remembered picking

up a chair, smashing it into whatever he could find. Will shouting *no no no*.

He remembered an object that Will had made: a geometric sphere about the size of a volleyball. Something about the workshop told Jack that this was what all the money had gone into. So he had taken to it with a chair, smashed it once, twice . . .

"Stop! You're killing the universe! Stop! St—!"

Jack's nails bit into his palms. That was the moment his past self had punched Will in the face. Will's dumbfounded expression—baffled, hurt, childlike—stayed with Jack for years. And then Jack had left.

Jack and Beth heard the motorcycle kick to life. Seconds later, Jack's past self roared past the alley in which they were parked, heading for Zed's place.

"Wait," Jack said.

Beth stopped, threw a questioning look.

Will called Jack's name, heartbroken. Then the sound of a car starting, and Jack caught a glimpse of his brother as he drove past.

That would be the last time he would see Will alive.

"You okay?"

He wasn't ready to say anything. Just needed a second.

"Remember what I showed you by the river, with the revolver? I couldn't die because it wasn't my time, and you couldn't have said anything to Will that would have—"

"Enough," Jack said. "Let's go."

The warehouse was no small affair: two stories tall and three times the size of the family home. Beth had a key for the front door, and pulled the ten-foot-high rolling mass of steel aside. It led into a smaller anteroom with a security door. Beth punched in the code, and the lock popped.

"My birth date?"

"'Fraid so."

"Jesus, Will. Security."

They moved inside. They took no more than a few steps before having to stop.

The majesty of Will's workshop made Jack believe in his brother's genius in much the same way that Notre Dame de Paris had made twelfth-century peasants believe in God. Vast and complex, everything with a purpose, the workshop was a meticulously ordered warren of raw technology. Jack appreciated the inner workings of that place as much as he could the inner workings of a person: the incomprehensibility was as unsettling as it was astounding.

Above and around: wonder. At his feet a spray of smaller items scattered across the floor, the smashed body of a laptop—evidence of the furious violence Jack remembered inflicting.

Directly in front of them was a glass chamber, thirty feet a side, atop a three-foot-high square platform beneath which was buried a jumble of heavy-duty technology. A canopy of wires and cabling attached the transparent box to scaffolding that housed two floors of unidentifiable machinery.

The door to the box was slid aside. Inside, at the center of the glassed-in space, was a spindly stainless steel dais. Delicate upraised pincers, designed to support something delicately and precisely, held nothing. On the floor next to the dais was the chair Jack remembered using to knock a geometric sphere from the grip of those claws.

He walked around the box, checking it out from all angles. Beth trailed along behind, glancing at her watch.

The sphere—the Countermeasure—lay on the room's insulated floor. A couple of its faces were now slightly deformed. An access panel had divorced itself from the housing.

Beth got close to the glass. "Oh Christ."

"I didn't know what it was." Then: "What is it?"

"It contains a self-replenishing chronon charge powerful enough to brute-force the M-J field back into shape."

Jack eyed the bent panels. "And what if it breaks open?"

Beth glanced at him. "Then an infinite number of your alternate selves cease to get along." She straightened, re-checked her watch. "Catastrophically."

She glanced at the device lying battered on the floor of the glass chamber. Something changed in her suddenly. Jack watched the tension drain from her, urgency fading.

"Beth?"

"Dr. Kim was credited with creating a self-replenishing source of power that was intended to be the heart of Project Lifeboat," Beth mumbled. "The Regulator."

Jack looked back into the chamber, skin flushing cold.

"Kim didn't create the Regulator, Jack. Will did. This is it. The Countermeasure and the Regulator are the same thing."

Something heavy thudded in the far wall: the security door was being deactivated.

"The Countermeasure doesn't go missing because we steal it, Jack. It goes missing because they do."

Jack grabbed her sleeve and pulled her behind the scaffolding that ran north-south between the box and the small eastern-side office.

Two people—a man and a woman—entered, the guy carrying a rubberized gym bag. With a finger on one ear the woman said, "We're inside."

Her counterpart muttered, "Aw no," and moved to the open door of the box.

"Looks like the device has been damaged, Actual."

Beth glanced at Jack and closed her eyes in despair.

Monarch.

"We can stop this," he whispered to her.

She shook her head, frustration turning to fury. *"You can't change the past,"* she hissed, softly. *"It's a fucking impossibility. We've* lost."

Looking through the gaps in the scaffolding, through bundles of wiring, Jack could tell the two intruders weren't decked out in the Monarch outfits he remembered. The logo was similar but cruder, and the uniforms were cheaper, dun-colored, off-the-rack.

Jack unslung his carbine. "You want to gift wrap it for them, or are you going to help me here?"

The guy carrying the gym bag stepped into the sterile room and picked up the Countermeasure, barehanded, without precaution or ceremony. "Yeah, it's pretty banged up."

Beth tensed, fingers flexing on her gun. With a glance Jack understood what had to happen.

As the guy left the room with the device, Jack and Beth swept out from behind cover, weapons level.

The woman spotted them, eyes wide with shock. Beth pressed one finger to her lips. The woman screamed.

The guy, whose back was turned, leaped, saw the guns, also screamed, and ran.

The muzzle of Beth's carbine followed him as he bolted for the door—sweeping across the woman's head as her finger tightened.

Jack leaped in, knocked her barrel skywards with the barrel of his own, a three round burst ringing out.

Beth wheeled on him, furious.

"You can't just *shoot him*!" he said.

Patience spent, Beth shouldered past the woman and out through the security door.

Bright sunlight resolved into shapes, and some of those

shapes turned out to be men with guns leaning against a four-wheel-drive, startled to action by the sound of gunfire.

Beth skidded to a halt, sixty feet from them, armed, as the entire team brought their weapons up.

The guy with the gym bag kept running, straight toward them. The Monarch crew were just guys in jeans, shades, and Monarch-branded T-shirts.

The runner was in the line of fire.

The space around the four-wheel-drive snapped and froze—a shimmering dome of stuttered time.

From the doorway Jack said, "Get the Countermeasure. I'll take care of these."

She took off after the runner, past the security team.

Jack headed straight for the mini-stutter when a gunshot rang out and a cannonball of force took him in the torso. He hit the concrete with a disbelieving cough.

Before Jack could refill his lungs, Paul Serene was on him.

"The machine changed you, too. I knew it had."

Paul's face was six inches from his own. This version of the face he knew so well was a little younger than the bastard who would kill Will in 2016.

"You're the second you," Paul said. "Not the one who rode away just now. You're from 2016. Which means Will's machine is intact. That has to be how you got here. Where is it?"

"It's good to see you too, buddy." He could feel the bruise forming, sharply and painfully, beneath the Kevlar, and then tickling as it quickly healed and faded.

Paul let go of Jack's shirt. Jack noticed that both of Paul's hands were pristine, normal . . . human. No sickness. So that first trip through the machine in 2016 hadn't made him sick. What had?

"Good to see you too, Jack. I have so much I need to tell you."

The runner had recoiled from the sight of the stutter bubble encasing the security team and kept on running. Countermeasure in hand, he pounded for the gap between the warehouses where Beth had parked the car. She didn't like the way that gym bag was bouncing around in his hand. If the Countermeasure cracked open it'd be game over.

"Stop!" she yelled.

She raised the carbine's barrel, cracking a warning burst over his head. The runner skidded to a stop. As he threw his hands over his head the gym bag containing the Countermeasure slipped from his fingers.

Beth recoiled, shielding her eyes as the bag hit the ground, hard.

Nothing happened.

"Stay down, Jack," Paul said. "This'll be over soon, and then we can talk. This is so weird, man. You won't believe it."

Just as suddenly Paul's weight was off him.

Paul folded himself back into a moment, propelling himself across the open ground and past his frozen security team. In a blink Paul tore the carbine from Beth's hands, flipped it, and jabbed her square in the forehead with the butt of her own weapon.

Beth's head snapped back and she went down. Jack heard her cry out and began struggling to his feet, breath burning in his chest.

Behind Paul, the security team sprang back to life as Jack's mini-stutter collapsed. Paul marched toward them, hand up, ordering them to hold fire. They were confused, but this would be a key learning experience for them. All in all, this was turning out to be a most beneficial day.

Paul addressed the guy with the gym bag, now gratefully relaxing against the hood of Beth's car parked between the buildings some fifty feet away. "Well done. You're safe now. Is that it, in the bag?"

The man was nodding, loose-jointed with relief. "Yes sir, yes it is. Thank you."

Past the security team, closer to Will's workshop, Jack got to his feet. The scene filled itself in: the security team covering him. Beyond them Paul, with Beth's carbine. Beyond Paul, Beth laid out flat, clutching her head. Past her, leaning against the car, the tech. At the tech's feet, the gym bag containing the Countermeasure.

Paul gestured to the waiting vehicle. "All right, technician. Get yourself to—"

Like a living thing the gym bag at the technician's feet leaped off the ground—the bag disintegrating instantly—and all the light in Heaven spilled out.

The self-replenishing source within the battered Countermeasure hosed out a density of chronon particles orders of magnitude greater than the environmental baseline. The technician—engulfed by a roiling, expanding distortion field—was rapidly reinvented by a flickering, shifting phage that swept from his center of mass toward his extremities, and raced upward toward his mind.

Eyes open, terrified and ignorant, he felt all that he was being replaced a thousand times over.

Paul shouldered Beth's carbine and shot the doomed tech through the head.

The tech's sickness vanished upon death, and he slid to the concrete fully human.

Silhouetted against the crazed, strobing light, Paul let the weapon slip from slack fingers. Caught within the Countermeasure's ongoing blast, the left side of Paul's body was already changing. His hand was reskinned by the same iridescent transformation that had claimed the doomed technician. Both terrified and entranced, Paul saw his flesh alternate between versions of itself, the shining facets of the sickness like shift-

ing windows on to alternate versions of his own flesh, nothing
constant, always changing, always different. The change crept
toward his shoulder, inch by slow inch, accelerating as Paul's
cells absorbed more and more of what the Countermeasure
threw out.

The roar of approaching trucks came to them from blocks
away, echoing off the closely packed buildings: Monarch
backup, responding to the emergency.

Jack was on his feet. Beth too. The light was blinding.

Beth received the worst of the blast. She had been caught
between the tech and Paul, much closer to the epicenter, twenty
feet from the Countermeasure. She faced Jack, her head a silhouette against that killing light, one transformed eye shining
like a dying star. Her teeth, clenched against pain, were
backlit.

The backup squads arrived as the warehouses and Beth's car
met alternate versions of themselves: fading in, falling apart,
building up, redesigning, self-defacing, flashing clean. The
first security team stood unmoving, trembling, hypnotized by
the vision.

The slowly expanding radius of oversaturation showed
catalogs of could-have-been. The sections of the warehouses
caught in the blast were raw brick, then pristine white, then
tagged with gang symbols, then gone entirely, then overgrown
and abandoned. One second they were made of corrugated
iron, the next they were a parking lot, followed by an outdoor
café. The car changed models and colors. Sometimes it wasn't
a car, other times it was a Bronco, or gone, or riddled with
bullets, or a motorcycle, or a solar-powered three-wheeled covered trike the likes of which Jack had never seen. The ground
itself changed, rioting and fighting with versions of itself:
concrete, blacktop, overgrown, lawn, mud . . .

Brakes were hit as the driver of the first backup truck spotted the anomaly, the three-truck convoy skidding to a halt out-side the oversaturation's radius. Armed men disgorged from the vehicles without order. Nobody advanced. No one wanted to get close. None of them understood what they were seeing.

Beth saw Jack. He was running to her. She brought both her hands up, intersected. T for Time-Out. Think Before You Act.

There was nothing he could do.

"Go." Her throat, the interior of her mouth, luminesced, flickered, snapped.

Then she turned and walked toward the mad light.

"Beth!"

She didn't look back. Her rescue rig sparked and crazed as it shielded her against the madness. Connections shorted out, sparked, burst into flame at elbow and shoulder. But it was enough to keep her going, to get her closer to the Countermea-sure before the change took her completely.

Discordant energy arced and flailed from vehicles and brick-work. Men stumbled backward, scrambling like scalded cats from flickering arms of violent energy that leaped and bounced from one surface to another.

The space between the warehouses had become a storm; a force Beth had to push against, and through. It cost her to do it, as every cell in her body was forcefully introduced to its countless others. Her brain revolted. She understood in mo-ments what it was like to be a thousand people all at once. A thousand simultaneous versions of herself. She saw infinite lives running parallel to each other; infinite futures in this life branching away from that moment. She held herself together, in this life, to finish what she had come here to do—to retrieve the Countermeasure, intact. She had given too much, lived too long, to be swept away by a torrent of potential and chaos before she had sung her final note.

She crouched before that fount of mad energy, and plunged

her flickering, shifting hands—hands she didn't recognize—into the roiling light.

The Countermeasure was in there, a thrashing, discordant sun. It plunged tendrils into her body and mind, showing her infinite possibilities, distracting her from the most important of all tasks, unmaking her capacity to be singular, introducing her to flavors of agony few people had ever known. Her rescue rig shorted out completely. Her hair caught fire, a corona around her head.

Sliding and fumbling across the surface of the Countermeasure, she was able to locate the damaged access panel. Using hands that were in the process of ceaseless reinvention, faster than she could process the changes, and with what remained of her strength and control, she forced the tiny hatch back into place, hoping against hope it would be enough.

It was.

The blinding glare vanished as Beth toppled to her side, the hot, heavy weight of the Countermeasure clutched to her chest.

"Beth . . ." Jack vaulted forward. The nearest security specialist fired his Taser. Jack tensed, and dropped like a side of beef.

Beth lay on her back, blue morning sky broken and wrong-colored in her new, changed, starlight eye. So many versions of her wanted to be known inside that singular body. So many lives. An infinity of other nows and heres; lives where she and Jack had walked away from this. Where this had never happened.

Men gathered, carefully, nervously, at the corners of her vision. She saw the surviving technician reach down to take the Countermeasure from her, eyes full of fear and misery.

She heard Paul howl. He staggered into view above her, all messed up, his arm and the side of his body a flashing, fractal mess. *What have you done to me?*

An aftershock pulsed. The world reinvented shockingly as something else, something alien, for just a moment. Returned to normal.

The technician took her prize and ran toward a waiting security team. The Countermeasure was gone, and with it any hope of repairing the M-J field.

One of the security team ventured to speak. "Sir, we should get you to a doctor immediately."

Paul ignored him, fell to his knees, got in her face, screamed again, "*What have you done to me?*"

Beth smiled, her teeth backlit, her left eye going nova. "Oh buddy," she said, with many, many soft voices. "I have not yet begun to fuck with you." She unzipped her jacket, with a strange *ping-snap* sound, showing Paul what she carried beneath: five one-pound bars of C-4 wrapped in Gorilla Tape, attached by nine inches of rubberized fuse to an M60 igniter. "This is just the load screen."

The fuse popped and hissed, throwing smoke in Paul's eyes.

So many futures ran to meet Beth, so many possibilities revealed themselves to her starlight eye. So many Jacks.

Jack ordered misfiring limbs to action, hauled himself off the ground. One of the security grunts had Tasered him in front of their vehicle, and Beth was too far away to reach. His heart died the moment he realized he had failed her again.

Paul leaped back, folded into a moment, and fled. His men were less fortunate.

One future in particular shone brightest, clearest.

Beth whipped her head to look at Jack, one last time. "Hey, Trouble? Trust the villain."

The first rule of a good disappearance: leave nothing behind.

"*Beth!*"

Supernova.

The C-4 kicked off. The three men gathered about her had no chance. The corners of both warehouses blew inward, top levels collapsing into lower. Beth's car bucked upward, the hood blown off, tires blown out, a ton of brickwork sloughing down onto it from both sides. Every window for a block blew out. The soldiers milling about thirty feet away went blind, deaf, and were blown off their feet. The technician, running for the third unit, tumbled to the ground, clutching the Countermeasure—then got up and kept running. Debris rained down for two blocks. Somewhere in the docklands a car alarm started wailing. The air was choked with atomized dust and brickwork.

Jack lowered his arm from his face, his ears ringing. Beth was gone. The men who had gathered around her were gone. The second unit were laid out: two of them clutching their heads and screaming, eyes destroyed, eardrums burst. The remaining three were motionless. The third unit had fled for the cover of their vehicles, sheltering behind their window-smashed truck.

Clouds of dark orange haze rolled across the scene, obscuring and revealing. Here men screamed, then they were gone. There bricks tumbled from the smashed face of a warehouse . . . and were taken away.

No sound, save the ringing in Jack's ears.

A dust-curtain breathed aside and there stood Paul Serene, some fifty feet away, his arm a shifting, sliding, starlight mess, his face fixed in a caught-red-handed little-boy expression of "what have I done?"

The clouds froze. Jack and Paul looked at each other—fate affording them privacy in this final moment. Jack raised his handgun, took his time centering the sights on Paul's head. Paul didn't move, didn't fight it. Jack's hand was as unsteady as it had ever been, muscles and nerves gone slack from shock.

He could barely keep the gun raised. After a few seconds he couldn't.

Paul seemed almost disappointed.

In one move the gun came up, level and braced.

On the other side of the iron sights, Paul's expression melted into one of mortal fear. He had no time to escape.

Fifteen feet behind Jack a thousand roars and screams folded into one. It should have been bass enough to rattle Jack's ribs, shrill enough to pain his ears. But the only place it resonated was within his mind. He turned to face the source of the discord and saw a thing that, surely, represented the final stage of Paul's sickness: humanoid, of uncertain profile, a stumbling, heavyset sketch of flashing, fractal insanity.

It moved toward Jack, raising one arm as it did so, to reveal the well of starlight in its palm . . . crowned by a row of fingers sharp and phasing.

So this was where it ended, then. But he wasn't letting Paul off the hook. Jack decided to take one last shot at changing the past. He wheeled around, raised his pistol, centered it on Paul's head and . . .

The creature's palm swept in from Jack's left and took him by the face.

20

In that place of violent, chaotic energy—in a moment suspended in time—the shining hand descended on Jack, and his world had exploded in pain.

He was a million Jacks, and none. He was pulled a million ways down a million branching paths of causality . . . but guided firmly down one.

Monday, 10 October 2016. 12:03 A.M. Two hours, relative, after Jack traveled to 2010.

Jack reassembled from nothing and crashed steaming, wet, and gasping, onto the ramp of Will's machine. His handgun reconstituted itself from nothing and hit the ramp with a clang. He opened his mouth and drew breath as if for the first time.

The room spun and veered. He was in the swimming hall. It was night; no light through the grimy upper windows. The lights that still worked were on. The tang of cordite lingered in the air, still fresh from the gunfight with Gibson and Chronon-1. It was a couple of hours after he had gone through Will's machine, back to July 4, 2010.

The ghosts of a thousand lives faded from his mind, coalescing into one. This one. The life where Beth was dead.

A sound came from his throat, from his chest, long and broken.

He heard voices. Sirens. He heard fear and panic. He understood that what he was hearing was the news.

He rolled onto his back, angled his head, saw two pairs of legs at the end of the ramp. High-tops. Angled up.

Riverport Newshour was exclaiming from its monitor. Lots of reds and blues and the occasional reporter snapping off bullet points, while clearly wondering if their job was worth what they were going through.

Jack's eyes traveled up the legs.

"Mother of crap," Nick said, softly. "You came outta nowhere."

Beth was dead. The world outside was going mad, and he felt nothing for it. Beth was dead.

Sofia Amaral was seated in a wheeled office chair, before the workbench, still alive.

His entire body felt like a single deep bruise. Nick tried to help Jack up, was batted away. Getting up hurt Jack like breaking bones. He needed it. It felt like something.

"Leave me alone."

Sofia wasn't looking well. Her coat was draped over her shoulders, her right arm bandaged with what Jack now recognized as Nick's shredded shirt. Nick was bare-chested beneath his Raptors jacket.

"She wouldn't leave," Nick said. "Said you might need her."

"I can speak for myself," she said, her voice faint, like wind over sand.

Sofia's olive skin had gone flat and damp and pale. When she spoke her voice was thin, tired. "Tell me how you did that. How you . . . reconstituted from nothing." She was more focused than her appearance suggested.

"Something grabbed me."

"Describe it."

Jack did.

"A Shifter. *The* Shifter, if it held a light in its hand the way you describe. That particular creature has been stalking Paul Serene for years. It features prominently in his nightmares, of which he has many."

"I've never seen them do anything but kill people."

"And I've never seen one tunnel a human being through time. Yet here you are." Ever the scientist, she asked, "What was it like? The journey?"

"I . . . remember remembering. Lives I've never lived."

"As Jack Joyce?"

Jack nodded. "I'd forget one as I remembered another. It felt like that happened . . . a thousand times? More?" He shook his head. "I can't remember."

"Alternate versions of you, living alternate lives in alternate timelines."

"The creature pushed me away from every other path. Right back here."

"The Shifter mimicked the process that takes place within the Promenade, and did so perfectly . . . but completely unassisted. The odds of your winding up at this place, at this moment, in this timeline, are so incalculably small—"

"—that it's basically impossible. It wanted me here."

"That would be a logical conclusion, but the question is why. If we accept that these creatures are capable of rationality, forethought, and strategy, I mean."

"This one always seemed pretty measured."

"The one Shifter Monarch possessed spent its days trying to kill us. It was rarely calm, unless left utterly alone within a stutter of substantial size. I never saw anything that suggested intelligence. I knew the man that creature used to be. Dr. Kim prized his mind above all. If he couldn't hold on to even a scrap of who he was . . . I don't imagine anyone could."

Jack crouched, retrieved his handgun from the ramp. Motioned to Sofia's injury. "No hospital was a stupid idea, Doctor."

She gestured to the screen. In a couple of minutes Jack learned that a container ship had severed one of Riverport's two major bridges, half the city had lost power, communications outages were being reported across the state, traffic accidents had reached pandemic levels and then ceased entirely, several buildings were on fire, at least one helicopter had crashed (into a church), casualties were being estimated in the thousands, the airport and bus terminals were choked, half the cops had walked off the job and as such the mayor had—within minutes—invoked martial law and outsourced peacekeeping to Monarch.

Nick sighed. "Sofia's been saying it's too dangerous to move, I've been saying she's in a world of trouble if we don't."

"This has been a night for miracles. Perhaps I'll get one of my own." She nodded toward the machine, or more specifically the space from which Jack had appeared. "So here you are. Did you find the Countermeasure?"

Jack shook his head. "Monarch was there."

Her face sank. "And Beth . . . ?"

Jack didn't answer.

Nick felt behind himself, found a chair, sat. Didn't say anything either.

Sofia suddenly looked ten years older. "Then there is nothing to stop Monarch."

Jack shook his head. "Monarch stole the Countermeasure. They still have it. Built Project Lifeboat around it."

Sofia sat forward. "I was told Dr. Kim created the Regulator. It was his great legacy. You're saying the Regulator is the Countermeasure?"

"My brother built it, in a workshop that's now what you people think of as Ground Zero. The casing cracked, Paul got a strong dose and Beth . . ."

Sofia slumped backward. "I'm such a fool. That's why Kim was never able to properly harness . . . he never really understood what . . . oh my God. I'm such a fool. It *was* all Dr. Joyce's work. All of it."

"Sofia," Jack said. "Where do they keep the Countermeasure?"

She fixed her eyes on him, anger sweeping away infirmity. "Floor 49. There's a security door in Paul's office. I'll draw you a map."

The Riverport swimming hall sheltered beneath the overpass. Rain slashed crazy, blasting down out of a night sky that couldn't make up its mind. The world outside was a chopped-up madness of lenses: myriad stutters popping up, lingering and vanishing at points across the city.

The elevated line above began to sing. A train was incoming, not far away now.

Monarch Tower was his destination, that train his ride.

Nick had gotten him a backpack from the cab. Riverport Raptors. Jack slung it, tightened it.

The stairs to the elevated platform were a block away. Jack warped.

The platform was dark, every lighting tube blown out. Jack was the only living thing stupid enough to be there. The freezing, wind-lashed platform offered a 180-degree panorama of a world tearing itself to pieces.

The bridge across the Mystic River was a smashed wreck, having risen too slowly to avoid a cargo ship stuttering right through it. The boat itself was a smoking, flaming ruin, sitting

idle in a river thrashing upon itself as multiple stutters threw its
motions out of synch with itself. Alien-colored lightning leaped
from earth to sky, clouds roiling like an off-black special effect.
Entire sections of the city had blacked out. The soundtrack
to all of this was alarms, sirens, horns. The platform's loud-
speaker system was still running, piping Riverport Radio, the
nighttime DJ rattling off disaster updates and urging people
to stay in their homes.

That's not going to help anyone, Jack thought. *Nowhere is safe
once the rules go out the window.*

The only solution now was Will's: Jack had to find the
Countermeasure and, somehow, use it to fix all of this. To
make things right.

The train was barreling its way toward the platform. Maybe
it was automated, or maybe the driver couldn't see the blacked-
out platform, or maybe they were just flooring it in the hope of
getting clear and getting out. Whatever the reason, the train
wasn't slowing.

He ran down the platform, climbed to the top of the rigid
iron safety fence that protected commuters from a straight
drop to the overpass below, grabbed the gutter of the shelter,
and bounced himself onto the pebbled roof.

Jack took three steps back from the edge, angled himself to
match the train's approach as best he could, waited. . . .

The train was three blocks away.

Waited . . .

Two blocks, moving fast.

Waited . . .

One block.

And warped.

In less than a second he sprinted forward, covered the gap
between the roof of the platform and the top of the train, and
kept running forward, covering enough space within that

folded second to match the train's speed. As quickly as he could he decelerated, before that second expanded, got low, dug in, and held on tight to the lip of the carriage he was atop.

The second unfolded and tossed Jack face-first into a hurricane, his fingers almost snapping off at the joints as the train's speed outmatched his by orders of magnitude.

He had to get the fuck off that train car.

He pulled himself forward, slid down into the gap between cars, and shouldered through the door, gasping.

His arrival was met with wide eyes and a few alarmed screams.

Passengers. Of course there were passengers. A handful in this car, and he could see others in the car down the line.

He felt that now-familiar pulse in his blood that said a stutter was coming.

This was the third-to-last car. Glancing behind him it looked like the others had been blacked out for the night. No other passengers. Small mercies.

An old man sat with a young woman. His eyes were fixed with sad concern on the world outside, while his pale paw of a hand patted hers.

A young guy in a suit was stabbing furiously at his phone while a middle-aged woman glanced at him with contempt.

A broad-shouldered father in a flannel overshirt held his small son tightly to his chest, glancing frantically from one window to another.

Another pulse kicked through Jack, harder this time. Stutter incoming harder and faster than any he had felt before.

Jack held on to a chrome support as the train's frame jostled and kicked. "What's the deal with the driver? Where's this train headed?"

The woman with the old man said, "Whoever's driving isn't answering the emergency intercom."

"Worcester," shouted the man with the child. "All stops Riverport, then express to Worcester. You from the company?"

"No," Jack said. "No. I'm not from the company." He let go of the support, leaned across a seat, and opened the window. Sticking his head out into the wind and rain he saw Monarch Tower slide around the bend, just a few miles away. He'd planned on getting off at the nearest platform, but if the train wasn't stopping then the train wasn't stopping.

The elevated line curved away to the east, shooting above what should have been busy nighttime streets. Jack saw very few people out there, a lot of trashed vehicles, and windows lit from deep within by flame. He could see the domed distortions of stutters dotting the landscape like pimples. As one popped another emerged. Conflict emerged wherever these new borders sprang up.

One mile from Monarch Tower the elevated line curved to the east. A big rig was making good time, horn blasting, looking to get out of town as fast as possible. Its trajectory would take it directly beneath the elevated line. As it got close a stutter snapped down, trapping the front of the cab, bringing it to a halt in a microsecond. The articulated trailer attached to it did not.

The trailer rear-ended the back of the cab, flipped forward like a giant blade, and became trapped in the stutter. When it broke the entire vehicle would smash into the elevated line . . . and that stutter didn't look like it'd be around for long, flickering as it was.

Jack pulled in his head and shouted: "Last car! Everyone into the last car!"

Nobody moved. Half a mile.

Jack pulled his pistol, fired a shot into the ceiling. People screamed and ran. Jack moved forward, fast. "Move! Everyone! Last car!"

The crowd surged into the back, the old man struggling to get out of his seat.

"I'm sorry about this," Jack said. "But we have to move."

The woman didn't question. Together they got the old man upright, looping one arm each around his shoulders, moving as fast as they could.

The few people in the second car were with the program, and almost nobody was in the third.

"Bunch up tight against the back wall! Tight as you can!" The old guy was doing okay. "Can you get him down there?"

The woman nodded. Jack removed the man's arm from around his shoulder to catch a glimpse out the window.

The stutter holding the truck in place broke, the trailer descending on the elevated line like a knife. Whatever it contained was big, heavy, and there was a lot of it. The rig went up in a fireball.

Jack whipped his head away, turned, and warped toward the terrified huddle of twenty-odd people at the back of the last car. Squeezing in close and tight he said, "I'm real sorry about this," and threw down a stutter shield.

The stutter shield anchored their tiny island of car and track in a bubble of frozen time, locked the rear of the car they were squeezed into solidly in place. The rest of the train was not so constrained.

They watched as the rest of the car deformed at seventy miles per hour, metal screaming, glass shattering, lights sparking and going dark as electrics were severed. The engine and every other car pulled away from that one violently, the line of cars straining and snapping their connections, fishtailing wildly. Then half their car tore off completely. Jack watched as the passenger train whip around horizontally, bolo-like, once. The engine seemed to remain stationary in space as the car-tail whipped around it, and then the centrifugal forces swung the engine around to smash like a mace through the front face of Monarch Tower.

The engine cleaved through the bottom two floors of the building, tearing open the black mirror to reveal the honeycomb of its innards. The tail followed up, slashing through and around the building like a whip.

"Last stop, I guess."

Jack's stutter had anchored the final car, the momentum now dispelled. He put his gun away.

Monday, 10 October 2016. 12:28 A.M. Twenty-eight minutes after Jack's return.

Jack had walked the passengers down the elevated line to the platform across from Monarch Tower. He left them there, with advice to stay put, as it seemed to be one of the few places that wasn't being pummeled by violently vacillating causality.

The thick, black cloud cover roiled and unroiled and re-roiled. Violet lightning froze, rewound, reflashed. The passengers watched as the train whipped back up from the wound in the Tower, reassembled mid-flight and seamlessly reattached to the car from which they had just escaped. Then it let go once more, tearing itself apart and brutally lacerating the Tower's face. Freezing. Back-stepping. Letting go. Superstructure sloughing down the Tower's chest, drooling shattered black glass. Sometimes the Tower front shattered without the train impacting at all. Sometimes the truck rewound and was delayed, yet the train flew free anyway.

It was more than just the world that was falling apart: it was the rules that bound the world together, the principles that gave meaning to the flow of time. Causality was becoming porous and weak, falling apart like a wet cake.

Jack took the stairs down from the platform at a run, reached the street, timed his crossing, and warped toward Monarch Tower before the truck could tumble past again. The train completed its arc, smashing through the building, and destroying the security doors and most of the facade.

The woman and her grandfather stood on the lip of the platform and waved to him. Jack almost waved back, when they stepped back from the edge, paused, stepped forward again, waved. Paused. Stepped back.

Science was even less his thing than Beth's, but Jack guessed that if he were standing next to them his subjective causality as it pertained to them would be fine, but at a distance his causality disagreed with theirs. In short, stutters were no longer separate and distinct things. The breakdown was becoming far more granular, finicky. Dangerous.

If it kept degrading at this rate, the universe's chronon levels would flatline and there'd be no coming back. He had to stop that from happening.

He ran for the shattered entrance.

The engine had separated from the line of cars, frozen in the act of wrapping themselves through floors three to five. The engine had paused halfway through the act of smashing through Monarch's lobby, the vast, open space that it used to showcase the successes of its various subsidiaries. The lobby was a museum to corporate achievement, a glossy space illuminated tastefully to better draw the eye to the contents of cases and displays.

Or rather it had been tasteful before a ninety-five-ton passenger locomotive had scythed diagonally through it all. The air was filled with concrete dust, glass shards, and flying shrapnel.

Jack ducked under the frozen train and out the other side, pulling his handgun.

The way out of the lobby and into Monarch's atrium had been shuttered by two-inch-thick steel security doors: bomb-proof.

Jack looked at the train. Looked at the doors. Looked at the train. Against his better judgment, he reached out and laid his palm flat against the overturned side of the vehicle.

He remembered how it had worked, under the Quantum Physics dome, reanimating Will. He had done it again, pulling Sofia into their hijacked chopper fifty floors above Riverport.

He imagined everything in black and white, while from his hands flowed Technicolor.

With alarming suddenness Jack felt his blood surge, his hand tingled sharply, and the locomotive trembled.

The security doors hissed apart, heavily. Two Monarch goons, strapped into the white half shells of prototype power armor, stood framed in the doorway. Auto-cannons slung under their arms sat ready; targeting lasers probed from shoulder-mounted micromissile pods.

They spotted Jack.

Jack held up his free hand, smiled, and gave a little wave.

The train launched right into them.

Jack climbed over the wreckage of the locomotive, shaky from the exertion of freeing the train from the stutter. He climbed through the shattered wall, avoiding fritzing electrics and past the tangled, half-buried remains of a security scanner that beeped forlornly in the haze. The train had tumble-chewed through the security station and clear into the atrium—the space that had, just a short while ago, played host to Monarch's night of nights.

Nobody had bothered to clean up. Raised stages, lighting rigs, bunting, videoboards, smashed glassware, programs sat there covered in concrete dust. Jack climbed out of the trench plowed by the train.

Overhead the atrium's clear ceiling let in all the mad light of a universe sundered by torsion. Dust, papers, and debris fell from forty different mezzanines, none of the wreckage conforming to gravity with any sense of unison or regularity. The acoustics carried the sporadic bark of gunfire, the occasional lonely shout or scream from the street. He saw the sporadic otherworldly flicker of Shifters prowling and vanishing along the mezzanines.

· Floor thirty-four vomited a gout of flame, a Monarch trooper falling, screaming, to the atrium floor—stopping before impact—rewinding, pausing, falling, and screaming again. The man's high-pitched scream slurred into a drawn-out howl as he pinwheeled upward toward a tongue of boiling flame that was quickly retracting into one of the upper levels. He merged with the flame in time to be drawn out of sight by it, the concrete balustrade over which he had flown piecing neatly back together behind it.

The elevator bays were transparent geometric tubes, all shattered, behind the circular reception area. Two contained the wrecks of elevators. The third was rendered opaque by smoke and burning debris.

Jack wasn't alone there: he shared the ruined space with kinetic statuary that had once been living people. Moving, jigging, and back-stepping all about him were dead people continually reenacting their final moments of life—all of them violent, all of them screaming as hideously as the man forever tumbling from the thirty-fourth mezzanine.

Jack felt weak, detached. Unleashing the train had taken it out of him. He was going to need a few minutes to regenerate his charge. It seemed to be taking longer, now that the world's chronon levels were a thin, spasmodic mess.

He made for the reception desk, hoping to find a stairwell door, moving and turning to avoid flailing arms, airborne droplets of blood, flying glass, flying bullets. It wasn't just Monarch troopers meeting their end there, but the workers needed to keep a place functioning. People who'd turned up to earn a paycheck.

The elevators weren't an option—they weren't rewinding far enough back to be usable.

Howls. A whole fucked-up choir. Shifters, up there, prowling the mezzanines. Jack figured he had no choice but to take the stairwell, but he didn't like his chances if he was caught in a narrow space with one of those things.

He moved to the reception desk, hoping to find a floor plan.

One of the creatures was waiting on the other side of it, maybe fifty feet away, writhing, flashing. It yowled softly, curiously. Its contorted body language, the cant of its flickering, flashing head, was that of something wanting something it was not allowed to have.

Another stood to the left, by the wrecked train.

Three more were off to the far right, hovering in the shadows. They saw him. Screamed. Flashed forward, close. Flashed again, closer.

Two more blinked in, flanking the Shifter fifty feet from Jack. Roared.

A third blinked in behind them, spread its arms, and the three Shifters flashed aside.

He recognized this one. It threw its head to the sky and loosed the sound of a hundred horses with slashed throats. Shining Palm.

"Hey," Jack said, very carefully. "You brought me here."

Every single Shifter lost its shit completely. The three to the right charged, flashing in and around the frozen, jigging corpses, on a killing path straight for him.

Shining Palm wheeled on them, shrieked. The three braked, rounded on him, and screamed right back.

Jack took his chance and ran.

He sprinted right, then warped past the reception area, giving the three clustered Shifters a wide berth. The exertion took it out of him, dropping him almost back to zero.

The three reacted, spun. Shining Palm leaped, slamming into their cluster, sending them scattering.

Jack pivoted, facing them.

Shining Palm retargeted.

"Hey now," Jack said, reasonably. "Back off."

It charged.

Jack leaped boots-first onto the bent knee of an inanimate Monarch trooper who was arched backward in death—

"Ugh."

—and jumped up, clawing for the falling trooper as he hurtled at half speed for the atrium floor.

"Time to be lucky," he gasped. "Please be lucky."

Jack's fingers scrabbled against cloth that was utterly immovable, managed to loop one arm around the man's midsection, the back of his flailing legs punching Jack in the face.

Froze. Jack almost came loose with the jarring stop.

Shining Palm swept both killing paws upward, as the trooper rewound.

At speed.

For Jack the next ten seconds were a lot like falling off a cliff while being punched in the face. When the flailing trooper hit his parabola, Jack's grip slipped. He continued upward, briefly, while the trooper redocked with his past. Jack missed the thirty-fourth floor entirely while sailing toward a slow-approaching thirty-fifth.

He grabbed for the glass-and-steel balustrade as if it were

all he had ever wanted. Got his forearms across, fell, bashing chest against the flat of it and his chin against the rail.

Stars. Flailing. Didn't let go. Felt nothing beneath his feet. A terrible and total nothing.

He let himself hang for just a moment, gasping.

Slipped his boots onto thirty-five and rolled himself over the rail. His back hit the ground hard. Just breathed as if he'd forgotten how to.

"Kill him!"

Ah, shit.

He slapped both hands against the slate-gray carpet, popped a shield, almost blacked out from the effort. Heard a ton of bullets *thwip* against the carapace.

He was done. Running on fumes.

"Fuck off," Jack said to the ceiling, flatly. "Whoever you are just fuck off."

"That shield has a half-life of about, what, ten seconds? Fifteen?"

Jack heard the *snick-snack* of weapons reloading. The subtle pneumatic hiss of German-engineered microhydraulics. The question mark whine of servos.

He sat up beneath his bubble.

"That's Jack Joyce," someone else said.

There were thirty guys and two Juggernauts—all of them rigged for stutter mobility. They'd been hauling ass and braked to a halt when Jack flipped over the railing. The ones bringing up the rear were swinging assault rifles back and forth like they were expecting to get jumped any second.

"Who gives a shit?" another said. "We're almost there."

The leader—a clean-cut kid with a movie-star complexion— shook his head. "Uh-uh. Shifters can't pass through the stutter shield, but *he* can. We can't leave him wandering around."

The kid opened up, barking a thirty-round mag into the shield, wide coverage. Hundreds of bullets waited for permission to splash Jack to paste, while the squad kept him covered with everything they had.

"Figure that half-life is down to about five," the kid said.

If Jack stepped outside, he was going to die; if he stayed put, he was going to die. He didn't have enough left in him for a warp.

"Four," the kid said.

Jack looked left and right: He was on a curved mezzanine, with the Monarch crew in front of him. There was cover behind the elevator bay to the right. To the left was all glass-walled meeting rooms along the full line of the gallery. Not enough charge in him to cover a warp of ten feet.

The shield trembled. So did the bullets.

"Three."

Jack glanced behind him. "Over the side," he mumbled to himself, thinking back to Paul's panicked face at Bannerman's Overlook six years ago. "Legs first."

The kid smiled. His buddies braced weapons.

Jack backed against the rail, got a firm grip.

The stutter watered down fast.

Jack tensed. . . .

"One."

The top half of the kid tore free and flew a messy twenty feet toward Jack before freezing mid-air, trailing wet red machinery.

Mad light. Howls.

The stutter shield collapsed as Jack leaped to the right, instead of backward, the designer railing blasted to slag by the simultaneous impact of a cloud of military rounds and at least one micromissile. Something hot—slag, shrapnel, or a bullet—blazed through his hamstring. The entire squad had now forgotten him, going full auto on opponents far more lethal than Jack.

Rising to one knee he came face-to-upside-down-face with the kid's shocked expression. He shuddered. "Tough break."

The squad had scattered like billiards.

Shifters were tearing them to pieces. Back pressed to the elevator bay, chest pounding, Jack scanned the mezzanine for a way to Paul's office on forty-nine . . . and found it. Security elevator—black-and-chrome edged. He fumbled in his pockets—trying to ignore the pain and keep the weight off his crippled left leg—and found Sofia's security laminate.

He glanced around the corner.

A trooper flew past at waist height and hit the railing, where his spine snapped like a gunshot, before flipping slackly into the void.

One Juggernaut wheeled in an awkward forty-five-degree three-step, targeting laser drawing a bead on one monster approaching at speed. The pilot spat his entire missile pod at the thing, a dozen micro-missiles *vip-whoosh*-ing in rapid succession down seventy feet of office hallway, clothing the thing in shrapnel and blooming flame clouds. To no effect.

The Shifter raised both arms, brought them down and through the Juggernaut's only protection: the front armor plate.

The man tried to wrestle free, had no chance.

A second Shifter zapped in from behind, grabbed the guy around the face and waist. And pulled.

The Juggernaut froze in a position of alarm, the trooper inside the suit froze mid-air; pilot and frame violently disarticulated.

A second Juggernaut pivoted and cut loose with its autocannon—pointlessly; 7.62mm rounds sprayed into the Shifters, wild rounds mowing down a handful of his workmates who were still alive.

Realizing he was a drowning man strapped to a multi-million-dollar anchor, the pilot activated the emergency release, stepped backward out of the exoskeleton, and ran—straight toward the elevators.

"No," Jack hissed. "Not here. Not here."

A seven-foot fractal silverback dropped on the pilot, crushing him.

Jack breathed a sigh of relief.

The Shifter snapped its head up, roared, and reached for him—palm filled with starlight.

"Oh fuck."

Jack warped. He didn't make it far, but he cleared the distance between elevator bays and the glass-walled rooms, the nearest of which were now bullet-riddled and shattered. He came out of the warp and kept running, old-school, his left leg bright red with pain. The security elevator was a hundred feet away and closing, the sounds of carnage behind him dwindling as the Shifters began to run out of people to butcher.

A quick look behind and he saw Shining Palm take down one trooper before one long swipe reduced a second trooper to a dead statue.

Seventy feet. The pain in his leg was receding; it took weight more easily.

Jack warped.

Thirty feet.

He was dizzy, seeing stars. Glanced back.

Shining Palm was thundering down the gallery after him, and behind him came a wave of other Shifters.

Jack warped—fifteen feet—and almost blacked out. Laminate in hand he swiped it through the slot.

Glanced back. Shining Palm was fifty feet and closing. Forty.

The security doors opened. Jack leaped inside, punched the Door Close button.

As they slid closed Jack noticed the chronon frame that bracketed the elevator—charged.

Ten feet. Doors closed. Jack braced for impact . . . nothing but howls.

The elevator climbed upward, its own rescue rig keeping it mobile despite universal stasis.

He collapsed against the wall, slid to the floor. He hadn't stopped to think the elevator might be as uncooperative as everything else in a stutter. Looked like Paul took that into account when he rigged the top floors with its own stutter shield.

"Good morning, Dr. Amaral," the elevator said. "You are not due at the office for another six hours and eighteen minutes."

A stutter shield that, Jack figured, was being powered by the Countermeasure.

The infoscreen told him it was 12:42 A.M.

The doors opened on floor forty-nine and Jack felt the chronon dampeners like the fug of a mild hangover. He'd have no advantages here if anyone tried to jump him.

Jack emerged into a hallway lit by recessed violet strip lighting and walked toward Paul's office without so much as a limp. His leg had healed.

Paul's door was fine mahogany set into a sci-fi housing. Sofia's card clicked in, got green-lighted, and the door's maglock released with a pleasing *thunk*.

Pistol gripped in both hands, Jack booted the door, sending it flying open hard enough for the handle to punch through the wall and keep it there. He stepped in briskly, scanning. He was alone.

Glass wall on one side, staircase curving up to living quarters on the other. Desk facing glass wall, big gnarled-looking expensive wooden chair . . .

Expensive art, expensive carpets, two-floor-tall bookshelves. Fully-equipped gymnasium on the far side.

Jack took Sofia's map, checked the layout. The Regulator was kept in a sealed chamber directly beneath her chronon labs, and was accessible through . . .

Behind the desk, flush with the wall, was an armored security door. Reinforced, two-inches thick, and the eruption of technology next to it suggested that nobody was getting in without everything including a urine sample.

". . . that suspiciously open door."

The door was wide open, the chamber beyond lit blood red.

Jack approached sidelong and slow, gun at the ready. Could be it just popped open when the building started freaking out. Or maybe someone had panicked and left it like this.

He glanced inside.

Broad and deep, Paul's side of the Regulator chamber ended at a thick transparent wall. That wall had a door—also open—and beyond that the chamber was walled with diagnostics. Two standing consoles faced the far wall, and set into the wall was a geometric depression.

Within that depression sat the thing Jack and Beth had gone through hell to find.

The Countermeasure had been reinforced since Jack had last seen it, back in 2010 when Beth had died. It was now gloved tightly within a reinforced titanium frame. Connectors and adapters had been built into it, conservatively, for the purpose of powering Monarch Tower's chronon-related vitals. Otherwise, beneath the pretty new dress, it was still Will's home-made dodecagon. It was a powerful thing for such a small object, no bigger than a volleyball.

He moved in. Nobody home. He stepped into the chamber proper. Everything quietly humming. Screens flashed blueprints of the entire Tower. Looked like Will's volleyball really was powering everything that mattered.

Jack got closer to it, puzzled out the clamps and catches keeping it in place, which panel governed the release mechanism.

It was the panel with the screen opened on REGULATOR HOUSING RELEASE: Y/N?

Jack closed his eyes, sighed.

"All right," he said. "Whatever you're going to do, do it."

Nothing.

"*Come on!* Door's open? Every safeguard on this thing's been disabled. *Do it!*"

Nothing.

REGULATOR HOUSING RELEASE: Y/N?

Jack stared at it, hating it.

"Fuck it."

Catches popped like gunshots. Electromagnets powered off, cabling popping free from every socket on the device.

A klaxon blared, deafeningly, once, and the lighting in the room shifted to blue.

FLOOR 49 STUTTER SHIELD: DEACTIVATED.

FLOOR 50 STUTTER SHIELD: DEACTIVATED.

CHRONON DAMPENERS: OFFLINE.

ELEVATOR MOBILITY RIGS: OFFLINE.

Howls.

Jack leaped toward the Countermeasure, tugged it from its housing. A little resistance, a lot of heat, and it clacked loose.

Jack held it, surveyed it, the salvation of humanity.

"I have no idea how to use this thing."

The Shifters were moving in.

Jack zipped the Countermeasure into Nick's backpack, slung it, and ran out of there.

There was only one person left who knew what to do.

The chamber's southern exit led to Paul's office, and a western exit was designed for quick access to the time lab. Jack took the latter. The security door led to a dog-leg hallway. He rounded the second corner, swiped his way through the door, secured it behind himself.

He stood in a glass-box control room, looking down on the sterile expanse of the Monarch time laboratory, safety areas marked out in black-and-yellow lines, a raised grill-floored diagnostic station on the far side. The machine itself—that smooth, high-tech donut—sat heavy on the right side of the lab. The time core—the one Monarch had airlifted out of Riverport University two nights ago—hung twenty feet above the center of the ring, cabling draping down to the Promenade, ready for automated lowering and connection.

The time lab had its own stutter-proofing: a series of discrete generators in each corner of the room, drawing a chronon charge from the same batteries that powered the machine. Insurance, and an escape route, against the main shield ever going down in the midst of a crisis.

Jack slapped the release button, setting the machinery downstairs in motion. He exited the far side of the observation deck, clattering down the stairs as the time core lowered carefully into position at the center of the Promenade.

It was still inching downward as the Shifters crashed through the corridors upstairs.

Reaching the time lab floor, Jack looped thumbs through the straps of his pack, pulling it tight against his back to minimize bounce, and sprinted for the machine. He got to the controls just as various connectors began jacking into the core. The controls lit up.

A swarm of crazed light manifested inside the glass-box control room.

Shifters flickered and phased into the lab.

Fuck.

It wasn't possible to go back any earlier than when the machine was first activated, which was around 4:15 A.M. the previous Saturday. Today was Monday. He gambled on 4:35 A.M. and activated the machine.

The Monarch machine was better made. The Promenade charged up immediately, the airlock levering itself open smoothly as the horde rolled out of the observation deck, already appearing here and there across the time lab's expanse. Jack warped for the airlock, up the ramp, spun, and slapped the release plate. The airlock began levering itself closed as that galloping, tumbling mass of schizophrenic carnage filled the lab, skidded, and barreled toward him, howling hatred.

Jack stopped. Someone was in the lab, standing unbothered, eyes on Jack as the horde flowed around him.

Martin Hatch.

The Shifters didn't acknowledge Monarch's CEO, didn't lay a claw on his finely tailored suit. Hatch watched the airlock close as the monsters flowed around him, galloping and tumbling for Jack, until he was lost from sight behind the strobing and shifting mass.

The airlock smooched shut as the first creature slammed into the door. The right door opened and Jack stepped into safety.

There was one person who could still make this work, and Jack had a plan to bring him back from the dead.

Fuck the laws of the universe.

21

Saturday, 8 October 2016. 4:35 A.M. Riverport
University, Quantum Physics Building. Two days
earlier. Twenty minutes after initial time machine
activation.

The silent trip around the Promenade ended with Jack stepping back into the night that changed his life forever. He expected commotion on his arrival, but the lab outside the airlock
was oddly quiet. Risking a peek through the viewplate, the
Riverport University time lab was as he remembered: ramp
leading down, time controls to the right. Stairs ahead, leading
up to a left–right platform. Glassed-in control booth up a short
flight of steps to the right from that, the way out up steps to
the left.

He triggered the airlock to open, then emerged.

"I'm telling you something just happened." Voices from beneath the machine. The two grunts who chased Will and Jack
on the night they got caught up in Paul Serene's madness.
"Someone's up there."

Two Monarch troopers, hunkered on either side of the access tunnel down which Jack and his brother had fled, glanced
up as Jack popped his head through the gap overhead. "Boo."

Jack had intended to freeze them in a stutter. Instead, shockingly, the causality within the confined space around the
troopers disconnected, reentangled incorrectly, and then
erupted in a violent contradiction that saw the skeletons of both

men spontaneously disarticulated. Joints interacted bizarrely with bone; physics reinvented itself while clashing with causal outcomes that existed only in foreign timelines. The men were refashioned savagely in the blink of an eye, pinballing with terrific force from surface to surface within that confined space. Death was instantaneous, and what slumped to the grill floor beneath the machine resembled abused marionettes more than men.

Jack recoiled. "Maybe I should have just said 'hands up.'"

His powers hadn't stopped evolving. He was still changing. What did that mean, and where did it end?

He dropped into the maintenance cavity and, with thumb and forefinger, gingerly removed the earpiece from one of the troopers.

". . . Physics Building. A couple of regulars are cleaning the lab, the rest of us are on the tenth floor."

"All right Donny, clean house, top to bottom. Catch you after."

"Copy, boss."

Gibson. His crew was about to sweep through the building and kill everyone inside. People whose jobs Paul had been trying to save. The ones Jack and Paul had passed on the way to the time lab the other night—this night. *People with families,* Paul had said.

Jack headed for the stairwell.

He passed the fifth, hearing a trooper in Reaper squad yell, "Grenade! He popped my grenade!" before air displacement from the detonation thumped the stairwell door in its frame as he passed.

He exited the Quantum Physics Building on the third floor and crossed over the ramp into the western administration building. This took him out from under the dome—the dome where everything went to shit and he and his brother fought for their lives. Were about to fight for their lives.

"Sir?" Donny piped up over Jack's earpiece. "The two strays from the time lab weren't among the bodies."

"Do what we do, Don. Lock it down. They'll be in there." Then, "Don? Go look out a window."

"Well shit, boss. Am I seeing what I think I'm seeing?"

"Wait twenty seconds, Don, then tell me what you see."

He moved as fast as he could, folding into moments and accelerating along straight corridors. In his earpiece and through the walls he could hear the successive thumps of Gibson's grenades striking the underside of the Quantum Physics dome, with Will the target. Time was running out.

Elevators were shut down. He found the admin stairwell, taking stairs five at a time, slamming out onto the ground floor, speeding down another corridor, emerging into a reception area and out into the night.

He'd kicked the rear door open onto a small parking area, knocking over a coffee can filled with old cigarette butts. Energy levels low now, he folded into a moment, zipped about a hundred feet toward the parking lot. That got him just outside the north side of the dome—the opposite side from the protest camp and Founders' Walk.

Guardian squad was scattered about inside the dome. A wide section of glass at ground level had already been blasted white by Gibson's last grenade—the one whose force had thrown Jack face-first into the grill of Gibson's BearCat.

He caught a glimpse of the camp. It was a flat mess, with very few tents left standing. Some of it was on fire. There wasn't a single kid in or around the camp, just a few stray troopers walking a circuit, being thorough.

Headlights flashed to life on the south side of the dome. Jack saw his bloodied past self rise to his feet in front of Gibson's BearCat as Monarch's number one chronon operative threw the vehicle into reverse.

That meant Monarch had Will.

Right on cue the sound of struggle on the steps inside. Two goons had Will by each arm and were dragging him down the central stairs, toward the north doors—about 150 feet in front of Jack.

Ducking down, he figured he had enough energy left to zip across that space fast and hard, which should be enough to take out the goon on the left. Getting the one on the right would come down to luck. He stayed low, waited.

The doors opened and out they came, Will protesting the whole time. "You're destroying yourselves! The . . ."

Jack launched at them—

—and never made it.

He'd covered twenty feet when a forearm swept across his path, collecting him from the throat, knocking his feet skyward, and slamming him back-first into the ground.

He couldn't breathe. Someone stood over him, adjusting his tie.

Hatch. He said just one word: "No."

Neither the troopers nor Will noticed, and Will was dragged toward a waiting BearCat.

Hatch glanced at the dome, then down at Jack. It was the same examining stare Hatch had used on him a short time ago in the Tower: unconcerned, as if wondering why Jack even existed.

Jack's thoughts were suffocated, strangled by his own half-closed windpipe. He struggled to sit up but a foot shoed in fine Italian leather gently pushed him down. Hatch waited, watching the BearCat pull away and tear toward the library, then turned his attention to Jack.

"All right," Hatch said, and removed his foot.

Jack blinked hard, tried to swallow, could barely form the question: "Who are you?"

He said it to the night air. Hatch was gone. Jack was alone. The fucker must have ghosted back into the western admin building. What was he doing here? Who had Paul partnered with?

Thunder rolled across the parking lot: the sound of the BearCat waking up, then peeling toward the library. No time for subtlety. Low on energy and struggling to breathe, Jack cut through the dome. Gibson and his own past self were already gone; the person he had been would already be at the library.

Jack accelerated toward the library. He only did one burst. He was going to need every scrap of energy that he could muster for what came next.

When a moment is witnessed the waveform collapses. That's what Will had said—and Paul. Events cannot be changed once those events intersect with and influence causality.

Jack ran straight at the particleboard barriers around the rear of the library, converted momentum to mantling, swung a leg over, and landed facing the open entry to the rear of the library, stripped of its door.

The room was perfectly square, empty save for limp lengths of plastic like the shed skin of giant snakes, dust and insulation.

The stacks were through the empty door frame to his left and beyond the south door Paul and Will were in the final moments of their futile conversation.

"But we don't have years for you to come to the same conclusion. We have moments."

That was it. Jack jagged left. . . .

"Actual," Paul said. "this is your Consultant. Trigger." And then warped out.

Jack rounded the corner in time to see Paul go out the main doors. His past self looked on in horror as Paul slammed into him, sweeping him out of the building as the first charges detonated upstairs.

Jack skidded on the smooth black-and-white flooring, fingertips trailing in the dust, and dashed forward as a curtain of debris descended.

Jack kicked into a slide as the top floor came down behind him, colliding with Will's legs at the same time as he slammed hands into the dust.

The weight of a building fell to earth on the spot where the brothers stood. The collapse kicked out a cloud that swept across the campus, obscuring everything in a thick, rolling shroud of pulverized marble, masonry, and concrete.

Jack coughed. "Will? Will!" He couldn't see anything. "Will!"

"I think I broke my watch."

Will was right there, sitting up beneath the flickering bubble of self-contained causality. Alive.

Jack crashed into him, holding on to him with everything he had.

"You, uh," Will said, with difficulty. "You're getting quite good at this." Then he realized: "You're not Jack. The Jack I met tonight had shaved. You have not."

Jack let him go. "This won't last long."

"I should be dead," Will said. "Same clothes, more stubble. I'd say you're, what, two days older? Three? You've come back in time. For me, for this. Meaning you thought I was dead. I should be dead."

"There's some space outside this bubble. I'm gonna blast us clear. I doubt anyone's gonna notice at this point."

"I *was* dead, to you, but you've saved me. The only way that could be possible is if . . . if between now and when you come back for me the world has every reason to believe me dead—if I never interact with causality between now, and two days from now. Which we can achieve if you and I now travel *forward* in time, bypassing those two days. Jack," Will said. "The waveform never collapses. I never die. What a brilliant solution to have formulated. *Well* done."

"Cover your ears." Jack shoved his hands through the bubble, and did to the wreckage what he had done to the two Monarch troopers beneath the time machine.

Tonnage blew outward.

Jack and Will emerged from the wreckage of the library into a world that had stopped moving.

They carved through the chalk-white atmosphere, making their way across the shattered ruin of the library and out onto the campus.

"I completely missed this the first time around," Jack said.

"Missed?" Will inquired, dusting himself off. They were walking briskly toward the Quantum Physics Building—and their way home.

"Yeah," Jack said. "She found me. And . . . oh man."

"She?"

Jack wasn't listening. Or walking. He'd seen something, on Founders' Walk, and was now running toward it. Will called after him, then followed.

Beth was frozen, marching along Founders' Walk with the unconscious body of Jack's past self slung over her shoulder. There she was, beautiful and alive. Unmoving. The fighter he'd fallen in love with.

Jack stepped closer to her. Here she was, so very much alive. "You knew her, didn't you?" Jack said to his brother.

"I've known Beth Wilder for seventeen years," Will replied.

"The first thing she did was save my life. Yours, too, actually."
Then, "You can't save her."

"You know what happened to her?"

"In 2010? I think so. I returned to my workshop at the dock
and the area was ruined. I saw the anomalies, recognized them
as the product of a Countermeasure breach. I'd hoped she was
alive, had taken the Countermeasure and returned to 2016—
but I knew the exposure would have killed her first. Then
Monarch bought out the entire area, and set up a chronon-
harvesting operation. 'Ground Zero' they call it. So, with
eleven years of work wasted and Armageddon due, I bought a
gun and tried to shut down Monarch's lab myself. Which
brings us here."

If Jack had heard, he made no sign. "She deserves to live."

"You have to let her go, Jack. We have a universe to consider."

Jack couldn't open his mouth to say a single word. He just
leaned into Beth, slid his arms around her, and held her as best
he could. Just for a moment.

He whispered something he wished she could hear, but knew
she never would.

22

Jack and Will clasped each other's hands as they walked the Promenade, side by side, in lockstep, staying in synch as they walked two nights forward.

"What you'll see is going to be shocking, Will. Fair warning."

"I've been prepared for this since you were ten. I'm confident I can handle it."

Arriving at the airlock they opened the seal and stepped into the first hour of Monday morning.

Jack checked through the viewplate. The airlock hissed, the seals depressurizing, and the two brothers stepped out onto the ramp.

The lab was vacant. They were alone.

"Oh," Will said. "I expected something more dramatic." Then, "Is that . . . music?"

What they heard was a lilting series of high notes, as though someone in a distant room were plinking on a xylophone, building from slow rhythm to something faster. Coming in under this simple score, abruptly, was the sound countless girders might make if they were bent and tearing beneath a weight they could no longer support.

The floor shifted alarmingly, betraying them as the far wall detached and slipped away without so much as a sound.

Freezing air rushed in and far below came the sound of hundreds of tons of concrete, glass, and iron waterfalling clumsily and catastrophically into the street.

Riverport—bucking, flaming, dying—laid itself bare to them.

Will walked across the buckled floor, toward the torn-open wall, perhaps drawn by something only he could understand. Something written in the pulsing, wailing, pointillist nighttime landscape spread before him. Or perhaps he was simply a man who was looking upon what he had done, and found himself overcome by the horror of it.

Jack reached for him, pulled him back from the ragged edge, and saw for himself what was becoming of the town that had raised him.

"Will," Jack shouted above the high-altitude wind. "Can you stop this?" He unslung his pack, opened it, showed Will the Countermeasure. "Can you?"

The sight of the device drew Will out of his shock. He nodded. "I can try. It's what I built it for. Yes. Yes, I believe so. I need to get under the machine."

Taking the device from the bag, turning it over in his hands, Will said, "The charge is unusually low."

"Monarch was shielding the top floors from the stutter with it, running some kind of dampener network. Probably running a bunch of other crap as well. I have no idea."

Will looked out across that terribly wounded city. "It . . ." He struggled to find the words. "Causality relies upon an agreed-upon sequence of events. This creates what we understand as the flow of time. The Fracture is inviting other potential realities to the mix. What was once a song is now a violent confusion. This building is falling apart beneath us."

"Well, actually," Jack said, "it's a little of that, and a little of me throwing a train through the reception area." He shrugged. "It was locked."

Will took the Countermeasure and headed for the time machine, when a voice said:

"Jack."

Jack scanned around: the corners, the control room above, no one was here.

Will didn't seem to have heard it, examining the Countermeasure as he walked to the machine.

"Jack?"

"Paul . . . ?"

Jack stopped cold. Paul was in the airlock, standing on the ramp, looking into the room with terror on his face. This wasn't the Paul whom Jack had seen drop a building on his brother; this was Paul as he had been the night he had first traveled through the machine.

Will carefully put the Countermeasure down near the story-high platinum-cased chronon reserve Monarch used to power the machine and began an examination of the power's routing to the Promenade.

As Jack moved toward his friend-who-had-been, a second figure materialized—standing at the bottom of the ramp. Martin Hatch.

This wasn't real, Jack realized. It was a vision, like the ones he experienced back at the house.

"You and I are destined to be great friends, Paul," Hatch was saying. "It is the honor of my life to provide all that you need to play your singular role."

Hatch opened an arm toward three men and women, waiting to escort Paul out of the room—toward a future that turned him into the man responsible for all that was happening to the world at that moment.

Jack watched young Paul Serene—baffled and lost—get shepherded away. Hatch took a cleansing breath, with the air of a man who had just crossed a major milestone.

Who the fuck are you? Jack thought. *You monstrous son of a bitch.*

Hatch moved to leave . . . and then stopped. His back straightened, curiously.

Martin Hatch glanced behind himself. Turned fully. Then took a step toward Jack.

Martin Hatch—years into the future—stood five feet before Jack Joyce, and appeared to look him right in the eye. Jack stepped back.

Slowly, carefully, Martin Hatch looked Jack up and down . . . and smiled.

"Who the fuck are you?" Jack said.

Hatch clicked his fingers . . . and the vision ended.

Jack was alone.

The stutter hit without warning. The intercom overloaded and exploded in sparks. The glass walls of the control room shattered, rewound, remained intact. For a vertiginous microsecond the floor vanished, sharing a moment with a world where the entire building had collapsed, before native reality reasserted itself—the spasm between what is and what could be knocking Jack and Will off their feet.

Across Riverport the skies bucked, energy flashed, shock waves kicked down streets and thrashed the river. Whole blocks lit up or went dark, most often vacillating between the two. The chorus of car alarms was a background song to whole streets opening up along their length, to spot fires and infernos. Jack had no idea what was happening on the ground. If this could happen to steel and concrete, what was happening to people?

"Jack."

"What is it, Will?"

Will looked up from his examinations of a rack of connectors on the corridor-ring. "Did you say something?"

"Didn't—"

"*Jack!*" The voice was wrong: layered, skitzing, fucked-up.

Paul Serene stepped off the stairwell to the control room, fifty feet from Jack. Broad-shouldered, and almost entirely consumed by the chronon sickness that was remaking him into something monstrous. Starlight flashed beneath his clothes. The flesh of his hands and neck was a shifting play of fractal light. When he spoke illumination poured from his throat. "Are you ready?"

"Jesus."

"Close enough." Paul spasmed, a flurry of multiple Pauls all at once. He was phasing from humanity to whatever the Shifters were. "You and I die here," he rasped. "But in doing so save a universe."

"Will, get that thing hooked up, and fast."

"I have it connected to the primary chronon flow. I think we're ready."

"Then do it!"

Paul snorted. "It makes no difference."

Will socketed the Countermeasure into the battery's main outflow and . . . nothing.

"Don't fight me, Jack." Paul was having a hard time keeping it together. "We stick together, right?"

It was then that Jack noticed the silver chain dangling from Paul's balled, luminescing fist: the chain attached to the bullet.

He raised that fist. "We've known each other all our lives . . . the universe . . . fate . . . arranged it just so. . . ." Paul shuddered. Multiple Pauls flashed and rioted for control of his friend's identity, and were beaten back by an excruciating force of will. "I know this because I've seen it."

"I've seen things, too, Paul."

"We are here now because my futures make themselves known to me . . . and I choose the futures into which I take the world. And I *know*, Jack, that this is where you and I end . . . because I've never had a vision beyond tonight. Beyond now. They all narrow to the same inevitable point. You fail, you die, I die, and Monarch triumphs."

Paul straightened up, then marched toward Will. "Give me the Regulator."

Jack warped to intercept. At the last second Paul wasn't there and Jack went careening into the diagnostic bank against the wall.

Paul stopped. "As I near my end the visions don't stop. The less time I have, the clearer they become, as potentiality narrows. You may attack as you wish . . ."

Jack warped, and again Paul wasn't there. Jack skidded, stopping short of tumbling into the maintenance recess.

". . . but I am beyond surprises."

Will ripped the Countermeasure from the machine, held it before him like a weapon. "I'll breach this before I let you take it. It almost killed you once, it can—"

The Countermeasure vanished from Will's grip, leaving him yelping and clutching wrenched fingers.

Paul held it, unconcerned. "This is meant for Martin Hatch, and the future."

Jack took a gamble. "In all those visions, Paul, do you ever see Hatch?"

Paul said nothing for a moment, then, "Martin has always been with me."

"And?"

Paul didn't say anything.

Jack smiled, didn't enjoy it. "That's what I figured. So what is it? What's off about him?"

Jack warped, Paul had moved, appeared farther down the lab, toward the breach.

"You know what I'm going to say, you know what you're going to say. Flip ahead. Tell me how this conversation plays out."

"Lives . . . are messy," Paul said. "Martin's . . . is not."

Jack blinked. "Meaning what?"

Will stepped up. "In all the futures you can see and choose from, Martin Hatch's actions never deviate?"

"He is the most focused man I have ever met. My life, all that I am, I owe to his clarity."

"Think about that," Jack said. "And . . ."

Paul's outline flickered, wavered, but not in the way that Shifters spasmed out. This was more of a superimposition.

". . . give me . . ."

The room tunneled and slowed, as a crowd of Paul Serenes— like ghosts, like after-images—stepped, moved, gesticulated, swung, ran . . .

". . . the . . ."

Not after-images: fore-images. Jack saw his own image dashing out, intersecting with Paul's. A million potentials exploding from all three men present to form a chaos of moment-to-moment potentiality. Too much to make sense of, so Jack narrowed focus down to what he needed: the device Paul now held.

Ghosts faded. The futures in which he made a play for the Countermeasure solidified. Paul intercepted or avoided him in all of them. In some of them Jack went flying out that breach.

He chose one where he didn't.

". . . Countermeasure."

He shot forward. Paul wasn't there. Jack knew where he was, feinted, counted on Paul making a bad choice from the futures he was seeing. Failed.

The game became one of seeing who could see deepest into the mesh of move and countermove and take action accordingly. Jack had far less experience, but Paul was being reassembled from the inside out.

Jack zipped toward him, failed to intercept, feinted, failed, swung for him, failed, outflanked, failed. Paul flashed for the stairwell, Jack moved to intercept, Paul saw it coming and jagged left and swung over the railing. Jack was already there, waiting. Paul swung, Jack grabbed for the Countermeasure, Paul was gone.

"You said we die here?" Jack gasped.

Paul nodded.

"Got a time on that?"

Paul warped forward, bringing down one flash-skinned hand, missing, following through on the momentum, and swinging the Countermeasure like a bowling ball into Jack's chest. Jack flew six feet and hit the deck hard.

"*No!*" Will scrambled toward them. "You'll breach it!"

Paul looked at the device in his hand as though he had never seen it before, an expression of animal confusion on his face.

"Paul?"

He glanced at Will, then, as if hoping to see understanding in another's eyes. "Wars, calamities, plagues, they were all prices paid to cause and effect, to lead us to this moment." He slung the silver bullet about his neck, beheld it. "I miss the little things."

He let it go. Looked away as it fell against his strobing chest.

Paul Serene shuddered, cried out, as the sickness extended farther up his throat, into his skull, and touched his brain.

Jack kicked off against the diagnostics, used what energy he had left to flash the distance between them . . .

. . . which Paul countered by warping at him, a half foot to the left, swinging an extended forearm into Jack's face. Jack went down, and the thing that had been Paul Serene followed up, driving a booted heel downward. Jack flinched aside, the boot cracking the floor near his head, pressed his hands to the floor and . . .

Paul dropped a knee into Jack's back. Jack buckled, smashed to the floor, realizing almost immediately that he could feel nothing below his waist.

Paul stepped backward. "You die here so that Monarch can succeed." He pointed toward the stairwell. One level up, phasing and flickering, was a Shifter. The Shifter. The Shining Palm. "That kills you." Paul drew out his handgun. "This . . . here . . . is the last vision . . . I ever had. . . ."

He was almost gone. Shifter Paul clutched for the bullet about his neck, tore it free, focused on it—the reminder he had carried for over twenty years: of friendship, his humanity. A reminder that nothing is to be taken for granted and that time is finite, so better get on living. It seemed to grant him some cohesion, some peace, some focus.

The sickness surged, Paul screamed. Jack pulled his handgun and fired. Agonized howls rolled out of the Shining Palm as potential actions condensed to singular realities, moment to moment, lacerating it. The bullet passed through empty air, sparked off the diagnostics.

"You're not all gone, are you?"

Paul was by the breach; Jack fired. Retargeted back, fired. The Shining Palm kept screaming, writhing, staggering, and flashing in microbursts down the stairs. Jack dumped his last magazine, tossed the gun aside, rolled.

The Shining Palm flashed across the space.

"You"—Shifter Paul gasped, tearing himself apart through the act of keeping himself together—"waste . . . time . . ."

Jack flipped on his back. The Shining Palm reached down and opened its flashing hand toward Jack's face.

"Not really." Jack gasped, rolled, flipped to his feet, and cannoned shoulder-first into Paul. The Countermeasure flew free from Paul's hands. Jack flashed, intercepted it, skidded to a halt, spun toward Paul.

Jack had the Countermeasure.

And realized the Shining Palm was now directly behind him.

Jack had dumped his entire chronon reserve in the warp-fight, and replenished just enough to snatch the Countermeasure from a rapidly deteriorating Paul. Now he was back at zero.

Paul came for him. Jack spun, hand over the Countermeasure's release.

"I'm pretty sure I can pop this. And I'm pretty sure that if I do it'll take out you and this thing behind me." Jack backed up, keeping an eye on both Paul and the Shifter. "Did you see this?" Jack said. "Can you see how this plays out?"

Paul, or whatever was left of Paul, was beyond language. It just held out one hand, reaching for the Countermeasure—a complex mind reduced to the last thing that drove it, perhaps.

The Shifter took one heavy step forward.

"I will do this. Will," Jack said. "Get behind something."

The Shifter roared, flexed that open palm, and lumbered straight for Jack—screaming.

Jack spun, Countermeasure extended in both hands, catch ready to pop. *"Stop!"*

Unexpectedly, the Shifter did exactly that. Its phasing, shining palm hovered two feet from Jack's face.

It did not move. It only growled, in a thousand voices, and strained its hand toward him.

Beth had done the same thing, in her final moment. *"Trust the villain."*

Jack looked. Beneath the distortion, resting within that palm that phased constantly through a thousand variations of itself, one thing remained constant. The flash of light at its center.

A single silver bullet. A reminder to take nothing for granted, that time is finite.

The Shifter made a sound, like a hundred abandoned dogs very far away.

"What . . . ," Paul croaked, horribly, "are you . . . doing . . . ?"

The head of the Shifter was a flashing fractal mess. This close to it, Jack could make out the face of the person it used to be. Had always been.

He lowered the Countermeasure, and stood aside.

Paul and the Shifter locked eyes.

The Shifter crossed the space between them with purpose.

Paul, human enough to be panicked beyond reason by this thing he had feared for seventeen years, brought up one useless, shifting hand as the Shifter's shining palm accepted Paul's, palm to palm, bullet to bullet, and Paul Serene met the thing he was fated to become, the thing he had always been—four-dimensional—existing at once across all times, midwifing the cause and effect that led to all things being as they are.

Including his own rebirth.

The sickness took him completely, his eyes locked with his Shining Palm self, and in that moment the two became one.

The Shining Palm, existing four-dimensionally, embraced Paul—embraced itself—at the moment of his/its own re/birth.

The Shining Palm had saved him in Monarch Tower. This was the same creature that had tunneled Jack through time, from 2010 to now, thereby ensuring that he would be here. That events would play out as they had.

That Paul Serene would become the Shining Palm.

Paul's ability to perceive and explore multiple oncoming timelines . . . all part of himself becoming four-dimensional.

Of growing closer to this thing he was meant to become. Had always been.

Things play out as they must. The universe won't be bargained with.

Both forms were lost in a corona of light as Paul's sickness took him completely.

Paul Serene was gone. The Shining Palm remained, but was changed. Uncertain.

Newborn. Flickering, phasing. It looked to Jack, studied itself, at the shining point of reflected light it held in its hand, threw back its head, and . . .

The stutter broke.

Rain and wind poured into the shattered lab with renewed ferocity.

"Jack!" Will ran across the expanse.

Jack was staring at the spot where his friend had been. "What just happened?"

"I'll explain later," Will said, gently taking the Countermeasure. "But if we're going to do this, it has to happen now. The next stutter that hits may well be the last."

Underneath the machine, Will decoupled a few fat, insulated wires from each other, using the Countermeasure as a go-between for the chronon flow between core and corridor.

"The Countermeasure is built to brute-force a recalibration of the M-J field," he said, "resulting in this timeline falling back in synch with itself. If it works we should see an end to the stutters. If that happens it means the field is no longer bleeding out, and universal chronon levels have restabilized." He made the final connection.

Jack gasped, toppled into the wall of the maintenance loop. Will steadied him.

"It's coming. A really big one." Jack held on to his brother, found his feet. "This isn't going to work if the Countermeasure isn't charged. Can you show me what to do?"

Will had lived his share of terrible moments, keeping his secrets, sacrificing his life on a long shot that maybe he could save the world. Jack didn't want to add another, but there was no choice.

Soberly Will pointed to the access hatch, about the size of a fist. "The device is hooked into the machine. I can activate it remotely from the control room upstairs. The depth of the maintenance well and the distance from the machine should protect me from the . . . effects."

"You turn it on, I do my thing. Easy."

Will nodded. "Jack . . ."

"Beth explained everything. Let's finish up here, then go get a couple of beers. You and me."

The two brothers left it at that, Will laying a hand on Jack's arm before climbing out of the maintenance ring.

The second pre-stutter blasted through Jack. It wasn't just the world falling to pieces. The next stutter that hit was going to start taking people apart.

"Will? Hurry!"

Twelve different jacks socketed into the core, eliciting a thump and bass hum from the corridor. The machine was online.

Jack held the Countermeasure in both hands, nestled awkwardly amid a tangle of wall wiring. Counted down from three. Thought of Beth.

Catches flipped, the hatch popped open and all the light of heaven spilled out. Jack plunged his hand inside, felt the Countermeasure's heat penetrate his cells.

Jack poured every particle of energy he had down his arm and into the Countermeasure.

Above him familiar distortion waves were building off the corridor-ring. The light grew brighter. In a room overhead William Joyce flicked a switch, and the corridor-ring activated.

The Countermeasure flared as bright as a sun, and Jack Joyce was lost in light.

23

It says something about the spirit of a town that even after disaster and calamity people take time to celebrate traditions. Though porches and stoops were shattered, lawns piled with gathered rubble and wreckage, jack-o'-lanterns sat on rails and steps, and cardboard witches dangled and turned from eaves. Halloween was a lot more homemade this year, but it felt good. A lot of people had left Riverport after the disaster, or were selling up, but those who remained were coming together as a community in ways that Amy had only ever heard her dad talk about in stories from when he was a kid.

"Riverport, oh Riverport, such a pretty little town."

Amy looked at the guy sitting on the bench to her left, next to her homemade stand. "You went to Riverport High?"

The man shook his head. "Nah, I'm from Jersey. Just visiting."

Shaved head, glasses, beard. Layered against the autumn chill in a two-piece suit and wool overcoat, just watching the river. O'Sullivan Park had a good view of the river, and at this time of day it looked like molten silver. From there you could watch crews rebuilding the bridge.

"Speculator, huh?" she said. "Come to see if there's money in reconstruction?"

The visitor glanced at her. "I ain't a speculator, sweets. Like

I said: just visiting. You really believe that stuff you're handing out?"

Her card table was stacked with flyers. Postdisaster they'd been a nightmare to get printed, and nobody was taking them. The sign she'd taped to the front of the table read I WAS THERE: MONARCH IS LYING. READ THE TRUTH. The flyers featured the high school photograph of Jack Joyce. FRAMED was stamped over his face in provocative rubber-stamp font.

Amy saw the paper folded in his lap, the one with the same front page as every other paper and Web site for the last few days. Martin Hatch's face, speculation about October 10, and the news that universities, labs, and agencies the world over were either losing or outsourcing key personnel to Monarch's new project: the project that was going to save the world.

"You really believe that stuff you're reading?" She threw his question back at him. He glanced at the paper. "This time last month I'd have thought the Meyer-Joyce field was where the Riverport Little League met on weekends. Then it's brownouts and blackouts all over, and then there's all that stuff on the Internet. Real smart people are saying it happened, and real dumb politicians are saying they need more evidence, so . . ."

"The Peace Movement, man. Four incidents, all those witnesses, all that footage? You don't fake that." Amy handed him a flyer. "Read it or don't. Your call." She started gathering the stacks, putting them into her backpack.

" 'Respect Existence or Expect Resistance.' Nice."

"It's yours."

"You givin' up?"

"I gotta take my neighbor's kid trick-or-treating."

"Weird place to be celebrating the night the veil between worlds is thinnest. Who the hell wants ghosts at a time like this?" He stood up. "Nice to meet you."

Amy kept shoveling pamphlets into her pack. "Sure thing."

The man turned, crumpled what was in his hand, and tossed it into the trash. Amy's last year in metaphor, right there. She zipped the bag, folded the table, and headed home. Passing the bench, she glanced in the trash, the bright red of the crumpled paper snagging her curiosity. What he had thrown wasn't her flyer. It was something else.

Fishing it out and unfolding it she found herself holding a balled-up return ticket to Thailand, made out to someone she knew.

Main Street and surrounds looked like Kabul with a Starbucks. Gas mains, power lines, infrastructure, cars and trucks, they'd all been fucked up beyond belief. To hear Sofia Amaral explain it, it was areas with densest populations that got it the worst. Something about the web of cause and effect being far thicker and more varied in any location with a lot of people. Those last few stutters had played hell there. The last one especially had gone beyond messing with things and really got to the people. The final hour of the disaster had been a spawning ground for heartbreak and horror stories.

Unexpectedly, sadly, beautifully, that was probably a big part of what was bonding people after the madness: a desire to make amends. Civilized people had lived the alternative, and the value of what they had became crystal clear. The people of Riverport had a cause now, and that cause was, for the time being at least, looking out for each other.

Hazard tape, construction signs, and warnings were taped or lashed across the frontages of more buildings than not. Street corners were piled with brick. Trucks worked twenty-four seven clearing the ruin. Signs were pasted on each block offering rewards for information. Each of those signs displayed two faces: Paul Serene's, and his own.

Jack adjusted his glasses and kept walking. He walked differently now, purposely, and when he spoke he angled his jaw forward just slightly. This changed his silhouette, it changed his face, it changed how he formed words. Sometimes that was all it took. He'd learned a lot from Beth. The Jersey accent was all her.

The shaved head, glasses, and beard were insurance.

Jack Joyce walked toward Beth's old house. The neighborhood hadn't been hit as badly as other places, mainly because it was low density. He stopped on the lawn and picked up the For Sale sign, then unlocked the door.

His phone vibrated, again. He checked it: another message from Will. The twelfth. Same as all the others.

Jack. DON'T. We need to talk about this.

He pocketed the phone, opened the door, and went inside.

From across the street, peering down the gap between two houses, Amy watched him pocket the phone, open the door, and go inside. Locking the door behind himself.

The house was empty, devoid of life or furniture. The basement was another story.

In the hours after the disaster Jack had taken advantage of the confusion. This is how the basement of that suburban house came to be equipped with a small amount of bleeding-edge chronon-related technology. Just enough to create a small, but very specific, effect.

Sofia Amaral didn't look up as he came down the steps. "Are you always going to be this relaxed about timetables?"

Jack took off his hat, hooked it on the bannister. "It got sunny."

Nick was leaning against the wall, seated on a folding chair. "She's been fretting. Gave me the third degree because it took twenty minutes too long to get Dad back home. He loves watching those Monarch crews build that bridge."

Half the space was bracketed off by the placement of four pylons: field generators.

Sofia turned in her seat, facing Jack, all business. "Working with Paul we conducted such . . . interactions . . . under much more contained conditions. You're certain the subject is reliable?"

"Yeah." Jack took off his coat, laid it across the back of a folding chair. He touched the bullet around his neck, out of habit. "I am. Did you take a reading on the M-J field?"

"I have."

"And?"

"Where once we had two days to live we now have five years. The field has not been repaired, but integrity has been restored and the rate of degradation slowed."

"Paul was right then. The end of time hits in five years."

"We were both correct. Your actions simply bought us more time. Let me point out, yet again, that this only further proves that past events cannot be changed."

"But you're helping me do this anyway, right?"

"If past events are immutable, which they are, the only thing that could be lost in this undertaking is your life. Also . . ." she admitted, "I would like very much to see him again. Even in his current state."

"So this is it?" Nick sat forward. "I get to see this thing? Pisser."

Jack stood before the squared-off space. "Okay. Do it."

Sofia dialed the output of the chronon batteries, popped the idiot shield from the activation switch, and then flipped it.

The space within the pylons hummed, inverted, then popped. Distortion waves pulsed off. The squared-off space held a neatly contained stutter.

Jack waited. "Come on," he muttered. "You're four-dimensional. You know you're supposed to be here."

Then, just like that, a six-foot fractal humanoid inhabited the space.

"Fuck me!"

"Nick!" Sofia snapped.

"Sorry."

The Shifter remained still, surveying Jack, outline flickering only slightly, then it raised its shining palm. Jack did the same. It was good to see him.

"Hey, Paul," he said. "You ready to do the impossible?"

One night in the recent past.

Will took his brother by the arm. "You have to let her go. We have a universe to consider. The dead, the living, and the yet-to-be-born."

Jack nodded, couldn't open his mouth to say a single word. He just leaned into Beth, and held her as best he could. Just for a moment.

He whispered something he wished she could hear, but knew she never would.

He whispered, "I'll come back for you."

ACKNOWLEDGMENTS

Sam Lake, Mikko Rautalahti, Tyler Smith, and everyone I worked with in my three years at Remedy. *Ad astra.*

Dmetri Kakmi, for his friendship and peerless editorial assistance. His acclaimed novel, *Mother Land,* is well worth your time. I urge you to pick it up.

Syksy Räsänen, theoretical physicist, cosmologist, and activist, with whom we consulted in developing the science for time travel in *Quantum Break.* His advice was crucial to the design of the machine and to several of its governing principles.

Nikaya Lewis, for architectural advice.

Ian Robertson for his friendship and military expertise.

The author C. R. Jahn for his encyclopedic knowledge of firearms and explosives. I recommend that you check out his horror novel, *The Outrider,* available on Amazon.